Other Books by Rachel Poe

*SECRETS FROM THE ATTIC*

# VANISHED SISTERS

# VANISHED SISTERS

*To Cloteal my card playing friend*
*Rachel Poe*
*2019*

# VANISHED SISTERS

## RACHEL POE

Published by Alabaster Book Publishing
North Carolina

This book is a work of fiction. Names, characters,
some places, and incidents either are the product
of the author's imagination or are used fictitiously,
and any resemblance of actual persons, businesses,
events, or locales is coincidental.

Copyright © 2016 by Rachel Poe

All Rights Reserved. No part of this book may be used
or reproduced in any manner whatsoever without
the expressed written consent of the author,
except in the case of brief quotations with
credit embodied in articles,
books, and reviews.

Published by
Alabaster Book Publishing
P.O. Box 401
Kernersville, NC 27284
www.publisheralabaster.biz

Cover Art: Rachel Poe

Book Design: David Shaffer

Editor: Tyler Tichelaar, Ph.D.

ISBN: 978-0-9861790-7-5

Library of CongressControl Number
2016939194

First Edition

For additional copies visit:
www.RachelPoe.com

Address all inquiries to:
Rachel Poe
P.O. Box 7480
Greensboro, NC 27417

In memory of Elizabeth Rae and Addie Lee Reel

My loving grandparents who lived in this valley and personally knew the sisters.

# ACKNOWLEDGMENTS

Along every pathway in life, there are always those who helped you, gave you encouragement, and were there to listen and even sometimes gently lead you in a different direction. For those friends and family, I feel truly blessed.

My thanks to Gary Hastings, retired Assistant Chief of Police and self-published author of four books, for his guidance in not only law enforcement questions, but in his shared experiences as an author.

My heartfelt appreciation goes to Mary Flinn, author of seven books, for sharing her knowledge and recommendations with me. I wish her great success with her literary endeavors.

Many thanks to my readers who have sent me letters, notes, emails, and made personal calls to tell me how much they enjoyed my first book, *Secrets from the Attic*, and to encourage me to write this sequel.

And most importantly, Tyler R. Tichelaar, Ph.D., for his help as editor, proofreader, and promoter of my book, *Vanished Sisters*. I wish I had had him on my team with my first book. His personal knowledge as an author as well as his many academic achievements are invaluable to me.

# ACKNOWLEDGMENTS

Along every pathway in life, there are always those who helped you, gave you encouragement, and were there to listen and even sometimes gently lead you in a different direction. For those friends and family, I feel truly blessed.

My thanks to Gary Hastings, retired Assistant Chief of Police and self-published author of four books, for his guidance in not only law enforcement questions, but in his shared experiences as an author.

My heartfelt appreciation goes to Mary Flinn, author of seven books, for sharing her knowledge and recommendations with me. I wish her great success with her literary endeavors.

Many thanks to my readers who have sent me letters, notes, emails, and made personal calls to tell me how much they enjoyed my first book, *Secrets from the Attic*, and to encourage me to write this sequel.

And most importantly, Tyler R. Tichelaar, Ph.D., for his help as editor, proofreader, and promoter of my book, *Vanished Sisters*. I wish I had had him on my team with my first book. His personal knowledge as an author as well as his many academic achievements are invaluable to me.

# PROLOGUE

AS PROFESSOR MARK Goodman rounded the old campus library, an unseasonably warm breeze touched his face and the scent of boxwoods surrounded him. His mind was flooded with childhood memories so vivid that for an undetermined period of time, he was lost in them. He could see himself and his older sister, Anne, walking barefoot down a dirt road, children again. He was lost in the memories of summers spent in the North Carolina mountains with his grandparents. The sun was warm on his face as he reluctantly followed his sister.

The dirt road was flanked with cornfields and pastures on their right and dense woods to the left, where ancient oak trees dappled the road with splashes of cool shade. Ditches and banks on either side of the road were overgrown with black-eyed Susans and Queen Anne's lace. Morning glories climbed the fence posts surrounding the pastures.

It was mid-morning as they skipped down the road, swinging their baskets of fresh baked bread as high in front as they could without losing the bread and as far behind as possible. A symphony of July flies played for them and a multitude of birds swooped and sang as they skipped along. They were making a yearly visit to see Aunt Ida and Aunt Eva, trade bread for butter, and hopefully, get a few homemade sugar cookies for their trouble.

Rachel Poe

When Mark thought back to his childhood, his happiest memories were those spent with his grandparents every summer. The rest of his childhood memories existed in bits and pieces of schools he had attended, friends he had played with, and places he had lived. They paled in comparison to the valley where his grandparents lived, tucked away in the mountains of North Carolina.

Mark was more than a little apprehensive about the visit. He would never have been brave enough to come alone. He was only five and his sister, Anne, eight. The memories of the sinister old house and the two old women who lived there could give him nightmares for weeks. But the cookies waiting for them were well-worth the anxious feeling in the pit of his stomach.

The image of that valley was etched in his memory. From Granny's kitchen window, you could see beds of marigolds, petunias, gladiolas, and candytuft around an old cedar tree, which shaded the kitchen window. Beyond the cedar was a view of the valley spread out before you and surrounded by gentle, smaller mountains that gradually rose into the mighty Blue Ridge Mountains in the distance.

A river, which to his knowledge had no name, flowed down from the high mountains, snaked its way down the middle of the valley, and disappeared at the southern end. A dirt road entered the valley from the wee village of Dovecote, which lay just beyond the mountain on the west side of the glen. The road crooked and wound its way across the valley, until it crossed the river in the middle and wiggled up the other side. Occasionally, the serenity of this scene was interrupted by the lonesome whistle of a train, entering from the mountain pass at the northern end of the valley and meandering around the valley's edge. Little attention was paid to the whistle; even the cows barely blinked, and the repetitive rhythm of their chewing was uninterrupted.

Camelot. No other word in his vocabulary could come close to describing this holy place of his childhood. No matter where Mark's life had taken him since, eventually the need to return haunted him because it restored his very soul. Until his seventeenth year, every summer was spent in this mountain Camelot. It was to this place that the scent of boxwoods took him as he walked across campus on that mock spring morning.

The visit to Aunt Ida and Aunt Eva was but one of the many memories that had so deeply etched his summer vacations with Granny and Papa into his memory. The two old maid sisters lived on a small farm atop a gentle mountain, which looked out over the entire valley. They were born on that farm and had remained there after their parents died, as if they were suspended in time. The farm, as well as the sisters, was untouched by the outside world. They were hermits and did not know, understand, or care what was going on beyond their mountain home. They worked like men with no hired help as they eked out a meager living from the small farm, which consisted of forty acres (mostly forest), two cows, a goat, three pigs, a dozen chickens, one rooster, an old hound dog, and two cats.

The long, winding, dirt road, which led to the dilapidated old farm, forked off the Old Hudlow Road, which crossed the valley, climbed the mountain, and led into Dovecote. The dirt road leading up to the house was wrought with holes and gullies. A car would have had a difficult time getting through. This did not matter, however, because Aunt Ida and Aunt Eva did not have a car. In fact, there were no powered machines of any kind on the place. Neither was there electricity, nor running water.

Mark was afraid of the sisters' sinister-looking old house and approached it timidly. It rose tall and dark, with a steep tin roof turned deep orange from years of rust. A stranger could have passed without seeing the house as it blended so completely into its surroundings of overgrown vines, huge boxwoods (which had never been trimmed) and thick, over-hanging trees. The old clapboard siding had turned almost black with age and the absence of paint. The house looked deserted, forgotten, and uninhabitable. No one would have guessed the two old sisters called this scary farmhouse home.

Mark and Anne followed a well-worn path through the boxwoods to the back porch where an old hound dog slept in the morning sun. The porch was open and unscreened—bare except for two straight back chairs, a tin tub hanging on a rusted nail, and a well where water was drawn at the far end of the porch. The plank floor looked as if a huge animal had chewed off the ends of the planks.

    Anne's knock and feeble "Yoo-hoo" was answered by total silence. The old hound dog raised his head, looked them over, and went back to sleep, unimpressed by the strangers come-to-call. Anne said the sisters must be in the barn. Mark came out from behind one of the boxwoods where he was timidly hiding, and then they made their way along a narrow, overgrown path to the ramshackle, old barn. Granny's warning, "Watch out for snakes," echoed in Mark's head. One barn door was missing and the other hung askew by one hinge. They squinted to see in the dark, smelly barn surrounded by waist-high weeds. Sunlight from the missing doors at the far end of the barn illuminated the silhouette of Aunt Ida sitting on a stool, milking a cow, her head resting on its side. Dust motes and flies danced in the beams of sunlight surrounding her.

    Anne knew the aunts were both hard of hearing so she didn't want to frighten them. She shouted, "Yoo-hoo" before entering the foul-smelling barn. Aunt Ida turned around, a frightened, suspicious expression on her face, and Mark saw Aunt Eva shyly peek around the other end of the barn. "It's me," Anne called. "Elizabeth's granddaughter, Anne; I've brought fresh baked bread from Granny."

    The children carefully chose their steps toward Aunt Ida. Mark hung back behind Anne, trembling with fear. Aunt Ida finished milking and wiped her hands on the dirty old apron she wore. As Mark peeked around Anne, Aunt Ida smiled at him with a toothless crooked smile that they, over the years, had become accustomed to. She walked toward them like a man, and they noticed that her old-fashioned, homespun skirt dragged the ground in places and she wore men's brogan boots, unlaced without stockings.

    The part of the visit that Mark liked least was about to happen. He was going to be kissed by both sisters. Aunt Ida came toward him with that toothless smile and a face so deeply rutted with wrinkles she resembled a wizened apple. Her outstretched, manly hands let Mark know to get ready. He braced himself, as best he could, as the indescribable smell of her reached him. Human sweat, cow dung, homemade lye soap, sour hay, and snuff assaulted him all at once. Her strong arms engulfed him as she gave him a wet smack on the cheek. Aunt Eva, the shy one, inched closer, came at him, hesitated as if she weren't sure she could do it, and then dove at him. This time, she was successful in planting another wet kiss on his other cheek.

"Laud hav' mercy," Aunt Ida declared. "Ya done growed sos we'd hardly noed ja. Ya just come on to tha house and set a spell. I mite can find a sugar cookie or two. Ya com'on now," she said as she led the way. "How's Miss Libeth a doin? Can't 'member tha last time I seen 'er."

"She's doing just fine," Anne answered. "She sent us to see if we could trade this bread for some of your sweet-tasting butter. Granny says you make the best butter in the county. You must have sweet cows."

Both women threw back their heads and let out belly laughs that came all the way up from their toes. "No, hon," she said, "hit ain't tha cows; hit's tha sweet grass theys et. Ain't no sweeter grass than on this here hill of iron. Folks come a fur piece to trade fer ire butter." Aunt Eva never spoke, but she had the sweetest smile that said she was so glad to see them.

They walked back to the house, which over time had acquired the same smell as the two sisters. The inside of the house was a lot like the outside, dark and sparsely furnished with wide plank floors that had never seen a mop, vacuum cleaner, or wax. A homemade, straw broom resting in a corner was the only cleaning the floors could ever hope for.

The only upholstery was a horsehair-stuffed sofa in the parlor whose hairs poked through the worn velvet fabric and stabbed your backside even through your pants. Mark timidly climbed on a tall stool in the kitchen as Aunt Eva disappeared into the root cellar (a cave dug deep into the ground under the kitchen floor) where milk and butter were kept cool even in the hot summer time. She reappeared with a jug of milk. After pouring them a big glass, she went to the corner cupboard and returned with a crock of huge flat cookies. This was what they had really come for; their mouths watered in anticipation. The cookies were made with unpasteurized milk, mill ground flour, raw honey, and real home-churned butter. No other cookie had ever tasted like the cookies of Mark's childhood.

Aunt Ida asked lots of questions, which Anne tried to answer between chewing and gulps of milk. "How's ya Pappy's garden adoin'?" asked Aunt Ida.

"Great, just great," Anne answered. "He said to ask if you needed green beans, squash, or tomatoes?"

"Weins got more beans than we can put-up, but I shore could use a peck of maters ta put-up. Tha dad-gum billy goat got in tha mater patch and ate near half my maters. Now I shore could use some maters."

"Papa said to tell you that if you needed anything, he would bring them first thing in the morning."

"At thar'll be just fine. Eva and me ken git 'em maters put-up a'fore tha sun gets too high of a morning."

Mark tried to eat slowly to make the cookies last longer, but they tasted so good he kept shoving them into his mouth as fast as he could. Aunt Eva didn't say a word, but she watched with pride as they gobbled up her cookies. She always let Aunt Ida do the talking.

When they had finished their treat, Anne announced they had better get on home so Granny wouldn't worry. Aunt Eva jumped to her feet and filled their basket with butter, a jar of homemade apple jelly, and more cookies. They waved goodbye and headed down the road for home with a smile on their faces and a basket full of cookies that would never make it home.

With a jolt, Mark realized he had been standing there staring into space. Students briskly passed by him as they hurried off to class. He took a deep breath of the boxwoods and smiled to himself, knowing he would never pass this way again without thinking of his Camelot. *I'm late,* Mark thought and hurried off to class. As quickly as he had left the present and drifted back in time, Mark was back again in the present and the past was but a precious moment floating on a gentle breeze.

# CHAPTER 1

WITH HIS SWISS Army knife, Mark cut and chopped his way down the overgrown dirt road. There was little he could see to remind him of the old road, which had been little more than a rutted path thirty years ago. Mother Nature had reclaimed the fields as well as the road. Huge tire tracks, probably from a tractor, had recently been made down the road—probably the only way a realtor was able to get in and check out the property. They continued to hack their way toward the old house and barn. *I wish I had a machete,* he thought.

His wife, Carrie, was not as enthused as Mark, but she tramped along behind him as Mark hacked at weeds and told stories of Aunt Ida and Aunt Eva on their ancient farm. "How much farther?" Carrie asked as she stumbled on a rock and landed on her backside in the weeds.

"Are you okay?" Mark asked as he helped her up and brushed the weeds and dirt from her clothes. "We should be seeing the roof soon, if it's still there."

"I think so; everything seems to be working. Boy, am I hot. It must be ninety degrees. I can see why this track of land is so reasonable; we'll need to cut a new road in just to get equipment in here. Are you sure we're on the old road?"

"I'm not sure; I think I remember it running along this

tree line. I'm going by the older trees. The land to our right was once pasture and cornfields. I can't believe how the trees have taken over. I suspect the house and barn have caved in by now."

"How did Anne hear about this land being for sale?" Carrie asked as they continued to chop their way through the underbrush and trees. "There's no sign out front."

"Because of her garden center in Marion; she talks to farmers every day, and most know her grandparents lived in Dovecote. Someone saw a sign on the property and mentioned it to Anne. He happened to come by as the realtor was putting up the sign. He was curious, so he stopped to inquire about the price and find out what happened to the sisters."

"I thought you said it had been on the market for over a year?"

"That's right; the realtor told the farmer that someone kept stealing the signs. They can't figure out why. She also said the two sisters had just disappeared several years ago. Everyone just assumed that relatives took them in. They were in their nineties and no longer able to keep the place up. The realtor told him they had been living on all the food they had canned. According to her, there was enough food here to keep them alive for years. The neighbors checked on them, but they have no clue what happened to them. The county sheriff came out and looked around, but he found no reason to suspect foul play. They just vanished into thin air.

"I want to have a look around myself, see what I can find, before we have any demolition done. As far as I know, there was no reason for anyone to want to harm the sisters. They had nothing of value that I know of. The little money they made selling their fruit, vegetables, and butter was used to buy flour and cornmeal for baking bread. The sheriff told the realtor he found evidence of teenage vandals trashing the place. There were signs of marijuana being smoked in the house. They were probably high and wanted to tear something up.

"The sheriff knew the kids who did the trashing. He had had trouble with them before. He rounded them up and questioned them. According to the kids, the house was deserted. Seems they were just looking for a good place to smoke pot and decided to look for hidden money they could use to buy more drugs. They claimed to have found no money or anything of value they could sell."

"Doesn't sound like a thorough investigation to me. Did anyone check with the relatives? Was the property walked to try and find them?" Carrie asked as she stepped on a small black snake. She screamed and ran back the way they had come. "Snake, Mark; get out of there!"

Mark laughed as he used a stick to pick up the six-inch black snake. "He won't hurt you, Carrie; he was probably asleep and we woke him. Hot weather makes them sleepy and lethargic. Here, want to hold him?"

"Not on your life; have I never told you I do not like snakes? Not any kind, friendly or otherwise." She kept her distance, ready to run. "You throw that thing in the woods or I'm heading back to the car."

"Okay, honey; I'm sending him on his way. Just stay behind me and I'll watch more carefully.

"You're right about the relatives. While searching the house, the sheriff discovered a crude last will and testament leaving the farm to a distant cousin. The relative had never met the sisters and knew nothing about what had happened to them.

"This is such a small community where everyone knows everyone else and their business. Even though the sisters were loners, they were well-respected in the community and checked on regularly. Lots of locals bought their butter from the sisters until they were too old to milk the cows and churn the butter. It was considered the best butter in the county. The sisters claimed it was because of the sweet grass that grew here in their pasture."

"Did anyone check the property to see if they fell off the mountain?" Carrie asked as she gingerly walked behind Mark and kept her eyes glued to the ground. Carrie knew this property held wonderful childhood memories for Mark, so she was prepared to see this adventure through. He had high hopes of building a summer home here because the property looked down on the whole valley. She, on the other hand, had reservations about being so far from civilization. The nearest grocery store was at least twenty-five miles away, and who would look after the place in the winter?

"The sheriff assembled a group of men from the community and walked the entire property, but he found no clue as to what happened to the sisters. The only time they ever left the property was to walk to market in Bethel every Saturday morning to sell their vegetables, and they hadn't done that in years. I remember seeing them many times in the summer, walking down the road with a sack over their shoulders, headed to market. Around four in the afternoon, here they'd come back carrying a sack of flour and cornmeal.

"The problem is, no one knows exactly when they disappeared. Someone just went to check on them one day and couldn't find them. He went back the next day and they still were not there. That's when people became suspicious that something was wrong."

"Look, I see a chimney...over there, Mark." She pointed up ahead to the right.

"You're right; I see it, too. Maybe the old house is still standing." They continued to chop and hack their way along and were soon looking at the old, dark, scary house. Mark remembered how frightened he had been as a little boy when approaching this house. Time had only increased its sinister appearance. The vines had taken over and climbed to the tin roof...now rusted through in spots. Parts of rafters could be seen through gaping holes.

"Gee, this looks spooky," Carrie exclaimed as she eased closer to Mark. "Are you going in? The floor could collapse with our weight."

"We'll go slow and test the floor before each step. Let's go around back and check out the whole exterior before we enter."

Mark led the way as he held back the overgrown boxwoods for Carrie to follow. As they rounded the house, Mark could see that the back porch, like the front, had collapsed, along with the steps. The only part of the back porch still attached to the house was the far end where the well stood. The well was holding up that end of the porch. The doors had fallen off as the screws rusted and the wind rattled them loose. Mark used a rusted tin tub to step up into the doorjamb.

As Mark stood there looking into the kitchen, his mind drifted back and he could see himself sitting on the tall old stool, waiting and hoping for a sugar cookie. The scent of the two old ladies remained in the house. The stool was in the middle of the kitchen floor, broken in several pieces. Funny, it didn't look as tall now, but to the little boy, Mark, it had been huge. The cookie crock was also on the floor, broken in many pieces. It made him feel sad, as if a wonderful memory had been stolen from him... ripped away.

He tested the floor before giving Carrie a hand up. The floor seemed very solid. "They don't make houses like these anymore." The timbers were huge and the floor planks thick and sturdy. They had lasted for over a hundred years, and he hoped he could salvage some of the timber to incorporate into his new summer home. The thought of owning a summer home of his own, here on this site, overlooking his precious childhood valley, would be a dream come true.

"Mark, look at that old iron stove." She was in awe of the entire house. "If the floor didn't collapse under the weight of that stove, it's not going to collapse. That thing must weigh a ton."

"You're right, but I'll bet it was reinforced under the house to ensure that it didn't give way. Look here; I want to show you something."

Mark opened a door to reveal steps going down into the root cellar where milk and butter were kept. Even after thirty years, there was still no electricity in the house. No pump had been added to the well to supply running water. It was just as it had been when he was here spending summers down in the valley thirty years ago.

This was where, in Mark's mind, he was sure he would find the sisters. He could see them going down the steep steps, one falling and the other reaching out to save the first, only to fall down as well. Neither would be able to get up, and they would have died there together. He aimed his flashlight to the bottom of the stairs. There was nothing there. The cellar was lined with shelves where canned fruits and vegetables were kept. The vandals had found the cellar too. The floor was strewn with broken glass from many shattered jars.

Mark felt so angry. What kinds of kids were we raising today? It had to be the drugs. Something had to be done to save our youth. Mark was a forensic anthropologist and taught at a university in Mississippi. He had seen some gruesome things in his life. He hoped the vandalism would not tarnish his memories of this place. He never wanted to forget his Aunt Ida and Aunt Eva.

Actually, they were not really related at all, but in his childhood, children didn't call adults by their first names. So he had been taught to call them "Aunt" instead of the more formal "Miss." He wished people still taught their children to respect their elders.

Carrie touched his shoulder and brought him back from his reverie. "Let's look at the rest of the house and have our picnic out back where we can check out the view of the valley."

"Sounds like a plan to me," Mark replied. "I've only peeked into the rest of the house. Anne and I were more interested in what was in that broken cookie crock. I'm afraid we'll find more vandalism.... Let's go see."

After checking out the rest of the house and, indeed, finding more destruction of property, they searched but could not find an entrance to the attic. The steep roof indicated a good-sized attic. Giving up the search, they assumed you had to enter the attic from an outside window. The attic would have to wait until they could find a ladder. They ventured out back to find the perfect spot where the view of Mark's valley could best be seen. As they settled, side-by-side with feet dangling from a huge rock, they shared their picnic lunch.

"You've prepared a feast, even wine," said Mark. "So what do you think of my valley? Would you like to grow old here with me?"

"Mark, I'd love growing old with you anywhere, but I do love this view and the fact that we aren't surrounded by a community of other retirement or summer homes. We can plant a garden, have horses, goats, and even chickens. This place is special to you and me too, since you have shared so many stories of your childhood here in this valley. It will be a place where our children and grandchildren can create their own memories that will last them a lifetime."

Mark pulled her down on the quilt beside him and kissed her tenderly. They lay there in each other's arms, gazing up at an ancient oak tree and the sky beyond, each thinking what a great place it was to spend their summers and a wonderful place to retire.

# CHAPTER 2

AFTER INDULGING IN a small nap, Mark and Carrie packed up their lunch remains and went back to the old ramshackle house to investigate further and check out the barn. Mark's intuition as a forensic anthropologist told him that there had to be clues here as to what had happened to Aunt Ida and Aunt Eva. He wished he had his forensic case with him, but it was too big to drag along as he slashed out a pathway to the house. He made a mental note to hire someone to bush hog the old road so he could get his SUV down to the house.

As they returned to the back porch, Mark thought, *I wonder if I can stand on the portion of the porch surrounding the old well? I sure would like to see down into that well.* He moved the old tin tub over to the remaining porch floor and climbed up, holding on to the side of the well. He wedged himself between the well and the outside wall of the house where the floor seemed sturdiest. "Hand me the flashlight, Carrie; I want to see if there's any water in this well. If there is, we need a sample for testing."

"Mark, be careful; that floor could collapse at any time. Do you really think the water is still drinkable? I wonder when this well was dug?"

"Don't know. It's been here as long as I can remember. The bucket is still here, but the rope looks rotten." He took the bucket and sent it down the well, causing the crank to turn rapidly. He heard a thud. "Uh oh, no splash; let's see if the rope is strong enough to bring the bucket back up." Mark took the crank and began to turn. The rope held for two turns and broke, sending the bucket and rope crashing back into the well. With his flashlight, Mark leaned over the well to try to estimate its depth. He only got a quick look at the bottom before he heard a bullet come whizzing just over his head. Mark jumped from the porch as he shoved Carrie to the ground.

"Don't move," he said as he reached for his backpack and retrieved his own gun, which he carried in case they might run into a bear or a rattlesnake. Never did it occur to him that he would need to defend them against another human. They didn't move or make a sound for several minutes. No one appeared, nor was there another shot. Mark motioned for Carrie to move under the house and stay there while he ventured out to take a look. Carrie shook her head furiously, begging him not to go. With hand motions, Mark indicated she should stay put and not make a sound. Carrie knew she was overruled, so she moved behind one of the rock supports. She pulled out her cell phone, only to find there was no signal, so she hunkered down and prayed.

Mark stayed behind the boxwoods, moving low and close to the house. He inched his way around to the front of the house, fighting the cobwebs and branches as they whacked him in the face. He wanted a view of the back of the house from the other side. Whoever fired the shot would not be looking in that direction. The shot had to have come from the woods behind the house. He had good cover from overgrown boxwoods almost all the way around the house. He stayed low and searched the woods for any movement. Nothing. He waited. After fifteen minutes, he eased his way back to Carrie.

He crawled under the house where Carrie still crouched. She moved beside him and whispered in his ear. "Did you see anything?" Mark shook his head and pointed to himself, to her, and then back toward the way they had come. He motioned for her to follow behind him. Before moving, Mark searched the porch ceiling. He was sure the bullet had to have wedged in the sagging porch roof. He could see where it had lodged, but it wasn't safe to try to retrieve it now. They needed to get out of there.

They crawled until they were able to sprint to the woods in front of the house. From there, they made their way back to the Old Hudlow Road where they had parked. They ran for their SUV and sped away toward the village in search of help.

The village consisted of a post office, railroad depot with no railroad tracks, a combination grocery store/barbershop, and a gas station. There were two churches, a community center, and about two-dozen homes along the main road. Other than several outlying farms on back roads, that was all there was for at least twenty-five miles. He remembered the realtor telling them that the for-sale signs kept disappearing. Maybe the locals didn't want any newcomers moving in. Mark decided to go on to Marion where his sister lived before reporting the incident.

*

THEY PULLED INTO Anne's Nursery and Garden Center and looked for Anne. She was helping a customer load fertilizer onto his truck. Mark helped her finish with her customer and followed her into the office. Carrie was already there waiting for them. Anne looked at Carrie and frowned. "You look like you've seen a ghost," she said. "You're white as a sheet; are you okay?" Carrie shook her head yes and pointed to Mark. Anne looked at Mark and said, "What's going on? You don't look good either. What's happened?"

"Someone fired a shot at us while we were looking at the Hawkins' property. We need to report this to someone, but we don't know whom to call. There's no sheriff or even a deputy in Dovecote. The locals keep stealing the signs, which makes us believe they don't want us there. We decided to come here and ask you whom we should call?"

"Oh no!" Anne couldn't believe what she was hearing. "I'll call the sheriff immediately and have him come here to talk to you." Anne picked up the phone and dialed a number. She asked to speak to Sheriff Brady and was put on hold.

"He's a good friend of mine," she said as she waited.

"We're both single and go out occasionally. We became friends after I reported several trees and plants missing from the garden area. He staked the place out one night and caught a couple of yard sale enthusiasts loading up plants to sell at their weekend yard sale.

"Hello, Blake; it's Anne; could you come over to my office right away? No, no, it's a little more serious than missing plants. My brother is staying with me for a week. He and his wife were checking out the Hawkins' property in Dovecote today. Someone fired a shot at them as they were looking at the house. Thanks, Blake; see you in a few minutes." Anne turned to Mark, "He's on the way."

Anne noticed that Carrie was still very pale. "Carrie, I'm going to get you something to drink; you don't look good."

Mark became concerned, too, and began to check her pulse. "Honey, are you okay? We're safe now. It was probably a hunter out hunting squirrels. As a boy, I used to hunt squirrel and rabbit in those woods."

"I'm fine, dear; it just dawned on me how close I came to losing you. We've been through so much; I just couldn't handle losing you now. Not now that I'm pregnant."

"What!" exclaimed Mark. "Why didn't you tell me?"

"I wanted it to be an anniversary present, but under the circumstances, I decided to tell you now because I really don't feel well."

Anne came back with a bottle of water. "Here, honey; drink some water and put your feet up on my desk. Maybe you need to go back to the house and lie down a bit."

"She just told me she's pregnant," Mark told his sister. "I think we need to have her checked out by a doctor." Then he turned apologetically back to Carrie and said, "I never would have dragged you into that wilderness if I had known."

Carrie took a big drink of water and cut her eyes up at Anne. "I'm as healthy as a horse now, Mark; please don't fuss at me. We've been through a traumatic experience. I just need to calm down. I'll be fine."

"She was a little queasy this morning," Anne added, "but that's normal since she's pregnant. If she doesn't start feeling better soon, I'll have Doc Wilson come over and have a look at her. He lives next door and he owes me a favor."

"You knew she was pregnant?" said Mark, suspicious that his sister did not act surprised by the news.

"Well...yes...she wanted it to be a surprise. I'm glad you told him, though; I couldn't have kept the secret for a month anyway. Now we can celebrate."

Mark laughed. "Carrie, there is something you need to know about my sister. Don't ever tell her anything you want kept secret. She is incapable of keeping a secret." He put his arm around Carrie and kissed her on the top of her head. "I'm so happy, darling; nothing could make me any happier. I'm going to make sure you take it easy. Anne, why don't you take her to your house and make her lie down?"

"No, Mark, I want to be here when you talk with the sheriff. He may want to ask me some questions."

"If he does, I'll call you; now please do this for me. You are very pale and we don't want to lose this baby. For me... please."

Anne took her hand. "Come on, Carrie; he's right. After all your body went through last year, you don't want to take any chances."

Carrie agreed and they left Mark to talk with the sheriff. As Anne and Carrie were getting into her car, the sheriff pulled in. When he came over to Anne's window, Carrie noticed how he patted Anne's arm as it lay on the doorframe. He held her arm a bit too long as Anne explained where they were going and then introduced him to Carrie.

"Miss Carrie, you go on with Anne and rest. Mark and I will get to the bottom of this mystery. Don't you worry; it was probably just a kid out hunting rabbits."

Carrie thought, *I think Anne and Sheriff Brady may be a little more than friends.*

\*

MARK STOOD UP when the sheriff entered and introduced himself. Sheriff Brady shook hands with Mark and said,

## Vanished Sisters

"Call me, Blake"; then they sat down to talk.

"I'm very glad that the girls are not here, Blake, because we have a murder to solve. Before the shot rang out, I was looking down into the well on the back porch and I know I saw human bones down there."

"Are you sure?"

"No doubt in my mind. I'm a forensic anthropologist, so I know bones when I see them. It's true that I only got a glance before the shot rang out, but there are bones down in that well. I'm sure we've found the Hawkins sisters."

Blake ran his fingers through his hair. "Let's go back out there and take another look."

\*

AS MARK AND Blake rode back to the Hawkins' farm, Mark took him through the events as they had unfolded earlier. He explained his connection to the sisters and ended by saying that the realtor was having trouble keeping a sign up on the property. Someone was stealing them. "Someone does not want that property to sell, and I think we now know why."

Mark and Blake followed the path that Mark had made earlier. When they came around the house to the side porch, Mark saw the well bucket lying on the ground. He reached out and stopped Blake. "That bucket was at the bottom of the well when we left. I'll bet you the bones are not down there either."

Blake told Mark to stay put until he checked out the house and surroundings. He drew his gun and entered the house. Mark had his forensic case with him and began to take pictures of the scene. There were many footprints around the area, and not all of them his or Carrie's. He wanted to look into the well, but he knew he needed to dust for fingerprints first. He examined the area around the well for clues. What, other than the bucket, was different from before? There was mud on the well encasement and the floor around the well. There must have been some water in the bottom of the well. He saw a fairly good heel print of what looked like a boot. Mark carefully preserved and bagged the print. Likewise, on the top of the well a partial hand was preserved in dried mud. It was too smeared for fingerprints, but he preserved and bagged it too.

Blake returned and holstered his gun. "Can I help? I know better than to compromise a crime scene. I was very careful in the house. I didn't see anything unusual, but you need to go through and see if anything has changed since you were here. Have you looked in the well yet?"

"No; I'm almost ready to take a look. I've got a few possible prints. The bones won't be there because there's dried mud smeared all over the well surface and the floor that wasn't here before. They were in a hurry and left many clues for us. Wonder how they got down there? I need to go down to see if anything was left in their haste."

"I have rope in the police cruiser," said Blake. "I'll run back and get it. I saw some trampled weeds behind the house. It looks like they may have dropped something from that end of the porch. Have a look while I get the rope."

Mark finished his search for clues and grabbed his flashlight. The bottom of the well was a quagmire of mud and rock. Muddy footprints were smeared on the inside walls of the well. They had used a rope. He hoped he was strong enough to let himself down into the well without breaking anything vital and hoist himself up again. He could see no bones, but there could be small bones that escaped their notice in the mud. He wasn't completely positive that Blake believed his story. He looked up to see where the bullet was imbedded in the sagging porch ceiling. The hole was now much bigger. They had taken the time to retrieve the bullet, which said volumes.

Mark jumped down to check out the end of the porch. Blake was right; they must have dropped the sack of bones from the end of the porch. The bent grass and weeds revealed a path that led into the woods. Daylight was beginning to fade; they probably wouldn't have time to follow the trail today. Mark looked up under the porch. From where he squatted, he could see the outside of the well encasement and on up under the house. A bag of some kind had been tossed up behind one of the rock supports for the house. He crawled forward and pulled it out. It was a burlap sack, and he felt sure it was empty. They must have brought more than one and threw this one up under the house. He was turning the sack inside out when Blake returned. Mark bagged the burlap sack. He would check it carefully later.

Blake had a nylon rope across his shoulder. "Did you find anything?"

"Just this bag; it's empty just like the well. The well bottom is only mud and rock with smeared footprints on the inside walls where they crawled out. Do you think you can hold my weight as I slide down into the well and then pull me out?"

"I hope so; we're about the same size, and I'm in pretty good shape. I brought some gloves to protect your hands." They returned to the well and Mark showed him where the bullet had been imbedded in the porch ceiling. "They went to the trouble to dig the bullet out?"

"They're afraid if we find the gun, the ballistics markings will prove who fired the shot. Or it could be foreign-made, which would open up a whole new set of possibilities."

"Well, daylight is fading; let's get me down in that well." Mark armed himself with his camera, evidence bags, a flashlight, and a trowel to move the mud around, in hopes of finding overlooked small bones. He wrapped the line around his waist and pulled on forensic gloves first and then the heavy leather gloves Blake had provided. Blake wrapped the line around a tree and held it taut as he slowly lowered Mark into the well. He prayed he could get Mark out without having to call for backup.

Mark inched his way down into the well. It was not a good feeling. He was glad he wasn't claustrophobic, or even worse, achluophobic, because the sun was going down fast.

As he reached the bottom, his tennis shoes slipped on some rocks, but he caught himself before he went down. With his flashlight, he searched the mud for even a toe or finger joint. It would prove that Aunt Ida and Eva had been down there. He was sure they would never be able to find the sisters now and give them a proper burial. He took pictures of the ground and the walls showing the skid marks of the well's previous visitors. For thirty minutes, he moved mud around, squeezing globs of mud between his gloved fingers and turned over rocks with no luck. It was time to give up and get out of there.

Blake was watching from above. "Any luck?" he yelled as if Mark were a mile away.

"Afraid not; guess it's time to see if you can get me out of here."

"I think I've got it all worked out; I've wrapped the cord around the crank shaft, and I'm going to try and crank you up. It looks pretty solid; we'll give it a try."

"Give me some slack. I'm going to rearrange the rope like a mountain climber; my hands and feet will be free to hold on to the sides. Maybe I can help by walking myself up the wall as you pull."

"Great idea. Let me know when you're ready."

Mark tried to tie the rope as he had seen climbers do, even though this was not the proper kind of rope. He did the best he could and prayed it would work. "Okay, let's try it."

Blake began slowly turning the well crank. The old oak shaft groaned as it wound the rope around itself. Progress was slow, but it was working. Fifteen minutes later, Mark's head appeared out of the dark abyss. He grabbed either side of the well frame and pulled himself up and out. He was covered in mud. "Are you sure you'll let me ride home in your car?"

Blake laughed. "I've got a body bag I can wrap you in."

"Because of my line of work, it won't be the first time I've used a body bag as a seat cover."

Mark used his flashlight to gather up all his equipment. The sun had gone down while he played in the mud at the bottom of the well. They were ready to leave when Mark's foot stumbled into the well bucket. At first, he didn't know what he had bumped into and directed his light to see. Mark picked up the bucket to sit it back on the well. His light shown into the bucket and there on the bottom was a bone. "Wait, Blake; I think I've found something." He had assumed the bucket was thrown out of their way, when actually they had used it to retrieve small bones. He bagged the whole bucket to be checked for fingerprints later, along with the tiny bone. He was sure the bone was a distal phalanx. He would come back tomorrow to search for something belonging to the sisters, from which he could obtain their DNA. A comparison would be made with the DNA he hoped to retrieve from the bone. This would give them proof the bones not only belonged to the sisters, but that the sisters were thrown into the well after they were murdered.

# CHAPTER 3

MARK'S MUDDY CLOTHES and feet were wrapped in a body bag as they drove back to Marion. "I hope Carrie is feeling better. She just told me today she's pregnant. I think I better try to call her."

"Wait a couple minutes," Blake suggested. "You won't get a signal until we're passed Mud Cut. Dovecote doesn't have a tower yet. Hopefully, by the time you build there, they will have one."

"I'm not sure Carrie will still want to build in Dovecote when she learns that we found the sisters in the well. She was pretty upset today; so was I, for that matter. I have such great memories of this place. It's like someone is trying to shatter my dreams. What do you know about the people who live in Dovecote now? Do you think they would try to frighten away a newcomer?"

"No, not at all. Most are hardworking, honest people. I never get a call from that community. Crime is nonexistent. The only problem is the community is drying up. Their kids are leaving. Only a small number of farms have been handed down to the next generation. As you know, all three farms in the valley are gone. Most of the land is rented to other farmers. The dairy on this side of the river was sold to a doctor from Raleigh. He hoped to retrieve from the bone. This would give them proof the bones not only belonged to the sisters, but that the sisters were thrown into the well after they were murdered.

# CHAPTER 3

MARK'S MUDDY CLOTHES and feet were wrapped in a body bag as they drove back to Marion. "I hope Carrie is feeling better. She just told me today she's pregnant. I think I better try to call her."

"Wait a couple minutes," Blake suggested. "You won't get a signal until we're passed Mud Cut. Dovecote doesn't have a tower yet. Hopefully, by the time you build there, they will have one."

"I'm not sure Carrie will still want to build in Dovecote when she learns that we found the sisters in the well. She was pretty upset today; so was I, for that matter. I have such great memories of this place. It's like someone is trying to shatter my dreams. What do you know about the people who live in Dovecote now? Do you think they would try to frighten away a newcomer?"

"No, not at all. Most are hardworking, honest people. I never get a call from that community. Crime is nonexistent. The only problem is the community is drying up. Their kids are leaving. Only a small number of farms have been handed down to the next generation. As you know, all three farms in the valley are gone. Most of the land is rented to other farmers. The dairy on this side of the river was sold to a doctor from Raleigh. He has built a nice summer home where the old farmhouse once stood. Don't know that I've ever met him. Your grandparents' farm was sold back to the railroad. They demolished the house and are renting the land. The Taylor dairy farm has been on the market for over a year. That community needs newcomers. It's a wonderful place to live. Try your phone now."

Mark dialed Anne's house phone. He was afraid Carrie might be resting and didn't want to wake her, so he was glad when Anne answered on the first ring. "Hey, Anne, it's Mark; is Carrie resting?"

"No, she's fine and sitting right here. We've been talking and cooking. Tell Blake to come on over for dinner. We have prepared a feast."

Mark turned to Blake. "You're invited to dinner; they've cooked a feast."

Blake gave a thumbs up. "Sounds great; tell her you'll be there in thirty minutes. We need to stop by the garden center and get your car."

Mark relayed the information and asked to speak to Carrie.

"I understand you're feeling better," he said when she came on the line. "Did you get any rest?"

"I did, and I feel like a new person. Can't wait to dive into this dinner your sister has whipped together. It smells scrumptious. Did you find anything? I've been worried; I wanted to call, but then I remembered there was no service in Dovecote."

"We did; I'll tell you all about it at dinner. We should be there in a few minutes. Love you."

"Love you, too. Bye."

"You two sound like newlyweds; how long have you been married?"

"Almost a year. We met under very strange circumstances. Carrie was trying to sell a family gravesite and was having it excavated, which is required now. They uncovered baby bones buried in a leather satchel. Turned out to be her half-brother. Her mother was hiding a previous life, from which she was forced to flee, to save her life. Her neighbor helped her get away and flew her to Thomasville, North Carolina, where the neighbor's brother took her in, gave her a job, and kept her secret.

"She met and married Carrie's father and lived out the rest of her life there. I helped Carrie dig for the truth, and we wound up in Kansas, where her mother was originally from. Carrie was almost killed while we were in Kansas, and she underwent extensive surgery to save her life. We were married several months later. Carrie was afraid she wouldn't be able to have children, so we're both thrilled about the news."

"Sounds like quite an adventure."

"It was. Carrie wrote a book about her mother's life; it's titled *Secrets from the Attic*."

Blake looked surprised. "I've read that book; I thought that scenario sounded familiar. I know the whole story. I think Anne gave me the book. I just hadn't made the connection. What a bizarre story that was. Has she written a second book?"

"She's working on one, but the past year has been a rollercoaster ride. I have a son, Tucker, who is a Down syndrome child, by a previous marriage. Tucker is seven and loves his new family. We have spent most of the past year getting settled on the university campus in Mississippi. We combined two households, along with a housekeeper and Carrie's elderly Aunt Mattie, who was the neighbor in Kansas who saved Carrie's mother. The past year has been a challenge.

"When Anne called about the Hawkins' property being for sale, we used it as an excuse to get away for a week. So you can see how upsetting today was for us. We had hoped to love the place, and we do, but getting in the middle of another murder case is not going to help Carrie have warm, fuzzy feelings about this property."

"I have a suggestion that might help. The village of Dovecote has a potluck dinner once a month for the residents of Dovecote at the community center. It's a popular event and fills up fast, but I'll make a few calls, see if I can get the four of us invited if they have room for us. If I can introduce you to the locals, then I'm sure Carrie will feel much better about living in Dovecote."

"That would be great," Mark said as they pulled into the garden center. "Meet you at Anne's in a few minutes."

Vanished Sisters

Blake agreed and added. "I need to check in at the station. It will take me about thirty minutes. Warn Anne that I'll be a few minutes behind you."

*

WHEN ANNE AND Carrie saw Mark carrying his shoes and his clothes covered in mud, they pointed the way to the shower. He didn't even stop to kiss Carrie. After a shower and clean clothes, he was ready for a hug from the girls. "Something really does smell good, and I'm as hungry as a bear. Blake will be along in a few minutes; he had to check in with the station. I really like him, Anne; could he be the one?"

"I'm not looking for the one, Mark; I've already had the love of my life. How can I ever settle for less? But Blake is very nice, and we enjoy each other's company. His wife died of cancer too, so we have a lot in common. We prop each other up when needed. I give him a hot meal once in awhile, and he repays me by taking me out to eat once in awhile. We're just good friends."

"Whatever works for you, Anne, but if you want my opinion, I like him."

"Me too," said Anne. "Time will tell. None of us knows what tomorrow will bring. Did you find anything new back at the Hawkins' place?"

Mark took a deep breath; he didn't want to upset Carrie, but neither could he hide it from her. "We did; someone had been there and removed something from the well. We think it was the bones of the Hawkins sisters."

"Noooo," Carrie moaned, as she closed her eyes and shook her head, "not in the well; please tell me they weren't thrown in that deep dark well?"

Mark put his arms around Carrie. "I know, honey; I didn't want to tell you. I'm afraid you will never want to go back there, much less build a summer house."

"Oh, Mark, it's so sad. You're right and wrong; I will never be able to get this experience out of my head and I feel their ghosts will always haunt the place. But on the positive side, they'll be friendly ghosts; we'll share our home with them. When we aren't there, I'll feel as if they're looking after the place for us. I just wish we felt more welcomed by the community."

"Blake says it's a wonderful community and that crime is nonexistent. He's going to get us invited to the community's potluck dinner this week so we can meet some of the residents and hopefully feel more comfortable about the neighborhood."

"That's great," Anne said. "I've been to a couple of those dinners; it was the best food I've ever eaten. All the veggies are straight from the garden and those women know how to fry chicken. I wish I knew their secret. Mark, you'll know some of the people there; not all of the old farmers are dead. There's a few still kicking, and some are the kids we played with when we stayed summers there. Remember Bill Burgess? He will be there. He's taken over the Burgess farm and turned it into a real showplace."

"I feel better already," Carrie said. "If we can make some friends in the community, it will make all the difference. I'm looking forward to it."

*

BLAKE CHECKED IN at the station and made a call to the State Bureau of Investigation. The agent Blake spoke to promised to arrange a flyover of the property and send two agents to walk the entire forty acres. The agent also wanted to talk to Mark and have his evidence sent to their lab since the bureau would be officially investigating the death of the Hawkins sisters.

The next day, Mark returned to the Hawkins' farm and met with the SBI agent in charge. They did a thorough search of the house and found hair samples from both sisters, a chamber pot containing dried urine, and an old shirt that had bloodstains on the sleeve. If they could obtain DNA from just one of these samples, they would hopefully have a match with the DNA from the one bone found. This would be the needed proof that the sisters were murdered and their bodies thrown into the well. Then would come the task of finding out who murdered them and why.

## Vanished Sisters

As Mark and the SBI agent searched the house and barn, two other agents, dressed like ordinary hikers, were investigating the woods and trails in and around the property. Together, Mark and the agent searched for a way into the attic, with no luck. They both made a mental note to find a ladder; however, if there was no way into the attic from the house, how could there be anything in the attic?

Carrie was given the task of calling the realtor to request the old road leading into the Hawkins' farm be bush hogged. She assured her an offer would be coming in the next day or so. The realtor agreed to have the drive mowed immediately.

\*

THE COMMUNITY HOUSE was alive with people and a fiddler was warming up as Mark, Blake, and the girls arrived. Anne and Carrie had made a macaroni casserole that morning for the potluck. As they all entered, the smell of food made their mouths water. Mark saw his old childhood friend, Billy Burgess. He went over to shake his hand and introduce Carrie. The first words out of Billy's mouth were, "I understand you're going to buy the Hawkins' farm?"

Mark was surprised by his statement, but he suspected that in a small community such as Dovecote, news traveled quickly. "We're thinking about it; haven't signed anything yet."

"I also heard you found the old sisters."

Mark was shocked, no one knew about the bones being found except the four of them and the SBI. Mark was sure the word couldn't have gotten out. "Where did you hear that?"

"There are no secrets in this community," he laughed. "Heard you found them in the well."

Mark faked a cough and said, "Excuse me; I need a drink of water." He took Carrie's arm, moved toward Blake, and informed him of what he had just heard. Blake and Mark looked at Anne.

"I swear I didn't tell a soul. Mark, I wouldn't tell something that might jeopardize finding out who murdered poor old Aunt Ida and Aunt Eva. Billy has a self-esteem problem; he's constantly trying to show the community how important he is. He's just guessing, or he stupidly let us know he's involved."

Blake gave Billy the once over. "Either he knows who killed the sisters or he has someone in law enforcement who feeds him information. I'll give his name to the SBI. Billy has a reputation of being very unpleasant if he doesn't get his way. Anne's right; he's a high school dropout who made it big. No one knows where his money came from, but he seems to have plenty."

Blake took Mark and Carrie to get cups of cider and introduce them to the community. Mark remembered some of the names from when he was a boy, but the faces had changed, a different generation. They settled at a table and ate dinner with the Cooper and Morgan families. Both families lived in the little village. Mr. Cooper was the postmaster and Mr. Morgan owned the service station.

Mr. and Mrs. Cooper were very nice. Elvis Cooper was a little on the stout side and Martha Cooper was definitely the cook who made him that way. She was as wide as she was tall. They were a jolly couple with six plump, rosy-cheeked children. They offered to assist Mark and Carrie in any way they could.

Butch and Ruby Morgan, a quiet but friendly couple, had no children. Both had worked in the sock mill in Marion until the mill closed. They took their life savings and opened the service station in Dovecote. Butch knew a lot about cars and Ruby ran the cash register and pumped gas when Butch was busy repairing a car. He also had an ancient tractor and would plow your garden for you in the spring. He told Mark he had bush hogged the Hawkins' driveway for the realtor and would smooth down the ruts for Mark if they bought the property.

They also met Minnie Sue Winkle and her husband Lester, who owned the grocery store/barbershop. Minnie Sue assured them she sold the freshest vegetables in the county. She was no more than 4' 5" and didn't weigh ninety pounds. You could have mistaken her for a child if it weren't for her deeply wrinkled face and white hair. Lester was 6' 3" and skinny as a rail. They looked like Mutt and Jeff. They were the friendliest and most talkative. Minnie Sue bragged that she didn't own a

## Vanished Sisters

superstore, but she had most anything you needed to survive. "My Lester here is the barber," she informed them, "but he only knows one haircut. He shaves it all off. He was a barber in the Army."

By the end of the potluck dinner, Mark and Carrie felt much better about the people in the community. They had been warmly welcomed into the village of Dovecote. No one other than Billy had mentioned the Hawkins sisters or even hinted at having heard rumors. Billy's remarks were very suspicious.

As they drove back to Marion, Blake and Mark talked in the front seat. "What kind of boy was Billy when you two were growing up?"

Mark thought a minute, reflecting on the past. "Well, I wouldn't say he was a bad boy, but he was the kind of kid who didn't mind stealing a watermelon out of someone's patch and smashing it, just to be mean. We never got into a fight or anything like that, but he did things I knew better than to do."

"I think I'll put him under surveillance for a few days and suggest that Ben, the local director of the SBI, have a talk with him. Maybe someone at the station heard me talking to the SBI. You can't keep employees from talking no matter how many seminars you have on the importance of confidentiality. You always have that one employee who wants to sound important by blabbing everything he hears."

*

THE NEXT DAY, Mark and Carrie made an offer on the property. To their surprise, the distant relative who inherited the property and had had it on the market for over a year, with no offers, suddenly decided to take it off the market. It was no longer for sale. The realtor was as surprised as Mark. "Could you give me his number and let me talk to him? Maybe I can change his mind."

"Well, I'm not supposed to, but anyone can look it up at the deeds office. If he asks where you got the number, tell him at the Registrar of Deeds."

"I'll be happy to do that; thanks for helping us. Here's

my card in case he calls back and has a change-of-mind."

Mark and Carrie left the realtor's office defeated and disappointed. In their minds, the Hawkins' farm was already theirs. They were hoping to go home and hire an architect to start designing a house for them. Mark had to know what or who had changed the distant relative's mind.

\*

MARK CALLED BLAKE; he was not in his office, but he returned Mark's call within minutes. "Blake, we've just been told that the Hawkins' property is off the market. I think someone got to him because there was no other offer. Someone made him take it off the market."

"Mark, I'm out at the property now. It was the SBI who told him to take the property off the market; it's only temporary. The owner told us he would accept your offer, if and when he was allowed to sell. The realtor faxed your offer to him, even though he had taken it off the market earlier.

"We have serious problems here, Mark. The two SBI officers are missing. They never reported in after they were dropped off. The property is now crawling with agents. The lab reports are back, and we have a match. The bone was from one of the sisters. We now have proof that the sisters were in the well."

"That's great news. Have they got a forensic man out there? If you need me, I've got my case in the car."

"I'm sure they do, but none as experienced as you are. I told them you were the forensic anthropologist on the Kansas farm, serial killer case. They were impressed and would love to have your expertise on this case. Can you extend your vacation another week?"

"Yes, my job description allows me to be loaned out to assist in multiple murder cases if I'm requested by the CIA, FBI, SBI, or Homeland Security. I'll contact the university immediately and arrange for someone to teach my classes for as long as I'm needed here. I'll be there as soon as I drop Carrie at my sister's."

"That's great, Mark; I'll inform the SBI."

Mark looked at Carrie. "Could you figure out what's going on from hearing one side of the conversation?"

"Pretty much. I could hear Blake's side of the conversation, too. Take me to the garden center. I can help Anne and it will give me something to do. I'll call Aunt Mattie to let them know we won't be home right away. I'm sure Aunt Mattie and Rosa can handle things. I'll talk to Tucker and try to explain that Daddy is needed here and assure him you will continue to call him every night as usual. You know Pete will check on them for us. At least we'll still be able to buy the property, whenever this mess is sorted out."

## CHAPTER 4

WHEN MARK REACHED Dovecote, Butch Morgan and several locals were hanging around the entrance to the Hawkins' property. They recognized Mark and motioned for him to stop. "What's going on, Mark? There's enough cops and SBI men in there to wage a war."

"Butch, I'm not sure. I was just asked to come out here. I'm just following orders."

"We heard they found the Hawkins sisters. Is that right?"

"I've heard that rumor too. Let me get in there and see what's going on. If they will allow me, I'll stop by the station and let you know what I can repeat, but I can't promise. I've worked with the SBI before; sometimes they're pretty tight-lipped."

Butch patted Mark on the arm. "Thanks, Mark; we're all a little confused and worried right now. I've had some real strange-looking customers lately, wondered where they came from. Maybe the SBI needs to know that."

"I'm sure that's important. They will probably want to talk to you. I'll pass on that information."

Mark eased his SUV on down the rutted drive and pulled over in the field behind several police cars. He saw Blake and moved that way.

Blake noticed Mark pull in and came to meet him. "The SBI are pretty impressed to have you working with them. Ben

Miller, the Western North Carolina Director, wants to talk with you. They've set up a makeshift command post in the house because it looks like rain. So far, we haven't found the missing agents. The flyover didn't turn up much."

"Did they use heat-sensing photography?"

"I don't know. Ben is requesting another flyover; maybe you'd better talk to him about that." They walked into the old parlor and Blake introduced Mark to Ben Miller.

"Nice office," Mark remarked as they shook hands.

"I can't believe this place has never been wired for electricity. We're checking to see if we can use the community building just down the road. I hope to have this mess cleared up before that's necessary, but just in case, we can't use this place after sundown unless we work by candlelight. We have twenty-five men searching the area, and I've requested another flyover."

Mark interrupted, "Request a photographer with a camera that uses heat sensing film. In this dense forest, we may pick up a few bears, deer, and big cats, but one may turn out to be your agents. Even if they're buried, the heat from their bodies will show up. It's worth a try; could save a lot of time."

"Sounds good; I hadn't thought of that. I'll call and see if we have one available; we may have to borrow one."

"I'm sure the Asheville coroner's office has one. Check with it first if the SBI doesn't have one."

Ben motioned for Mark to sit down in one of the straight-backed chairs he had found around the house. "I need to talk to you about your old friend Billy Burgess, as soon as I make this call."

Ben used a radiophone with no problem. He did need to call the Asheville Coroner's office, and was assured that a helicopter would be in the air within the hour.

"Now, Mark, Blake tells me Billy Burgess knew the sisters had been found and you were trying to buy this property? Blake has Billy under surveillance, but so far, he hasn't even left the ranch. Do you think he could have been involved in the removal of the sisters' bones from the well?"

"I couldn't tell you. I haven't seen or heard from him since I was seventeen and spending my last summer in the valley with my grandparents."

Concern and determination furrowed Ben's brow. "I went to see him this morning. I asked him how he knew you had found the sisters. He gave me the same answer he gave you. I pressed him and he became a little nervous, said he couldn't remember who told him. During the conversation, Billy crossed a foot over his knee. I couldn't help but notice how closely the heel of his boot matched the print you took from the porch around the well.

"We believe he is somehow involved in this murder. At the very least, he knows something. I didn't want to arrest him because we don't know enough to make it stick and he could lead us to others. He doesn't strike me as the type who would do away with two old ladies for no reason. Something is going on here; the vanished sisters and our missing agents prove that. I want my men back, and I want everyone involved arrested."

"How can I help?"

"I want you to go see, Billy. Play dumb; tell him you don't understand what's going on over here. Use the fact that he knew about the sisters being found to ask if he might know who owns the property and why he would take it off the market. Get him to show you around the farm. He definitely has an ego the size of Texas when it comes to that ranch, as he calls it. Don't let him know what you do for a living. Just say you teach at a university. Keep your eyes and ears open and see what clues you can find by just looking around. You know what to look for."

*

MARK USED THE excuse that he had no phone service to stop by Billy's without calling first. No one answered the door, even though Billy's truck was in the drive along with a brand new Lexus, probably his wife's. Mark decided to walk out back toward the barn looking for Billy. At least he could use that as an excuse if he were caught snooping. Billy's farm was a much bigger operation than Mark remembered. There were three barns instead of the usual one. Cattle and horses had been added. Billy's father had been a crop farmer, mainly corn and tobacco.

Vanished Sisters

Mark walked past the barns out to where the fenced pasture began. He watched the cattle huddled together under a shade tree and slowly took in the entire farm. Everything was neat, clean, up-to-date, no peeling paint, no sagging barn doors, no overgrown weeds around the barns; the entire place spoke of prosperity. Billy was a successful farmer, or should he say "rancher"?

Mark ventured back toward the house and peeked in the first barn. Horses—this barn was entirely for horses, and he had some beauties. He walked past the stalls rubbing the noses of show quality horseflesh. Toward the back of the barn were bigger, working horses, probably used for herding the cattle. He saw an office toward the barn's rear and knocked on the door. No answer. Mark looked around to make sure no one was coming up behind him and tried the door. It was locked.

He came out of the barn but still saw no one. *Surely, Billy has hired hands to help out around here.* He moved to the next barn and opened the side door. "Hello," he hollered, but no one answered. He heard a calf bawling for his mama. Several newborn calves were in different stalls along with several empty stalls. The last two at the end had newborn kids in them along with their mama goats. The loft was full of hay and feed sacks, as was the first barn—nothing out of the ordinary.

Mark was very impressed. He remembered Anne saying that Billy had dropped out of high school. To run an operation this big took a certain amount of know-how. He didn't remember Billy's father even having a horse on the place, much less cattle. He had to wonder how Billy went from being a dirt farmer's son to the owner of an operation this size. *Where did he get the money? He sure didn't get it from his father. Maybe he married money?*

Mark came out of the second barn and looked around; still no one in sight. He moved to the third barn and thought he heard voices coming from inside. He tried the door.... It was locked. Before knocking, he listened and realized they were not speaking English. What was it? He first thought it must be Spanish. Everyone hired Mexicans; they were cheap labor and good workers. But no, it wasn't Spanish. Mark knew Spanish when he heard it, even though he didn't really speak the language. This was a language he had never heard before. He was about to knock when someone tapped him on the shoulder.

"There you are," Mark said, looking into Billy's angry face. He ignored Billy's expression and continued as if they were still best friends from long ago. "I got no answer at the house, and I've been walking around your wonderful place. I found no one in the horse barn and no one in the calving barn. I was sure you were in here because I heard voices. Unfortunately, they seem to be speaking Spanish and I didn't understand. I was about to knock and ask if you were around."

Billy's shoulders relaxed and his posture changed from suspicious to friendly. "What brings you out here, Mark? I thought you would be long gone by now?"

Mark let his shoulders droop and looked sad. "No. I'm disappointed, but still here. I wanted to see if you could help me. The property has been taken off the market and I don't know why. I wanted to call the owner to see if I could talk him into changing his mind. I remembered you saying there were no secrets in Dovecote. I thought, maybe, you might know the owner and why he took the property off the market. I wouldn't think that finding the sisters would make him decide not to sell. We had hoped to have our offer accepted this morning and be on our way home to hire an architect. Now, we're at a loss. We were going back to get packed up when I decided to leave Carrie at my sister's house and give it one more try; that is, if you can help me?"

"Come on up to the house. I'll fix us a cup of coffee." He put his hand on Mark's back and cleverly moved him away from the barn. "I know why the SBI are crawling all over the place, but I'm afraid I don't know who now owns the property. But I may be able to help you find out."

Mark played dumb. "What do you mean the SBI are crawling all over the place? Blake said they're investigating the murder of the sisters. Is that what you meant?"

Billy stared at Mark for several seconds too long. Mark could see the cogs of the gears moving in Billy's brain. When he said he knew what was going on up on the Hawkins' property, he was sure Mark knew about the missing agents—and the many SBI agents who were there to try and find them. If Mark didn't know about the missing agents, how could Billy know? Again Billy had said too much. Mark now knew that Billy knew about the missing agents, but how?

Mark decided to go on with his ignorance-of-the-facts mode. They continued to walk toward the house. "I'm not sure they will ever find the murderers of the Hawkins sisters. The case is too cold. Do you have any idea who would murder them or why?"

Billy tried to feign a "Who me?" expression. "Don't have a clue, Mark; those old ladies never hurt anyone. Can't for the life of me figure that one. It was a real shock to the community. Probably some teenagers hopped up on dope."

They settled at the kitchen table and were drinking coffee. Billy had the phone book out, looking for a number. He picked up the landline and dialed. "I have a friend at the Registrar of Deeds; I'm sure he will give me the number. Hello, Sadie, my lady; is Bert around?" He waited with his hand over the phone. "That Sadie is a real looker, like to take her out in the barn.... Hey, Bert, I need a phone number."

Mark noticed he didn't even say who was calling. They knew him by his voice.

"I don't have a name; I need that too. I need to know who owns the Hawkins' property in Dovecote and his number." Billy waited and rolled his eyes. He was obviously getting some flack. "Just do it, Bert; what's one more breach of protocol?" Another pause. "He's getting it for me. He's a lackey." A minute later, he began to write a name and number. "Thanks, Buddy. I'll put in a good word with the boss." He hung up and handed Mark the name and number.

"Nice to have friends in high places," Mark said. "With a spread like this, I guess you deserve a little clout. I'm extremely in awe of your place here. I would never have guessed you for an equestrian. Some of those horses are show quality. How long have you been in the horse and cattle business?"

"What you really mean is how did a dropout like me get to own a ranch like this? Well it's not what you know; it's who you know. I guess you're some kind of big-shot doctor or lawyer?"

"No, just a teacher. I didn't mean it the way you took it. How would I know you were a dropout? If you are, you're to be commended for what you've achieved with your life. Are you married?"

"Sorry; I'm a little touchy. Everyone, including my parents, thought I was a flunky and would never become anything but a pothead. To answer your question, yes, I was married, no children. She didn't like country life...moved on to bigger and better things. Tried to make me sell this farm and give her half. I showed her."

Mark could see the hostility just under the surface. This was a man with low self-esteem. He constantly had to be proving to others (but really himself) how successful he was. Mark continued to brag on his accomplishments. "Don't you wish your Dad and Mom could see you now? They would be so proud. There's not a farm or ranch in this state that could touch this place. I love how you've kept the original farmhouse and redesigned it to suit your modern needs. It's beautiful."

"Thanks, Mark; not many around here will admit that to me. I appreciate you saying those things."

"How did you get started in the cattle and horse business?"

"I went out west after Mama died and worked on a ranch for a while. Saved my money. When my Dad died, I came back, started small, and increased my herd every year. It's hard work, but I love it."

Mark felt the conversation waning and said, "I sure appreciate the name and number. I'm going back to Marion and call this man. Maybe we can come to some kind of understanding. I really want that farm. It looks down on the valley where I was the happiest. Carrie even likes it and wants to plant a garden. We'll see." Mark stood and offered Billy his hand. "Thanks again, and I hope we'll be neighbors someday."

Billy stood and took Mark's hand. "Me too, Mark; hope to see you again soon."

# Vanished Sisters

*

MARK WENT PAST Dovecote and headed for Marion. He was afraid if he went to the Hawkins' property, Billy would know within minutes that he went straight to the SBI. He was sure Billy had a spy in the sheriff's office. He went to his sister's garden center, locked himself in, and called Blake.

"Hey, Blake, Mark here. I feel I need to warn you that I'm pretty sure you have someone in your office feeding Billy information. Billy knows about the missing agents, but I'm not convinced he's actually done anything wrong."

"I'm sure you're right, Mark. I think I know who our snitch is. It's not the first time I've suspected him of passing information. I'll have a talk with him and threaten to fire him if I even suspect he has leaked confidential information. As of right now, he is on administrative leave. How did the meeting go?"

"Okay, I guess. Do you know how Billy became so successful?"

"Rumor has it that either his dad won the lottery and didn't tell anyone, or Billy got into drug trafficking while he was in Texas. He physically abused his wife until she left him. Most people get out of his way when they see him coming."

"I saw that anger firsthand today. He caught me snooping around. I convinced him I was just looking for him because I needed his help to find the owner of the Hawkins' property. He had no trouble finding out with one phone call to the county Registrar of Deeds. He didn't even have to tell them who he was. They knew his voice and did exactly as he told them."

"That's interesting. Sounds like our Billy is somehow getting his hooks into public officials. Not a good thing. I think you need to tell Ben what you've told me. We're waiting for the flyover; should be here any minute."

"I'll call him now, Blake; I didn't return to the house because I didn't want word to get back to Billy that I went straight to the SBI. I think I need to stay away from there until Ben decides what to do about Billy."

"Good move, Mark. I'll come by Anne's tonight and fill you in on the flyover."

Mark called Ben and repeated most of the conversation he had just had with Blake. Ben asked him whether he was able to see much of the ranch.

"Yes, I did, and I was surprised at the size of his operation. There are three barns behind the house. One is for horses and has a locked office in the back. One is for calving, and the third is a mystery. It was locked and I could hear voices inside speaking a language unknown to me. Billy found me at the door of the third barn, which is closest to the house. I managed to persuade him I was only looking for him since no one answered the door at the house. He guided me away from that barn and didn't offer to show me inside. The windows were shuttered from the inside. I admitted I had been in the other two barns looking for him, which didn't seem to bother him. We went to the house, had coffee, and chatted."

Mark repeated everything that was said in the conversation and suggested he needed to find out what was going on in the barn closest to the house. He explained why he hadn't come back to the Hawkins' property, and Ben agreed he should stay away until they could get a warrant and check out the barn.

*

AFTER MARK LEFT Billy's ranch, Shahin came to the house. He was furious. "What have you done, you stupid infidel? You have jeopardized our entire operation." He slapped Billy across the face. "If I didn't need you, I would kill you right now. We need to transfer everything in that warehouse down to the secret room. Let's go, asshole. If they find our meth lab, you will go to jail. First, the SBI shows up asking questions; now this friend shows up poking around and asking more questions. I sent you to the community dinner to find out what they knew. Instead, you shoot off your mouth and tell them you know about the dead sisters. You are a liability, Billy. I can't afford to have you arrested and questioned."

Shahin had hidden cameras all over the farm. He could see not only what was going on in the house and barns, but he could hear as well. He knew the SBI would be back with a war-

rant. He and his men had to clear out as fast as possible. They would live in the cave until they could get the weapons from the sister's attic, then move everything to the safe house that even Billy knew nothing about. Billy had no idea how many Al-Qaeda operatives were now in America, and Shahin knew Billy would never know, because if arrested, the stupid infidel would spill his guts to the police.

*

THAT AFTERNOON, BLAKE called Mark to let him know the flyover had been a big success. They had found more than anticipated. Several marijuana fields were found on and around the Hawkins' property. The chopper surprised the field hands, as they hacked away at the marijuana plants. They scattered into the forest; however, not before aerial photographs were obtained of the workers and the fields. They all seemed to be foreigners. At first, the photographer assumed the workers were Mexican, but on closer observation of the aerial photographs, they were not sure who they were. Their clothes suggested they were from the Middle East.

"We didn't find our men, but we did find a new shallow grave, possibly the sisters'. Ben wants you to accompany his agents and be there to retrieve their bones and make the identification. We have commandeered the community house and are using it as our headquarters and morgue. He needs you there by six in the morning.

"Ben and a swat team of officers are on the way to Billy's farm, as we speak, to search and seize any evidence. Ben suspects that trafficking in marijuana is how Billy supports his new lifestyle and ranch. If I hear anymore tonight, I'll call you. I'm hanging around the station because I expect to have Billy residing here before morning."

Mark was quiet; ambivalent feelings filled his mind. He felt glad the sisters might be recovered and would have a proper burial, but he was sad for his childhood friend who had chosen the wrong road and would now pay for his bad decisions. When Mark had worked for the Davidson County Coroner's office, he had seen every day the consequences of the bad decisions people made. Now he taught other future forensic anthropologists how to discover, process, and report on others' mistakes, while respecting and caring for the victims' remains.

"Mark, are you there?"

"Yes, Blake. I sure hope the remains turn out to be the sisters. They deserve a proper burial. As for Billy, he's an adult; he had choices to make and he chose the wrong path. I'll be there first thing in the morning. Please do call me if you hear what the search at Billy's uncovered. I'm curious to hear what was going on in that barn."

Carrie had been listening to Mark's side of the conversation. When he was off the phone, she asked, "They've found the sisters?"

"Not positive, but we hope so. I'm going with the agents to recover the bones in the morning. They've set up a temporary morgue at the community house. I think I have everything I'll need to process the bones and make the tests that will confirm their identity. Unfortunately, they did not find the missing agents, but that could mean they're still alive. Can you do something for me tomorrow?"

"I sure can; I wish I could come along with you. I love Anne, but there isn't much for me to do at the garden center. She doesn't have time to entertain me, and I sure would like to get back in that house and make a list of possible things we could incorporate into our new house. It would fill the house with memories of the sisters. I wouldn't feel as if we're demolishing everything that was theirs.

"That house is solid. The wide plank flooring could be saved for sure. And the rock supports could be incorporated into a rock façade. I wish I could get into that attic. Surely, there's a way to get up there without going up a ladder on the exterior? If the rafters are as solid as other parts of the house, we could use them as beams in the den or kitchen. They are weathered and aged, just what I want to give the house a primitive feel along with lots of Aunt Mattie's antiques."

"Sounds warm and inviting," said Mark. "Just the feel I wanted for our summer home. What I was going to suggest is that you borrow Anne's car and come out there tomorrow. I want you to go into the village and talk to Mr. Cooper. Ask who we see about having the sisters buried in the little church cemetery near the sister's property. They would be close to home, and it's such a quaint old church. Maybe you could pick up some lunch and we'll go through the cemetery, check out the dates on some of the tombstones, and go through the house again. I need to be there very early, and I doubt we'll get back with the remains before lunch. I don't want you going through that house alone."

"Oh, Mark," said Carrie. "That sounds like fun. I'll come on over around eleven, talk to Mr. Cooper, and come on to the community house."

# CHAPTER 5

MARK ARRIVED AT the community house around quarter-to-six. Miss Minnie Sue had arrived at five. Coffee and sausage biscuits were ready for the men as they came in. The community house had a fully equipped kitchen; someone would have coffee and biscuits ready every morning and serve a hot lunch at noon for as long as the investigation continued. Minnie Sue said it was the least the village could do to help out. This was the community Mark remembered from his childhood. He wished he could call Carrie and tell her to forget bringing lunch. He didn't want to miss the local fresh vegetables, and he was counting on fried chicken.

Mark had settled at one of the tables and was enjoying his coffee and biscuit when Blake arrived. He came straight for Mark. "Where did you get that?" he asked, pointing to the coffee and biscuits. Mark laughed and sent him to the kitchen. He returned with a mouth full of biscuit. "Boy, do I miss having a wife to cook for me. My wife made biscuits just like these. I should have gotten two. I'm afraid they're going to run out."

"Don't worry, Blake; the ladies in the community are going to do this every morning as well as serve a hot lunch. We need to pray this investigation lasts a long time. I hope Carrie will learn to bake biscuits like these. How did the bust go last night?"

"Not good; the place was cleaned out. Either someone warned him or he doesn't believe your reason for paying him a visit. Either way, Billy Burgess lives to deal another day. We'll get him. How do you feel about going back over there? Ben wants you to go over the place thoroughly for traces of drugs. Billy is still at the station answering questions for the SBI. We need to get over there now and be done by the time they release him."

"Let's go; I'll follow you. I have all my equipment in the SUV. By the way, will you call Carrie for me? She was going to bring lunch for us around eleven. I think she would rather have lunch here at the community house, instead of fast food."

"No problem; is she at the nursery or house?"

"I think she'll be at the nursery because she's going to borrow Anne's car."

\*

THE BARN WAS not a barn at all—more like an empty warehouse. Mark knew there was clean and then there was clean. This room had been vacuumed, but he knew vacuums didn't filter the air and pull dust from the baseboards and corners. He went to work with his own vacuum, after collecting evidence from the bathroom and kitchenette. He had a case full of evidence and was packing up when the barn door slammed open and Billy walked in.

Billy went straight for Mark. Mark braced himself for the worst. "What the hell are you doing here?" Billy yelled. His face was blood red and you could almost see smoke seeping from his ears.

Blake intercepted him. "Now, Billy, you know we have a warrant; better cool down."

"What's he doing here?" Billy sneered, giving Mark a vicious look. "I should have known I couldn't trust you. I thought you said you was a schoolteacher?"

Mark remained calm. "I teach college, Billy; I teach forensic anthropology."

"What the hell does that mean?"

"It means I find clues that criminals think they've hidden. I examine bodies and skeletal remains to discover how they died, which helps law enforcement find the perpetrators. It's a science that law enforcement depends on to put the criminals away. If you're innocent, there won't be any clues here for me to find and you will go free."

Billy stood rigid...face red...hands clenched in fists. He stared at Mark with hate in his eyes for at least thirty seconds before abruptly turning, marching out of the barn, and slamming the door.

"Well...." Blake blew out a breath he had been holding so long his chest hurt. "I could almost use that as a confession. Unfortunately, 'almost' doesn't get it. I'm afraid you've lost a friend for life.... Sorry. Are we ready to go? The team is waiting for you to retrieve the sisters' bones."

Mark looked sad. "Yes, I'm ready. I don't think I need his friendship, now or ever."

\*

THIS WAS TURNING into a busy day. Mark arrived back at the community house and climbed onto a four-wheel vehicle, similar to a golf-cart. He held on for dear life as the SBI agent headed for the woods with two other four-wheel go-carts following behind. They sped down mountain trails and made their own trail when necessary. They were heading straight up now. Mark couldn't look down. At one point, the vehicle almost turned over. "Slow down, son, or I'm going to throw-up on you." Mark was not feeling well at all. After thirty minutes of this hair-raising thrill ride, they finally came to an abrupt stop. Mark got out and promptly lost his sausage biscuit.

"Sorry, Mark; I was just trying to get us back in time for lunch. The ladies were frying chicken when I left."

Mark bent over and retched again. Someone handed him a bottle of water and he rinsed his mouth. The agents unloaded his case and led the way to the gravesite.

"I'm driving back," Mark announced. "These ladies

## Vanished Sisters

have never been in a motor vehicle before, and I don't intend to subject them to a ride like that even if they are dead. They've been murdered, thrown in a well, dumped in a burlap bag, and buried in a shallow grave.... It's time for a little respect."

"Sorry, Mark; we forgot you knew these ladies. You're right; they deserve a gentle ride back to their home."

Mark didn't reply but began digging with his shovel, after looking for clues as to who had done this. He carefully retrieved Aunt Ida and Aunt Eva's bones. The ride home was quiet and as slow as a funeral procession...just as it should have been. A storage room off the main gathering room of the community house was already set up for Mark, and he began the task of uncovering how these ladies died.

When Carrie arrived, Blake told her they had found the sisters and that Mark was a little upset. Carrie slipped into the back room where Mark was working. She came up behind him and put her arms around him. "I'm so sorry, Mark." He faced her and returned her hug. A tear escaped his eye and he buried his face in her neck and kissed her. "At least we can give them a nice burial. Did you have time to talk to Mr. Cooper?"

"I did. He's taking care of everything and asked that we let him know when we would like to have the service. The little church has a minister who travels to several small churches in the area. He knew the sisters and had visited them many times. He has a service here once a month. Sometimes he has to preach three sermons on Sunday, to make sure each church gets at least one sermon a month."

"He must be a very dedicated man," Mark replied. "Not many ministers would take on that mission."

When Mark had finished with the sisters, he placed their bones in special bags and said a prayer. He and Carrie walked up to the little church and meandered through the graveyard. Some of the graves dated back to the Civil War. Mark found a slightly sloping spot with a view through the woods to the sisters' property. He hoped they could be buried there.

"Hello there," someone called. They turned to find Mr. Cooper walking toward them. A day and time for the funeral was decided. Mr. Cooper was sure no one owned the plot Mark had found. "I will take care of everything. I have already called the funeral home used by everyone around here. They will pick up the sisters when you're ready. The community has decided to pay for the funeral entirely and provide a meal after the service. We want to show our appreciation to you as well as honor the sisters."

Mark and Carrie were overwhelmed. Mark felt like he had come home and never wanted to leave. They walked back to the community house for lunch.

\*

BILLY SAT AT his desk. His office door was locked. There was something he had to do before it was too late. His head was fairly clear; he had not had any drugs today, so his hands were beginning to shake. Shahin and his men had left after clearing out the lab and supposedly cleaning any residue of meth or marijuana from it. Billy knew he had little time left. They would come for him soon. He knew too much. He had told the police nothing about Shahin and his friends, but he knew Shahin would not trust him to keep his mouth shut.

Now that Mark had gone over the meth lab, Billy was sure he would either be arrested or killed...today. Shahin was watching the ranch and was aware that Mark had entered the lab. Billy's whole world was falling apart. He hoped they killed him before he was arrested.

With pen in hand, he began to write. He was leaving a letter under his desk blotter, knowing the SBI would find it. It was a complete confession. He explained his drug habit, as well as how he had become addicted and controlled by terrorists. Yes, they were terrorists, but he had not figured that out until the first shipment of arms arrived. By then, it was too late; his own ego and the drugs had destroyed his entire life.

This was his last chance to do something right. He hoped he could free Sarah of any involvement with either the ranch or the terrorists. *God knows, she deserves something from me,* he thought. She had tried so hard to make him see the truth and to get him off drugs. He believed she had truly loved him at one time, but he had destroyed her love and given her a scar on her face she would take to her grave. Every time she looked in the mirror, she would remember what a total failure he had become. He hoped leaving the ranch to her would somehow let her know he did care for her. He was just too weak to turn his life around.

*

BEN CAME IN to have lunch and sat down with Mark and Carrie. "I've sent all evidence samples to the lab. We should know tomorrow if we need to arrest Billy. I have someone watching his ranch in case he decides to run. I also requested tapes of different Middle East languages. I want you to listen to them and see if you can zoom in on the language you heard spoken in the barn. It will help us know who we're dealing with.

"With our borders unsecured and illegals pouring in, it's the ideal cover for terrorists to slip through. This could be nothing more than a marijuana farm, or it could be a means of supporting terrorist activities. We need to find out. The problem is, they know we're on to them and they'll go-to-ground and lay low for a while. We plan to use every device known to the criminal justice system to find out what is going on here. Have you learned how the sisters died?"

"Bullet to the head. Gang style. My guess is they found the marijuana fields on their property. I'm sure they wouldn't have known what it was, only that someone was on their land. The sisters may have surprised the workers, and the workers killed them to keep them from reporting the marijuana."

"Possibly. We may never know why they were killed," Ben added. "As old as the sisters were, anyone would have known they were harmless. Maybe they wanted to store marijuana in the house, thinking it was deserted. I mean, who would have thought anyone lived there. They could have surprised the sisters in the middle of the night, thinking the house was abandoned."

"You may be right, Ben," said Mark, "but there would always be the risk that someone from the village would check on them, find them missing, and report it to the authorities. We don't know how long they were dead before someone came to check. They could have used the house for storage or even lived there until one day the teenagers showed up to use the house to hide and smoke pot. Maybe then they moved out and disappeared into the mountains. You're right. We may never know what happened.

"I think Carrie and I will go over and take another look. As many times as I've been through that house, I can't believe I would have missed evidence of someone other than the sisters living there. But if the house was lived in, I should be able to find evidence to support that theory. Maybe I've been looking for the wrong things. Want to come along?"

"No, I need to check in with my agents who're combing the forests around Dovecote. I talked with the service station owner. From the description Butch gave, we may well be dealing with Middle East terrorists. When you listen to the language tapes, let him hear them too. If you both pick the same language sample, we're in business."

*

THE OLD HOUSE stood tall, cold, and dark as they eased down the rutted road and parked out front. Mark carried his forensic case along to look for clues that the house had been lived in by someone other than the sisters. "It's so quiet back here, Mark; the only sound you hear are the birds. I can't wait to spend our first summer here."

"That's all we'll ever hear, except for an occasional distant train whistle. This village will never turn into a vacation haven; I'm worried it will disappear completely."

The scent of the sisters that still lingered in the house was a warm welcome as they entered. The smell made him think they were still there.

"Mark, can I wander around, or do you need to check the place out first?"

"Go ahead; there have been so many people in here already that your walking through won't make any difference. I doubt there is anything here, but I'll have a look anyway. I'll start upstairs in the bedrooms. When we searched for DNA evidence, I think I would have found proof then of other inhabitants."

It looked as though the sisters had shared the same room, probably the same room they shared as children. While Mark went over the beds, Carrie checked out the closets. It looked as though the sisters were not overly fashion conscious. They had only one change of clothes. Carrie pushed the clothes aside and examined the walls. Anne had mentioned that some old homes had hidden stairways in the closets that led to the attics. There was no secret staircase here. She moved to check out another bedroom. There were three, two nice-sized bedrooms and one small one.

She went into the small room, which was probably a nursery. There was no furniture in that room. She suspected vandals had stolen anything of value. Carrie secretly hoped she might find something to remind them of the sisters. She opened the closet, which was empty, and checked out the walls. Nothing there. She moved on. The third bedroom must have been the parents' room; it had a bed, dresser, and armoire. Carrie thought the armoire, even though it was very primitive, could be used in their new home as a reminder of the sisters. Maybe even the old iron bed and dresser.

The parents' clothes remained in the closet. An old, wool, moth-eaten coat hung on a wooden hanger by a thread. The pants were just as bad. Two dresses hung beside the coat and pants. They were long, homespun, and plain. The moths had liked them too. Carrie pulled the garments back and checked out the back wall. Nothing. Disappointed, she looked down at the floor and noticed tracks from men's boots. She looked back over the room and found more tracks, all leading to the closet. "Mark, could you come in here?" she called.

Mark had found a couple of dark hairs...the sisters had white hair. He noticed heavy boot prints in the dust on the floor, but that could have been the pot-smoking teenagers. He stopped what he was doing and went to see what Carrie had found.

"Look!" Carrie pointed to the muddy footprints.

"Yes, I found them in the other room too. They could be

from the kids who were in here looking for things to sell."

"But look where they're all going. They all go to the closet."

Mark frowned. "You're right; what's in the closet?"

"Nothing except a few old, moth-eaten clothes probably belonging to the parents. So why do they all lead there?"

Mark moved to the closet. He felt the wall. He knocked on the back wall, then the sidewalls. He examined one end of the closet closer, banging on it harder. He took out his Swiss Army knife and used the large blade to try to pry out one side of the wall. It moved.... He looked at Carrie. "Can you get your fingers in that crack and pull? Mine are too big."

Carrie stuck one finger in and decided hers would fit. With both hands side by side along the wall corner, she pulled as hard as she could, and the whole end of the closet opened up like a door. Inside were stairs leading up to the attic. Carrie started up, but Mark pulled her back and motioned for her to be quiet. He pulled out his gun, which he had worn that morning in the woods. He slowly moved up the stairs with Carrie close behind.

As Mark's head reached the attic floor level, he stopped. Slowly, he raised his hat and held it there for a few seconds. Nothing happened. He eased up and took a look. "Oh, dear!"

"What is it, Mark!"

"Guns. Go back down; it may be booby-trapped. I need to go get Ben."

\*

MARK LEFT CARRIE there to make her list of things she wanted removed before the house was demolished. He jumped in the SUV and headed for the community house less than a quarter of a mile down the Old Hudlow Road. He found Ben on the phone. He waited impatiently pacing up and down. He was having second thoughts about leaving Carrie alone. When Ben got off the phone, Mark told him what he'd found. Ben immediately called for backup. Four agents were just minutes from the house on their four wheelers; they would meet them at the house. As Ben and Mark headed back to the house, Ben said, "I

want you to go over every weapon in that stash. They will have fingerprints on them. We probably won't find a match in our U.S. database, but we may have luck in international."

Mark, Ben, and four other agents entered the house.... No one was there. The guns were gone...Carrie was gone. Mark ran frantically through the house, calling her name while the other agents headed outside. The backup agents saw movement in the woods and ran on foot to see which way the possible terrorists had gone. When Mark could find Carrie nowhere, not even in the well, he and Ben jumped on one of the four-wheelers and headed for the woods. They caught up with the agents on foot. The agents pointed the way for them to go. "Get the other four-wheeler," Ben called. "We'll try and catch up with them." One agent jumped in the back of Mark and Ben's vehicle as the other three ran back for the second four-wheeler.

Ben was on his radio, calling for more backup. Mark was driving and moving at a fast pace, he thought, until minutes later the other four-wheeler caught up with them and sped past. Mark sped up, but knowing he didn't have the experience the agents had with these vehicles, he didn't try to catch up, just follow.

After several minutes, they saw the other vehicle abandoned...no one in sight. They stopped too. "Where did they go?" Mark asked.

Ben spoke into his radio. "Where are you?" he demanded. Ben pointed down the mountain. "They threw Carrie off their vehicle when they realized we were catching up. They say we'll need a helicopter to get her out. She has multiple broken bones. She's unconscious but breathing." Ben made the call for a helicopter.

Mark was halfway down the mountain after hearing the words, "threw Carrie off." When he reached her, his first instinct was to take her in his arms. The agents stopped him. "No, Mark. I know you want to hold her, but you could cause more damage. We have help on the way. Her pulse is good, but I think she may have hit her head on something as she came down the mountain.... She's unconscious."

Mark touched her face. "Carrie, wake up. It's me, Mark; open your eyes. Carrie," he yelled, "look at me!" Her eyes popped open and she stared at Mark for a few seconds, but she didn't seem to see him. Her eyes closed again. He looked at the agents standing around her. "That's a good sign; she isn't in a deep coma. I think she's going to be okay."

\*

IT SEEMED FOREVER before they heard the chopper. One of the men sent up a flare. The helicopter hovered over them and sent down a cage with a back and neck brace. Carefully, they prepared Carrie for transport. As she ascended to the helicopter, Mark said. "Tell them to send it back down for me. I want to be with her."

"Sorry, Mark; they won't move her out of the cage; it could cause more damage." Mark was devastated. He looked up to say a prayer and saw a line with a hook and strap on it coming down. He smiled as the agents fastened him into the straps, put his foot in the hook, and up he went. He was too concerned for Carrie to be afraid. Later, he wouldn't believe he had done that without even thinking.

The emergency medical team worked with Carrie as they flew to Asheville General Hospital. She opened her eyes once, reached for Mark's hand, and closed them again.

As they landed on the hospital's helicopter pad, a trauma team was waiting with a gurney. They placed the cage on the gurney and ran with her to the emergency room.

\*

MARK SAT IN the waiting area and prayed. His mind went back to a year ago in Kansas, another hospital, where he had waited to hear whether Carrie would live or die. He felt sure she would come out of this okay, but what about the baby? He had forgotten to tell EMTs she was pregnant. He ran to the check-in desk. "Would you please tell the doctor that my wife is pregnant?"

"They will ask her," the attendant told him.

"She was unconscious when they brought her in. She

can't tell them," he said. The nurse was up and running back to the treatment room to relay that information.

When Mark returned to the waiting area, Anne and Blake were coming in the door. Behind them came Ben and two of the agents. He told them he knew little about her condition. "She did regain consciousness for a few seconds on the way to the hospital; she knew me and held my hand."

Anne sat down beside Mark, encircling her arms around him. "I feel sure Carrie will be okay, Mark." Anne was saying a prayer as she tried to console him. She couldn't stop the memories of their experience in Kansas from flooding her mind. She knew he was doing the same. This baby meant so much to them. If they could have a baby, the tragedy of the past year might finally be put to rest.

Mark stared at the floor and shook his head. "But what about the baby? She's been through so much, Anne. I just pray she hasn't lost the baby. She was so happy when she discovered she was pregnant. Her biggest fear, after all she went through in Kansas, was that she might not be able to have a child." A tear trailed down Mark's cheek.

"I know," Anne said, "but it's in God's hands now. All we can do is pray the baby will survive."

Mark blamed himself. Why had he left her there alone? The men must have been hiding in the attic the whole time they were there. He and Carrie must have shown up just as the men came to get the guns. There had been so much going on in that house with the SBI using it as a command base. The terrorists, or whoever they were, had been forced to leave the guns and hope they would not be found. This case was becoming more involved by the minute. Mark turned to Ben and asked, "Were any of the agents able to get a look at the men who took Carrie?"

"Not really; as soon as they caught sight of them, they saw Carrie go flying from the vehicle. We don't know if she jumped, or if they threw her off, hoping the distraction would allow them to get away. Did you get a close enough look at the weapons in the attic to determine their make and quantity?"

"They were covered with clear plastic. It was a bit opaque, but there was no doubt they were guns. There were at least a dozen AK-47s, and it looked like there were several missile launchers behind them, and even more behind the launchers that I couldn't see. It was a major stash. In my opinion, we're definitely dealing with terrorists. What have you heard from the lab report on Billy's barn?"

"Traces of marijuana and meth. Agents are picking him up now. I'm hoping we can scare him into talking; maybe offer him a deal. Finding this weapons stash puts a new light on the whole picture. It does look as if drugs could be a definite means of funding terrorist activities. When you combine the unknown foreign language with the fact that Butch described them as Arabs and now these weapons, then if it walks like a duck and quacks like a duck, we must assume we're dealing with a duck.

"They couldn't have picked a quieter, more out of the way place than the mountain forests around Dovecote. If the sisters hadn't vanished, causing the property to go on the market, who knows when or if they would have been discovered before we were facing a major catastrophe. I'm afraid it's time to get the FBI involved and probably the CIA because of international implications. We've got more than we can handle alone."

*

THE DOCTOR APPEARED in the waiting area and called Mark's name. "Come on back with me," he said. Mark followed as the doctor explained, "We've given your wife a thorough exam, and the bottom line is, she's going to be fine. She has several broken bones, a concussion, and multiple cuts and bruises. She is fully conscious and asking for you. So far, she has not lost the baby. We were careful with the x-rays, and hopefully, she and the baby will be fine. She has suffered a traumatic experience, and along with the concussion, needs rest and quiet for the next week.

"She says you're visiting your sister. I would suggest she not travel for at least a week. The trip from the hospital to your sister's will be trauma enough. Because of the baby, we want to be cautious with painkillers. She will stay overnight so we can monitor her and the baby for twenty-four hours. This will be a bad night for her, and you can stay with her if you wish. She assures me she can get along without pain medication. If she changes her mind, there are drugs we can give to help her through the night without harming the fetus. If tonight goes well, we'll release her tomorrow after lunch. They're casting her arm and leg now and you can sit with her."

Mark wasn't about to leave Carrie to suffer through the night alone. He suspected she would get little sleep. She had to be in terrible pain, but he also knew Carrie. He knew she would suffer anything to protect this baby.

*

FOUR SBI AGENTS cautiously approached Billy's house. One had been watching the house since Mark left with the possible evidence. There was always the risk Billy would run. They needed to know what he knew about the Hawkins sisters, the fields of marijuana, and the foreigners working for him...or was he working for them? Before knocking, each took a different side of the house. A search warrant was obtained in case they needed to break down a door. The house was quiet; Billy's truck sat in the driveway. There was no answer to the agent's knock. The agent tried the front door—it was unlocked. He radioed the team that he was entering the front door.

With gun drawn, standing to one side of the door, he reached over, pushed open the door, and waited. Nothing happened. He entered the house low to the ground. From the front door, he could see Billy seated at the dining room table, his head resting on folded arms. "Billy Burgess, you're under arrest." The agent held his gun with both hands aiming for Billy's head. He took another step closer. Billy didn't move. "Billy, do you hear me?" No answer. The agent spoke into his shoulder radio, directing the other agents to enter. One came in from the back, the other two through the front. They all stood staring at the pool of blood on the dining room table. The agent in charge lifted Billy's head. He had a bullet hole between his eyes. There was no gun in sight. He had been murdered just like the sisters.

"Someone got in on your watch, officer," the agent in

charge accused.

"I can see that. From my post on the ridge, no one could enter or leave without my knowledge. There has to be another way in and out of this house. Let's search the basement."

The entire house was searched, and then they moved to the basement. There was only one way in and out. The basement was completely underground and only accessible from the house stairs. It was used as an office with bookcases along one whole wall. There were no closets; the room was just one big rectangular shaped room. "No way out of here except the stairs," said one of the agents.

"I wouldn't be too sure of that," said the agent responsible for watching the house. "Let's take a closer look at this wall of shelves." He started at the far end and worked his way along the shelves, moving objects, feeling the underside of the shelves, and checking to see whether books were really books. About halfway up, he felt a button under a shelf. When pushed, one quarter of the wall opened up to expose a tunnel leading to the woods at the side of the house. "I knew there had to be a way in here. I don't sleep on the job."

## CHAPTER 6

SHAHIN AND TALIB drove their four-wheel vehicles, purchased for moving marijuana on back trails, into what looked like a normal copse of fir trees. They emerged on the other side of the copse at the mouth of a huge cave. Their vehicles were no larger than a golf cart with a good-sized truck bed, loaded with weapons. Rasin and Amir were already there waiting with their load of arms. They had made it back safely. Shahin worried about the American woman. She had seen their faces, knew they were foreigners, but how could she live through being thrown from a vehicle down a mountainside? He was sure she was dead, and her fall had succeeded in stopping their pursuers. The arms were far more important than the life of an infidel. He would have killed her anyway, after they had all raped her.

Several men came from the cave to help unload the arms and remove their tracks from the mountain trail to the cave. It was almost time for prayers; then they could rest. They had spent days watching the house. After getting the bones out of the well, they had planned to go back for the guns, missile launchers, and bomb-making paraphernalia. However, the man they shot at, hoping to scare him away, came back with an armed policeman. They prayed to Allah that the secret door to the attic would not be discovered.

No one had been to the house in the past twenty-four hours. It looked like they had moved down to another building on the main road. Now was their chance to retrieve the weapons. Things were not going well. They had stupidly underestimated Billy's ability to keep his mouth shut. He had to be dealt with before they collected the weapons and made their escape to a safe house.

They had just entered the house when Mark's SUV pulled up out front. They ran for the attic and closed the secret door behind them. Hidden back behind the weapons, they waited for the infidels to leave. The woman called to her husband. He began banging on the walls of the closet and found the secret attic door. With guns drawn, they had waited, knowing if they fired, the agents would be upon them in minutes. The weapons would be lost. Footsteps were heard first ascending, then descending. They held their breath. The SUV had sprung to life...they were gone. But they would be back, and soon; they had seen the guns. The men sprang to life, rushing down the secret stairs weighed down with weapons.

*

CARRIE HAD BEEN making notes. She had been left behind, thinking she and Mark were alone in the house. Help was only a quarter of a mile down the Old Hudlow Road—she would be fine here alone. He would be back in minutes. It might be her last chance to go thoroughly through the house and decide what could be saved before demolition. Suddenly, she heard noises coming from the attic. Before she could think, they were there, facing her. For one long pregnant pause, they stared at each other in shock. Everything in Carrie's brain screamed...run! Before her feet would move, she was knocked to the floor. *Oh, God!* she thought. *I've seen their faces.... They'll kill me.*

One of the men dropped his weapons and grabbed her. He barked orders in a language she was sure she had heard on the evening news, shouting threats into the camera. She was rushed from the house and forced to run toward the woods. Once behind the bushes, her hands were tied behind her and she was secured

## Vanished Sisters

to one of the four-wheel vehicles. Men continued carrying out armloads of guns and other strange-looking weapons from the house. They all ran back for more. She struggled to untie the knot, but they were back before she could free herself. After the weapons were loaded, she was wedged between two men in the last vehicle. It sprung to life and lunged forward. Through the trees, she thought she saw men running toward them.

Traveling at what Carrie thought was a much too excessive speed for such narrow walking trails, they began to climb a mountain. They kept climbing for what seemed an eternity, and both men kept looking back, fear in their eyes. Suddenly, the one on her right began to shout to the driver. She was sure help was coming. The driver shouted back, ordering the other man to throw her off the vehicle.

Like a sack of potatoes, Carrie was heaved from the four-wheeler. For a moment, she felt the terror of flying through the air, completely helpless to break her fall. But she had been lucky and landed in a pile of leaves. She tried to stand with her hands tied behind her, lost her balance, and began to fall and roll down the mountain. *Oh, God*, she had prayed, *stop me from falling and protect my baby.* It felt like she had been rolling and tumbling forever. Her head crashed into one tree as her leg slammed into another. She continued to roll down the steep descent. With a thud, she abruptly landed against a huge tree. She knew from the pain and angle of her left arm that it was broken, and then she had drifted into unconsciousness.

*

CARRIE WOKE AND looked at the clock on the wall for the umpteenth time. It was morning and she had actually slept for two hours. Mark was beside her in a recliner sleeping. He had helped her make it through the night without painkillers. She didn't know whether her pain level was better or she had become accustomed to the pain. She felt like hell. She stroked her abdomen with her good hand. *Hang in there, little one. You're going to be fine*, she thought. She looked at Mark; he had not moved, but his eyes were open, watching her.

"How do you feel?"

"Somewhat better, I think. I need the bedpan; where's that darn button?"

"Here you go," he said, handing her the clicker as he got to his feet and stretched. "When the nurse comes, I'll go find a bathroom and freshen up."

When Mark returned, aides were giving Carrie a sponge bath, changing her bed, and delivering her breakfast. After her vitals were taken and she was propped up in a fresh bed, her food was arranged so she could maneuver with her good hand. "Honey, you go find something to eat. I can feed myself. Thank God, it was my left arm that's broken. I'll be fine."

Mark was reluctant to go. "Let me get the tops off for you and see if you can reach everything." She looked so much better. It had been a rough night.

"That's a lot of food," she said after he opened everything.

"Remember, you're eating for two." He rubbed her tummy. "You haven't had anything since lunch yesterday. I'll bet the little one is hungry even if you're not." Mark kissed the top of her head and left to find the cafeteria.

\*

AS MARK LEFT her room, a man came up to him and flashed an FBI badge in his face. "Remember me?" he asked, smiling. It was David Durham, the FBI agent Mark had worked with in Kansas.

Mark smiled and shook his hand. "How are you, David? You're not in Kansas anymore. No pun intended."

"No, got a promotion and transfer to Asheville. We've been called in on the case you're working on. I need to talk with you and Carrie, when she's up to it. Have you had breakfast?"

"Just going to get some; let's talk while we eat. Promotion, huh? You deserve a promotion for the work you did on the Masters' farm back in Kansas. I was impressed. Are you the new director for Western North Carolina?"

"Yes, and I love it here. My first time in real mountains."

# Vanished Sisters

"Have you been briefed by Ben?"

"Yes, last night. I have bad news. The SBI went in to arrest Billy Burgess and found him dead. Executed gang style just like the sisters. They found a tunnel from the house to the woods beside the house. Billy's accomplices took care of the only witness we had who could lead us to them and got away without a trace."

"I hate to hear that; Billy and I were friends as boys. He just went down the wrong road."

"It happens every day. Unfortunately, that's my job security. We'll never run out of bad guys who took the wrong fork in the road."

"You know, he had a wife. She might be able to tell you something. He revealed to me that they parted under hostile circumstances. She tried to make him sell the ranch and split the profits. His remark to me was 'I showed her.' Locals say he was abusive, but they didn't go into detail."

"We're going through his house now; I'm sure the wife's name will come up. Hopefully, we'll find an address too."

Mark stirred his coffee. "Did your office have any idea this kind of terrorist activity was going on in our area?"

"I'm afraid so. When the deluge of children from South America and Mexico hit our borders, our country was inundated with terrorists. The flood of children was planned for that reason, but the powers-that-be turned it into a humanitarian crisis, which created a cover for them.

"They're here for one reason. To set up cells, recruit home grown losers who want their fifteen minutes of fame, and to use them to wreak havoc across this country. They're not only here; they're in every state in the union. Life as we have known it is about to change. Several have been discovered and arrested. They should have been sent straight to Guantanamo where they could have been strenuously questioned, but they were quietly shipped back home only to try again. I feel like we're working with one hand tied behind our backs."

"This is not the kind of world I wanted to bring a new life into. I fear for our children, but we can't live in fear of the future. We would be surrendering to their plans. What can we do except try to continue as normally as possible?"

"I don't have an answer for you on that one, Mark. I stay after my congressman, do my job, and make sure the terrorists I find don't survive to fight another day. I love this country and will do what is necessary to make it safe."

Mark looked at his watch and realized he had been gone an hour. "David, I need to get back to Carrie. This conversation has been very enlightening." He gave his hand to David. "I look forward to working with you again."

"Likewise, Mark," he said as he shook Mark's hand. "Let me know when Carrie feels like talking."

"Why don't you come back with me and I'll see how she feels. It would be to your advantage to talk to her as soon as possible, before her memory fades."

\*

WHEN MARK AND David entered Carrie's room, Anne was there with clean clothes for Carrie. Her old clothes had not survived the trip down the mountain and the examination of her wounds.

Mark hugged Anne and kissed Carrie. "Are you up to talking to an old friend?" he asked his wife.

David stepped from behind Mark and asked, "Can't you stay out of trouble?"

"David Durham, what are you doing here?"

"Heard you were in trouble, again, so I got on my white charger and came to save you."

"I'm afraid you're a little late. I could have used you yesterday." She laughed as she reached for his hand. "It's good to see you again. Have you met, Anne, Mark's sister?"

David took Anne's hand, said hello, and noticed she had the same deep blue eyes as Mark.

"Is this an official visit, or did the news of my tumble down a mountain make it all the way to Kansas?"

"I'm afraid it's official; do you feel like talking about your tumble down the mountain?"

"I had a rough night, but I'm feeling much better today.

## Vanished Sisters

Not sure how much I can remember, though."

"I'll say goodbye for now," said Anne, "and let you two get down to business. It was great meeting you, David." She reached out her hand. "Come by the house any time you need to talk to Mark or Carrie."

"Thanks, Anne." He took her hand. "I may need to take you up on that, and I'm glad I got to meet you." Anne left with Mark to allow David a few minutes to question Carrie.

"I have a few questions. Did you get a good enough look at their faces to pick them out from pictures of previous offenders? There aren't more than fifty or so. We only have those whom the State Department has designated as known terrorists."

"I might be able to; it's worth a try."

"Good. I have the list with me on my iPad, but first, I also need to know if you can describe the weapons you saw?"

"I don't know what you call them, but I can describe how they looked. Mark saw the guns before he went for help, so he may know what they are. There were lots of boxes of stuff, and I did see the words 'dynamite' and 'ammunition' on several boxes. There were also clear plastic bags of wires and mechanical things, as well as guns. I'm afraid these men are going to blow something up, unless you get to them first."

"That's what we're working toward. The pictures also include weapons we suspect you saw. Maybe these photos will help you pinpoint the ones in the stash. I don't suppose you understood the language they spoke?"

"No, but I'm pretty sure it's the same language used by the terrorist group that claimed responsibility for the recent bombings in England and France. I don't know if they all use the same language. The announcer said they were part of the Muslim Brotherhood and were threatening to wage a jihad. They shouted that the establishment of a Sharia-based society would eventually rule the world. Does that help?"

"It sure does. I'm going to let you look through these pictures while I step out and ask Mark a few questions. I'll be right back," David said as he took his iPad from his briefcase and arranged it so she could click the pages with her good hand.

David left the room to find Mark, who was just outside

the door with Anne and Blake. Blake was introduced to David. Blake and Anne excused themselves, explaining Anne had brought Mark's car and Blake was giving her a ride back to Marion. "I'll see you when you get to the house with Carrie," Anne added. "I have everything ready for her, including a wheelchair and bedside potty. We'll have her back on her feet in no time."

David and Mark discussed the weapons that Mark had seen in the attic and then went back in to check on Carrie.

"I've found a couple who look similar to the two in the vehicle I was riding in, but I can't say for sure. They looked older in person than in these pictures."

David looked at the pictures, made notations, and said, "Thanks, Carrie; you've been a tremendous help. Now, I will get out of here and leave you to get some rest. If I have any more questions, I'll come to Marion. I understand you will be there for at least another week? Is that right?"

"Yes, David; come down and have dinner with us one night. Anne is a wonderful cook."

David thanked them both again and agreed to come by to see them before they went back to Mississippi.

\*

AS BLAKE AND Anne drove back to Marion, she sat in the front seat of his police cruiser. "Thanks, Blake, for bringing me home. I could've ridden home with Mark and Carrie."

"I know, but I wanted to be alone with you for a few minutes. With Mark and Carrie there at the house and this on-going investigation, I haven't had a chance to be alone with you. I miss our talks and just being with you. I'm afraid I'm becoming accustomed to having you around. I think I may be falling in love with you. There, I've said it; how do you feel about that?"

Anne had not expected this. She secretly thought she felt the same, but she was afraid to admit it even to herself. Each had lost a spouse to cancer. Anne felt she had lost her soul mate and was sure Blake felt the same about his wife. How could they now settle for less? "Well, I have to admit I've grown accustomed to having you around too. But I think we're lonesome for what we both had and are searching for someone to fill that void, but we need to be careful we don't make the mistake of settling for someone."

Blake took a deep breath and let it out dejectedly. "I'm sure at some level we are doing exactly that, but isn't that what everyone is looking for? Even if we hadn't been married before, we would be looking for someone to love and share our lives with. I think I know what you mean. You don't think you will ever be able to care for another man the way you did your husband. You feel you're being disloyal even to try. You would be admitting he could be replaced. Am I right?"

Anne stared out at the road ahead. She wasn't sure she liked him putting her innermost feelings into words. "It's more than that. I would feel like I was cheating you by not loving you as I did him. We each deserve to find that feeling again with someone else, eventually. Do you really think you love me the same way you loved her?"

"No, Anne, because you are you...not her. I don't want to find a substitute for her. Our love will be different, yes, but just as deep, just as special because we are different. We are not the same people we were with them. I don't want to see you throw your life away looking for the perfect replica of your husband. I can never be that person—wouldn't want to try—and I don't expect you to be a clone of my dead wife. You are special in your own way, just as she was special in hers. We will each cherish our memories of our past loves, but they are gone and we must live on. Live on and, hopefully, love again."

"You make it sound so easy to give your heart again."

"It is easy, Anne, when you meet someone who awakens feelings you thought you would never feel again. I think you're denying that you're human and want to love again. You're making our feelings for each other into something complicated when it's so simple and natural. We have grieved for over a year for what was. Now we need to look to tomorrow and embrace what could be."

"Maybe I'm just not ready, Blake, but I do know I don't want to lose your friendship and companionship. I need to think about what you've said. There is truth in everything you've said.

I just need more time to let go of the past and start looking forward to the future. Will you give me more time to figure myself out and take a good look at what we have or could have?"

Blake took her hand, placed a kiss on the palm of her hand, and said, "Of course; I'm sure when you think about what I've said, you will feel the same."

Anne said nothing more, but she was afraid she didn't share the same depth of feeling Blake had expressed. She hoped some day she would, but she couldn't will herself to feel what wasn't there. She knew what it was like to be loved and cherished, and she didn't want to settle for less. She would rather live alone with her memories.

*

AFTER LUNCH, CARRIE was released from the hospital. After twenty-four hours of surveillance, the doctor was optimistic about the baby's chance of survival. Mark and Carrie left the hospital feeling positive and full of hope for their baby. Carefully, Mark settled Carrie into the backseat with her left arm cast propped on the back of the backseat and her right leg cast propped on pillows. Off they went down the mountain to Anne's house.

Blake was there to assist in helping Carrie out of the car and into the house. By the time she was resting in bed, she was exhausted and fell right to sleep.

# CHAPTER 7

DAVID RETURNED TO FBI headquarters in Asheville with the disturbing news he had received from Mark and Carrie. According to their information, he was facing two well-known, heavily armed terrorists who obviously had a plan of action. The question was: What was their target? Was it nearby, or were they only using this remote area as a hideout to prepare for the attack?

David filed his paperwork and left for Dovecote. He wanted to see the Burgess' ranch for himself. One of his teams had been there since before sun up, going through the entire house and barns. As he drove down Interstate 40, he tried to put this whole situation into perspective.

The terrorists knew they had been seen and the mountain areas around Dovecote were being searched. Would they try to move their operation to a different location? Or would they hunker down in hopes the FBI would eventually assume they had moved on? With all the weapons they had to move without being seen, they might stay put and wait for the FBI to move on.

David knew, because four-wheel vehicles were being used, they had to be located in an area where not even a standard SUV could travel. Also, by traveling the mountain trails using these small vehicles, they avoided being seen moving the marijuana from field to warehouse. The mountains from Dovecote to

Asheville had few roads leading into the forest areas. You were no longer in farmland, but dense forest. Roads were cut in only to areas where mountain homes were located.

David stopped by the Hawkins' property to have a look around before going to Billy's ranch. Why were the guns stored in the old Hawkins farmhouse? Could this have been a drop-off place? The long dirt road into the Hawkins' property was near a main road and obviously accessible by four-wheel vehicles from the terrorists' hideout. Maybe the arms supplier was told the house was empty. Anyone seeing it for the first time would certainly think so. Maybe when they delivered the arms, they had run into the sisters and had to kill them. The well was a close and convenient place to get rid of them. It made sense.

The service station in Dovecote had had several customers who looked foreign, filling up their four-wheel vehicles as well as additional gas cans. No one knew where they came from or where they lived. According to the service station owner, they spoke few words, never looked him in the eye, or bought anything except gas.

\*

THE TERRORISTS WERE having a discussion in the cave as to whether they should stay there or move to their safe house, a deserted farmhouse deep in the forest, unknown even to Billy. Shahin was summarizing their situation. "We have been seen. As you know, the forest is crawling with infidels. I don't think they will find our cave, but someone could stumble on it by accident just as Billy did as a boy. It will be very difficult for us to get from here to our SUVs. We can't take a chance on using the small vehicles—too much noise. They must be left in the cave. We can afford to lose the vehicles, but we cannot afford to have the arms discovered. We were ordered to move the arms over a week ago. Our Muslim brothers will be concerned. If we do not show up soon, they will assume we have been discovered and move to another safe house. Our cell phones are of no use here. We must move to the safe house immediately.

"We will need to travel at night. This will be difficult, but

## Vanished Sisters

we will manage. Each of us will need to walk out of here with many pounds of weapons strapped to his back. Our emergency escape SUVs are hidden ten miles from here. We must move slowly and quietly. We will leave tonight. We have several hours before sundown, which must be spent wisely. The vehicles and fuel must be covered in plastic and buried. Any evidence that we were ever here must be removed. Everything must be packed and ready to travel by sundown. I will go ahead, check out the trail, and signal with the call of an owl for you to proceed.

"We must shave, cut our hair, and wear our American camouflage clothes. If seen, we will look more like them. When we reach the vehicles, we must first check out the surrounding area. The engines can be heard from a quarter of a mile away and bring the infidels down upon us. If all looks safe, the SUVs can be uncovered and loaded with the weapons.

"When we reach the safe house, before driving in, we must first check out the house to determine if it is still safe. We will park a mile from the farmhouse and walk in to see if our fellow Muslims are still there. If they have been found or moved, the place could be under surveillance. If all is as it should be, we will return for the SUVs and move the weapons to the barn with the others."

*

THE FBI TEAM was going over Billy's house inch by inch. They had worked their way down to the basement, while Ben and his SBI unit were going over the barns. "How's it going?" David asked as he walked into the basement.

Brent, his second in command, added a book to the finished stack he was working on and came to meet David.

"We've found tons of information that will allow us to reconstruct how and why this farm was involved with terrorists. But, so far, we've found no information on where they are or what their target might be."

"Where does the underground tunnel lead?"

Brent pointed to the side of the house. "About a hundred yards into the woods on this side of the house. It's just an escape route in case the terrorists needed to get in or out of the house without being seen."

"Find any info on Billy's wife?"

"Yes, I have an address and phone number for you. Her name is Sarah Kindle. She went back to her maiden name after the divorce. She lives in Statesville, about halfway between here and Winston-Salem. She works as a receptionist for a furniture manufacturing company; been there for three years. Her uncle owns the company. His name is Alfred Kindle, and the initials of his company show up repeatedly in emails and documents we've found. May be a connection there."

"Good. Forward that information to Geraldine, our computer whiz; see what she can find on the uncle before we approach Sarah. I don't want to tip our hand to Sarah and have her warn her uncle before we're ready to make a possible arrest. We may want to set up a sting and let them lead us to Mr. Kindle's dealers. I'll have someone at their employment office first thing in the morning. We need an agent in that warehouse. Continue with what you're doing. I'll check on Ben and his crew to see if they've found anything."

*

BEN WAS IN the back office of the equestrian barn when David walked in. "Found anything interesting?"

"Come in and have a seat; I have something you need to read."

David sat down and began to read a letter, which began: *To Whom It May Concern*. "This sounds like a confession; where did you find this?"

"Right here on the desk, tucked under the desk blotter. He knew we would go over this office. He wanted this letter found."

David began again at the beginning:

> They will be here soon to kill me. I know too much. When Mark heard them talking and reported it to the SBI, the handwriting was on the wall. They

## Vanished Sisters

blamed me for running my mouth about the sisters. I was so stupid gettin involved in this whole mess. I done this to myself, cause I hate rules. Don't want nobody telling me what to do.

I left home cause my Pa was always telling me what to do. I got a job on a ranch in Texas, and got heavily into drugs. The drovers I worked with got me on Marijuana first. They would give me a joint whenever they lit up.

The ranch I worked on was really a drug warehouse. It was a real ranch, but the owners made more money moving drugs. The Mexican cartels would pay illegals to carry the drugs over the border, leave it with my boss and disappear into the US with enough money to start over. The U.S. cartel would pick it up, refine it and move it to dealers to sell on the street.

I noticed that the illegals were not all Mexican. I first met Shahin on the ranch. He was from the Middle East and spoke perfect English. He stayed on the ranch a while and asked me lots of questions about the mountains of North Carolina. He began by telling me how much smarter I was than the other men. He taught me about his religion and how they would rule the world one day. Everything he said sounded so right and cause I hated my own country cause of all them rules and laws, I began to see things his way. I played right into his hands.

One day I got this letter saying my Daddy was dead and I got the farm. By then, I was into cocaine and Shahin was in total control of my brain. They told me I could be a big rancher in North Carolina and we could be partners and start our own drug business while using the farm as a cover, just like my boss was doing. They paid my way home and had the cash to get started on our own business. My head was in the clouds. I was so pumped. All I thought about was how everyone in Dovecote would know who I was and respect me. I was going to be rich and important.

The next thing I knowed, more of Shahin's friends come and he made them partners. Shahin said we needed people we could trust working on our new ranch. I was so stoned I believed everything he said.

We first began buying cattle and planting marijuana in fields surrounded by forest. It didn't matter who owned the land, we made sure the land was deep in the woods. Dovecote was the perfect place. No businesses sept one grocery store, one service station, a post office and a few farmers who only farmed on the flat land. No one ever moved to Dovecote.

We became rich overnight. Shahin had connections in the drug world. He took me to Statesville and introduced me to a furniture manufacter who would move all our marijuana for us and pay us big bucks. He was the middleman for the drug cartel. I met his niece while I was there and fell madly in love. We was married a few months later.

Sarah was purty, but she wanted me to get off drugs. She didn't like Shahin and his friends and began to try and turn me against them. At first I tried to get her on drugs so I could bring her around to our way of thinking. She didn't want to have nothing to do with drugs and bugged me about the drugs I used. I began slapping her around to try and scare her. Finally she left me and tried to take half my ranch.

Shahin told me to beat her and threaten to kill her if she ever come to the ranch or talked about the ranch. I got really high on drugs and went to see her. I beat her so bad her face was scared for life. She was so scared of me she agreed to take the money I offered and keep her mouth shut. Her uncle gave her a job in his furniter business, so he could keep an eye on her. She has no idea her uncle is in the drug business. She don't even know the ranch is a front for drugs.

I never questioned Shahin until the first shipment of arms arrived. Shahin asked me about the Hawkins farmhouse. He thought it looked deserted and I agreed it must be, cause I hadn't seen the sisters in years. I told him about the two old sisters who used to live there but was sure they died years ago. Shahin told me he needed a deserted place near to a main road, where he could have arms delivered.

I asked him why he was buying guns? He said we could make big money selling guns. I was all for making more money. I didn't guess until then that he and his friends was arming Muslim terrorists. Shahin and his Muslim friends are living in a cave in the mountains. Now that they have the weapons, I think they will be moving them soon. They never told me where they was going.

One of Shahin's friends killed two hikers who showed up at the ranch and walked into the meth lab, cause I forgot to lock the door. There bodies are buried in the woods, beside the fence near the trees in the pasture. All the meth and marijuana is stored in a secret room under the meth lab. There is a switch under the counter. It opens a secret elevater shaft leading down to the storage room. There is also a secret tunnel from the house basement to the woods. There is a button under a bookshelf half way down the room that will open the entrance.

I want this to be like my last will and testament and leave the farm and everything on it to my ex-wife Sarah Kindle.

I'm sorry I have made such a mess of my life. I deserve to die. Please tell Sarah I'm sorry.

The letter was signed and dated. David wasn't sure it would be considered a legal document. It was sad. Billy had been used because of his property and because he was stupid—exactly what the Islamic extremists had been looking for. Unfortunately, Billy did not know where they were going, and if David's guesstimated timeline was correct, he was sure the terrorists would be making their move tonight.

David shared his thoughts with Ben. "We have three priorities facing us that need immediate attention: First, we need to know what's in that underground room. If it's full of drugs and marijuana, someone's waiting for a promised shipment. We need to set up a sting and catch Mr. Kindle with the goods. One of my agents will be applying for a job in the Kindle warehouse first thing in the morning.

"Second, we need to get Mark down here to retrieve the bodies of the agents and take them to the Marion coroner's office for autopsy. With someone as experienced as Mark right here, there is no need to send the bodies to Raleigh.

"Third, we need to coordinate as many men as we can muster and have them in the forest around Dovecote before dark. With the FBI, SBI, and local law enforcement, I feel certain we can do this."

## Vanished Sisters

# CHAPTER 8

MARK'S PHONE RANG as he and Anne were playing cards with Carrie, who was bored out of her mind. He went into the kitchen to answer. David filled Mark in on what they had found. "The one thing Billy didn't tell us was the location of the cave. We plan to have every available officer in the woods around Dovecote tonight."

"David, I may be able to help; I remember Billy taking me to a cave one summer. I know the general direction, but I'm not sure I can lead you to the actual location. We were rabbit hunting near the Hawkins' property when he said he wanted to show me something. I think it was about a mile from the sisters' house, but that was over thirty years ago."

"That's better than nothing, which is what we have now. Get yourself over here as soon as possible. We'll gather at the community house. Our men who have been in these woods since the two agents disappeared have seen nothing but a couple of bears, a skunk, and a plethora of deer."

Mark went in to change clothes. As he strapped on his revolver, Carrie asked, "What's going on? Have they found the terrorists?"

"No, but David thinks they are living in a cave around Dovecote and may be going to move the weapons tonight. I remember Billy showing me a cave many years ago. David wants me to look at a map of the area and pinpoint the general location of the cave. He thinks the terrorists could be using that cave. Don't wait up for me. I may be there overnight. They found the two agents; I need to bring them back to the coroner's office in Marion for an autopsy."

"Mark, this is getting scary. How did we get in the middle of this?"

"Because I remembered my valley and how peaceful it was when I was a boy. Terrorists have invaded my valley. I just hope it will be peaceful again after we round up all the Islamic Extremists. I pray we find them before they use those weapons on unsuspecting, innocent people."

He was dressed in black cargo pants and a black T-shirt and sweater. He came over to kiss Carrie goodbye. "Don't worry; I'll be well-protected."

"I know you will; I'm just jealous you get to be in the middle of all the action while I sit here trapped in these two casts. I wish I could be there too."

"You've been thrown down one mountain, so let's not push our luck. Remember, you're going to be a mommy and need to take care of yourself and the baby. I'll be back as soon as possible. I would say, 'I'll call you,' but as you know, my phone will be useless."

"Use Blake's; I want to know what's going on."

"I'll try, I promise." He kissed her and asked Anne to take care of his girl.

\*

MARK LOOKED FOR a familiar face as he walked into the community house. He saw Blake and moved that way. "Hey, Mark, David's looking for you; he's in the kitchen meeting with the leaders. He's trying to coordinate local law enforcement with the SBI and the FBI. Come on; I was sent to watch for you and bring you into the meeting."

"Are you waiting for sundown to get going?"

"No, since you know it's a mile or so from here; David

wants to get men positioned in those woods while we still have daylight."

"Good idea," Mark said as he followed Blake into the kitchen. David had tacked an aerial photo to the wall, showing Dovecote and the surrounding forest. Everyone was intently looking and listening to David as he shared his plan of action.

"I'm thinking we need to get in place before sundown and stay off the trails after dark. We'll use night vision, keep out of sight, and remain silent. Do not break silence unless you have a visual. Each leader will have a copy of this map. I will position each group as soon as Mark arrives."

Mark raised his hand. "I'm here, David."

"Good. Come on up and take a guess at the cave's general location. I know it was years ago and you might not remember the exact location, but an approximate guess will help tremendously. We don't have time to actually try to find the cave. I will position my men near the trails around that area and wait to see if we can intercept them as they try to leave. I doubt they will make a move until dark.

"Local law enforcement will park their vehicles on all roads leaving from this general area marked here, no matter how remote. Some of these roads are no more than trails, but if a vehicle can pass through, we need surveillance there. Hide your patrol cars as well as possible. Stop all vehicles leaving the area. Have your weapons drawn as soon as you see or hear a vehicle approaching. These men will shoot their way out if they have to. They have already killed two old ladies, two SBI agents, and thrown Mark's wife down a mountain."

While David was talking, Mark was going over the map, trying to trace with his finger from the Hawkins' property to where he thought Billy had led him. Seeing it from an aerial view helped in one way, but not being able to see peaks and valleys clearly was confusing. David turned to Mark and said, "What do you think, Mark?"

Using his finger, Mark drew a circle around a section of the map. "I'm pretty sure the cave is within this perimeter, but it was a long time ago, and I am sure there are many caves in these mountains. I could be totally wrong."

David gave him a marker and asked Mark to draw a circle around that area on the map. David then drew another circle outside the circle Mark had drawn. "Thanks, Mark; a guesstimate is better than nothing. I think if you are reasonably close, we can cover all surrounding trails and wait for them. We have enough men to cover the area around your circle and the outer perimeter."

David began assigning sections of the circle to the team leaders. He gave each group a number, which corresponded with the number of its section on the map. "Each leader will take four men and a map. Spread out, but keep the leader in your line of vision. Let's move out. Remember, do not break silence unless you have a visual. When you signal that you have a visual, everyone will check his map and head for that section. Good luck, men."

Mark stood there, not knowing what he should do next. Was he included in the search? He tapped David on the shoulder. "Where would you like me?"

"Mark, I have another map of Billy's ranch. I have pinpointed the graves of the two agents. I need you there, bringing in our agents. I don't want to take any chances with your life. You have helped us greatly and we need you where your expertise can best be used—recovering our fallen men. I would like for you to wear a radio, but only use it if you're in trouble." As he attached the radio to Mark's shoulder, he explained that Mark's radio would put him in touch with Blake. "My team's radios will be using a different frequency to ensure no outside interference can jeopardize our stakeout. I've alerted the morgue in Marion and they're expecting you. I'll check with you in the morning. Good luck and thanks again."

Mark was relieved; sitting in the woods with the mosquitoes all night was not his favorite thing to do. But that is what he would have done, if they had asked him. He grabbed a cup of coffee and a donut and proceeded to Billy's ranch.

An officer stopped him as he pulled up to the locked gate. "State your name and business on this property, please," said the officer.

"I'm Dr. Mark Goodman, and I'm here to retrieve the

slain bodies of the two SBI agents. Here is my identification and a map given me by David Durham, director of the local FBI."

The officer looked at his ID and map. "You may proceed to the house; an officer will accompany you to the gravesite and assist if needed." As he pulled up to the house, the officer was waiting and told Mark to follow him. He followed the officer across the pasture to a fence that separated the pasture from the woods. Mark pulled in beside him. They shook hands and introduced themselves. The officer said his name was Danny Davis and he had some experience with retrieving cadavers.

"That's helpful; do you work with Blake?"

"Yes, he's my boss. We've worked together for ten years. I have the greatest respect for him; he's a fine man."

As they unloaded Mark's equipment and walked toward the fence, Mark asked, "How long ago did his wife die?"

"Oh, I'd say over a year ago. It nearly killed him. She had cancer, you know. She fought a long battle, but it finally got her in the end. They had no children. The cancer was in her female organs, which was probably why she never conceived. We're all hoping that Blake and your sister, Anne, will someday get hitched. They both live with the same grief. Both of them say they're just friends, but sometimes that's the best way to fall in love."

Mark lifted his case over the fence and climbed over. He chuckled to himself. The officer was a romantic. "I like Blake; wouldn't mind having him for a brother-in-law. I think they would be good for each other. But they're the only ones who can make that decision."

"Agreed, but we can hope, can't we? They're still young enough to have children. I hope it works out for them."

They walked into the glen and up near the top of a ridge. "Over here, Mark; I think I've found the spot. Must not be too deep with all these rocks piled on the grave."

Mark checked the grave thoroughly before touching the first rock. He pulled on his gloves and began taking pictures. As he worked, he asked Danny about the farm. "David said there was a secret room under the meth lab. Did you discover how to enter the secret room?"

"Yes, only because Billy left a letter telling us where to look. It's full of marijuana and street-ready meth. That's why we're still here day and night—to protect the goods and see who shows up to get them. There was a secret stairway down into the room from the meth lab and an elevator for transferring large loads of marijuana for safe keeping until it was picked up."

Mark snapped pictures from all angles. "I can't believe I missed that. I went over the entire room." He took close-ups of footprints. He found many, but since he was not the first to find the grave, he was sure some were the footprints of fellow officers. He checked the area for any clues or blood and found none. The agents had probably been in the ground for five days or more. Slowly, he removed the rocks and handed them to Danny, who stacked them over to one side.

"Mark, the stairs and elevator were artfully hidden in the walls; nothing was visible. It took us the better part of a day to find them and we knew what we were looking for."

Danny was right. The grave was shallow, about three feet. The ground was crisscrossed with huge roots, which made digging difficult. Whoever had buried the agents had given up and covered them with rocks to keep animals from digging them up. The progress was slow and the sun was going down as they retrieved the bodies and placed them in body bags. They worked silently now, each reflecting on the lives of these brave young men.

They were ready to transport them to Mark's truck when they heard what sounded like muffled voices. Mark and Danny were not aware that the graves were no more than a few yards away from a trail. Something or someone was on that trail. Danny heard them too and motioned for Mark to move behind a rock. They slowly pulled the body bags behind the rock. A terrible thought kept going through Mark's mind. *I've sent them to the wrong cave. There must have been another cave on this side of the valley. What should we do?*

Danny motioned for Mark to call Blake; he was going to move toward the voices to try to see which way they were going. Mark moved further away and called Blake.

"Blake here. You okay, Mark?"

## Vanished Sisters

"Yes," he talked softly, "but the terrorists are over here; we can hear them on a trail just above us. Danny and I are at the gravesite, above Billy's ranch. There must have been another cave other than the one Billy showed me."

"We're on the way; I'll alert David. Stay out of sight, and don't try to apprehend them."

\*

SHAHIN HAD CHECKED out the next two hundred yards and given his men the okay to move forward. Danny was sitting beside the trail behind a tree. As they quietly shuffled by with huge packs on their backs, Danny silently watched them. When they had passed and moved another hundred yards, Danny made his way back to Mark.

"Mark, I'm going to follow them and see which way they go. You stay here and wait for Blake and the others."

"No, Danny.... If you go, I go. Blake and the others will follow. I'll leave a note with the direction we went in."

"Okay, but hurry; we don't want to lose them."

Mark scratched out a hurried note, giving the location of the trail and the direction they followed. He placed it on a rock beside the bodies and secured it with a small rock. They hurried back to the trail and carefully followed behind the terrorists. They followed for a few hundred yards and almost ran into them. They were just standing there, with their backs to Danny and Mark, waiting. Mark and Danny crouched on the trail just a few yards behind them and waited.

After several minutes, they heard an owl call and the men began to move again. They were leaving the trail now and heading up a ridge. Danny and Mark had to drop back some. They had no trouble following quietly behind them on a smooth trail, but now they were moving through dried leaves and the noise seemed deafening. Maybe the terrorists couldn't hear them because of their own feet shuffling through the leaves. They were cresting the next ridge when, again, they came to a halt. Mark and Danny stopped and stood perfectly still. They would be heard for sure if they moved. The sound of an owl came again after several minutes. The men began to move again. A pattern became obvious; someone was checking out the trail ahead. This went on and on for what seemed like hours.

Where were the SBI, FBI, and the police? They must be close behind them by now. Then Mark remembered they were no longer on the trail. The officers would continue down the trail unless they happened to see where they veered off, which wasn't very likely in the dark. They were on their own. They continued to follow with stops every few hundred yards until they came to a clearing and the men began to drop their loads. Danny motioned for Mark to get behind a tree.

They watched while the men spread out, as if looking for someone or something; they sniffed the air. One of the terrorists came straight toward Mark and Danny. They held their breath and prayed. He stood still just feet from where Danny and Mark crouched behind a tree. He seemed as if he were listening. After several heart attack minutes, he returned to the others. Mark and Danny let out a breath that had been choking them and continued to watch as the men quietly talked.

Mark whispered, "Should we try to call?"

"No, I've been sending a signal. They should be able to figure out that we left the path back there. It may take them a while to backtrack and find where we left the trail."

"What do you think they're doing?"

Before Danny could answer, everything went black; they had been knocked out cold, never seeing or hearing their attacker.

\*

BLAKE BROKE THE silence order and called David direct. "What's going on, Blake? You just jeopardized our entire surveillance." Blake broke in. "You're in the wrong place!" he yelled. "Mark just called; the terrorists are above Billy's ranch. He and Danny saw them. There must be another cave. We need to get everyone over there now. The trail is just above the gravesite. I've been getting beeps from Danny on their location. I know the only road they can take out of there; it's off the Old

Hudlow Road by the old gristmill. I'm halfway there now. I'm going to need backup. There are about six of them, and they're moving the arms stash."

"Copy that, Blake."

David barked orders into his radio. "We're on the wrong side of the valley. I want everyone back to the vehicles, double time. I want all SBI agents to the ranch. The terrorists are on a trail just above the gravesite. They're moving the arms. Mark and Danny are there now. I want all FBI to the gristmill on the Old Hudlow Road. Move out!"

David was worried; he knew it would take an hour for them to get out of these woods, get to their vehicles, and arrive at the new locations. He prayed Mark and Danny wouldn't try to follow the terrorists, but his gut told him that was exactly what they were doing. It's what he would do.

*

BLAKE'S PATROL CAR and several others arrived at the gristmill. Blake pulled his vehicle across the dirt road where he was sure the terrorists would exit the woods. He knew of no other way out. He positioned his men where they could shoot the tires of the vehicles as the terrorists tried to escape. Blake and three of his men moved on foot into the woods along the dirt road.

As they carefully moved into deeper forest, one of his men remarked, "You know, Blake, about three years ago, a logging company came in here and took down a good bit of timber. They made their own logging road about five miles down the Hudlow toward Bethel. It's almost grown up now, but a big SUV could get in and out of there."

Blake stopped dead still. "Why didn't you tell me about this thirty minutes ago?"

"Sorry; I just remembered it."

Blake barked orders into his radio. "I want two cars at the old logging road about five miles toward Bethel. Park one vehicle across the entrance and prepare to fire on any vehicle trying to exit."

# Rachel Poe

\*

SHAHIN WAS CONVINCED these two men were the only ones following them, but he knew they must have alerted others. "We can't waste any more time; get the trucks uncovered and loaded; we need to get out of here."

The two extended cab trucks with over-sized tires were hidden behind a copse of evergreen trees. They were covered with small trees and branches left by the loggers. To anyone walking by, it looked like a large pile of brush waiting to be hauled off. The men were dead tired after lugging the weapons for ten miles, but they swung into action, and within thirty minutes, they were moving slowly down the logging road with no lights.

Mark and Danny were thrown into the bed of a truck along with the weapons and covered with a tarp. Shahin wanted to get information from these men. He needed to know how much Billy had told authorities while he was in custody. He would then kill them and bury them in the forest.

Danny regained consciousness first. He knew he was either in hell or alive; heaven couldn't be this uncomfortable. Their hands were tied behind them and their feet bound; they couldn't move. His head was lying on the butt of a rifle. He tried to move. The pain in his neck was acute and made him groan. *Why didn't they kill us?* he asked himself. He looked around for Mark, who was lying at his feet. Danny squirmed around and worked his way toward him. "Mark," he called, "can you hear me?"

Mark was gradually coming around, but the pain in his head made him long to return to the unconscious state. He heard his name being called and tried to look around. Something was jabbing him in the ribs. He tried to move when he heard his name again. He painfully remembered what had happened. "Danny, is that you? Where are we, and why didn't they kill us like the others?"

"We're lying on a pile of weapons in the back of a moving truck. I think I'm going to be sick."

Vanished Sisters

"Wish I could help you, buddy, but I'm a little tied up at the moment." He heard Danny wretch. The terrorists would be angry when they found puke all over their weapons. Mark feared they would wish they had been killed before this was over. He thought about Carrie and the baby. He would never see his precious little girl. He didn't know why, but he was sure they were having a girl. He could see her in his imagination. *Please, God, let me live to see my little girl,* he prayed.

\*

SHAHIN LED THE way. They moved slowly down the logging road until they came to the Old Hudlow Road. He pulled out slowly. Seeing no one, he turned on his lights and picked up speed. About two miles down the road, he passed two police cars barreling past them. They had managed to escape unnoticed, thanks be to Allah.

\*

JEB SLOWED DOWN and looked for the logging road. He pulled into what looked like a possible entrance and got out. With his flashlight, he examined the area. Tire tracks—and they were fresh. Small saplings had been recently scraped and bent over as the vehicles passed over them. He called Blake. "I'm afraid we just missed them. There's evidence of a vehicle's passing by here very recently. We passed two black, extended cab trucks with oversized tires a couple of miles before entering the logging road. At two in the morning, they had to be our suspects."

Blake shook his head, stomped around, and said, "Shit! We missed them." He called David. "Be on the lookout for two black, extended cab trucks with oversized tires. We think they just came out of a logging road about five miles past the gristmill. How far away are you?"

"Almost to the gristmill. We're turning around; I think we just passed them." David ordered his entourage to follow him as he made a U-turn in the middle of the road. "We're going after the two trucks we just passed. Hold your fire; they may have Mark and Danny with them. We're going to try to run them off the road if they refuse to stop."

*

AFTER PASSING A string of black SUVs, Shahin knew they had barely escaped detection. They needed to get off this road and find a less traveled one toward Marion. The safe house was past Marion, up Highway 23 toward the Blue Ridge parkway. He made a turn onto old Highway 221. It was narrow, winding, and slow, but a safer choice.

*

BEN AND HIS men reached the ranch and proceeded across the pasture. They saw Mark's SUV and Danny's cruiser parked by the far fence. They headed for the gravesite and found Mark's note. "Why didn't they stay put like Blake told them?" Ben was scared; he ordered one of his men to take the bodies of the murdered agents to the morgue in Marion. He quietly prayed that Mark and Danny had not met the same fate. He thought of Carrie and the baby; he had to find them alive. *Please, God, let them be alive. Help me find them.*

He got on the radio and called Blake. "We're at the gravesite. Mark left a note saying they were following the terrorists. I just heard you on the radio say the suspects got away. Where are Mark and Danny? We'll start up the trail from this side, and you try to follow their tracks from that side. Maybe we'll find them. Did you see the bleeps from Danny's phone earlier? If we had been on the trail then, we could have possibly followed them. I get no response from either receiver."

"Ben, we've found where the trucks were hidden. Two of my men found Mark and Danny's radios on the ground near where the trucks were hidden. They left those radios as a message. They have Mark and Danny. Let's meet back at the community house and regroup."

David was sure they should have caught up with the

trucks by now. They must have turned off somewhere. He listened to Ben and Blake's conversation and decided to return to the community house to come up with a new plan of action.

# CHAPTER 9

DAVID STOOD IN front of a tired and disappointed group of men. He was also discouraged, tired, and angry about this evening's failed attempts to capture or stop the terrorists. "Men," he said, then thought, *How do I begin?* He paused and began again. "First, I would like to thank each and every one of you for the magnanimous effort I have seen here tonight. We're living proof that different levels of law enforcement can effectively work together. We failed...yes...but we came so close.

"Mark and Danny are missing. We have two dead agents lying in a morgue in Marion. Two innocent sisters were murdered in the night simply because they just happened to be asleep in their own beds. These terrorists must be stopped. I want you all to go home, get some rest, and be back here tomorrow at eight o'clock. I want your input as to how we should proceed from here. Good night."

Ben and Blake joined David. Ben suggested the three of them meet at seven for a private brainstorming session before the others gathered. David agreed and asked Blake whether he would accompany him to give Carrie and Danny's family the bad news. Blake agreed and said he had planned to anyway.

\*

CARRIE COULD NOT sleep. It wasn't her leg or her arm that kept her awake, but the not knowing what was going on in Dovecote. She had this nagging feeling that something just wasn't right. She knew Mark would have called if he could. It was the not knowing that worried her. She hated to wake Anne just because she couldn't sleep, but lying there alone was driving her crazy. She was about to call out to Anne, who was in the next room, when the doorbell rang.

She heard Anne hit the floor and run to the door. Carrie wanted to fly out of that bed, but she had to calm herself and wait. She heard Blake's voice and another man's that sounded like David's. *Oh, dear God, what has happened to Mark?* she thought. Tears filled her eyes as she waited for the door to open slowly. Anne, David, and Blake entered her room. Her light was already on, and she began to sob uncontrollably when she saw the look on the three faces.

"He's dead, isn't he?" sobbed Carrie. "Oh, dear God. No...no...no!"

Anne, with tears running down her face, took Carrie in her arms. "No, Carrie, we don't know that. They don't know right now where he is. Now dry your eyes and listen to what David and Blake have to tell us."

"I'm sorry." Carrie wiped her eyes. "Tell me what happened."

Blake and David took them through all that had happened since Mark had left the house earlier in the day. Carrie and Anne continued to cry silently as they listened to the events that had taken Mark from them. David, however, did not tell them that they were sure Mark and Danny were in the terrorists' hands. That would have been the same as admitting they were dead.

After hearing the front door close, Anne crawled in bed beside Carrie and they talked and cried for what was left of the night. Sleep finally captured them for about an hour before they smelled coffee. Anne got up to find Blake pouring himself a cup. It was four-thirty. "I thought you went home, Blake?"

"No, Anne. I couldn't leave. I dozed on the sofa. I figured if Mark found his way out of those mountains, he would get himself back here if he could. I wanted to be here in case that happened. Can I pour you a cup of coffee?"

Anne came to Blake and he held her in his arms. "When this is all over, we need to have a serious talk."

Anne looked up into eyes that were as moist as hers. "Yes, we do, Blake; it's long overdue." He pulled her deep into his arms, kissed her, and held her against him longingly.

Anne reluctantly pulled away. "What about Danny's family?"

"I'm going there first thing this morning," he said as he poured her a cup. "As soon as I finish this coffee, I'm going home, get a shower, change uniforms, and go see Danny's folks before I go to the meeting with David. Danny isn't married, and his parents are old. I couldn't see waking them in the middle of the night."

Anne took the coffee. "I need this; I'll take Carrie a cup too. Coffee always helps. Keep us informed today even if you have no news; we need to feel connected."

"I promise I will," and he took her in his arms again and held her close. "It's going to be all right, darling. Now, I need to get out of here." He kissed her one last time and was gone.

Anne was confused about her feelings for Blake. She cared deeply for him, but she wasn't sure whether her feelings were as deeply felt as Blake's seemed to be. They had both suffered the same loss. They had been there for each other to listen and console. He seemed to be ready for a serious relationship, but Anne was just not there yet.

\*

MARK AND DANNY had maneuvered around to where they could talk above the noise of the big engines, the wind whipping around the cab of the truck, and the flapping tarp that covered them. "Do you have any idea which direction we're going in?" asked Mark.

"Yes. I managed to see through a crack in the tarp. I think we just went through Marion. I could see the tops of buildings, and it looked like home. We're climbing now. We have to be on Route 23 going up toward Boone. Can you loosen the rope on your wrists? I've been trying, and I think I've stretched them a little."

"Me, too. I can almost pull my hands out."

"Don't; we need to pretend we're still out cold when we get where we're going. Hopefully, they'll dump us someplace and go to bed. They've been up all night too and carrying heavy loads for miles. Hopefully, if that happens, we might get a chance to get away."

"I think I still have my cell phone in my cargo pants pocket. It's one of those pockets inside a pocket with a Velcro seal. They either didn't search there or missed it. Maybe if we manage to get away, we can call for help."

They were back in the woods again, on a dirt road bumping around on top of the weapons. This continued for several miles. Finally, the trucks came to a halt. They heard doors opening and the sound of men griping, only in a different language. Someone lifted the tarp and punched Mark and then Danny. They didn't move or open their eyes. The men laughed and left them there. They heard the sound of guns being readied—*ammo being shoved into revolver chambers. Dear God, we're going to be shot just like all the rest,* Mark thought. Instead, the voices moved away.

Mark's hands were free. He was about to raise the tarp when Danny grabbed his hand. They heard a cigarette being lit. Someone had been left to guard them. They heard him move away from the truck, then the sound of a man peeing. Danny reached down and untied the rope around his feet, then helped Mark untie his. The guard was coming back to the truck. They heard him yawn and sit in the truck. Mark took a quick glance and could see the back of the man's head through the rear cab window. He was in the front seat with his head eased back against the headrest. He took a last drag on his cigarette, flipped it to the ground, and yawned again as his head lolled to one side. They hoped he was asleep.

Danny eased over the side of the truck. Mark looked one last time at the man before slipping over behind Danny. They ran back down the road. Danny suggested they might be too visible out in the open, so they moved into the woods and started to climb a small mountain. Mark had no idea which direction they were going or where they were. They continued to climb until they were so tired they had to stop and rest.

Mark was bent over, breathing hard as he tried to catch his breath. "You know they'll have to come after us. We could ruin their entire plan if we get away. I wish I knew our location."

"We're somewhere between Marion and Boone. I'd say about halfway. The dirt road we just left looks more like a driveway than a road. I wonder if there's an old deserted house at the end of that road. They have to have a place where they can stash the weapons and hide out. When they get back to the trucks and find us gone, they'll head the same way we did. They will expect us to run back the way we came. If we move toward the house instead, we could avoid them, check out the house, and try to find our way out of here from the opposite direction."

"Sounds logical to me. Let's see if I have a signal on my phone. Being half way up this mountain may help." Mark found his cell phone still in his pocket. He turned it on. The battery was almost gone. He didn't have much of a signal either, only one bar. It was worth a try. He dialed Blake. It rang twice and Blake answered. "Blake, it's Mark; we've escaped and are in the woods between Marion and Boone." The phone went dead. "Well, at least they know we're alive and what direction to start looking. Let's go see if we can find our captor's hideout and keep from being recaptured."

They had not gone far when they heard voices. Slowly and quietly, they eased down a steep rock incline and slid down between two big boulders. There was a small crevice between the boulders just large enough for the two of them to slide into. When they backed into the fissure, they were totally hidden.

They listened and ventured a peek through the heavy foliage in front of them. They were looking down into a glen. Their hiding place was just above an old farmhouse. They could hear the babble of a brook running through the glen just below and between them and the farmhouse. Behind the two-story house were out buildings and a barn that had seen better days, but was sturdy enough to hide weapons. They crouched behind the heavy foliage and watched. These were not the same people who brought them here, but they had the same Middle Eastern look.

Danny whispered, "We're in a good position here with the mountain behind us and good cover in front. Let's stay here for a while and watch to see if our friends come back. If they do, we'll know they've given up and we can skedaddle out of here and find the road we came in on."

*

BLAKE STARED AT his phone. He checked his calls received to make sure he wasn't imagining the call he had just received. He was on his way home to get a shower. He called Anne. "Anne, I just got a call from Mark. His phone went dead after only a few words, but he managed to give me his general location before it died. I need to call David. I'll call again later when I know our new plan. Tell Carrie we think he's fine."

Carrie was sitting up in bed, staring out the window. Anne had never seen her so depressed. "Carrie, I have good news."

Carrie jerked her head around, wide-eyed and hopeful. "What? What have you heard?"

"Blake just got a call from Mark. He only got in a few words before the phone went dead, but he managed to get in his general location. Blake is calling David now to get a team out there to find Mark and Danny." Anne sat on the bed and took Carrie's hand as tears threatened to fall. "We have hope, Carrie—real hope. Danny is a seasoned cop; I know he'll get them home safely."

Carrie stared at Anne. "He's just lost in the woods? They just have to go pick him up?"

"Well, it's not exactly that simple. He was only able to give his general location before the phone went dead. Blake feels sure he knows about where they're located. He's going to call us back when he has more information. You need to relax and take a nap. You need your rest. I'll wake you if he calls with more information."

Rachel Poe

\*

BLAKE CALLED DAVID and relayed the information received from Mark. "We now know about where they are. I'm going to the tax office in Marion to see if they can give me locations of any abandoned farms in that vicinity. There are many old home-places that have been abandoned throughout the area. The children inherit the property, don't want to farm it, and can't sell it. They can't afford to keep paying the taxes so they're abandoned. If there are taxes owed on properties, the tax office will have a record. Can we switch the meeting to my office? We'll be twenty-five miles closer to Mark and Danny's location."

"Sounds good; I'll get the word out to my men and Ben; we'll see you in one hour. This is the break we needed."

David had emailed a report of the evening's failed attempts to his superior in Washington. David was a stickler for getting his reports out as soon as possible while the facts were still fresh in his mind. He never allowed himself to go to sleep until the report was written and forwarded. After talking to Blake, David immediately emailed this new turn of events. This was the break they needed. They now knew where the terrorists were relocating and could monitor their movements.

The phone call from Mark, however brief, confirmed four things. One, Mark and Danny were alive. Two, they had been captured by the terrorists, but had possibly escaped. Three, they were in possession of valuable information. And four, the FBI was back on the terrorists' trail. David felt rejuvenated, saved from failure.

\*

MARK AND DANNY had drifted off when they heard a door bang. Both came upright and stared at each other. Their first thought was that they had been discovered. They looked around, but saw no one. Peeping through the heavy foliage, they saw the two trucks parked in front of the old house. Several other vehicles had joined them as well. This must be their command center, but they were leaving. Evidently, they had given up on finding Mark and Danny and knew they would return with more men.

Danny was angry. "We can't let them get away. What can we do? We have no weapons and no way to alert the FBI. We can't just sit here and watch them sail out of here."

"It's been four hours since I called Blake; surely, he has alerted the SBI and the FBI. They must be looking for us. Maybe if we created some kind of disturbance to draw attention to this place."

"Do you have any matches?"

"No, and I don't think we want to set the forest on fire... do we?"

"How about we blow up some dynamite? We know they have boxes of dynamite on those trucks."

Mark was skeptical. He wasn't sure how experienced Danny was in dealing with terrorists or explosives, but he knew he himself wasn't a trained law enforcement officer, nor did he know anything about explosives. Danny seemed to know what he was doing. Mark remembered what David Durham had said: *I love my country and will do what is necessary to keep it safe for our future generations.* Mark's thoughts went to Tucker and his unborn child. "Okay, Danny, what do you have in mind?"

"Well, I've just been sitting here thinking. I have a little experience with explosives. I'm Marion's only officer who knows how to disarm a bomb. If I can get my hands on the right stuff, I think I can create a small fireworks display. Everything I need is on that truck right in front of us. I just need to get down there and pick up a few things."

They looked out again. The small troop of men was moving toward the barn. The trucks, which had brought them, were just sitting there loaded and covered. Other trucks were backing up to the barn.

"Now is our chance," Danny said quietly. "Can you imitate the call of a blackbird? You know, 'Caw, caw, caw'; can you do that?"

Mark looked at him as if he were crazy. "I guess so; why?"

"I'm going down there and do a little pilfering from those trucks. You watch the group loading the trucks at the barn. If you see someone coming this way, give out three caws. Got it?"

Mark was reluctant but said, "Got it!"

Danny patted Mark on the shoulder. "We make a good team." He slowly began to slide down the thirty-foot rock incline and drop into the creek at the foot of the mountain. He crouched on the bank for a few seconds before sprinting about twenty feet to the trucks. Mark kept his eyes trained on the barn. Danny was lifting the tarp that covered the truck bed. He recovered it and went to the second truck where he began to fill his pants pockets until they were bulging.

Mark saw one of the men headed back to the front of the house, so he tried to make the bird sound, but nothing would come out. He cleared his throat and tried again. This time, "Caw-caw-caw" came out loud and clear. He watched as Danny dove under the truck and hid behind one of the big tires.

The man stopped by the truck, lifted the tarp, threw something in, and replaced the tarp. He stopped long enough to light a cigarette and went back to the barn.

Danny was watching the man's feet from his low vantage point. He eased back to the truck and continued to rummage for what he needed. He was now filling the front of his shirt. Mark wondered how he was going to get back up the mountain.

The last thing Danny lifted from the truck was two AK-47s and several clips of ammo. He recovered the truck bed and headed for a small lean-to shed on the other side of the house. He tried the door and went in. It was empty except for a couple of boxes and a few burlap bags. Mark waited. What was he doing? Maybe he was going to assemble everything in the shed. That made sense. There wasn't room to work where they were hiding in the rocks.

Several men were headed back to the house now, so Mark did his birdcall again. A hand came from the door of the lean-to with a thumbs-up signal. *All right!* Mark thought.... *What next?*

\*

DAVID, BEN, AND Blake were meeting in Blake's office. The other agents milled around, drinking coffee, eating donuts, and waiting to get their orders. In all, they had almost fifty men. The three superior officers were looking over a map Blake had prepared. He had marked three farmhouses with barns in the general area Mark had indicated. "This one," Blake pointed out, "is too close to the road. They will be looking for privacy. This one," he moved his finger to a different house, "is too small I think. Barn isn't more than a shack. But this third one is a two-story farmhouse back in the woods, tucked down in a holler. It has several out buildings and a good-sized barn. I'm betting my money on the third house. It's also just about halfway between Marion and Boone."

David and Ben nodded their heads in unison. "Let's drop off men here, here, and here." David made circles on the map, indicating the drop points. "They can work their way through the woods and get into position to catch anyone who tries to run when we pull in. The house will be surrounded. Let's move out. If they haven't found Danny and Mark by now, they'll be packing up and getting out of there."

After going over the strategy they had decided on, twelve vehicles loaded with men, arms, and ammunition quietly slid out of Marion and up Highway 23 toward Boone. The men were busy testing radios, loading guns, and donning bulletproof vests.

\*

AS THE CARAVAN neared the first drop-off, David's cell phone rang. It was the director. "Good morning, Director Greenstreet; did you get my email with the latest turn of events?"

"David, I have just had a conversation with the president." David could hear the condescension, the self-importance in his voice. Greenstreet delighted in bantering around his hallowed connections to the President. It was a well-known joke that Greenstreet's nose had a permanent tinge of brown to it. Madam President was fast getting the reputation of being soft on terrorism, and Greenstreet believed whatever she told him to believe. David felt an ominous pronouncement coming, and he almost wished he had not answered the phone.

"It is the belief of the President that other agencies may be involved, and they may have agents imbedded in the Boone cell. She has asked me to order you to stand down. We feel more harm than good could come from confronting these possible terrorists at this time."

"Possible terrorists? Director, they have two of our men, although they may have escaped. We received a cell call from one of them, but the line went dead before we could get anything except their general location. We're in the process of recovering them now. We're sure we know where they are. I'm sending in men to try to either pick them up or help them escape. We will use extreme caution and will refrain from interfering with the terrorists unless we feel our men's lives are in danger. In that case, we will do what needs to be done to save their lives."

"David, you're walking a tightrope here. Your job could be on the line if you refuse to stand down. I want you to be forewarned. My hands will be tied if this goes badly."

"I understand that, sir. I will report back to you when we have more information."

Before dropping off the first group of agents, David relayed the information he had just received and gave the order to stand down unless they thought Mark and Danny's lives were in danger.

Ben, who had worked in the North Carolina area for some time, recommended David call Adam Wentworth, the local Agent in Charge with the CIA. David had yet to meet Adam, but he had heard he was tough on terrorists. He made the call. Adam listened as David filled him in on the situation and activities of the last few days.

"I'm afraid you've stumbled on a cell I was not aware of. The CIA is the agency to which Greenstreet alluded. We had two agents imbedded in the Boone cell. We now know they have been compromised. We are 99.9 percent sure they are dead. Their phones have been destroyed. We have received no communication in weeks. Madam President knows this and should have informed Greenstreet. The CIA should have been informed of this new cell along with details of how and where they were

## Vanished Sisters

discovered. That has not happened.

"We have agents in the woods around this farmhouse. They have not seen the imbedded agents for some time. Word has already reached me that something is amiss. My men are watching your men as we speak. We will stand down and allow you to retrieve your men. We are there if you need us.

"After 9/11, the CIA, FBI, and Homeland Security pledged to work together to prevent another 9/11. The last administration and this one have failed to keep this pledge. Instead, they vie one agency against the other, depending on which one humors them the most. Greenstreet is ambitious and plays right into their hands. He will do anything to make the CIA look bad, even taking credit where credit is not due.

"Evidently the two cells are joining forces to plan a major attack. Proceed to try and recover your men. What radio frequency are you using to communicate with your men? I want to listen in as this recovery attempt progresses. I will be in constant communication with you, and send in manpower if it is needed."

The first men were dropped off on the front side of the house. The men had to climb the ridge and descend the other side to get to the house. Blake, leading the convoy, used back roads to get behind the house and drop off the second and third group. They returned to the main road and tried to find the driveway into the house. Two agents were dropped off to check out the house. There was always the possibility that this was the wrong house. Blake found an old logging road about a quarter of a mile down Highway 23 and led the motorcade out of sight, to wait.

\*

MARK WAS GETTING nervous. The terrorists were almost loaded and ready to pull out. He wished he had a way to get one of those guns. Danny eased his head out of the shed. Using hand signals, he gave a thumbs-up, pointed toward the terrorists, lifted his shoulders, and splayed his hands palms-up as if wanting an answer. Mark moved a branch to the side so Danny could see him and give him a thumbs-up that it was safe to come out of the shed. Danny motioned to Mark that he was going down the drive and for Mark to make his way to meet him. Mark nodded his head yes and returned a thumbs-up. He saw Danny take off running down the driveway with a gunnysack over his shoulder. Mark climbed out of their hiding place, moved up the ridge, and made his way down the other side to meet Danny.

Danny could hear Mark running through the dried leaves and made his way toward the sound. They met halfway up the ridge. "Follow me, Mark; I have a spot picked out where we can see them leave and toss dynamite into the truck beds." He handed Mark a gun. "Can you use one of these?"

"Yes, I'm familiar with this weapon."

"Good; here's an extra clip. I want you in those rocks up there." He pointed to several large boulders just above them. "I'll stay here where I can toss the dynamite into the trucks. As soon as I do, get ready to hide behind the rocks because there's going to be a huge explosion. Men will start pouring out of the trucks. Your job is to help me prevent them from getting away or coming after us. They're all armed."

"I understand," Mark answered as he headed up behind the boulders. He turned. "Where are you going to take cover after you throw the dynamite?"

"Hopefully, I'll have time to climb up there with you. I can move pretty fast, and I gave myself enough fuse to allow a few seconds to take cover."

"Be careful, Danny; there's a lot of dynamite in that truck."

"I'm always careful; I'll hear the doors slam and the engines start; I'll be ready."

The CIA operatives were getting nervous. What were these two cowboys about to do? They couldn't let them blow these terrorists and probably themselves to smithereens. Just as they were about to intervene, two unknown men went past their hiding place and grabbed one of the cowboys. They shoved a badge in front of his face.

Mark was intently watching the house as the terrorists milled around waiting. Two men were doing something to the front door. *Oh, holy shit*, he thought. *They're booby-trapping the house.* The whole house will probably go up when the explosives in the trucks blow. Mark was about to go down and tell Danny when a hand came over his mouth and an FBI badge appeared in front of his eyes.

The agent smiled and said, "What's going on here?"

"We're about ready to blow those trucks to kingdom come as they exit the driveway. They're moving to another location. They tried to find us, but we found a good place to hide and watch the house. They assume we have gone for help and are making tracks out of here. Danny pilfered dynamite from the trucks and is ready to throw it in the truck beds as they try to escape."

"Oh, shit," the agent said as they heard the first truck engine start. The first truck was moving, and Mark and the agent watched as Danny started to light the first fuse. The agent literally jumped down to where Danny stood, grabbed him by the throat, and held him down as he pulled the fuse from the stick of dynamite.

"Don't move. FBI." He held Danny down as he alerted David. "The terrorists are moving out; there are six trucks to be followed." He released Danny. "Sorry, Danny, but not today; there may be CIA agents imbedded with this terrorist cell. The CIA thinks they're dead, but we can't take any chances. They would be killed, along with tons of knowledge about this and other cells all over this country."

Danny collapsed. "Thank God you got here in time. I just didn't want them to get away. I was going to make sure none of these terrorists would ever hurt an American citizen."

"I know, Danny, and I agree with you all the way. But they will have to live another day. They won't get away; we have vehicles ready to follow them."

The CIA operatives breathed a sigh of relief and remained out of sight.

The trucks had all pulled away. Mark came down to where Danny and the agent sat on the ground talking. "Don't go in that house," Mark warned. "I watched them booby-trap the front door just before they left. I'm sure all other doors are also wired. We need a bomb squad in here before we can process the house."

"Not to worry," said Danny. "That's the simplest type of bomb to disarm. I can handle it if I have the right tools."

The agent laughed. "Danny, we leave those things to the professionals. I'm sure you're very capable, but this is too big to take a chance on losing you or the evidence left in that house."

Danny and Mark smiled and waved as a string of black SUVs came down the driveway. Thank God they were safe and the FBI had stopped them from making a terrific mistake.

David called in a report to the Director of the FBI, informing him that his men had been retrieved, the terrorists were on the move, and they were being followed. The director ordered David to stand down. "Do not follow; if you're seen, you could compromise the operatives."

David could not believe his ears. "Just let them go without trying to see where they're going? Sir, I have talked with the CIA; they advised...."

"You presumed to go over my head? How dare you! When I give an order, I expect it to be followed to the letter. Now back off; the FBI is in charge of this operation."

"Yes, sir," David answered. He then decided to ignore Greenstreet's order, continue to follow the terrorists, and ask forgiveness later.

David switched to the radio frequency Adam was listening on. "Adam, are you there?"

"I'm here; are you still following the terrorists?"

"Yes, sir; I have four vehicles keeping them under surveillance. They're good and won't be detected. I was ordered by my superior, Director Greenstreet, to stand down and not follow. I have ignored that order. He informed me that the FBI is the lead agency here. I suspect I will be fired."

"Knowing Greenstreet, you're probably right. Call me if you need confirmation that I rescinded his order. I will inform my superior; he will handle Greenstreet. The FBI may have found and been in control of the Dovecote cell, but you are in my territory now. This is the mother cell in North Carolina, and the Dovecote cell has obviously joined forces with it. This was probably their intention from the start. We appreciate you informing us of the Dovecote cell, but the CIA is in control here. You are now under my jurisdiction. However, let's don't tell Greenstreet; he so loves to be in charge.

"I'm sending you an evidence response team to go over that house. It may take an hour to get them there."

"Sir, we have Mark Goodman with us, and we have everything he will need to start processing the house and out buildings. We have a bomb squad on the way. Mark watched as they booby-trapped the house. Shall I have him begin or wait for your team?"

"How the hell did you get him on your team? I've heard he's the best there is. Did you read his book on the Kansas case?"

"I was there, Adam, and I had the pleasure of working with Mark and Pete Gunter on that case."

"I'll cancel that response team; they will only be in his way. Give me a full report when he has finished."

"Will do."

# CHAPTER 10

THEY HAD HEARD nothing since Blake's early morning call. Carrie was alone and scared; Anne had gone in to work to check on things. She called Pete, Mark's best friend and mentor. He insisted on coming up to be with her in case they got bad news. After landing in Asheville, he would rent a car and drive to Marion. She hoped he would be there by lunch today.

Peter Gunter was Mark's college professor, friend, and now his colleague at the university where Mark taught. Mark and Pete had become close friends in Kansas when he came out to help Mark with a huge burial site of murdered, illegal immigrants.

Mark had agreed to go with Carrie to Kansas in search of her two missing half-brothers. While searching for the boys, Mark had uncovered a serial killer's graveyard. Her brothers had been victims of this horrendous killer. Mark and Carrie had fallen in love while going through the terrible ordeal.

Pete had become Carrie's surrogate father, and she loved him almost as much as she loved Mark. She remembered fondly their first meeting. As he had gotten out of his rented SUV, she couldn't help but think: *He looks like Dr. Livingston, right out of the jungle.*

Carrie walked up and down as best she could with casts

on her left arm and her right leg. She could not stay in bed another minute. Why had they heard nothing since Blake's early morning call?

\*

THE BOMB SQUAD was called in from Asheville. It would take an hour for it to arrive. Danny wanted to show the squad that he was capable of handling the situation, but David didn't want to take a chance on either Danny blowing himself up or losing the valuable information that might be in that house. There was no way of knowing whether the terrorists wanted to kill their pursuers or blow up evidence they had to leave behind as they hurriedly tried to avoid capture. As they waited, Mark asked Blake whether he could use his phone to call Carrie and Anne. "Sure, please do; I promised to call, but things got so intense."

"That's putting it mildly," Mark replied as he dialed Carrie.

\*

ANNE HAD GONE to check on things at the garden center. She and Carrie cried every time they looked at one another. She needed to get her mind on something other than the possibility of losing her only brother. Should she call her parents? No. Why put them through the agony she and Carrie were going through? She hoped Pete would get there soon; she didn't want Carrie alone for very long. If she fell, she might lose the baby. At the very least, she would be on the floor until Anne got home. She called one more time to be sure Carrie was okay.

"Hey, sug; I'm just checking in. I haven't heard anything; have you?"

"No. I'm pacing the floor."

"You promised you'd stay in bed until I got back."

"I know.... I'm going nuts. Why doesn't Blake call? Hold on; I've got a call coming in!" She put Anne on hold. The call was from Blake. "Hey, Blake, we're going nuts; have you found

Mark?"

"Yes, darling, I've been found."

"Mark! We've been so worried. Are you all right?"

"I'm fine; just hungry and thirsty. We're still at the house where we were taken. The terrorists have left, but I need to go over that house with a fine-tooth comb. It will be a while before I can get away, but I wanted you to know I'm fine. I will tell you the whole story when I get home."

"Thank God you're okay. Pete is due any minute; he's coming up to hold my hand and give Anne a rest."

"That's great. I wish I had him here to help me go over this house."

"You want me to tell him? You know he would love to be in on this frightening mystery."

"I couldn't begin to tell you how to get here. I'll talk to David and see if he would like Pete in on this. Tell Anne that Blake will call her as soon as he gets a chance...lots going on here. I need to go, love; I'll see you soon, I hope."

"I love you, Mark."

"Love you too."

Carrie switched back to Anne to let her know Mark was fine and Blake would be calling her as soon as he could. They were having a good cry when the doorbell rang. "I think Pete's here," said Carrie. "I'll see you soon." She disconnected the call. Then, with tears streaming down her face, she opened the door and fell into Pete's arms.

"Oh, dear God," said Pete. "Don't tell me you have bad news?"

"No. On the contrary, these are tears of joy. Mark has been found. He just called and assures me he is fine—just hungry and tired. They're still at the house the terrorists were using. He has to process the house to see if they left anything that might give them a clue as to what these religious heretics are up to. He said he wishes you were there."

"I'm sure he's dead tired. How do I get there?"

"I have no idea and neither does Mark. He's going to talk to David Durham, the FBI agent in charge, and see if he'll agree for you to assist Mark. Remember David? We met him in Kansas. He's now the FBI director of Western North Carolina. He'll call back if it's approved. How about a cup of coffee?"

"Great. I remember David. I can see why they would promote him; he was very thorough and professional."

"I agree. Have you seen Tucker, Aunt Mattie, and Rosa? I miss them so much. I'm ready to go home."

"They're fine; I went by yesterday and got a biscuit fix. Aunt Mattie is making biscuits and freezing them for me so I can have one every morning."

Carrie laughed. "Pete, you are a mess."

Pete patted Carrie's tummy. "How's my granddaughter?"

"You know?"

"Yeah. Mark couldn't keep a secret if his life depended on it."

Carrie thought to herself, *Must run in the family.*

"I agree with Mark; we both think the baby will be a girl. How are you coping with the casts and crutches?"

"Much better now that Mark is safe and you're here. I've had a lot of time to work on my new book. It's almost finished, even though I had to learn to type with one hand."

Pete put his arm around Carrie and gave her a big hug. "You know, you and Mark are the son and daughter I never had, and now I'll have a granddaughter. Tucker will be so excited."

The door opened and Anne came in. She hugged Pete as if he were a long lost friend, even though she had never met him. "I feel like I've known you all my life, Pete. Carrie and Mark never stop talking about you. I hope you know you are loved by these two?"

"And the feeling is mutual. They're my kids now."

Anne's phone rang. "Finally, it's Blake," she said as she excused herself to answer the call. She immediately turned back as she said, "Yes, Blake; he's right here," and handed the phone to Pete. "It's for you," she said with a disappointed look on her face.

Pete listened for a minute and said, "Putting the address in my GPS app as we speak; I'll be there soon." He handed the phone back to Anne. Pete was grinning from ear-to-ear. "They need me; I'll be back with Mark as soon as we process that house."

Anne and Carrie shared an eye roll and a smile. Carrie gave him a kiss and told him to give it to Mark. "How about I just tell him? It might embarrass him if I kiss him."

"Whatever.... Go and try to be home for dinner."

"You know I'll do my best."

*

THE BOMB SQUAD had finally arrived and was taking a look at all the doors and windows. The entire house was wired. The terrorists had obviously hoped they would suspect the doors and try to get in by a window. This was going to take forever. Mark and Danny had each crawled into the backseat of an SUV and were taking a nap after eating three energy bars and drinking a bottle of water.

Mark woke with a start and looked to see how long he had been asleep. Forty minutes; surely they had cleared the house by now. He crawled out of the SUV and stretched.

"It's about time you woke up," said Pete. "They're almost ready for us. Checking all the closet doors in the house now. Even the kitchen cabinets were wired. We're dealing with some nasty Arab nuts."

Mark hugged Pete and told him how relieved he was to see him. "I'm so tired that I was afraid I'd miss pertinent evidence."

"Never happen; remember the Masters' house. You went over that place after being at the hospital with Carrie all night and all the next day. You'll be fine. Let's go see if we can get started."

Four hours later, they had gone over the house and were ready to start on the barn. The bomb squad had swept the barn clean, as well as all the out buildings. So far, they had found nothing of importance except many fingerprints and some papers taped to the inside wall of a box spring. They were sure the imbedded agents had skillfully concealed these papers, knowing they would be found. Residue from explosives was found in the attic and the barn, but that was to be expected; that was where they were hidden. With what was in the trucks and what they could assume was stored in the attic and barn, the terrorists had enough arms to supply a small army.

As they were leaving the barn, Pete stopped Mark and pointed to something on the ground just inside the barn door and to the side, almost completely covered by straw. It was a cell phone. Pete bent over, and with gloved hands, he picked it up by the corner and placed it in a plastic bag. "If no one here has dropped a cell phone, we may have found important information."

David met them. "Found anything?"

"Mostly usual stuff, except for some papers found in a box spring. Couldn't read them; either encrypted or in a foreign language. Pete found a cell phone in the barn under some hay by the barn door. Could be good info, if no one here dropped it."

David smiled and said, "Both are probably from the CIA operatives. The cell phone switch is a last ditch effort. Probably what got them killed. When imbedded agents feel sure they're compromised, they will use drastic tactics to leave information behind. One method is to switch cell phones with the terrorist, if the cells are enough alike and they get the chance to make a switch. They pick up the terrorist's phone instead of their own and drop it someplace at the last minute to be found by law enforcement. There's only one problem. To get away with this, the agent has to be either desperate or a good pickpocket. He has to get his own phone back so the terrorist finds his missing and blames himself for being careless. If he fails, and the terrorist realizes he has the other man's phone, the undercover agent is immediately under suspicion. Not good; the agent is usually toast. It's a gamble, but maybe the agent knew it was worth a try. The phone will tell us."

Five hours later, as Mark and Pete were packing up, Mark said, "I want to walk through the house and barn one more time."

"Mark, you know we did a thorough search; what's bothering you about the house?"

"They had to have had a reason for being so sure the house would blow up. There has to be something in there they

I don't care for you enough? Maybe. I guess I thought when I said the magic words, 'I love you,' we would automatically hop in bed just like in the movies. I suppose I thought, somewhere down the road, we would decide to make it legal or go our separate ways. I'm sorry; I see now you're made of better stuff. I don't want to lose you, but I'm not ready to make a commitment yet. Can we continue to see each other as we have been?"

"Yes. I don't want to lose you either. Even if we do decide not to get married, I want us to always be friends. Maybe time will change your reservations about marriage and mine about being a cop's wife."

Blake took her hand again and they walked back to Anne's house. He kissed her again and was gone, but he wasn't gone from her life. She decided not to worry about it. Time would tell her what to do.

\*

MARK AND PETE were re-hashing the day's events when Mark yawned. "Son, you need to go to bed, and this old man could use some shut-eye as well. Let's hit the hay."

"It has been a long day. Do you need anything?"

"No. Anne has me all set up in the guestroom. I'll see you in the morning. What time do we need to be at the morgue?"

"I told Blake we'd be there at seven. Anne will have breakfast around six-thirty. See you at breakfast."

Mark sneaked into bed, trying not to disturb Carrie. She was all propped up with pillows under her leg and arm as well as her head. He could hardly find room to slip in beside her. "It's about time you got to bed. You've got to be dead tired."

"I am; Pete was wound up like an eight-day clock. He had to go over everything that happened today, and he wanted to know everything that led up to today. I finally couldn't stifle my yawns any longer, and he got the message. Are you comfortable?"

"I may be a little too close to the middle. If you come around and pull me over a little, you'll have more room."

Mark slid one arm under her pillow and the other across

her tummy. "I'm just fine, love; just happy to be here. I was afraid I would never see you again. I actually saw our little girl in my mind. I can't wait to see if she looks like I imagined her."

"What did she look like? And what makes you so sure the baby will be a girl?"

"If she were going to be a he, I would have seen a boy... wouldn't I?"

"What did she look like?"

"She had my dark blue eyes and your light complexion and blonde hair. She grasped my little finger and wouldn't let go." He kissed her cheek. She turned her face to him and he kissed her mouth softly. "Guess there won't be any hanky-panky until you get out of these casts. I would feel like I was making love to a mummy."

"It would be difficult. Goodnight, my love."

\*

THE ENTIRE VILLAGE of Dovecote came to the sisters' funeral. The minister, who knew the sisters, talked of their hard life on the farm as they labored to eke out a meager living. He told funny stories as well as painted a beautiful picture of their dedication to God, to Mother Nature, and to each other.

"The only doctor either ever encountered was when Aunt Eva had appendicitis and the local doctor was called. She was rushed to the hospital where an emergency appendectomy was performed. When she woke, she immediately dressed and began walking home, twenty-five miles away. When she was missed, the doctor was called and he found her halfway home. He had to insist she let him take her the rest of the way.

"I don't think either sister ever darkened the door of a church. However, in my years of preaching in this community, I have yet to meet more devout believers in our Lord Jesus. The Bible was the only book I ever saw in their home, and they read their Bible every night by candlelight. They lived on what the Lord provided.

"Aunt Ida and Aunt Eva never knew what it was like to have electricity, running water, drive a car, own a tractor, or even buy new clothes. But they were the happiest two ladies I have ever met. They wore secondhand clothes and shoes, which they obtained by trading butter, milk, or homegrown vegetables. Charity was never accepted.

"They loved company and always had homemade cookies and the best pound cake I have ever tasted for anyone who came to call. They never attended school, but they were taught to read and do arithmetic by their parents. As far as they knew, that and the good book was all anyone needed to know. No false idols or worship of things for the sisters, just pure faith and love of our Maker.

"As they grew older, neighbors plowed their garden in the spring and checked on them. No one could believe the awful fate these beautiful sisters encountered as they slept peacefully in their own beds. This community will never forget Aunt Ida and Aunt Eva. They will live forever in our wonderful memories of two sisters whose whole life was a testimony of how God will take care of us if only we have faith in Him and allow Him to work in our lives. He even arranged for them to go to heaven together. Amen."

After a sweet prayer at the gravesite, the entire village walked down to the community house and celebrated Aunt Ida and Aunt Eva's lives by enjoying a wonderful lunch prepared by those who had loved them.

Mark and Carrie, along with Anne, Blake, Ben, and David, were among the mourners. The community had accepted the newcomers to Dovecote and would be there for them if they ever needed anything.

## CHAPTER 12

CASEY WENT OVER the diversion plan one more time with his new partner. Harry was FBI, but the local Statesville police were also involved. David had arranged the whole sting. "Okay, Harry, you will drop me off well past the entrance at eight o'clock. I will approach the shrubbery from the far end and avoid being seen by the cameras. I'll make my way to the front door, moving between the shrubbery and the building. The night watchman will be asleep in his office, just behind the reception desk inside the front door. You will begin banging on the glass door, screaming you know your wife is inside with the night watchman. You will pretend to be overly intoxicated and acting like a jealous husband who has caught his old lady cheating on him. If necessary, to get the watchman's attention, use a rock to break the glass. He will call 911. A police cruiser will be around the corner and respond when the call comes through.

"When the police arrive, and the watchman comes out, you start accusing him of having an affair with your wife. The police will draw you both away from the entrance, so I can slip from behind the shrubbery and enter the front door. By the time the policemen have filled out the bogus report, I will have taken a look in the locked warehouse, slipped back out the door, and hidden again behind the shrubbery. The police will pretend to haul you away to jail, but they will actually drop you around the corner where you will leave my car. I will meet you back at the car and our job will be finished. Are we in agreement?"

"Sure, Casey. Sounds like a piece of cake; are you sure you can open the warehouse door?"

"I'm pretty sure; I've had time to look it over when no one was around. If I can't get it open, I'll abort the whole thing and get out of there. As soon as you see me slip out the front door, you tell the officer you need to take a pee, which will tell him I'm safely out. I'll meet you around the corner."

"Sounds good. When are we going to put on this little performance?"

"Tonight. I'll pick you up at seven. We will go over it one more time, before you drop me off and the curtain goes up."

*

AT EIGHT O'CLOCK, Casey was in place behind the shrubbery as Harry began pounding on the front door. He had doused himself in whisky to enhance the illusion of being drunk. He looked around for a rock when his knocking produced no watchman. "Shit, where's a rock when you need one," he mumbled. Casey tossed out a good-sized rock from behind the bushes. Harry picked it up and began banging on the door just as the watchman came out of his office. "Where's my wife?" he shouted. "I know she's in there! You open this door. I'm going to whip your ass! I said...open this door!"

"Mister," said the watchman, "I have no idea who your wife is and I have called the police. You step away from this door. If you break this glass, I will be forced to defend myself. I have a gun."

A police cruiser pulled up out front and the officer slowly got out. "Step away from the door and put your hands on top of your head," said the officer as he and his partner moved halfway up the sidewalk. "Now what seems to be the trouble?"

"Officer, I wasn't doing nothing, just minding my own business."

The watchman then opened the door and came outside.

"He was banging on this door, accusing me of having an affair with his wife."

The officers drew them halfway down the walkway away from the door as Casey slipped inside unnoticed and headed for the warehouse.

"He's a liar; I know he's got my wife in that office."

"Officer," said the watchman, "you are welcome to come inside and see for yourself. I'm the only one here."

"That won't be necessary," said the officer. "I can see and smell that this man is intoxicated and confused. We need to fill out a report."

"If you don't mind," said the watchman, "I would feel better if you handcuffed this man before I come any closer."

The officer asked Harry, "Are you going to cooperate, or do I need to cuff you?"

"I ain't done nothing wrong, officer, but I ain't gonna give you no trouble," Harry slurred.

The officer moved them to the police cruiser where he put Harry in the backseat with the door open. The watchman and two officers stood outside, filling out the paperwork. Harry could see the door from his location so he could signal the officer when he saw Casey exit the building.

*

CASEY MADE FOR the locked door, and he was halfway down the main warehouse when he heard a growl. *Oh, shit, a watchdog!* Casey double-timed it to a large crate and jumped up. The dog sprung into the air, trying to get to him. He knew this Doberman would eat him alive, but he only had so much time to get to the door, open it, look inside, relock it, and get out of there. He loved animals and couldn't bring himself to hurt the dog. He pulled out his taser gun and leaned over as if to pet the Doberman. When the dog lunged for him, he caught him in the side of his neck. He gave him only enough to stun him for a few minutes.

Casey jumped down and ran to the locked door. He fumbled with his lock picks, trying one and then another and another until finally the tumblers gave way and the door opened. He grabbed his flashlight and searched the room. Empty...completely empty. He relocked the door and turned to leave, only to come face-to-face with the Doberman. Casey could see the dog was still groggy. His eyes were not focusing, and he swayed from side to side. Casey was sure he could outrun the still sluggish dog. He sprang at the dog, causing him to hesitate; then he ran for the exit. As he ran, he looked back to see the dog coming faster than he had anticipated. Could he make it? He was almost there. He lunged at the door, slid through, and closed it. That is, except for part of his pants leg that remained firmly locked in the dog's teeth.

Casey knew he couldn't open that door again; it would only give the dog time to get a better grip on his pants, as well as his leg. At least the mouthful of Casey's pants was keeping the dog from barking. He pulled as hard as he could and finally heard a rip. He was free and crawling for the outside door. He paused to check the night watchman's location. His back was to the door. Casey slid out and crawled behind the bushes. He heard Harry say, "Hey, man, I need to take a piss."

The officer said he was almost through, closed his report book, and thanked the watchman. "We'll take him down to the station and let him sleep it off. Sorry to have bothered you. As always, call us if you need us."

\*

THE AUTOPSIES WERE completed by around eleven. David was already there to meet with the local director of the CIA. Mark, Pete, and David decided to get a bite of lunch before the meeting. David had worked with Pete during the Kansas investigation, and he looked forward to seeing him again. They found a table in the corner of the local café and ordered. "So, Pete, how does it feel to be back on a real case again?"

"It feels good. Don't get me wrong; I love teaching, but the real satisfaction in our profession comes when you actually help solve a case and get to see the bad guys put away. How's the investigation going? Or am I asking the wrong question?"

"Sort of; I'm not at liberty to discuss the case right now. It all depends on how my meeting with the CIA goes today. So far, no one has fired me. That has to be good news."

Mark noticed the expression on Pete's face change. He was frowning and looking across the room. Mark followed his gaze. He too was surprised to see Blake escorting a very pretty woman into the café. He was holding her arm as he guided her to a table, obviously unaware of anyone else in the room. Blake's back was toward Mark, and he could see the woman's face. Blake was clearly flirting with the woman from the expression on her face. He reached over and took her hand. She did not resist. Mark and Pete exchanged a look of concern.

"What's going on?" asked David. "Did I miss something?"

"Blake just walked in with a woman on his arm, and he's obviously flirting with her. Pete and I thought he and Anne were seriously involved. Guess we were wrong."

"Are you going to tell Anne?" Pete asked.

"I don't think so; she will find out soon enough. I try to stay out of affairs of the heart unless it's mine or Carrie's."

"Well, I, for one," announced David, "am glad to hear it. I've wanted to ask Anne out since I met her in the hospital. Do you think she would go out with me?"

Mark and Pete perked up. "I don't see why not; why don't you ask her?" Mark encouraged.

"I have to go back to Asheville tomorrow morning; do you think she would go out to dinner with me tonight?"

"Call her now; she's at the garden center. I'll call out the number as you dial."

David was a little self-conscious, but he had put his foot in it, so now he had to follow through. "Okay," he said as he took out his phone.

When Anne came to the phone, David nervously began, "Anne, this is David Durham; do you remember me?"

"Sure, David; is everything all right?"

"Yes. This is purely a social call. I'm in town until tomorrow morning and wondered if I could take you to dinner tonight?"

Anne was flabbergasted. She remembered meeting him and thinking what a nice man he was. She liked his eyes and his smile. She and Blake had agreed to be friends and give it time. This was just what she needed to validate her feelings for Blake. Neither she nor Blake had, to her knowledge, dated anyone else. Maybe this would put her doubts to rest. Maybe this was why she had this nagging doubt about Blake. There was no one to compare him with except her husband, and Anne knew Blake would never measure up in that comparison. Was she trying to convince herself to settle for Blake? With all these unanswered questions...why not go to dinner with David? "David, I would love to go to dinner with you tonight."

Mark and Pete were trying to act as if they weren't listening, but they were both leaning closer to hear every word.

"Can I pick you up around seven?" He paused. "Great. I'll see you then. Goodbye until tonight."

Both Mark and Pete were bug-eyed with surprise. "Sounds like she said yes?" Mark inquired.

"She did! I was ready to be turned down. This is great. I need to get back for my meeting. Shall we stop by and speak to Blake as we leave?"

Pete answered, "I really think we should; don't you Mark?"

Mark could see he was outnumbered. "Okay, but let's be nice. For all we know, she could be his sister. Maybe he and Anne broke up last night? They went for a long walk; Blake didn't come in to say goodnight, and Anne looked very unhappy when she came in."

As they approached Blake's table, the woman looked up, smiled, and batted her eyes at the three approaching men. Blake turned to see the recipient of her smile. The look on his face told all. He stood and introduced the lady. Mark, Pete, and David acted as if nothing were wrong. They chatted with Blake for a minute or two, then said they would see him back at the station. Beads of sweat were popping out on Blake's forehead.

\*

ADAM TAYLOR BRADFORD was a tall, bulky, imposing man. His shaven dome made him look like a Russian Cossack. David was not a small man, but he felt small standing next to the CIA director. He could see why this man intimidated everyone. David decided not to be intimidated as he extended his hand and said, "David Durham; call me David," and invited him into an office he had commandeered for the meeting.

By the time they reached the office, they were both on a first name basis and ready to get down to business. David began by handing him the evidence and his report. Adam took a few minutes to peruse the report. He looked up at David and boldly said, "So, what's on this phone and in the encrypted report?"

David was shocked, to say the least, and didn't answer immediately.

"I know you've had your own men look at the evidence; I know I would. I would be disappointed in you if you hadn't. So let's talk about what we need to do with this information."

David relaxed, his confidence regained; Adam had used the word *we*. They began going over all the information in the report and cell phone. David brought Adam up-to-date on the Dovecote cell and how it was discovered. "They're still in my territory. I hope I'll be allowed to take part in apprehending these terrorists. We know the Kindle Furniture Mfg. Co. is a front for drug trafficking. Alfred Kindle knows there's a shipment of meth and marijuana on that ranch. He thinks or hopes we haven't found the secret room under the meth lab. I'm sure he's being pressured to produce the goods.

"Mr. Kindle's niece is Billy's ex-wife. He wrote a confession/will, which I would like you to read. In the letter, he leaves the entire ranch to her. He also states that she knows nothing about the drugs. She supposedly doesn't even know her uncle is a drug trafficker.

"I have an undercover man working in the Kindle warehouse. Last night, he managed to get into the warehouse after hours and check out the locked portion of the warehouse. It was empty. Kindle has already made a trip to the ranch to try to see Billy. We have not announced his murder. The public only knows the ranch is under guard and Billy has been arrested.

"Before we approach Ms. Kindle, our inside man is going to get to know his niece to try to determine what she knows. According to Billy, she is totally against drugs. They were only married for a year, and she may not have had time to figure out the situation. Billy was abusive to her and she left. She has a permanent scar on her face from his last beating.

"We're hoping she will help us find incriminating documents, before finalizing this sting. If successful, we will catch Mr. Kindle with the goods that now reside in the secret room."

Adam listened intently to David's report. He was impressed with David's leadership qualities, his attention to details, and his eagerness to work together for the good of the country. He looked David in the eye as he spoke. "First, we don't have time for the imbedded agent to get chummy with Sarah. Pay her a visit now; show her the letter. Also explain that because Billy made his money processing drugs and selling them through the ranch, everything will be confiscated and she will be left with nothing. Emphasize that Billy and her uncle are to blame for her loss. Strongly suggest that if she doesn't help us, it will appear she is involved, which could result in her being charged as an accessory.

"Second, we need to move fast on the safe house near Poplar Creek. This report only confirms what I already knew. They are ready to carry out bombings in Charlotte and Raleigh. Other cells are in various stages of doing the same thing in other states. Some have already been quietly found and eradicated. You have not heard about these cases because we have orders from the White House to keep them quiet. They don't want the public to know how many terrorists are in this country. From tips by family and private citizens, we know this cell has at least three homegrown converts. We fear they will be used to blow up the targets.

"Third, there is little we can do about the powers who back these terrorists. They have unlimited funds and own politicians at the highest levels. Our only recourse is to fight them by infiltrating these cells, learning their next moves, and trying to stop them before we have another 9/11. I want you on our team. Your director does not. He suggested you be fired, which tells us volumes. But I have my own influence with Madam President. You will not be fired, and you will report to me first.

"Do not give Greenstreet pertinent information about the terrorists. Let him think he has succeeded in causing us to back off. Give him only information about the drug sting. The terrorists will not be using Kindle again because they know he has been compromised. They're already back in business and have found another source to move their drugs to dealers. I do not mean to imply that Kindle is no longer important. He needs to be indicted along with all his customers. I am simply saying he is no longer our number one objective."

"Do you have a plan for stopping this cell? I had hoped the need to move their operation to Poplar Creek would have slowed down their progress."

"It did, but they are sitting on ready; they have the weapons and all the money they need to attack, disappear, resurface, and attack again. They are on hold, waiting for their superiors to supply them with the targets. We need to know the exact targets before they do. I have new intelligence that may help us with that. Also, we need to know who these men are. As you know, we have a terrorist watch database, which needs to be kept up-to-date. We need to identify these new radicals.

"It would be nice if Mark could somehow get in that house at Poplar Creek to sweep for fingerprints and DNA. The information he gleaned from the Boone house was extremely helpful. The Poplar Creek cell is new to us. We need to know the identity of those men. As soon as we know the targets, we go in, either to capture or kill everyone in that cell. This venture will be reported as a drug bust and only a drug bust. The truth, according to the President, would only put the general public in a state of panic."

\*

BLAKE STOPPED BY the garden center to see Anne. He was sure Mark would say something about his lunch date; he didn't want to lose Anne. She was just the kind of woman he wanted to marry; however, he was not ready to commit to another relationship right now. The lunch date meant nothing. She was known for being easy.... He had his needs...didn't he? What was he suppose to do?

Anne was watering plants as he pulled into the garden center. It was almost closing time. He got out of his cruiser and walked over, trying to read her expression. Had Mark called her? "Hey, Anne, having a good day?"

"Hi, Blake. I sure am.... How about you?"

*She didn't seem mad*, Blake thought. *Maybe Mark kept my secret. After all, we're both men...with needs. Maybe Mark understands.* "Not a bad day; was hoping I could take you to dinner. Maybe get a burger at Smiley's?"

"Oh, Blake, how thoughtful of you, but I've already made plans. Maybe some other time."

Blake didn't understand; she was always ready for a burger at Smiley's after work—she wouldn't have to cook. "Mark taking you out? Carrie must be doing better with her crutches?"

"No. David Durham asked me to go to dinner. You know the local director of the FBI—the one who came with you the other night to tell us about Mark being missing."

Blake felt immediately jealous and had difficulty hiding his feelings. "Yes, I know who he is," he snapped. "Why does he want to take you to dinner?"

"Well, I don't know, Blake; he's in town for tonight and probably doesn't want to eat alone. He and Mark are good friends. Maybe he's just being nice to Mark's sister."

"I thought we were an item, Anne; why are you going out with someone else?"

"Blake, didn't we decide last night we were going to continue as good friends? We agreed neither of us is ready for a commitment and decided to give it more time."

"But David's in law enforcement too."

"Blake, I'm having dinner with him, not marrying him. Why are you being so defensive? We're not engaged; if you wanted to take someone to lunch or dinner, I would understand."

*She does know*, thought Blake. "So Mark told you, did he? I thought he was a better friend than that; guess blood is thicker than water. She means nothing to me; it was just a lunch date."

Anne stared at him, confused, not understanding what he meant. Then...the truth dawned on her. "So you had lunch with someone and Mark saw you? You came over to ask me to dinner to see if Mark tattled. Well, he would never do that; we don't stick our noses in where they don't belong. This is kind of the pot calling the kettle black, isn't it? Blake, we have no claim on each other. I'm not upset about you taking another woman to lunch. In fact, I'm asking myself... 'Why am I not upset about you taking another woman to lunch?' I should be angry, but I'm not. I don't want to lose you as a friend over this silliness. We've been through so much together this past year. As far as I'm concerned, we're friends for life, no matter who we see or don't see. You were there for me, and I was there for you. Let's not lose sight of that."

Blake felt ashamed. "You're right, Anne; I'm acting like a jealous kid. Forget I even came by. Have fun tonight and I'll talk to you in a couple days."

As he pulled out of the garden center, Blake knew he had ruined any chance of ever marrying Anne. He just hoped he had not destroyed every ounce of respect she had ever had for him. Maybe in time, he could regain her respect. But in his heart, he knew they would never be more than good friends. To make things worse, he really liked and respected David.

# CHAPTER 13

DAVID WAS ON time. Anne offered him a drink so he could visit with Mark and Carrie for a few minutes. While Anne prepared drinks, David took Mark to the back porch, presumably to view Anne's garden. "I needed to get you alone for a few minutes," David confessed. "I need a place for a private meeting with Billy's ex-wife. A place where she will not suspect she's meeting with the FBI, nor will anyone else who might be following her. I'm going to have my undercover agent ask her out for tomorrow night. The CIA wants this loose end taken care of as soon as possible. We need to be concentrating on more important matters. Do you have any suggestions?"

Mark frowned as he thought; he didn't know Marion very well, but he did have one place in mind. "If we can get Anne's approval, you could use her office at the garden center. The agent could say he's stopping to pick up a plant for his mother's birthday and get her to come in with him to help make the selection. He could say the owner is a friend of his and is staying open until he gets there to pick out a plant."

"Do you think she would mind? It sounds like a good plan. If someone is watching her and they walk out with a plant, no one will be the wiser."

# Rachel Poe

\*

DAVID HAD SUGGESTED they drive to a small steakhouse he had found by accident one day while driving through Boone. They settled in a cozy corner and placed their order. The noise level was louder than David remembered, but it was a college town and this was Friday night. He was glad of a corner table where they could talk. He felt comfortable with Anne—just as he had felt the first time he had met Mark. He immediately felt like family, and that feeling was there with Anne too. They talked freely about childhoods and families and laughed a lot. He had never married because of his job. How could he ask a woman to put up with his hours and the danger involved? He needed a friend he could talk to, and Anne was a good listener. Maybe that was what he had instantly liked about Mark.

As they drove back to Marion, he approached the subject of her office. "Anne, I need to ask a favor of you, and it has nothing to do with me asking you out tonight. I found out about this after we talked and made plans. I ran this by Mark and he suggested I ask you for help."

"Wow, this sounds intriguing; ask me."

David, without giving the particulars, explained his need for a private meeting place. "I will need you there to make the story believable. It shouldn't take more than an hour. Could you help me out?"

"The local mafia isn't going to rush in and shoot up the place, are they?"

David laughed. "I certainly hope not. I didn't know Marion had a mafia; I'd better look into that."

"I'm sure they don't, and I'll be happy to help out. What time will he drop by with this young lady?"

"I'm going to ask him to bring her by around seven. He'll knock on the door for you to let him in. Tell him you've picked out several plants and have them in your office. I'll be there waiting and take it from there. You disappear until we're through, and then I'll help you lock up and we'll go get a burger or something."

"I can handle that, but why not come back to my place?

I'll have Mark do burgers on the grill."

"Sounds great, but I owe you another dinner for putting you through this."

"Most assuredly; when you're down this way again, let me know."

\*

DAVID CALLED CASEY to bring him up-to-date. "I need you to ask Sarah out immediately, and instead of taking her out to eat, bring her to meet me. We're running out of time. We need her help, even if it necessitates threatening her with aiding and abetting. If she doesn't know the truth, she will after I get through with her."

"Sounds like things are heating up. Where should we meet?"

"I've arranged for the use of a friend's office. No one will suspect if you are followed."

David went over his plan and Casey agreed to ask Sarah out for the next night. "I'll tell her I need help picking out a plant for my mom and promise to buy her a hamburger if she'll help me."

"That's perfect; Anne will show you to the office where I'll be waiting. Should we say seven?"

"We'll be there; I've been flirting with her, so I'm pretty sure she'll take the bait."

\*

AT SEVEN THE next night, David and Anne talked as they sipped coffee and waited in her office for the knock on the door. "How long have you been in the gardening business?"

"About nine years. When my husband was diagnosed with cancer, we were told it would be a long battle. We gave up hope of having children and started this business. He knew he wouldn't be able to work more than a year or two longer, and he wanted me to have something besides his pension to live on. I've always been a gardener, and Marion had nothing like this to offer, so we gave it a try."

"Looks like you've made a success of it?"

"So far...so good. The farmers keep me going. The flowers are seasonal, of course, but adding feed keeps the farmers coming all year." Just as she finished speaking, they heard a rap on the front entrance. Anne looked at David. "Show time," she said as she went to let Casey and Sarah in.

Casey smiled as if he had known Anne all his life. "Thanks ever so much, Anne. I let Mother's birthday slip up on me, but I know a plant will always make her happy. This is Sarah Kindle," said Casey, making the introductions. "Sarah, this is Anne Frost, a good friend of mine and Mother's. Sarah is here to help me make a decision."

"I've picked out several I think she would like. I put them in my office so the staff wouldn't sell them by accident. Follow me."

As they entered Anne's office, David was waiting with his badge in hand. "Come in," David said and showed Sarah his badge. Sarah looked scared and backed away. Casey was right behind her and flashed his own badge. "Sarah, there is no need to be afraid. This is David Durham, the district director of the FBI, and he needs to tell you some things about your ex-husband. You are not in trouble."

"This doesn't make sense," Sarah declared. "Why was I not asked to come to your office? Why meet in a garden center?"

"Very astute of you," David replied. "We were afraid you might be followed. We need your help, and we don't want anyone to know we've talked to you for your own protection. You'll understand after I've told you all I know about your ex-husband and your uncle." David offered her a chair.

"Thank you," she said. "I'm a little weak in the knees. I thought I had Billy behind me. I heard he was arrested for drug trafficking, but that has nothing to do with me or my uncle."

"I'm afraid it does," David replied.

"Sarah," Casey consoled her, "just listen to what he has to say and be completely honest with him. When you know all the facts, you'll understand."

Sarah looked at Casey suspiciously. "You talk.... I'll lis-

## Vanished Sisters

ten. I make no promises."

David was worried; this meant she knew something and was either involved or afraid of what they would do to her. He had to find the truth. "Did you know Billy was dealing drugs and the ranch was his cover?"

Sarah stared at David, panic clearly present in her demeanor. She seemed to be weighing her choices and finally decided to be honest. "Not while I was married to him. I knew the foreigners were up to something. They had total control of Billy and wouldn't allow me in certain parts of the ranch. I tried to get him off drugs, only to be slapped around and ordered to do as I was told. The slapping escalated into beatings, and I received this scar from the last beating. I've had nothing to do with him since. He paid me ten thousand dollars, gave me a divorce, and told me if I went to a lawyer for more money, he would kill me."

David believed she was telling the truth, but he felt she knew more. Her demeanor said she was afraid of someone. Maybe she was afraid of what Billy would do to her if she talked. He had to get her to open up. "Billy is dead; you have no reason to fear him ever again." He could see from her reaction that she didn't know.

"How did he die? I was told he was arrested and in jail awaiting his trial. I was afraid I'd be called to testify at his trial. My uncle went to see him, but they said he wasn't allowed to have visitors."

"That's because he was never in jail; he was executed by the foreigners who worked for him. Or maybe, it would be more correct to say, he worked for them. He slipped up and talked to someone he was not supposed to talk to and was killed because of it. I have a letter Billy wrote just before he was killed." David handed her the letter and gave her time to read it.

As Sarah read, David and Casey watched her. Tears came to her eyes, and she angrily wiped them away. By the end of the letter, she was crying uncontrollably. Casey put his arm around her and offered her some water.

"He was not all bad; Billy had a good side. He just got in too deep because of drugs and he couldn't get out. He was as much a victim as I was. I will never see a dime from that ranch, will I?"

"No. Because of the drugs, the government will confiscate everything. I will allow you to go in and take any personal items you want before the government takes over. I have been ordered to get estimates on the animals, house, and property. We will work something out, but you can't be seen going into the ranch right now. We know it's being watched. Agents are living on the ranch to care for the animals and protect it from vandals. Did you know your uncle was involved?"

Again, Sarah began to cry. "I can't tell you what I've found; my uncle will kill me. I suspected something; I didn't know what, so I've been snooping, and Billy's letter confirms my suspicions."

"Sarah, we're here to help you, not get you killed. If you don't help us, you could be arrested with the others as an accessory after the fact. Are you willing to help us?"

"Yes, but I'm scared. What can I do? I'm only a receptionist."

"Tell us what you've found."

"Only a locked file cabinet in a closet in my uncle's office. I found the closet door open one day and looked inside. That door is always locked, so I wanted to see what was in there. There was only a file cabinet, which was locked as well. I heard him coming and quickly sat down in a chair. He was very angry and wanted to know what I was doing in there. I told him I was waiting to talk to him. I made up a story about needing more money because I wanted to go to college at night. He knew that wasn't true—he pays me well. He told me to try and get another job sitting on my backside (not his choice of words) and see what they would pay me.

"I left his office pretending to be insulted and have never gone back there. As I left, he said never to enter his office again unless he called me. I do know there's a part of the warehouse that's kept locked. Also, shady-looking characters have been coming to see Uncle Alfred lately. They come out of their meetings red-faced and angry."

"Do you know the names of these shady characters?"

"No. I'm not told when they're coming. They just appear, and Uncle Alfred is always at my desk to usher them into his office. You can't hear what's being said in his office from the reception desk. The night watchman's office is between the reception area and my uncle's office, but I could hear loud, angry voices."

"Could you hear if you went into the night watchman's office?"

"I don't know; I've never tried. After my first attempt at snooping, I've been afraid to do anything. The day Uncle Alfred caught me in his office, he was like a different person. I was, for the first time in my life, afraid of him. He looked at me suspiciously as if he didn't trust me."

"Is your uncle always there? Could you alert Casey when he goes out? We could do the snooping for you if Casey could get in there and install a listening device."

"I suppose...when he goes to lunch. He's usually gone a couple of hours. That's when I decided to snoop around. I was caught because he unexpectedly came back. I think he remembered he had left the closet door unlocked. I would be too scared to try listening. He has informers in the warehouse who tell him everything. What if one of them walked in while I was listening?"

"Isn't there a bathroom behind his office that you use?" Casey asked.

"Yes, only Uncle Alfred, myself, and the night watchman use that bathroom. It also has an entrance from Uncle Alfred's office."

Casey made a suggestion. "There's a plunger in the warehouse bathroom. When you call me, I'll bring the plunger and say you called for someone to unclog the toilet. Do you have a way of telling your uncle when he has a call?"

"Yes. His desk phone beeps and a light comes on the line he is supposed to pick up."

"If your uncle or one of his informers comes in while I'm bugging the office, hit the buzzer. I'll go into the bathroom, come out with the plunger, and announce that the clog has been removed. Will that make you feel better?"

"Yes. I think that will work."

"Good," David said. "Here is what I want you to do. After Casey has bugged the office and your uncle has returned, you will knock on his door. Tell him a lawyer has contacted you and told you Billy is dead and you have inherited the ranch. Act happy and excited. If he asks how he died, tell him from an overdose of bad drugs obtained in jail."

"He'll be suspicious," Sarah replied. "He knows there are agents on the farm; he did tell me that much. He went out there to see Billy. A guard stopped him from entering, told him Billy was in jail, and the ranch was under guard."

"Yes. That's why we're going to give him partial truths," David explained. "Tell him that all of Billy's money will be confiscated by the government because Billy's large bank accounts were linked to money laundering. You will inherit the ranch only because the FBI could find no sign of drugs being manufactured or sold from the farm."

"Do you think he'll believe that?" Sarah seemed skeptical.

"Yes, because he'll want to believe it. He is desperate to get his hands on the drugs we found in the secret room under the first warehouse. They did a good job of cleaning out the warehouse, but our forensic man found traces, and Billy told us about the secret room in his letter. Uncle Alfred will want to believe he still has a chance of getting his hands on that shipment of drugs. He is being pressured to produce the goods he promised. They're worth a million dollars.

"I want you to tell him the lawyer will inform you when to come to his office and sign the papers, giving you possession of the ranch. We will listen to his conversations as he tries to make plans to have the drugs picked up and delivered to the warehouse. We will allow him to move the drugs and step in as the drug distributors are picking them up. We will be killing two birds with one stone."

"What will happen to me?"

"There will be no way anyone can trace this back to you. Unfortunately, you will lose your job. Like the ranch, the government will confiscate the furniture business and property, as well as your uncle's money. Does Alfred have family?"

## Vanished Sisters

"He has an ex-wife and grown children. None live in this area. According to him, they only show up when they want money."

"He has no family other than you working for him?"

"No. My mother was Uncle Alfred's only sister. When she was dying, she told me to go to him and ask for a job. I had just graduated from high school, and there was no money for me to go to college. I don't know who my father was; he got my mother pregnant and left town; they were very young. Uncle Alfred has always looked after us. My mother worked in the sock mill here in Marion until she got sick."

"Well, maybe he had a good side too."

"Yes, he did, but he has changed over the years; he's become bitter and mean—I guess ever since he got into the drug business. Who knows what makes people do the things they do?"

"I agree, but we need to get you out of here with a potted plant in hand. You will receive an official-looking letter from a non-existent lawyer's office. It will tell you to come to the lawyer's office to sign papers, which supposedly give you possession of the ranch. Show the letter to your uncle so we can see what he does with the information. Give Casey the names of those warehouse workers who report to your uncle so he can keep an eye on them. If anything happens that you think I need to know about, tell Casey and we will set up another meeting.

"We appreciate your help, and after this all goes down, I will try to find you another job. Thank you again for your assistance. I'm sorry we had to meet under these circumstances."

Sarah stood and thanked him for offering to help her find another job. Casey picked up the plant Anne had ready for them in case they were being watched.

*

ANNE CALLED MARK and said to put the burgers on; they were leaving the garden center now. As they drove to Anne's, David began to relax. "That went better than I thought it would. I believe she's telling the truth and will work with us. Sorry we messed up your evening."

"Not to worry. I got some things done I'd been procrastinating over for a long time. Our evening is only just beginning."

David smiled to himself; he liked Anne, but he had to be careful not to fall in love with her. She was everything he was looking for in a wife. For years, he had guarded his heart because of his job. Lately, he was becoming weary of the constant pressure and politics he had to deal with on a daily basis. He wanted children and a wife to come home to. He was pushing forty and suspected Anne was too. He had a dream in the back of his mind and was working toward that new goal. Maybe there was a way to simplify his life and still be in the law enforcement loop.

# CHAPTER 14

THE MEN GATHERED around the outside grill and talked while the burgers cooked. Mark and Pete were anxious to hear how the meeting with Sarah had gone, but they were reluctant to ask. Pete took the initiative. "How did your meeting go, David?"

"It was a brilliant idea. Anne was happy to help, and I think we have a plan that will work." David explained how the meeting went and shared his plans to set up a sting that would not only catch Alfred Kindle but the distributors of the drugs as well.

Mark flipped the burgers and took a sip of beer. "You feel you can trust this Sarah Kindle?"

"Yes, I do; she's scared, but she admitted she was suspicious and had done some snooping. She found a locked file in Mr. Kindle's office closet. I'm sure everything we need to put him away will be found in that file cabinet. I would like you to be there to go over his office as well as the warehouse. He has had many meetings with drug traffickers in that office. Their fingerprints will help us identify and put them away for a long time. We need the files in that closet."

"Well, that answers my next question," Mark said. "I needed to know if I'm still needed here?"

"Definitely. After this sting hopefully proves successful,

we're on to the terrorist hideout in Poplar Creek. Adam Bradford, the CIA director, has the terrorists under surveillance. The move has slowed them down a bit, but we need to move on this as soon as possible. Can you arrange to stay on for another couple of weeks?"

Mark looked at Pete. "Do you think there will be a problem?"

"Not at all; this is more important. I'll be leaving in the morning; I can cover for you. I can also take Carrie back with me if you wish."

Mark looked doubtful. "I'm not sure you can get her to leave. She likes being where the action is, and she wants to get back in the Hawkins' house. She needs to take more measurements and check out the soundness of some of those beams and floorboards. She's found a reliable carpenter here in Marion who will help her make decisions on what can be used in our new house and what's not worth saving."

"Have you made an offer yet?" asked David.

"Yes, and it's been accepted. We'll close as soon as the lawyers get all the title searches done and the bank approves my credit. The SBI released the house after the terrorists moved out of the area. We plan to hire an architect as soon as we get home. Carrie did some drawings in her free time here to give the architect an excellent idea of what we want."

"You might want to check out some architects in Asheville; it's the summer-home capital of the state. I can ask around if you want?"

"Mention that to Carrie at dinner. I'm sure she hasn't thought about hiring a local architect. And speaking of dinner, these burgers are ready. Let's eat."

*

WHILE THE GUYS cooked burgers and chatted, Anne and Carrie had a heart-to-heart talk as well. Anne confided to Carrie about the talk she had had with Blake and his lunch with another woman. "He actually told on himself. He was so sure Mark had told me about his little lunch date. I know who the woman is; she works at the police station and has a questionable reputation. After I told him I wouldn't be his mistress, he wasted no time finding someone who would."

"Anne, you were lucky to realize who Blake really is before you let the relationship go any further. Some men are capable of faking an entire relationship. They want someone to take care of them and have their children while they are free to continue having extramarital affairs with seemingly innocent women friends. I was lucky to see that tendency in my first husband and make sure there were no children involved. I am positive Mark would never do that to me. We're soul mates and will be until the day we die."

"I think you can count on that, Carrie. He had a bad first marriage too, and I know, without a doubt, he worships the ground you walk on. It's because of him and my father that I know there are good men out there. I can wait for the right one. I was lucky to have a good marriage with Ken. I won't accept anything less. Blake accused me of looking for a clone of Ken, but he's wrong; I just want a good man, not a cheat. I want a man I can look up to and respect. Without respect, there can never be the kind of love that lasts a lifetime."

The door swung open and the men entered with the hamburgers. "Hope you're ready because the burgers are."

"We are. Those burgers smell wonderful; let's eat."

During dinner, David couldn't take his eyes off Anne. She was beautiful in a comfortable, warm way. She looked up at David and caught him looking at her. Their eyes met, and each knew, instantly, they would be friends for life. Anne's feelings for David were becoming stronger. She had convinced herself the love she had felt for her husband was a once-in-a-lifetime encounter. She had almost settled for less with Blake, but God had intervened and shown her a different path. She planned to put this relationship in His hands and see what He had in store for her and David.

David smoothed the moment over by saying, "Anne played her role perfectly tonight. She could be an actress."

Anne smiled. "It was an adventure for me; I enjoyed helping. I hope everything works out for Sarah; she seems like a shy, innocent little creature."

"I agree; she is innocent and, unfortunately, another victim of Billy and his grand scheme to get rich. I've asked Mark to stay on for another couple weeks; hope that won't be an inconvenience for you, Anne?"

"Not at all. I enjoy having someone in the house. I'll be lonely when they have to go. I'm so glad they're going to be able to build a summer home on the Hawkins' property. I know we're going to have some wonderful summers to look forward to, especially now that we have a little one coming."

Pete swallowed a huge bite of burger. "I'll be getting out of your hair tomorrow morning, Anne; I need to get back. I appreciate all the care you've provided while I've been here." He turned to Carrie. "If you need to get back, Carrie, I can give you a ride home."

Anne laughed, "I don't think you could get her out of here without Mark if he wanted her to go, which he doesn't. And you are welcome here anytime you want to return. You're good company, and you appreciate my cooking."

"That I do. Old bachelors don't get a lot of good, home cooking. We appreciate every mouthful."

"She's right," Carrie piped in. "Besides, I have an appointment with my orthopedic doctor next week. I might as well stay and see how my bum leg and arm are coming along. I'm halfway there. I also have a meeting with a contractor recommended by the Dovecote locals. He's going to help me make some decisions that will affect the construction of the new house."

David took the opportunity to say, "While you're in Asheville, you may want to check out some of our architects. We have some outstanding summer homes in the area designed by local architects."

"Great idea. Do you know any personally?"

"No; haven't been here that long, but I can ask around if you like."

"That would be great. I'll bring my drawings."

The evening was like a family get-together. David hadn't felt more at home since he last visited his mother. From now on, he would find lots of excuses to get down to Marion as often as he could. His heart was tugging him closer and closer to Anne. He prayed he was doing the right thing. He didn't want to lose her, but he also didn't want to hurt her by encouraging her feelings right now. He was in a quandary, and all he could do was turn it over to the Lord.

\*

ONE OF DAVID'S lawyers was set up in an office in Marion along with a secretary and even a sign out front. The letter went out, stating Sarah should call for an appointment to sign final papers, which would deed the ranch over to her. Fake papers had also been drawn up in case Mr. Kindle decided to come with her. The sting was coming together. The ranch house and all the barns were bugged. Care was taken to make sure the spies Mr. Kindle had watching the ranch saw nothing out of the ordinary. The cattle and horses had been sold and removed. Sarah's uncle Alfred had greedily taken over for her and accompanied her to the lawyer's office.

Casey had the warehouse under surveillance and Alfred's office bugged. Recordings of Alfred's meetings with drug traffickers told them how to anticipate his every move. He couldn't wait to get his hands on the marijuana and meth.

The plan was to move the drugs on the first night Sarah was the official owner of the ranch. The SBI moved out as Sarah and her uncle arrived. As Alfred's spies left the woods surrounding the ranch, the FBI moved in to watch, record, and follow the drugs all the way to the Kindle warehouse.

At precisely midnight, with no headlights, a large truck entered the ranch property. Kindle was waiting. He had unlocked the barn and opened the door and elevator to the secret room. The transfer took less than an hour, and then they were on the move. Kindle rode with his henchmen back to the warehouse.

Instead of following behind the trucks, even at a safe distance, old cars and trucks were parked along the way and followed only until the next waiting vehicle appeared behind the first. The first then turned off at the next road and the second continued to follow. This cautious method of surveillance was set up all the way to the Kindle warehouse.

As the truck made a hairpin turn, at a remote section of road, they ran into a roadblock. The drug traffickers were taking no chances of being caught moving the drugs from the warehouse. They had decided to take the drugs by force and avoid paying for them. There was no room to turn around. A line of thugs, with guns drawn, stood across the road. Another truck pulled behind them, hemming them in.

"What the hell is going on? We've been set up. That bitch; I'll kill her." Kindle was sure the men were FBI, and that Sarah had set him up. He got out of the truck with his hands up. He was shot through the head instantly. The traffickers knew this was Kindle's last shipment and no longer needed him. He was now a liability. Kindle's truck driver and henchmen tried to run, only to be cut down in a spray of bullets.

As soon as the FBI agents following the truck saw a second truck across the road, they knew the Kindle truck had been hijacked and called for all agents to move in. The drug dealers were trying to leave with the goods. The two agents moved in on foot and shot out the tires of both trucks, preventing them from leaving with the drugs and giving backup more time. The agents were taking fire and took cover behind their vehicle. Within minutes, the drug dealers were surrounded and a gun battle ensued. The drug dealers were trapped in their own trap. One of their two survivors attempted to climb the steep mountain to the right while another tried the down-the-mountain exit on the left. Both were shot in the leg and handcuffed.

Within an hour, the scene was secured. The perpetrators were handcuffed and sitting in the back of an FBI patrol car. The bodies were transported to the morgue. Mr. Kindle was dead, as well as two of his men. Only one remained alive but badly wounded. He was transferred to the Asheville hospital along with the two wounded drug dealers. If Kindle's man lived, he would make a good witness. Hopefully, a plea could be arranged in return for the ringleaders' names. The road was then reopened and the drugs taken to a safe place.

## Vanished Sisters

*

AT THE WAREHOUSE, David, Mark, and Casey waited and listened to the chatter on their radios. David left immediately to go back to the ranch and pick up Sarah. Until all drug traffickers were apprehended, Sarah's life would be in danger. She would be suspected of turning her uncle in to the FBI. David needed a safe place to hide Sarah until loose ends could be tied up. Of course, his first thought was to take her to Anne's. Mark agreed and was left at the warehouse to dust Kindle's office for prints and help Casey pack up all the files in the locked closet.

*

DAVID CALLED ANNE. "Sorry to wake you, but I have another favor to ask."

Anne was not sure she knew whom she was talking to. "Who is this?"

"Sorry, Anne; it's David. Were you asleep?"

"No. What's wrong?"

"The sting went down tonight and a few absurdities crept in. Sarah needs a safe place to hide for a few days. Could you possibly let her stay with you? I can't go into details, except to say her life is in danger."

"Sure, David; bring her here. I have an extra room now that Pete went back to Mississippi; she'll be safe here."

"You're the best, Anne; we'll be there in an hour."

When David arrived at the ranch and knocked on the door, Sarah opened it almost immediately. She was waiting for someone to tell her how the sting had gone down. From the look on David's face, she knew something was wrong. "What happened? Did you arrest all of them?"

"Not exactly, but we will in the next couple of days. We need to hide you until all suspects have been arrested. Anne, the lady at the garden center has an extra room and has agreed to let you stay with her. We need to get you out of here right now."

## Rachel Poe

MARK WAS ABOUT through with the file cabinet in the closet when he and Casey heard someone coming down the hall. They backed into the closet and Casey turned the lock on the door from the inside. Only a key would open it from the outside. The doorknob was rattled. They heard a string of profanity and then someone said, "We'll have to break it down."

Casey had called for backup as he and Mark pushed themselves back into the closet as far as they could. With guns drawn, they waited.

They could hear the men going down the hall to the warehouse. A few minutes later, the men returned and an ax came through the top panel of the door. Again, again, and again the ax chipped away at the door until a hand pushed through and unlocked it.

Without looking at the other end of the closet, one man went straight for the files while the other two waited outside. Casey placed a gun to the back of his head. "Make a move and you're a dead man," said Casey, using his most convincing voice. The man put his hands up and Casey pushed him into the office. The other two reached for their guns as Mark appeared behind Casey and said, "I wouldn't do that if I were you. Drop your guns; put your hands on your head, and kick the guns toward me." The two men complied and raised their hands. Mark picked up their guns.

An angry voice coming down the hall yelled, "What is taking you so long?" The fourth man entered the office and came to an abrupt halt.

"Come in and join the party," Casey said. "Take your gun out, place it on the floor, kick it over to me, and stand over here with the others."

As the man, who appeared to be the boss, took his weapon out, he whipped it around to fire, but Casey was quick and fired first, knocking his adversary to the ground. Mark kept his gun on the other three, ready to fire if either moved. Backup came pouring in the door, took charge, removed the three men, and called an ambulance for the fourth.

## Vanished Sisters

*

WHEN MARK FINALLY made it home and into bed, Carrie woke and asked whether everything had gone well. Mark replied, "Yes, darling; everything went well. Go back to sleep." To himself, he thought. *I didn't know when I became a forensic anthropologist that I would need to put my life on the line every time I turned around. What a day.*

## CHAPTER 15

ANNE AND SARAH helped Carrie into the backseat of Anne's SUV. Sarah had offered to help Anne get Carrie to her orthopedic and OBGYN appointments in Asheville. They were then going to interview an architect and look at some of the homes he had designed in the area.

Carrie's orthopedic check-up went well and then they went on to see the gynecologist. As Carrie dressed after the exam, her anxiety level rose. The doctor had listened for the heartbeat longer than Carrie thought was necessary. She worried something was wrong and wished she had asked Anne to remain with her for the examination.

Dr. Beth Kent knocked softly, entered the room, and took a seat facing Carrie. "I'm sending you for an ultrasound. I suspect I may be hearing two heartbeats. Do you have twins in your or your husband's family?"

Carrie was speechless. She tried to think and was sure that neither of her parents had ever mentioned twins in their families. Mark had never mentioned twins in his family either.

"I don't think so; at least not on my side. I'll check with my mother-in-law about Mark's side of the family. Are you sure?"

"No. That's why we're going to have an ultrasound. It's right here in the building and won't take long at all. Come with me and I'll show you the way. They'll call me when you're on the table."

As Carrie and Anne watched the monitor, tears flooded their eyes. The fetuses were so tiny, but they looked fully developed. Anne held Carrie's hand and cried with her. The door opened and Dr. Kent entered. "What do we have here?" she said as she looked at the monitor. "With all you've been through recently and in the past year, I wanted to see for myself that these little ones were developing at a normal pace."

"Then you knew all along I was having twins?"

"I knew you were either having twins or your baby had a very unusual heartbeat. I had to confirm it, and thank God we have this tool to help us. You are further along than you guesstimated. I'd say you're close to four months."

"I was guessing three, but my last period was no more than spotting. Guess I was pregnant then?"

"Yes, I suspect you were, and the development of these little ones proves that theory."

"Oh, Anne, I'm so glad you're here with me. I wish Mark could've been here to see his babies. Can you tell the sex of the babies?"

The technician answered, "One is a girl for sure, and I'm trying to get the other one to turn so we can see better, but the second baby seems to be taking a nap and won't cooperate."

"That's perfectly fine; we know Mark has his girl and the second one will be a surprise. Oh, Anne, I can't wait to tell him. Should I call him?"

"Why don't you wait? They'll give us a copy of the ultrasound. I want to see the look on his face when he realizes you're having twins."

\*

MARK WAS AT the morgue doing autopsies on the previous night's casualties, wishing Pete had not gone home so soon. He was working with Dr. Ted Morris, the Marion coroner.

"Were you there when these poor stiffs were shot?" asked Ted.

"No. I was at the warehouse, dusting for fingerprints. That was enough excitement for me. These guys were just petty thieves; we need to get the ones who hired these thugs. Hopefully, some of the prints I took will identify the ringleaders. We also have several in the hospital and in jail, who will probably talk to avoid prosecution."

Mark and Ted had finished with the first cadaver and moved on to uncover the second. Mark did a double take. This was the cop Blake suspected of passing information to Billy. Since the local police were not in on last night's bust, he wondered whether Blake knew. He made a mental note to call him later.

*

IT WAS LATE in the day when Mark and Ted finished. They sat in the breakroom and shared a cup of coffee. "Mark, I'm impressed with your skills. Most forensic anthropologists want to leave the autopsies to guys like me; they're only interested in retrieving the bodies. I guess as a professor you need to be up on all aspects of your profession?"

"We know how these blokes died. The mystery is not there, but when we're looking for a cause of death, I can really get involved. I love to solve the mystery. New and more advanced testing methods are being discovered every day."

"I remember when I was young and enthused about my job, but I'm looking forward to retirement now, and the enthusiasm is gone."

"The students keep me on my toes, and I have to keep up with every new aspect of the profession. I want my students to graduate with the latest knowledge available."

As Mark and Ted were talking, David came in. "How's it going? No surprises, I hope?"

"No, David. We found no surprises except one of the men worked for Blake. Blake told me early on he suspected he was giving Billy inside information and was going to put him on administrative leave. Guess he went to work for the other side, or he may have worked for both sides. Since the local police were not in on last night's sting, someone needs to call Blake. I can call him tonight unless you would rather talk to him."

"I would, Mark; that raises questions that only Blake can answer. All I need is the man's name. I'm headed over that way now to try to get information out of our new residents in the local jail. I'll talk to Blake. If we can get just one of them to talk, we can make a few more arrests before we close this phase of the investigation."

"Good," Mark said as he got to his feet. "I think I'll go home unless you need to go over the autopsies."

"No problem; you go on home. However, we do need to sit down and discuss our next venture; things are moving faster than we anticipated."

Mark wearily ran his fingers through his hair. "I'm looking forward to being part of that bust. Maybe we can finish the job Danny and I started."

David laughed. "I hope we won't be disappointed. The CIA represents the international aspect of this investigation. Adam's men are in those woods watching every move they make. Ben and his SBI agents are teaming up with us to make sure no one gets away. I have some ideas of how you can be valuable to this operation."

"Sounds exciting but dangerous. Are you coming by tonight to see Anne?"

"I was trying to find an excuse to come by. Would you be available to talk later?"

"Sure. I'm cooking salmon on the grill tonight; I'll tell Anne you were coming by to talk and I invited you to dinner. She will be thrilled."

"So you don't mind that I'm seeing Anne?"

"Couldn't be happier. You couldn't have come along at a more opportune time, and I know for a fact that Anne considers you a good friend."

"I'm happy to hear that; I feel the same about her. See you around sixish, and I'll bring the wine?"

*

BLAKE SAW DAVID and motioned him into his office. Blake had been in the interrogation room most of the morning. One of the drug traffickers was singing loud and clear. They were trying to get the second one to confirm what the first one had confessed. He wasn't cooperating. Blake gave David a copy of the signed confession. David was not surprised by the names he saw; he had been after these drug dealers for some time. David looked at the rap sheet on both men and asked Blake whether he minded giving him a go at the one who was not cooperating. Blake agreed and asked for the inmate to be returned to the interrogation room.

David walked into the interrogation room as if he were a doctor entering an examination room with a patient. He was reading Luther Burton's rap sheet as he entered. He sat down across from him and continued to read. Luther watched him curiously as he sat slouching in his chair, a defiant expression on his unshaven face. David continued to read for another three minutes, ignoring Luther completely. Finally, David looked up, offered his hand, and introduced himself. "Luther, I'm David Durham, District Director of the FBI. Good to meet you."

Luther was expecting anything except respect from his interrogators, so he was momentarily flustered. Caught by surprise, he took David's hand and David gave him a firm handshake. "Luther, I see here you've worked for Tony Spirio for several years?"

Luther looked confused, and before he knew what he was saying, he said, "Yes, sir, I have."

Confession number one; David continued as if he had confessed to eating a hamburger for lunch. "We picked up Spirio this morning. I'm afraid he's going away for a very long time. Your name was on his list. Spirio a good man to work for?"

Luther swallowed hard; he was processing what David had said. It sounded to him like Tony had ratted on him. He was also thinking this could be a trick. This guy had him all confused, but one thing he knew, he wasn't going to prison if he could help it. With Tony in jail, how could he depend on Tony to get him out? Tony had always pulled strings to get him out. Maybe he was taking everyone down with him. Luther's mind was spinning; he decided to see whether he could get more information.

Luther pretended to be thinking this over before answering. "He's a good boss. Takes care of his drivers. That's all I do for him; I'm just a driver."

"Really? It says here you worked as Mr. Spirio's bodyguard and muscleman. He speaks very highly of you and your talents. Calls you his enforcer. Is he right about that?"

"He's a good-fer-nothin' liar! All I ever did was drive a truck and maybe ruff a few guys. Believe me; I seen plenty."

Confession number two. David was on a roll, and Luther continued to spill out answers to every question David asked. They now had enough information to put Mr. Spirio away for a very long time, if they ever found him. David thanked Luther for his cooperation as if he had given him much needed instructions on how to repair his car. David assured him every possible avenue would be used to get him a lighter sentence because of his cooperation. David again thanked Luther and offered his hand for a parting handshake. Again, Luther shook his hand and truly felt he had a friend in David Durham.

Blake had a smile on his face as David left the interrogation room. "You're a pro all the way, David. That was some performance."

David smiled and assured Blake, "It only works if the accused has been thoroughly hammered by previous detectives. They come in expecting more of the same, and you catch them off-guard. The letters FBI seem to put the fear of God in them as well. It's all psychology. By the way, Mark has one of your men over at the morgue. He was driving the truck for Alfred Kindle. Mark said you suspected he was feeding Billy information."

"Johnny Grimes?"

David checked his notes and confirmed it was John Grimes. "Was he still on your payroll?"

"No. I did a little looking into his work record and decided to let him go. Guess he went to work for Billy full time."

Blake wanted to ask him about Anne, but he didn't know how to turn the conversation around. He finally said, "How are Mark and Carrie doing?"

David could see the tension in Blake's jaw as he asked about Mark and Carrie. He suspected he really wanted to know how Anne was doing. He held no animosity toward Blake and felt no personal triumph over the fact that he was now seeing Anne. He wanted to ease Blake's mind. "They're fine; they all speak very highly of you, Blake, and I want you to know that Anne and I are just friends. I think she is trying to work something out in her mind, and I have no idea what the outcome will be. I hope whatever happens, we can remain friends."

Blake offered David his hand. "You can bet on that, David. Look forward to working with you in the future."

They shook hands.

*

THE GIRLS WERE waiting when Mark came home. "You three look like the canaries who ate the goldfish. Why are you all grinning? Do I have egg on my face?"

"No," said Carrie. "I have something to show you."

Anne was ready with the camera as Carrie pulled the ultrasound from its envelope. She handed it to Mark.

"They did an ultrasound?" he asked. "Isn't it a bit early for that?"

"No. The doctor thinks I'm almost four months. An ultrasound can be done at any stage of pregnancy. I've been pregnant at least three weeks longer than I thought."

"Was I right? Is it a girl?"

"I'll let you decide; you're the doctor in this house."

Mark took the ultrasound from Carrie, a big smile on his face. He looked and then looked again. His eyes got big and watery as he realized there were two babies. "Are we having twins?" he asked as a tear escaped.

"Yes, Dr. Goodman; it sure looks that way," said Carrie as Anne snapped Mark's picture.

Mark took the ultrasound to the light and studied the picture closely. "One is a girl for sure, but I can't tell about the other. Did they tell you the sex of the second baby?"

"No; that one was asleep and didn't want to be disturbed.

The technician tried to make him move with no luck."

"You said, 'him'; do you feel like the second one is a boy?"

"I don't know, but not knowing adds a little mystery to the pregnancy.... I like that. I don't want to know; do you?"

Mark took Carrie in his arms and kissed her tenderly. "I don't care as long as they're healthy. I love you, Carrie, and I'm so happy we're having twins."

Sarah had to see the expression on Mark's face when he looked at the ultrasound. She then went to her room and allowed the family to enjoy the moment. She prayed someday someone would love her as Mark loved Carrie.

Anne was taking pictures and praying life would not pass her by without giving her a chance to experience the thrill of having a baby. Mark had not noticed Anne; he was so intent on the ultrasound. He heard a click as he kissed his wife. "Anne, what are you doing?"

"I'm recording this moment for posterity. You will thank me some day."

"Oh, by the way," Mark added, "I asked David to come to dinner. We need to go over some things after dinner. I didn't think you would mind," he said, giving her a knowing grin. "He's bringing wine."

Anne blushed, "Of course I don't mind; I'd better go change."

"Why? It's just David," Mark teased.

Mark, still holding Carrie in his arms, gave her another kiss and said, "I think we have a budding romance here, and I couldn't be happier. Twins. I just can't believe we're having twins."

"As far as I know," said Carrie, "there are no twins in my family; are there any in yours?"

"None that I know of. I'll have to call Mom and ask. We haven't told them you're pregnant; they'll be shocked."

"I wish my mom were here. She would have been such a wonderful granny."

"Well, we'll just have to let Aunt Mattie take her place. Have you told Mattie?"

"No. I keep thinking we'll be home soon, but it looks like we'll be here a couple more weeks, doesn't it?"

"At least. Are you going to wait to tell her?"

"Yes. If I told her over the phone, she would be calling every day, wanting a play-by-play of my progress."

*

DAVID ARRIVED AROUND six-fifteen, wine in hand. Anne rushed to get the door. Mark pretended to try to outrun her. "Mark," she said, with a warning finger pointed at him, "I'm still your older sister; behave or I'll tell Mom."

Mark backed off, laughing. "Only kidding, sis, and you look gorgeous," he teased.

Anne opened the door. "Hey, David, so glad you could make it for dinner."

David gave her an awkward little hug and handed her the wine. "I hope Mark's invitation to dinner didn't cause problems. I'm happy to get a chance to see you again. Remember, I still owe you a dinner."

"No problem. We'll have to make plans for that dinner soon. Come on in; I'll open the wine." She checked out the bottles. "By the way, this is one of my favorites."

The dinner was delicious, and they shared the news about the twins with David. David was obviously touched by the news and a little jealous of the close, loving relationship between Mark and Carrie.

"That's wonderful news. I have to admit I'm jealous of you two. I've never married because I could never ask a woman to put up with my hours, or the danger I face every day. I'm not getting any younger, though, and the job seems to get more dangerous every day. I actually am having days when I wish I had chosen a different field. I want to get the bad guys off the street, but I also want to be a husband and father before it's too late. I need to look at alternatives and soon. Sorry; didn't mean to put a damper on your good news."

Mark shook his head. "Not a problem, David; we're honored you feel comfortable enough to share your feelings with us. Have you ever thought about teaching at the FBI academy?"

"I have; I just don't know if I want to be completely out of the loop. The adrenaline that flows when I'm on a case is almost addictive. I'm very interested in the analysis of the criminal mind. That's a whole new field, and it intrigues me. I've taken several night courses, and I've read everything I could get my hands on about this new field of law enforcement. I have a second degree in psychology; guess that part of me is surfacing here."

"Wow! That does sound intriguing." Anne joined the conversation. Nothing he could say would make her happier than hearing he was thinking of changing jobs. "Psychology was my major too."

"That's psychic," said David. "From the very first time I met you, I've felt we were on the same wavelength. I bet you talk to your plants like I do."

Anne laughed. "I sure do, and sometimes they talk to me. Usually telling me they need water."

Everyone laughed and they returned to lighter conversations as David and Sarah helped Anne clear away the table and fill the dishwasher.

Sarah had been very quiet during dinner. She felt like a fifth wheel and was sure they wanted to get rid of her as soon as possible. "Mr. Durham," Sarah began, "do you still feel my life may be in danger? I feel like I'm taking advantage of Anne and her family."

Anne spoke up. "You certainly are not; we love having you here. You have been a great help to Carrie as well as me at the garden center. In fact, if you want a job at the garden center, you can consider yourself hired. You seem to be very knowledgeable about plants as well as office procedures."

"I would love that, Anne, but I would also like to get back to my own apartment when Mr. Durham thinks it's safe."

"Well, Sarah, one of the reasons I wanted to come over tonight was to let you know about several arrests we'll be making tonight and more tomorrow. If all goes well, you'll be able to go home tomorrow. I'll call and let you know. Do you feel sure you want to work for Anne? I can keep looking for something else if you want me to?"

"No, thank you, Mr. Durham. I would love to work for Anne. I want to start classes at the Community College here in Marion, and I feel sure Anne will schedule my hours around my classes...won't you, Anne?"

"You can bet on that, Sarah. You know from our conversations that I think college is an excellent decision. You can use my computer to check on classes. We'll sit down tomorrow and discuss salary."

*

MARK AND DAVID took a walk after dinner. David wanted no one to hear this conversation. "Mark, we're trying to get a couple spies into that farmhouse. The CIA tells me they've captured a dangerous Islamic extremist coming across the border. They're keeping it quiet. Want to get as much information from him as possible before the powers-that-be find out and invent a reason to send him back to the Middle East. They've discovered he's an—information runner—for lack of a better term. He was on his way to Poplar Creek with information too important to be trusted over a cell phone. They're expecting him. The whole operation, it seems, hinges on his information.

"We're going to replace him with a CIA operative. This agent is from the Middle East, speaks the language, and understands the way the terrorists think and act. His objective is to obtain information on their capability to inflict chaos on the American public and to see what Shahin will do with this new information.

"This was a huge windfall for us. The captured terrorist was carrying target sites for Shahin, from leaders of Hamas. These documents confirmed Shahin as the leader of all the North Carolina cells. The ranch was a training facility where radicals were trained and sent out to maintain safe houses all over this state. Experts have altered these papers to give us more time. Rayyan, our operative, will accompany Shahin to visit these targets before finalizing their plans.

"If he can get everyone out of the house, I want you in

## Vanished Sisters

there getting fingerprints and hopefully information on these other cells. We need to identify these Islamic radicals who were already at the Poplar Creek house. We'll then compare the new fingerprints with the fingerprints you lifted from the Boone farmhouse. This will allow us to estimate how many total members we're dealing with. After you have completed your findings, our men will bug the house. We'll then be able to monitor their activity and know when to make our move.

"I'm sure some of these men are on the CIA's database watchlist. They change their names as they move around to keep us from knowing whom we've taken out and whom we need to be looking for. We suspect some of these men have been here before. They were captured, sent back home, and have reappeared. Their only reason for being here is to kill as many Americans as possible. If all goes as planned, we'll not only know who they are but the exact time they plan to put their murderous scheme into action. We can then make our move knowing we have all the information we're ever going to glean from this cell."

"When do you plan to introduce this agent to our fanatic friends?"

"He's here now, observing the comings and goings of the cell, as well as coaching a second agent to be his partner. When he feels he's familiar enough with their patterns and is sure this agent can carry off the charade, he will walk in and introduce himself. He will actually be wearing the clothes of the captured terrorist."

Mark had an uneasy feeling in the pit of his stomach. "It seems an impossible task to convince everyone to leave that farmhouse. Aren't they still producing meth and growing marijuana? They won't just shut down their operation and leave their arsenal of weapons unguarded."

"Rayyan has a plan, and having a partner will help with its feasibility. I won't ask you to go in until the farmhouse is safe. This is another reason Rayyan has not made himself known to Shahin. We must all be on the same page and know exactly what Rayyan is attempting to do and how. We need signals so he can alert us if things are not going well. This all has to be worked out before we send him in."

"I understand now what you meant when you talked about the adrenaline rush. I'm feeling it now. But I must admit I'm scared. I've never been exposed to terrorists before. However, I feel we're living in an undeclared war zone, and I want to do my part for my country."

"Mark, if you weren't scared, I would be concerned. Men who aren't scared make mistakes and put others in danger. We call them cowboys and won't tolerate them in our ranks. As much as I like Danny, he's a cowboy. If he had thrown one stick of dynamite into just one truck, you both would have been blown up with the trucks, the house, and probably the side of the mountain. His intentions were good, but his knowledge was lacking and dangerous."

Mark felt a little sick at this new information. He thought to himself, *Should I just say, "No, I can't do this? I'm about to become a father, and I want to spend the rest of my life with Carrie watching our children grow"?* He then realized he wanted his children to grow up as free as he had. If they didn't stop these men now, his children might never know what it felt like to be free to follow your dreams.

"As soon as Rayyan feels we have an attainable plan, I'll bring you into our ranks and we'll instruct you in how we plan to pull off this whole charade. When Rayyan hands Shahin the papers with his instructions from Hamas, Shahin will make plans to visit the actual target sites, study the areas, and finalize his plan of action. Rayyan will suggest his partner be left behind to guard the farmhouse in case any locals wander into the site. Then and only then will you be sent in to obtain as much information as possible.

"Do you think Pete would come back and help you? It would make the job go faster. Our goal is to get you out of there as soon as possible. Now that Sarah is returning to her apartment, Anne will have room for Pete. Give him a call and see how he feels about coming back. He may have had all the excitement he wants for a while."

"That would simplify the situation; I'll give him a call."

# CHAPTER 16

MARK WAS FILLED with ambiguity. He did and he didn't want to do this. *I'm just scared*, he told himself. *I need to talk this over with Carrie.* "David, can I talk this over with Carrie? I don't feel right doing something this dangerous without letting her know what I'm considering."

"If I had a wife—which is why I don't—I too would have to discuss it with her. But I would not give her any information that could put her in danger. Think of it this way: What if Carrie were kidnapped because the enemy thought—being your wife—she might know information? Then ask yourself this: What pertinent facts have I given her that the enemy might need to know to alter their plans?"

"This isn't going to be easy," Mark replied. "I'll need to think this over carefully before I talk to her. I trust Carrie not to say anything to anyone, even Anne, about what we discuss in private. However, the news about the twins is definitely going to be on her mind. Her mothering instincts will kick in and affect how she looks at my being in a dangerous situation. I haven't told her about the incident at the warehouse when Casey and I were preparing to force the file cabinet open and the thugs showed up. I figured it was over and I survived, so why worry her about it?"

"I agree; it's in the past, and you had no reason to believe anything was going down that involved you or Casey. If you had told her, it would definitely color her opinion about what you're considering now. Just be careful, Mark; I know you will handle this discreetly. You may decide not to do this, and that's okay. I can always pull a forensic technician from our lab. I know you would do a better job, but I fully understand where you're coming from."

David and Mark were almost back to Anne's. They saw the girls sitting on the front porch. They could hear their soft laughter as they discussed girl things. Mark and David changed gears as they approached and leaned on the porch railing. "What are you lovely ladies doing out here in the dark with the mosquitoes?" asked David.

Sarah stood and said, "I, for one, am going to bed before they eat me alive. Goodnight all."

"It's such a perfect night; we just couldn't resist sitting and rocking while listening to the night critters," Anne answered as she wondered what they had been talking about. She knew the terrorist situation wasn't resolved and that David would be involved until it was. "Did you enjoy your walk?"

"We did," answered David as he held out his hand to Anne. "Would you like to take a turn around the block?"

Anne stood, David took her hand, and they walked down the steps together. David smiled as he slipped Anne's hand under his arm.

Carrie reached for her crutches. "Enjoy your walk; it's time for Mark to put me to bed. Hope to see you again soon, David."

"Have a good night," David replied. As they walked away, they heard the screen door open and close and David knew Mark had a difficult task ahead of him as he discussed with Carrie his involvement in the next phase of their plans.

*

AS CARRIE AND Mark were getting ready for bed, Carrie asked. "Do you think Anne and David are getting serious?"

Mark turned down the bed and winked at her. "I sure

hope so; David is an intelligent, caring man, and I think he likes Anne. How would you like to go out to our new property tomorrow? Just the two of us and a picnic lunch." He wanted to sleep on all the information David had given him. There was no need to say anything to Carrie until he was sure he wanted to do this.

"I think that would be great. I haven't had time to tell you about the carpenter's findings and suggestions. He went by the property and did a thorough inspection of the place. Explaining his findings will be so much easier if we're there where I can show you the things he wants to use in the new construction. I really like him. Elvis says Mr. Tate is the best carpenter in the county and we should hire him to build our new house. I'd like to see several things he has done and have you meet him before we make a decision. I was impressed with his knowledge and his demeanor. He is definitely country, but he knows his stuff."

"You know more about design and working with artisans than I do, and I trust your judgment explicitly. Maybe we can see some of Mr. Tate's projects in the area. We'll have time if you feel up to that much activity."

"I think I can handle it. I'll call Mr. Tate in the morning. Maybe he can get us in a few houses to see his detail work and you can meet him."

\*

THE NEXT DAY as they walked through the sisters' old house, Carrie pointed out different structural pieces that could be saved. "I want those joists used as exposed beams in the kitchen. The flooring over most of the house can be used as flooring in the new house. The great room walls will be paneled with the ceiling boards from the old living room and dining room. Mr. Tate says he can turn them into tongue-and-groove paneling." Carrie continued to point out items that could be reused in the new construction.

"This is unbelievable; how can hundred-year-old wood still be reusable?"

"This wood is hard oak, and hard rock maple, which will probably still be here after we're gone. It's never been treated with chemicals, painted, or varnished. The thickness of the wood is much greater than any we could buy today."

"What about the rock you hoped to use. Is there enough to do what you wanted?"

"Yes, the front steps, porch, crawlspace walls, and front façade will be rock. Mr. Tate found a rock wall on the back of what used to be the sisters' garden. It was completely overgrown with honeysuckle vines. He's sure the sisters dug the garden themselves and saved every rock they encountered while digging. Between the supports of the old house and this rock wall, there will be more than enough rock. And best of all, Mr. Tate says he can save the root cellar. Another memory saved for us to enjoy."

"This is amazing; I can't wait to see what the architect comes up with after seeing your drawings. When can we expect to see the blueprints?"

"He promised to get them to us in three weeks, and that was a week ago. He said the floor plans and other drawings I did would make his job easy. Are you getting hungry?"

"Yes. Are we finished with all you have managed to save of this old house?"

"I think so; come...we can eat our lunch out back, while looking out over our beautiful valley."

As they settled on a quilt and laid out their lunch, Mark poured the wine and reached for a sandwich. "Carrie, I need to talk to you about something."

"Oh, dear, this sounds ominous. Does it have anything to do with David and his plans for capturing the terrorists?"

"Yes; how did you know?"

"After you and David returned from your walk last night, you had that deep furrow in your forehead that you only get when you're truly worried about something. I'm sure it had something to do with your talk with David. What does he want you to do?"

"I can't tell you—for your own good—but it could be dangerous. I have never worked under these conditions. David is doing this country a great service, and I want to be part of his plan. That's all I can say."

"Why is it so important to you?"

"Because it will be my contribution toward keeping this country safe and free for our children. That's about all I can tell you, except I want your thoughts on this and, hopefully, your support. If you're totally against me taking part in this plan, I won't do it. I just couldn't make this decision without talking it over with you."

Carrie stared at Mark; their eyes held for what seemed a lifetime. What was she going to say? He obviously wanted to do this and wanted her to agree, but everything in her shouted for her to say, "No, don't do this." But if she said no, would he feel hen-pecked and disappointed? Yes, he would. If she said yes, gave him her support, and he was killed, would she blame herself for the rest of her life as she raised her children alone? Yes, she would...there was no easy answer to this dilemma.

A breeze picked up and blew napkins across the quilt. Mark scrambled to catch them and anchor them with the wine bottle. Carrie felt the breeze touch her face as the scent of honeysuckle drifted along with the breeze. She saw the house they wanted to build, but would she build it if Mark were not here?

"Oh, Mark, what do you want me to say? Do you want me to say, 'No' so you will have an excuse to tell David no? Do you want me to happily say, 'Go-ahead, darling; have fun with your war on terror'? I'm torn between selfishly saying, 'No, I don't want you to do this,' and being the supportive wife who says, 'I want you to do what your heart and sensible mind tells you to do.' I want to make you happy, Mark, and I want the man I love with all my heart to be here with me to raise our children. I wish you hadn't even asked me. Then, I could really be mad if you get killed. No. No, I don't mean that." She shook her head and wiped the tears as she looked out over their valley.

"I'm so torn," she continued after a moment. "I'm even more frightened because you can't give me a clear idea of what you're about to do. My imagination automatically sees the worst-case scenario. 'If I can live with the worst,' I tell myself, 'maybe I can handle anything in between.'"

"I'm sorry to do this to you, Carrie; I know it isn't fair. But the truth is, I could die of a heart attack tomorrow or get hit by a truck as I cross the street. When it's my time to go, I will go, as will you. If everyone turns a blind eye to what's happening in this country, we will no longer live in a free society. Our children could grow up in a much different world than we did, and I fear it won't be for the better. I just feel the need to do something to try to stop the madness."

"Well, if you feel that strongly, there is only one thing I can say, 'Do what your heart and sensible mind tell you to do.' I'm proud of you for wanting to do this. But I am also scared I will lose you. I love you so much, Mark."

Tears welled in their eyes as they reached for each other. They lay on the quilt, holding each other for several minutes. Carrie spoke as she tried to control her sobs. "I don't want to know when this plan is going to happen. Just do what you have to do and tell me when it's over. I want to pretend this conversation never happened. I want to go on as if terrorists were not imbedded in our beautiful mountains, plotting to kill us."

"That's exactly what we should do. To do anything else is to be defeated before they even attempt to hurt us. We're going to look at houses today and decide on a contractor for our beautiful summer home. With God's help, we will spend many summers here, watching our children grow up."

"You are so right; God laughs at all the plans we make because He knows 'He holds all our moments in His hands and gives them one by one.'"

"That sounds like a poem; where did you hear that?"

"It was from a poem, but the author was unknown. Let's clean up this mess and go look at some houses."

"One last thing, Carrie—you can't talk to anyone about what we've discussed. Not even Anne. Promise?"

"I promise; I will tell no one," she said as she tried to summon courage from the very depths of her soul. "But I will say plenty about this to my Lord. Every day until you tell me it's over, and then I will thank Him for the rest of my life."

Mark pulled Carrie up on her one good foot and helped her with her crutches. He hugged her close to him and whispered in her ear, "I love you, Carrie." Then they were off to meet Mr. Tate and look at houses.

# CHAPTER 17

ANNE AND SARAH sat in Anne's office, discussing Sarah's future. Anne was worried she couldn't pay Sarah enough to cover her bills and pay for her classes. "Are you sure working here will be enough money to pay for classes?"

"There was an insurance policy that my Uncle Alfred had, naming me as beneficiary. It's not a fortune, but enough to supplement my income here until I get my degree. I'll be able to stay in my apartment and support myself for four years, if I'm frugal with my money."

"What do you plan to study, if I may ask?"

"I want to be a nurse and help people. I want to work with newborn babies. With my face, I will never marry again or have a family of my own, but I can help new mothers with their babies."

"Oh, Sarah, don't say that. I don't even notice the scar anymore. Now that I know you, I just don't see it. You are a beautiful person, Sarah, and I want to help you in any way I can. You can work full-time when possible and we will adjust according to your classes. Please, don't sell yourself short. That scar can be removed by a good plastic surgeon someday when you're making good money as a nurse. But I'm sure you'll meet someone in school who sees who you really are and, like us, will not see the scar. Only the beautiful person you are."

"I hope you're right; if I do meet someone who isn't repelled by my scar, then I will know he truly loves me."

"That's right, Sarah; very few people can say that. Your scar could be a blessing in disguise."

\*

A TOP LEVEL meeting was being held in David's office. Ben, the local SBI director, Adam, the local CIA director, and David were going over the known and unknown specifics of the upcoming terrorist sting operation. David was leading the discussion. "I want to go over every step of our plan and look for flaws. Rayyan and Anthony (alias, Saheb) will be here in a few minutes. I first wanted us to have some time together to bring each other up to date on the progress being made and any additional information you may have obtained since our last meeting. Ben, you go first."

Ben opened his notebook and began his report: "My team has been keeping an eye on the meth lab and marijuana fields, their production, and movement to dealers. A buyer from New York has replaced Mr. Kindle. The drugs are being transported in a grain tanker. The company is bogus, of course; the owner is listed as James M. Saunders of Saunders and Sons. The company is a cover for mafia operative Benny Angelo, who is on the FBI's most wanted list. NYPD has been informed and is keeping Saunders and Sons under surveillance, but it will not make a move until after our operation is completed. We've managed to get two of our agents hired as laborers in the marijuana fields, which has given us good information.

"One agent was able to get into the meth lab, which operates from a shed attached to the house. He reports that the operation is of considerable size and produces enough meth to warrant a weekly pick-up. He has actually seen and photographed cash changing hands. There is no bank account. The cash is stashed in the house and used as needed, which is pretty standard for these operations. It's highly unlikely the workers in the fields and the meth lab will leave the farm while Rayyan accompanies the leaders to scope out the target sites in Raleigh and Charlotte.

## Vanished Sisters

"We need to come up with a plan to get these workers out of the house and slip Mark in there long enough to get the information we need and have our man wire the house and barn for audio and video."

David interjected here. "I've thought of a possible scenario, which I want to run by you when Rayyan and Saheb get here. They can best tell us if it's feasible; they know these people and how they think."

"I agree," Ben said. "If Rayyan can finagle it so our two agents stay to work in the field, we will only need to find a way to get the meth lab workers out of the way. That's about all I have now," Ben concluded.

"Adam," David asked, "what do you have to add?"

Adam opened his folder and began. "Capturing the Hamas operative was the ace we needed. I'm trying to obtain information about our captive and authenticate the intelligence he's given us. Of course, there's always the possibility that he's feeding us misinformation.... Everything must be checked, and that takes time. But I feel confident our two undercover agents are capable of pulling off this sting. The papers they carry from Hamas reveal objectives in Charlotte and Raleigh as well as targets for other cells.

"His job is to inform, prepare this cell, and move on to the next cell, which is Wilmington. The objectives for this cell are airports, and the Wilmington objective is the port. With the information we have, I have no doubt we can prevent both operations from succeeding if our operatives are properly informed and trained to pull off this sting. Intelligence gathering is the key.

"As Ben has stated, getting Mark in there to garner every fingerprint he can will tell us who we're dealing with and what we can expect from them. We have an extensive database of terrorists, with their known importance within the Muslim Brotherhood. Knowing who they are tells us the level of information we may be able to obtain from them."

As Adam concluded his report, David's assistant tapped on the door to let them know Rayyan and his partner had arrived. David asked, "Are we ready to add the agents to our meeting?"

Both Ben and Adam gave a nod, so David asked his assistant to show them in. Rayyan and Saheb entered, shook hands with their superiors, and took a seat at the table.

Adam took the initiative and asked, "How soon will you be ready to infiltrate our objective?"

Rayyan took a deep breath and proceeded as spokesman for his team. "As far as language, mannerisms, and appearances are concerned, we're ready. We wait only to obtain as much intelligence information as possible. We await your decision as to whether we are as informed as we possibly can be before we infiltrate and begin our objective."

Adam ran his fingers through his hair. It was obvious the weight was on his shoulders. "I'm almost 100 percent sure we have garnered all the information we're going to get from the captured terrorist. Our only snare is: How are you going to get everyone out of the house, so we can send in our forensic team? If you don't have a plan, David has an idea to share with us."

Rayyan raised his eyebrows and looked at David. "I have a plan, but I would be happy to hear David's in case it's better than mine. My plan involves wasting one or more of the meth workers. If I suggest that everyone leave, Shahin will become immediately suspicious. I'll advise leaving one meth technician and two field workers (our agents) at the house. I'll also prepare for a small explosion to take out the meth techs and allow us to get in the house. It will appear as if he made a stupid mistake and blew himself up. The controlled explosion will not cause the operation to come to a halt, or damage the house. It's simple and workable."

David smiled. "Your plan is identical to mine; a meth lab can be a hazardous place to work. His death will not be suspect. When shall we put this plan into action?"

Everyone looked at Adam. "If you feel confident you can pull this off, let's set the plan in motion this week." Adam looked at Tony, who had not said a word. "How about you, Tony...I mean Saheb...how do you feel? Are you ready and confident you can pull this off?"

"Yes, Rayyan has trained me well, and I believe the longer we wait, the greater the chance of being seen observing the house and possibly compromising the whole plan."

Adam was impressed. "I agree wholeheartedly; let's get this sting in action. I have only one request. I have already lost two agents to those reprobates; if at any time you suspect things are going wrong, send us the signal and get out of there. We will rush the house and end it there. I'm sure the house is wired with explosives; these radicals do not plan to be taken alive, which is fine with us, but we do not want you two caught in the middle. Is that understood?"

All heads confirmed with nods. The meeting then switched to a discussion of the minute details of the sting; signals were gone over again as well as different scenarios and how they would be dealt with. Hours later, the meeting was adjourned; Rayyan and Saheb were ready to walk into the farmhouse.

*

DAVID CALLED MARK and asked him to meet for lunch. They met at the Marion Market, where local produce could be bought and deli sandwiches ordered. It was only open in the summer, and several tables and chairs were outside where they could talk privately. The market was always busy, and it would be easy to spot anyone being overly attentive to their conversation.

With corned beef on rye, chips, and a root beer, they chose the farthest table and attacked their sandwiches. David began the conversation as he washed down his sandwich with a last swig of root beer. "Things are in place and I need to bring you in. Rayyan has signaled that everything is going as planned. The terrorists, along with Rayyan, are leaving the farmhouse this Thursday. One meth tech and two field hands will be left to guard the house. The field hands are our men and will take out the meth tech with a controlled, small explosion. You will then go in and get as much information as you can without leaving any evidence that you were there. Are you still sure you want to be a part of this sting?"

"I am. I've talked with Pete, and he awaits my instructions. I'll call him today and get him on the road. With two of us, we'll be able to do a thorough job in a smaller amount of time."

"That's fine with me. He's as thorough and efficient as you are. We feel lucky to have you both. I'll pick you and Pete up Thursday morning at five. Bring anything you remotely think you'll need. As soon as you're finished, our agents will make the call to Shahin and inform him of the explosion."

"Sounds good. Can you come over for dinner Wednesday night? I'm sure Pete will have questions."

"I was hoping you would ask; I've been so busy, I'm afraid I've ignored Anne. I'll bring her favorite wine; then maybe she'll forgive me. As soon as this case is put to bed, I plan to take her to my favorite restaurant in Asheville."

"I don't think Anne feels you need forgiving; she just wants to make sure you're safe and haven't forgotten her."

"Mark, I think after this case is completed, I'm handing in my resignation. I'm sure when my Washington superior realizes what really went down here, and that he was deliberately left out of the loop, I will be fired. I have enough savings to get me by until I complete my Psychology of the Criminal Mind course at UNC-Asheville. Adam has offered me a job with the CIA and I can work from anywhere I want to live. I'll be doing a lot of traveling to crime scenes, but won't be in on the action. That will suit me just fine."

"I can't tell you how happy that will make Anne. I know she cares for you, David, and worries about the danger you face every day."

"I care for her too, Mark. I plan to tell her my plans tonight. I want to spend more time with her and get to know her better. We seem to have clicked from the first time I met her. I don't know where this is going, but I can tell you I've never felt as comfortable and close to any other woman in my life."

\*

ANNE WAS THRILLED to hear that David was coming to dinner. She rushed around getting a special dessert prepared. Mark and Pete teased Anne about the pie. Pete had arrived the day before and was excited about being included in the case. He had many questions and looked forward to talking to David.

Vanished Sisters

When the doorbell rang, Anne rushed to open the door and welcome David. He gave her a sheepish grin and handed her two bottles of wine. "Sorry I haven't been very good at keeping in touch; please forgive me."

Anne took the wine, looked at the label, cocked her head to one side, and smiled. "Well, with this wine, I'll have to forgive you. Come on in, David; I know you've been busy. I'm just glad you had time to have dinner with us tonight."

David greeted and shook hands with Pete and Mark. Carrie, still on crutches, came forward and gave him a hug. "We haven't seen enough of you around here, David. I was thinking of asking you to be the twin's godfather, but you need to show up more often to qualify."

"I would be honored, and I promise to do better in the future. How are you feeling and when do you get those casts off?"

"Couple more weeks and I'll be free again. At least the casts have forced me to rest and allowed the babies to recover from the tumble they took with me down the mountain."

"Everything has a silver lining. Can you have a glass of wine?"

"No, but I'm sure going to enjoy that apple pie Anne made for you."

David laughed and everyone gathered in the kitchen as always to be together with the cooks. As Mark handed David a glass of wine, he suggested they go to the deck and put the steaks on the grill. Pete followed and the three gathered around the grill to admire the steaks. It also gave them a chance to talk while the girls fussed with the rest of the meal.

David said, "Pete, are you good with helping us out again?"

"David, I'm always happy to get my teeth into a real case. If you don't mind an old geezer tagging along, I'm happy to help in any way I can. Mark has filled me in on the situation. Can I ask you a couple questions?"

"Sure; that's why I'm here."

"First, are fingerprints our first priority when we go in there?"

"Yes, we need to put fingerprints with faces and names.

I realize dusting for prints leaves residue and takes time; if you can't clean a surface thoroughly, go for fingerprints on glasses that can be lifted easier. Take lots of photos of anything you think may be important. Look for hidden closets where weapons can be stashed. Check barns for weapons. The two most important pieces of evidence we need are the identities of these men and any information that will lead us to other cells. This house will most likely be destroyed, so this is our only chance to obtain as much information as possible."

"I understand," Pete said. "My second question is: Will we be able to communicate with you while we're in there? Do we take evidence if we find it?"

"Take nothing...just photos...you were never there. And yes, we will be in constant communication while you're in there. I would be in there with you, but I know I'd be in the way, and you need to be in and out as soon as possible."

"You're right; we need to operate alone without any distractions. We'll work as quickly as possible, but it will be helpful to ask questions if we have them."

"One more thing: We don't anticipate problems, but as you know, things can change or go wrong. As you move through the house, keep in mind that you may need to get out of there at a moment's notice. Keep all of your equipment close at hand in case this scenario becomes a reality. I don't want anything left behind that could jeopardize this project or possibly put Rayyan and Saheb's life in danger. Are we ready?"

Mark and Pete locked eyes and both gave a thumbs-up.

# CHAPTER 18

AFTER DINNER, DAVID asked Anne to go for a walk. "Let me get this kitchen cleaned up and—"

"No you don't," Mark and Pete chimed in together. "We'll clean the kitchen; you two go...go for a walk or something." Mark grinned and shooed them out the door.

"Well," Anne said, "I guess we had better go for a walk... or something."

David grinned. "When Mark asked me to dinner, I mentioned I needed to talk to you. Guess he thought I wanted to propose or something."

Anne looked panicked. "You aren't...are you?"

"No, relax; it's a bit early for that." He paused and then added, "Don't you think?"

"I sure do," Anne replied a little too firmly, and then she realized how it sounded. "I mean...I agree. It's a bit early for that."

They both laughed and David draped his arm around Anne's shoulder as they slowly walked down the lane.

"What I did want to say is that I'm sorry I've not called you lately just to talk and see how you are. I have you on my mind all the time, thinking I will have time later to call but later never comes. I find myself finally home, after another dinner meeting, asleep in my chair. I wake up and stumble to bed. This has been my routine for the past few weeks. I promise as soon as this case is over, things are going to change."

"What kind of change are you talking about?"

"After this project is finished, I'm going to resign my job with the FBI. As I think I mentioned before, I'm working on a degree in the Psychology of the Criminal Mind." He explained a bit more about the course and his job offer with the CIA.

"That sounds exciting." Anne reached up and held the hand that was draped across her shoulder. "You're getting to the burnout stage in your present job, aren't you?"

"You definitely could say that. My job no longer satisfies my heart's longings. I want to see more of you, Anne. I want us to have time to get to know each other. How do you feel about that?"

Anne didn't answer immediately; she was trying to get her emotions under control. She finally said, "I think I would like that a lot, David."

"We'll just let things happen naturally and not rush into anything. But first, I need to finish this degree and put the FBI behind me. My time in the next couple months will be stretched, to say the least, but I don't want someone else stealing you away from me. Can you be patient for a while longer?"

Anne smiled up at him. "I'm not going anywhere, David; I'll be right here whenever your life settles down enough to see a future."

They both had become aware of a growing bond between them. It was undeclared but, nevertheless, a growing physical thing that increased in intensity every time they were together. The bond was of respect, admiration, desire, and love—a bond that would endure forever.

*

AS MARK AND Carrie prepared for bed, Carrie was curious. "What do you think David wanted to tell Anne tonight?"

"Now, Carrie, let's not get into their business. If Anne wants you to know what they talked about, she'll tell you. I, for sure, have no clue what they talked about."

"This thing...the thing you're going to be involved with, it's going down soon, isn't it?"

Mark looked frustrated, but he knew she was worried. "Carrie, we agreed we wouldn't talk about that. You agreed that I should do what my heart tells me to do, and I explained why you don't need to know facts. What has changed?"

"I'm scared; that's what has changed."

"I can't say I'm not scared, but David has promised me I will not be put in any danger. I trust David; don't you?"

"I guess I do; I'll just be happy when the whole thing is over. You will tell me when it's over, won't you?"

"Absolutely, we'll celebrate." He tried to change the subject. "How are the house plans coming?"

"The old switch-a-roo game, huh?" Carrie laughed and Mark couldn't stifle the grin on his face. "Things are moving along. I've been to the architect twice to look at the working plans. I've made a few changes, tweaked a few areas, but overall, I'm very pleased. We should have the plans in a couple weeks.

"Mr. Tate has finished his other projects and is taking no other clients until our house is finished. He accompanied me to see the plans and pointed out the changes we needed to make. He seems very anxious to get started. I've given permission to start dismantling the old house. He's moved a metal storage building onto the property to store the materials we want to save. After the house is completely demolished, the land will be sculpted in preparation for the new foundation."

"I hope they won't bulldoze over the sisters' root cellar. Let's drive over there tomorrow and see how things are going. Maybe take a picnic lunch. I want to show Pete the old place before it's completely dismantled. Do you feel up to riding out there?"

"Sounds lovely to me. Pete will love the old house the way it is and want us to remodel instead of building a new house. We must reassure him that we need a bigger house so he'll have his own room when he visits."

"Good night, love."

\*

# Rachel Poe

CARRIE SMELLED COFFEE and eased out of bed. She found Anne on the back porch, having a brew. "Want some company, or are you enjoying quiet time?"

"I would love company. Have a seat—I'll get you a cup of coffee."

"Two more weeks and you won't have to wait on me anymore. Won't you be thrilled?"

"Carrie, you're no trouble. You've managed to master those crutches, but you can't use two crutches and carry a cup of coffee at the same time, no matter how adept you are."

Anne returned with a steaming cup for Carrie. "Any plans for today?"

"We're taking Pete out to see the old place before they begin dismantling the house. Why don't you take the day off and come with us? We're taking a picnic lunch."

"That's tempting; let me go by the office to see how things are going. I'll call and let you know if I'll be able to join you."

"I wish David could join us; I really like him." Carrie was trying to maneuver the conversation around to last night's conversation.

"That would be wonderful, but he's extremely busy right now. I suspect something is going on with the terrorists, but he can't talk about it. He's leaving the FBI after this thing...whatever it is...is over. I'm so relieved. He wanted to let me know he hadn't forgotten me, and we won't be seeing much of each other for a while. He asked, in a roundabout way, if I would be patient and not date anyone else. Isn't that sweet?"

"David is a thoughtful person. What did you tell him?"

Anne gave Carrie a look. "What do you think? Carrie, I think I may be falling in love with David. I can't imagine going out with anyone else. Blake was such a disappointment. I was ready to give up on men. And then along came David. It's as if the Lord were trying to tell me, 'Not that one...this one,' when He made me see Blake for who he really is."

"I'm so happy for you, Anne. I think David's leaving the FBI because of you. I think he's falling in love with you, too.

Vanished Sisters

You make a handsome couple. If you want my opinion, he's worth the wait."

"I always want your opinion, Carrie. I just don't want to get my hopes up, only to be disappointed again. I've decided if this is meant to be, it will be. I'm just going to wait and see what happens."

Mark stumbled out onto the porch. "What are you two talking about?" He gave Carrie a warning look. "I feel like an omelet; can I fix anyone an omelet?"

Anne said she had already eaten and had to get to the office. "If I can get things going and join you for a picnic, I will. If I can't, I'll call you within the hour. Have a good morning and enjoy your omelets." She dropped her cup in the sink as she headed out the back door.

Mark looked at Carrie. "You didn't, did you?"

"No, darling, we did not, but she thinks something is happening soon. David wouldn't talk about it, but her instincts tell her plenty. I didn't say a word; I promised you I wouldn't, and I won't."

"Thanks, love; how about an omelet?"

"I could eat two; remember, I'm eating for three." Mark laughed, shook his head, and said, "Right you are, my love, and we need those little tikes to be healthy."

Pete soon joined them and the whole omelet discussion was repeated again.

\*

ANNE GOT TO the office before the rush of the day began. She turned on her computer and checked on several orders to see whether they had shipped. She noticed she had an email. *Probably a supplier telling me my shipment is back ordered,* she thought. She clicked on "mail" and waited. To her surprise, it was from David.

>   Good Morning, Anne,
>   
>   Hope you had a good night. Just wanted to say hello and give you my email address. Even though I

will be super-busy for the next month or so, we can at least say good morning and goodnight every day. I couldn't get you off my mind last night, even though you assured me you would wait for me to get my stuff together. I promise I will make this up to you in the coming months. Our first date should be special. Think of the best restaurant you have ever been to and that will be our destination.

Have a great day, Anne, and know this: I think I love you.

Love, David

Anne reread the note several times and tried to control the tears that were gathering. *Carrie was right; David is worth waiting for,* she thought as she quickly answered his email.

Good Morning, David,

I've got mail! What a special thing to do. I too had a difficult time getting to sleep last night. I think I love you too. Time will tell. I've decided if we are meant to be, well then, we will be. I said a special prayer for you and went to sleep.

Be safe today and know that someone special is watching over you.

Love, Anne

Anne called home and said she was on the way. She was taking the day off.

*

THE DAY WAS perfect, and Anne's feet barely touched the ground as she walked with Pete. She was investigating the old farm with Pete, while Carrie and Mark talked with Mr. Tate. Mark wanted to be sure he remembered the old root cellar was to be saved.

"What do you think, Pete; isn't that a great view? See the little knoll over there? Our granny and papa's house once stood there. Mark and I have wonderful memories of that valley. I knew when it came on the market he would be interested. It's as close to going home as you can get. The kids will love being here in the summer."

"It's beautiful, and I'm looking forward to visiting in the summer. Wonder if they would let me live here and take care of the place in the winter? It doesn't get too cold here, does it?"

"No, not too bad. We do get snow, but if you're prepared, you just hunker down and wait it out. If you have plenty of wood close at hand and lots of food, you're in high cotton. I love to be snowed in; gives a body time to reflect on life, read a good book, and bake a cake."

Pete laughed. "I'm not too good at baking, but I promise I'll keep Twinkies in the freezer at all times."

When Carrie and Mark caught up with them, they were in the old barn. Pete was checking out the timbers. "Mark, this barn is about to fall down on its own. Not much to save here."

"You're right, Pete; this is where the garage will be, with a breezeway porch connecting it to the house. There will be guest quarters above the garage and a tool shed attached to the back."

"Anne and I have decided I need to live here in the winter and be the caretaker," said Pete. "A garage apartment will suit me just fine."

Anne and Pete watched Mark to see his reaction. "Darn good idea," Mark agreed. "I was wondering what to do with you when you retire. I'll just ship you up here."

"Suits me," said Pete. "In my spare time, I'll build my granddaughter a dollhouse and a treehouse for my grandsons."

Carrie laughed. "What if you have two granddaughters?"

"I'll build the treehouse anyway; Tucker will love it, and I suspect the girls will be tomboys anyway."

"Well," said Carrie, "now that we have Pete's retirement decided, let's go have a picnic."

\*

DAVID WAS GOING over the plans yet again; there could be no mistakes. This was his last case with the FBI and he wanted every *i* dotted. He knew his director in Washington would find every excuse to criticize this operation. David wanted to be sure his resignation was handed over before the director could fire him.

Rayyan had touched base several times. He had been imbedded with the terrorists for seven days. They were on schedule. The plan was to leave on Thursday morning. Rayyan had managed to get them to accept his suggestions. The meth man to be left behind was not the brightest of stars. It would be easy to convince Shahin he had blown himself to pieces.

Both Rayyan and Saheb were going with Shahin to visit the Charlotte and Raleigh airports. They would spend one whole day at each airport. Dressed as casual travelers, they entered the airport two at a time to scope out the surroundings, noting the busiest times of day, as well as the most populated areas. Rayyan had easily convinced the cell he was the one they had been waiting for, the one with the targets. The two undercover agents working in the marijuana fields were to make sure the meth worker was eliminated and signal for Mark and Pete to enter.

David called Mark to confirm he would pick them up on Thursday morning. "Everything looks like a go, Mark; do you and Pete have everything you'll need to process the house?"

"I feel sure we can handle it. Pete brought the new MG-P4 digital still camera from the school lab, which will allow us to obtain fingerprints easily and quickly. We also have a couple of other ways to obtain prints without using powder. We lift some with fingerprint-lifting tape and another method called fuming for prints. The location of the prints will determine which method we use. We will also take fingerprints and DNA from the dead meth tech."

"Sounds like you two know what you're doing. I'll pick you up around 5 a.m. The terrorists will leave the farm around that time. They may be ready for us when we arrive."

\*

MARK WAS AWAKE at 4 a.m. He had successfully slipped out of bed without waking Carrie. Pete was up and had coffee ready. They had quietly moved all their equipment into the trunk of Pete's SUV the night before. As they finished cereal and coffee, Anne joined them. "What are you guys doing up so early? Going fishing?"

Mark looked at Pete as if a lightbulb had gone on. "Yeah," he said. "Got to get out early if you want to catch the big ones."

"Where you going?"

"Don't know," Pete jumped in. "David is picking us up at five; he's found a good spot he wants to show us."

Anne knew David had no time for fishing right now. "Okay, guys; David said nothing to me about you all going fishing. Something has happened, hasn't it?"

Pete and Mark locked eyes; neither was sure what to say. Pete shrugged his shoulders as if to say, "We're busted." Mark looked up at Anne, who was staring at him, impatiently waiting for an answer. "Well...we decided pretty late last night. David texted me and said if we wanted to go fishing to be ready at 5 a.m. So...here we are. That's all we know."

There was a small knock on the back door. Anne rushed to open it with Mark close behind. David saw Anne and froze, as Mark said, "We're ready to catch some fish, David. Hope they're biting this morning."

David recovered, gave Anne a peck on the cheek, and said, "They're always biting at Lake James. I've found a great cove that has never failed me. Are we ready to go? I've got enough equipment for all three of us. Let's move out."

Mark and Pete were out the door before Anne could ask any more questions. David gave Anne a hug, told her to have a great day, and was gone. They reminded Anne of little boys making a quick exit before their parents could stop them.

Anne was not buying it. She rushed to a front window and watched them transfer Mark and Pete's equipment to David's car. Fear gripped her heart. Something was going down today. She was watching them pull away and saying a prayer as Carrie came up behind her. "What's going on? Where's Mark? I can't find him." She automatically peeked out the window to see what Anne was watching. "Was that David's car that just pulled away?"

"Yes. He picked Mark and Pete up early to go fishing, *they said,* but I just watched them transfer Mark's forensic equipment into David's car. Do you know what's going on? They obviously aren't going fishing."

Carrie instinctively knew and felt sick. Anne was right—something was going down today and Mark would be in grave danger. She felt a little better knowing Pete was with him. Maybe together, they could get the job done faster and get home safely. Carrie was staring into space, saying a silent prayer, when Anne invaded her private thoughts.

"Carrie, do you know anything about this?" Anne suspected that by the way Carrie reacted, she knew where they were going.

Carrie could hear Mark's voice saying: *Don't share this with anyone, not even Anne.*

"Carrie, I can keep a secret, especially if someone I love is in danger. Tell me where they're going. I love Mark and Pete and David; I have a right to know."

Carrie stared into Anne's eyes for several seconds as her mind tried to decide what she could tell her. She didn't want to betray her promise to Mark, but she had to tell her something. "Let's sit down; my knees are weak. Let's get a cup of coffee and try to figure out what's going on."

As they settled at the kitchen table, cup of coffee in hand, Carrie began. "I honestly don't know where they're going. Mark would give me no specifics. Mark and Pete are helping David with a case; that's all I know. It's why we've stayed here so long. David needed Mark's help. I, too, suspect something is going down today, but I honestly don't know what."

"David alluded to me that he was still working on the terrorist case, but he wouldn't elaborate. I suspect whatever is happening today will end his career with the FBI. I'm going to work, and I want you to come with me. I need to be busy, and I don't want you here worrying by yourself. I have plenty that you could do on the computer, placing and tracing orders, while I work the counter. It will be better for us to stay busy."

Carrie agreed and reached for the box of cereal Mark and Pete had left open on the kitchen table. She felt like a robot, going through the motions, as her mind raced, trying to convince herself that Mark would be fine. She wanted to send him a text saying, *Be safe.... I love you*, but she knew his phone would be turned off. *Pray,* she thought. *Just keep praying all day.*

## CHAPTER 19

DAVID DROVE TO his temporary office in Marion. He fitted Mark and Pete with hands-free radiophones attached to their shoulders. He instructed them on how to use the phones and again went over the plan and their objectives. As they prepared to leave for Poplar Creek, David received a call saying the terrorists had left. The second phase of the plan was beginning.

\*

THE METH TECH who was left to run the lab was a homegrown convert, looking for his fifteen minutes of martyrdom and all those virgins. He left the lab as soon as the SUVs pulled out of the drive. He entered the house and proceeded to fix himself another cup of coffee. He then went into the bathroom and stayed for forty minutes. After coming out of the bathroom, the small, ferret-faced man went upstairs and started going through his fellow Muslim's personal things. He pocketed cigarettes, money, and other small personal items that wouldn't be missed right away. He found a porn magazine, sat down on a bed, and began to look at the pictures, smiling as he thumbed through the pages.

He had generously offered to stay behind and keep the meth lab operating, but his real reason was a chance to run. He was having second thoughts and knew they would never let him go. He knew too much. He needed money and knew there was cash stashed in that house somewhere. He checked his watch. It was almost nine; he needed to hurry. The marijuana workers would be back to the house around lunchtime. He needed to be packed up and away from there before they came in at eleven. He finished his magazine and started looking for the big money. He searched for another thirty minutes and decided to take what cash he had found and get out of there.

The marijuana field agents were livid. They needed for him to get back to the lab so they could activate the small explosion. They wanted to get Mark and Pete in and out of the house as soon as possible. The agents continued to wait. If he didn't get off his duff soon, they would have to switch to Plan B.

David was on his way to Poplar Creek when he received another call. The agent explained the situation. David was frustrated, but he told them to give the tech another thirty minutes before going with Plan B.

From a porch window, they watched the ferret as he searched the downstairs. What was he doing? He headed upstairs again and came back down with a sack full of something. They decided it was time to make a move. As they entered the house, the ferret froze, obviously scared out of his wits.

"Where you going?" asked one of the agents.

The ferret pulled a knife and rushed them. "I'm getting out of here and you better not get in my way. Move aside; I've had all the Muslim bull I want to hear. They can blow themselves up if they want to, but I have other plans. I was stupid to get involved with you nuts in the first place."

The agents knew they couldn't let him go; he knew information that could be valuable to the FBI. This changed their whole plan. One of the agents pulled a gun from his ankle holster. "Put down the knife and lie down on the floor."

The ferret-faced little man was so scared he began to cry. "Let me go. Please.... They'll kill me. I don't want to die."

One agent took the knife and watched the ferret as the other agent called David and reported the new turn of events. "I'm pulling in the drive now," David informed the agent. "We'll take him into protective custody and see what he knows. Bring out everything he's stolen. You can honestly report you saw him leaving the house with a sack over his back. You were coming in from the fields; he was too far ahead of you to catch him.

"Disarm the explosives in the lab and leave no evidence that you were ever there. I'm sending Mark and Pete in now. I want no one in there while they're processing the house. As soon as they head to the barns, move in and bug the entire house and lab. Mount cameras only where they positively cannot be detected."

\*

MARK AND PETE carried everything into the house and set it down on a rug in the front room. There was no furniture in this room. It was used for prayer. They pulled on rubber gloves and together did a walk-through. Evidence of the ferret's rummaging through drawers and closets was evident. They decided to leave everything as they had found it to confirm the agent's story. They opted to begin in the kitchen where dirty dishes were left on the table—a wealth of fingerprints. They moved methodically through the house, working together to save time and keep from missing anything.

They finished downstairs and moved up the staircase. The handrail was photographed extensively and fingerprint tape used in many places. There were five bedrooms upstairs. They made their way into each, missing nothing. They worked around the messes the ferret had made. Mark found a stash of cash stuffed into the box springs of a bed. The ferret had missed his pot of gold. They left it as they found it after photographing the money. They found Rayyan's fake papers from Hamas along with other papers, which they also photographed and returned to their original positions.

"This room must be the leader's bedroom," Pete remarked. "Let's check the closet closely; this one's a master carpenter and expert on creating hidden spaces."

"You're right; if there's a secret space, it will probably be in this room where Shahin can keep an eye on it." They moved

## Vanished Sisters

around the closet, slowly feeling the walls. "Stop!" Mark shouted. "I've found something and I think it's booby-trapped."

Pete used his penlight where Mark pointed. He could see a catch with an attached wire emanating from the back of the catch and disappearing into the dark. It was cleverly placed and would not have been noticed by the novice eye. "I've seen this device before, and I'm sure I can disarm and rearm it again. Please step out of the closet just in case I screw up."

"I've disarmed this same device before. It's pretty basic; want me to do it?"

"No, I want you to step out of the closet and protect yourself. I'm not getting ready to be a father; you are. And besides, Carrie would never forgive me. I'll give you an all clear."

Mark didn't argue; Pete was right—no need to take unnecessary risks. He stepped into the hallway and waited. It only took a few seconds before he heard Pete shout, "All clear!" The fake closet wall hid the stairs to the attic, just like the Hawkins' house. They carefully made their way up the narrow stairs. The attic was large, tall enough to stand in, and filled with explosives. Shahin had been busy constructing vests for the suicide bombers. Several other backpack and small luggage bombs had been assembled and were ready to kill Americans in the Charlotte and Raleigh airports. Pete was holding the objects open for Mark to photograph the inner components. The luggage and backpacks had been wired to be detonated from a distance, using a cell phone.

Mark spoke into his phone, describing to David what they had uncovered. He explained how they had found the attic and the magnitude of explosives hidden there. David was not surprised and asked them to take as many pictures as possible. "How close are you to moving to the lab and barn?"

"We're ready to move out now, as soon as we replace the booby-trap device."

The meth lab was a dirty, disgusting mess. Mark and Pete wanted out of there as soon as possible. As they lifted prints from several items, a rat ran over Pete's foot. They took many photographs in case they were needed in court. The terrorists could be put away for many years on meth and marijuana charges alone. Mark had processed meth labs before, but this had to be the worst. They finished up and moved on to the barn.

The barn looked dilapidated on the outside, but once inside, they found evidence of Shahin's carpentry talents there as well. The old loft had been shored-up and a new ladder propped against the edge of the loft. Mark ventured up and took a look. Under the hay were multiple cases of rapid-fire weapons, missile launchers, rifles, pistols, and tons of ammo. Some were American-made and some Russian-made.

They found a pitchfork, moved the hay back, and photographed the entire arsenal. Some of these, Mark was sure, had been in the Hawkins' attic. They were proceeding to inspect the rest of the barn when Mark heard David's voice in his earpiece. "I need you out of there! Just got a signal that some or all of the terrorists are coming back here for the night. We knew Shahin had expressed that preference, but Rayyan objected. I suspect, at the last minute, Shahin pulled a control maneuver on Rayyan. Pack up and get out of there."

The two agents appeared to help carry equipment. It was obvious they didn't have much time. David also entered the barn to rush them as much as possible. They threw equipment in the back of David's SUV and jumped in as wheels were rolling. Mark looked back to see the two agents dragging branches over the drive to cover their tracks.

\*

DAVID PULLED INTO a nearby field and turned toward the woods. They sat hidden by shrubs and trees as they watched three black trucks pass and turn into the farmhouse drive. "We can watch from the top of that ridge," said David, pointing the way. They quickly climbed the ridge and lay flat on their stomachs.

They watched as the two agents came from the house to inform them their suicide bomber had flown the coop. Shahin was visibly angry and kicked the tire of his truck. The agent continued to talk, probably telling them that the escapee had stolen a sack of things from the house. Shahin rushed into the house as

David turned on his iPad. The house's interior was there on the screen, and they could hear every word that was spoken. Mark couldn't understand what they were saying, but the reactions and facial expressions were a close-enough narrative.

Mark turned to David. "You understand what they're saying?"

"Some, yes; I've studied the language, but they have as many dialects as the mountain people of North Carolina." Mark and Pete watched as David switched from camera to camera. Shahin was headed to his room. He first checked the mattress and box springs to be sure the money was there, and then he moved to the closet. Once assured the closet device was still activated, he returned downstairs as several men came in, shouting angrily. They had obviously found their possessions missing. Shahin seemed to calm down, assured that the ferret had only taken incidentals from the house. Shahin must have signaled for everyone to meet downstairs. David switched cameras as all the terrorists appeared in the living room. They could see Rayyan and Saheb looking as angry as the real terrorists. Shahin called for quiet. He began to talk rapidly, and no one moved a muscle, including Mark and Pete.

David pulled out his phone and dialed Adam. "The house has been bugged; turn on your iPad. Something is going down. I can't understand all Shahin is saying, but I think the bombings have just been moved up." David had kept Adam informed all day as things progressed and events changed. Adam was watching now and translating as Shahin spoke.

Shahin feared the deserter would go to the local authorities, so he wanted to bomb the Charlotte airport tomorrow, move to another safe house near Raleigh, and wait for things to settle down. This meant they would be pulling out for Charlotte as soon as they could load up the weapons. One detail would go to Charlotte while the other moved the remaining weapons to Raleigh.

Adam barked orders to David. "Have the place surrounded; we'll go in as soon as possible and take this cell out. Bring in the local police to place roadblocks as far from the entrance as possible."

David made the call for immediate reinforcements from the FBI, as well as the SBI and local authorities who were on standby. "How long will it take your men to get here?" asked Mark.

"Some are already here. He looked around and said, "Jake, where are you?" To Mark and Pete's amazement, a bush to the right of them appeared to levitate as legs grew from underneath the bush. They looked closer to see a man actually wearing a bush. When sitting or squatting, he was totally camouflaged.

"How many men are here right now?" David asked the bush.

"Twenty FBI and at least twenty SBI and CIA," answered Jake-the-bush. "We've been following your radio feeds all day. I felt things might be going bad, so I called in more men. If we need to, we can take them out right now."

"Good call, but let's wait for Adam to give the order. We need men in place along with vehicles, helicopters, and roadblocks, in case any slip through our net."

While David and Jake were talking, Pete elbowed Mark. "Guess we're here for the duration. Let's keep our heads down and let the big boys handle this."

Mark, not happy about the situation, agreed. "That's what I was thinking."

*

ANNE AND CARRIE were on their way home. They had tried to stay busy and not think about what Mark and Pete were doing, but they could stand it no longer. Carrie finally said, "Let's go home; maybe they're there waiting for us."

"I'm with you, but I don't think there's a chance that has happened."

When they reached the house, Anne hurried inside as Carrie followed slowly with her crutches. The house was empty. Anne returned to help Carrie. "No one here; let's turn on the TV and see if anything has happened today. I'll fix us an iced tea." As they settled in front of the TV, Carrie's phone beeped, alerting her to an incoming text. With shaking hands, she pushed the necessary button to receive the text. The message appeared: *Can't leave yet; fish still biting. Don't wait up for us and don't answer this message; you'll scare the fish. Understand? We're fine.*

"What did he say?" Anne was close to hysteria, her voice rising several octaves.

Carrie was trying to think as Anne grabbed the phone and read the text. "Anne, I can't believe you did that." She reached for her phone.

"Sorry; I'm totally out of control; I need to calm down. That message is total bull. They aren't fishing."

"Yes, Anne, you do need to calm down. He's telling us not to worry; they're fine.... They just won't be home any time soon, maybe not tonight. Here; calm down and read it again."

"Forgive me, Carrie." She began to cry. "I'm so afraid something will happen to take David or Mark from me. I never expected to feel this way ever again. I don't want to lose either of them."

Carrie swung her good arm around Anne and held her close. She knew exactly how Anne felt, but the text had put her mind, at least, at ease. "I know, Anne, but I feel sure they're going to be fine. Let's fix dinner together and go ahead and eat. There's no way of knowing when they'll be home."

*

MARK AND PETE watched as the field behind them came alive with agents. They appeared to be preparing for battle. Adam and Ben arrived and, along with David, discussed their next move. It was almost dark. "We've got four men in there; it's time to signal them to get out," David suggested.

The agents were wearing chips under the skin of their shoulders. Adam agreed and David activated the chips, which vibrated just enough to feel like a muscle spasm, virtually undetectable by anyone except the chip's owner. The vibration meant to get out as fast as you could.

Rayyan and Saheb were purposefully sitting on the floor at the back of the room. Shahin was going over the plans for tomorrow. He had his two remaining suicide bombers in front of everyone, praising them and assuring them that by this time tomorrow, they would be in paradise and the whole world would hear of their heroic deed. They would be revered martyrs and never forgotten.

Rayyan and Saheb looked at each other. Rayyan cut his eyes toward the kitchen. They began to back out of the room. When they reached the kitchen, they stood and eased out the back door. They held their hands in the air as they ran toward the woods, signaling, "Don't shoot."

The two agents who worked in the marijuana fields had been sent back out to work after reporting to Shahin; they were now safely back among their fellow agents.

As soon as the agents reached safety, Adam spoke into a loud speaker, "You are surrounded; come out with your hands up." They watched David's iPad as the terrorists went into action. They each knew what to do. Weapons appeared from nowhere. The living room rug was removed to reveal a trap door. One by one, the terrorists disappeared into a black hole. David warned his men that the terrorists were escaping under the house, but no one appeared and no weapons were fired.

"We missed that one, didn't we?" Pete admitted. "I pulled the rug up, but not all the way back. I was looking for hidden papers."

Mark shouted to David. "A tunnel...they have an escape tunnel just like at the ranch!"

David immediately ordered helicopters with searchlights in the air. They came from nowhere and circled just above the treetops. It reminded Mark and Pete of another time in Kansas when the FBI were in hot pursuit of Masters, who had entered Mattie's house right under the police guards' noses. Again, they sat helpless in the middle of what seemed like a war zone. Pete leaned over to Mark and said, "I wonder how many autopsies we'll be facing tomorrow?"

Mark was having the same thoughts and knew they would be busy.

One helicopter opened fire and reported the terrorists escaping from what looked like an underground tunnel about one hundred yards behind the barn. Fire was being returned as a grenade missile launcher was fired toward the helicopter. The near miss caused the chopper to swing around, reposition itself, and fire a return volley. The missile launcher was taken out. Ground agents moved in and surrounded the terrorists, who refused to give up. A heated battle ensued as the terrorists tried to return to the cave. Two agents followed the terrorists into the cave as an explosion erupted, sending them flying through the air. The entire house went up in a huge ball of fire, sending flames over a hundred feet into the air. Seconds after the house blew, the barn erupted into another fireball. Waiting fire trucks moved in to try to prevent the surrounding forest from exploding into flames.

Pete ran his fingers through his unruly crop of white hair as he and Mark watched the battle. This was mind-boggling. He lay on his stomach, propped up on his elbows as he watched a missile barely miss one of the helicopters. He was amazed as the helicopter swirled around, fired back, and hit its target. These terrorists were not giving up. They were firing senselessly at anything and everything. The agents were trying to stay down, yet return fire, and take these guys out. Pete was thinking this was more excitement than an old man needed. He wanted to be home, safe in bed, and pretend this was a bad dream.

It felt like they were watching a television show or a movie. They couldn't comprehend the magnitude of what was happening right before their eyes. When the house exploded, they were sprayed with burning cinders. They scrambled to back away from the intense heat.

When the fires were calmed down and the agents able to assess the damage, all terrorists and two agents were dead, plus five agents wounded.

*This is America*, Pete thought. *Things like this don't happen here...not in America.* But the sad truth was, they were happening. What happened on 9/11 was out there for everyone to see, but how many more would-be 9/11s had been stopped quietly in the nick of time...like today?

Small battles were being fought right here on American soil while the public was told lies. Lies to keep the general population from panicking. Mark wondered whether it was good or bad to keep the public in the dark. Maybe if they knew, they would be more interested in demanding that the President get tougher on Islamic extremists.

It was almost morning before David gave Mark and Pete a ride home. After the hostility ended, Mark and Pete were busy again. What bodies could be found were lined up for them to fingerprint, collect DNA from, and photograph. Tomorrow, they would perform autopsies on the bodies they could find. They had no idea how many were caught in the tunnel. Rayyan would be able to help with the total number of terrorists who lived there. Before they could leave, all photographs, fingerprints, and DNA samples were turned over to Adam to be sent to the lab for analysis. They would know exactly who these men were and check them off the list of wanted terrorists. David would not go to bed this night. A full report would accompany his resignation. He wanted his resignation on Greenstreet's desk when he came to work only hours from now.

Agents were left to guard the crime scene, and barricades prevented anyone from entering the property. Local news agencies would appear bright and early as rumors leaked out. The word "terrorist" would not be used. As far as the public would know, this was a drug bust, a meth lab that had blown up. The farm would be off limits until the marijuana fields were cleared and the ashes sifted through for pieces of bodies or weapons.

Fake names would eventually be released to the press. None of the names would sound the least bit foreign. And in a couple of weeks, no one would even remember the war that had raged in the sleepy little village of Poplar Creek.

## CHAPTER 20

AS DAVID GAVE Mark and Pete a ride home, he explained that Carrie and Anne must never know that terrorists had been killed and a plot to destroy the Charlotte airport averted. It was just another drug bust and one more day in the life of an FBI agent. David had a room at the local hotel, which doubled as his temporary office in Marion. He longed to be there, get a shower, a cup of coffee, and begin his report to his superior.

He pulled up in front of Anne's house. The porch light was on, but the house was dark. David gave Mark and Pete his final request. "Get four hours sleep and report to the Marion morgue. You have a grueling day ahead of you. Adam is flying in help from his team of CIA medical examiners. The bodies are under guard at the Marion morgue. Adam and I will meet you there. Adam will take over as your director. As of eight o'clock this morning, I will have officially resigned. Pray there is no fallout from tonight. I have a strange feeling—can't really explain it—maybe I just need a couple hours sleep. Thanks for your help."

As David helped get their equipment to the front porch, the lights came on inside the house. Carrie and Anne opened the front door. Before either had a chance to say a word, David took charge. "Don't say a word; don't ask any questions. Let Mark and Pete get a shower and four hours sleep. They have a rough day ahead of them tomorrow. We will talk tomorrow night."

Carrie and Anne shook their heads in unison as Mark and Pete passed by them with their equipment and headed for the showers. Anne remained at the door. Her eyes locked with David's. "I'll see you tomorrow, Anne," he said, but he wanted so desperately to take her in his arms. Instead, he whispered, "I love you." He was so exhausted that Anne could barely hear him.

She nodded her head yes and said, "I love you too; get some rest, my darling. Goodnight."

\*

DAVID THOUGHT BACK over the decisions he had made. He had lost two men, two were in the Asheville hospital, and three had been released after being treated for minor injuries. He knew he would be on the receiving end of a stiff lecture from the Director of the FBI, even though he was acting under CIA orders in a top secret, joint agency sting. He couldn't think of anything he would have done differently. He finished his report and letter of resignation, held his finger in mid air for several seconds, and then clicked SEND. As the sun chased darkness from the sky in the east, he laid his head down and was asleep before the sun actually peaked over the horizon. He had trained himself to wake automatically in two hours. With tomorrow behind him, he could look to the future and plan a life with Anne.

\*

ANNE AND CARRIE quietly had their breakfast on the porch. They didn't want to wake Mark and Pete until eight o'clock. Carrie stirred her coffee, deep in thought. She was thankful to have Mark safely home, but worried about where he was going today. She had made up her mind she would ask no questions, just be thankful for the few hours she'd had him beside her last night. He was so exhausted and emotionally drained. He had dropped into bed, hair still wet, reached for her, held her close, and gone immediately to sleep. Pete had looked the same and gone straight to his room. She wanted to be reassured that the terrorists were dead, but she would wait until Mark was ready to talk.

Anne finished her last drop of coffee. "I'm going to work; call me when they've left. If you want to come to the office and keep busy, I'll come back for you. I wish I had asked David to stay here last night. He looked so tired and defeated, but I'm sure his work was not finished. I think he's handing in his resignation today. He wants a complete report of what happened yesterday to accompany the resignation. That probably took him most of what was left of last night. I pray this is the end of his career with the FBI. Maybe we can finally have a normal friendship and begin to get to know each other." She kissed Carrie on the top of her head. "Are you okay, honey? You're awfully quiet."

"I'm fine, just deep in thought. I'll call you when they've gone. Keeping busy would be the best thing to do."

When Anne had gone, Carrie hobbled inside and fixed another cup of coffee. She hadn't slept very much last night, not until Mark was there beside her.

\*

CARRIE WAS GOING to wake Mark when Pete came downstairs. "I was just going to wake Mark. There's coffee in the pot; help yourself."

"Thanks, Carrie; this old man is going to need a lot of coffee today."

"Guess you can't talk about it?"

"No. But I can put your mind at ease by saying we will be at the Marion morgue all day; that's all I can say."

"Thanks, Pete; that does put my mind at ease. I'll wake Mark."

Mark was dressing when Carrie entered their bedroom. Their eyes locked. Mark could see the questions in hers, and Carrie could see the warning in his. "Pete's up; he let me know where you would be today, and that's all he said. I'm relieved to know you won't be in any danger. I'm not going to ask any questions. I know someday you will tell me what happened yesterday. Until then, we will just pretend you went fishing."

Mark looked relieved, closed the space between them, and held her close. "I love you so much, Carrie. What are you going to do today?"

"Anne is coming back for me; she has computer work for me to do. It will keep me busy. Can we expect David for dinner?"

"From the remark he made to Anne last night, I would count on it. I'm sure he will at least come by. He's meeting us at the morgue; I'll be sure to invite him." He lifted Carrie's chin, kissed her on the nose, and headed for a cup of strong coffee.

\*

DAVID WAS WAITING when they arrived at the morgue. Mark told him he looked like hell, and David returned the compliment. "Get any sleep?" Mark asked.

"Two hours. I'll be able to sleep good tonight once this day is over."

"How about stopping by for dinner tonight?"

"That would be great. I want to tell Anne I've officially resigned from the FBI."

Pete had been very quiet. He was not as young as these two, and he was still reeling with the memory of what he had witnessed the day before. He wanted to get today behind him and get back to his safe little job on a peaceful college campus. In his heart, he knew this country was a little safer today than it was yesterday. However, it scared him to know what had happened here yesterday was happening all over the country. "Okay, let's get this show on the road," he said. "The sooner we finish, the sooner we can put this nightmare behind us."

Mark put his arm over Pete's shoulder. "You up for this, Pete?"

"If I weren't, I'd let you know. I'm glad Adam is bringing in a few relief pitchers. Let's see what we have and get a plan before my coffee wears off. Wouldn't want to doze off in the middle of an autopsy."

David slapped Pete on the back. "I'll make sure the coffee in the breakroom is strong and plentiful. That's the least I can do to help you guys out."

Adam arrived thirty minutes later with three medical examiners in tow. He showed no sign of having been up all night, but he went straight for the coffee. With six medical examiners, including Ted Morris, the Marion coroner, maybe they could finish this job in one day, but Mark wasn't betting on it. They paired up into three teams, thus allowing three cadavers to be autopsied at one time. At times, all six were working on one cadaver if there was a problem. Otherwise, the teams worked separately.

Around eleven o'clock, the doors to the morgue flew open and in marched the Director of the FBI, followed by an entourage of armed federal marshals. He walked over to where David and Adam were watching the autopsies and announced, "David Bryan Durham, Adam Taylor Bradford, you are under arrest for an unauthorized act of war on American soil. You have the right to remain silent and anything you say can and will be used against you in a court of law...." Both men were handcuffed by federal marshals and escorted out of the building. They were placed in a waiting government SUV, then taken to the Asheville airport, where they boarded a waiting government jet—destination: Washington, D.C.

Mark and Pete, as well as everyone else in the room, were in shock. How could the Director of the FBI arrest the North Carolina Director of the CIA? It wasn't possible. Immediately, one of the CIA medical examiners left the room to make a call. Within seconds, he was talking to the Washington bureau of the CIA, explaining the actions that had just taken place. Damon Wentworth, the Director of the CIA, along with a team of lawyers, would be waiting when the Director of the FBI arrived.

The arrests had placed a pall over the whole team at the morgue. Everyone liked and respected David and Adam. To see them treated this way, as common criminals, made everyone feel angry and helpless. Mark wondered what would happen next. Was David facing a long and drawn-out trial?

\*

DAMON WENTWORTH CALLED an immediate meeting of his legal advisers. His blood pressure was climbing by the minute. Jason Greenstreet had over-stepped his boundary this time. Damon knew Jason was following the President's orders. He was her yes-man and shared her soft views on terrorists. The President had been elected with campaign donations from Arab countries...they now owned her.

The CIA director was a thorn in the President's side. She wanted to get rid of Damon, but she knew he had an ace up his sleeve he could play at any time. He had copies of emails with impeachment written all over them. He watched his back and surrounded himself with people who were loyal to their country and him. If anything happened to him, she would be exposed and she knew it. She could have her little temper tantrums, throw things across the room at grown men to demoralize them, and get her way, but it wouldn't work on Damon Wentworth.

Damon's first order for his legal team was to make formal complaints to the Director of the FBI and the President. Second, he wanted both men released immediately. They would not spend one night behind bars. President Warren could bring all the charges she wanted against Adam and David; Damon and his team would see them in court.

If the truth were known, the American public would give David and Adam a parade, not send them to prison. Damon knew their accusations wouldn't stand up in court. His second ace was clear. If need be, he would tell the American public the truth or make sure the real story was leaked to the press. The President didn't want the American people to know terrorists were actively working in every state in the union. Damon had her just where he wanted her.

President Warren and Jason Greenstreet wanted to ruin David's reputation in law enforcement for ignoring their order to stand down. She knew the conclusion of this little scenario would never be printed, but the press would be all over the arrest of trigger-happy David Durham, ex-FBI. His reprimand would be headline news for weeks. Again, she was in the dark. She didn't know the CIA had already hired David.

## Vanished Sisters

MARK TOOK A break to have a coin machine pimento-cheese sandwich. The bread was stale and the pimento-cheese was one-day away from being moldy. However, it did stop his stomach from rumbling. He considered calling Carrie. He wanted Anne to hear about David from someone she trusted—not from the evening news. He didn't need to give her details, just let her know David would not be there for dinner and tell her the basics of what had happened. He knew how devastated he felt; he could only imagine how Anne would take the news.

Pete came into the breakroom and headed for the coffeepot. He looked at Mark and shook his head. "What is this crazy world coming to? David saved hundreds of lives and they arrest him? Anne is going to be heartbroken."

"I was just getting ready to call Carrie and let her tell Anne before she hears it on the news."

"Do it. Blake will hot-foot it over there to tell her as soon as he hears. He probably already knows. He would love to put David down by telling Anne her new boyfriend is in jail."

"You're right; I didn't think of that." Mark grabbed his cell phone and called Carrie.

Carrie was entering orders when her cell phone rang. She saw it was Mark and answered.

"Carrie, I've got some bad news for Anne, and I want you to tell her. I don't want her to hear it over the phone or on the evening news. David and Adam have been arrested by federal marshals and taken to Washington."

"Jesus, Joseph, and Mary! Why?"

"We don't know; we think there's a riff between the CIA and the FBI. David and Adam are caught in the middle. I'm afraid it will be all over the news tonight. The truth will never come to light, but David's reputation, as an FBI agent, will be ruined. Not that he will care at this point, but he does care what Anne thinks of him. Tell her he has done nothing wrong and we will all stand by him until he is exonerated of whatever charges they have trumped up against him. I don't know where they're taking him or if he will be able to call her anytime soon. Just tell her to have faith in David and hang in there. I will see you later, love."

Carrie sat for several minutes, trying to think of the best way to tell Anne. There was no good way; she might as well get it behind her. She clicked on the outside microphone and asked Anne to come to the office. As she waited, she asked the Lord to give her the right words. This just wasn't fair. Anne was in love with David. This just couldn't be happening.

Anne was taking her gloves off as she came in the door. She had been out back planting pots with a mixture of different pants, colors, and textures. She was an artist when it came to arranging plants together. "What's up? That computer acting up again?"

"No. Sit down; I just got a call from Mark. He wanted me to let you know that David won't be coming to dinner tonight."

Before she could continue, Anne said, "He's all right, isn't he? Although, I'm not really surprised. Whatever happened yesterday was a big deal, and I'm sure he'll be involved in the aftermath for several days."

"Yes, he will. Anne, there is no other way to say this. David and Adam were arrested today by federal marshals and taken to Washington. That's about all we know. Mark thinks this has something to do with the rivalry between the CIA and the FBI. David and Adam are caught in the middle."

Anne was on her feet. Tears sprang to her eyes. "No. No! They can't do this to him. This is a total screw-up. How could anyone think David Durham would do anything intentionally wrong?"

Carrie stood, hopped over to Anne, and placed her good arm around her. "Honey, we know he did nothing wrong, and he'll be released as soon as they know all the facts. However, Mark thinks it will be all over the evening news, both locally and nationally. He wanted to prepare you before that happens. Mark said to tell you to hold on to your faith in David and hang in there. Let's pack up and go home. Can someone close up for you tonight?"

"Sarah is here today; I trust her to close up. Call her in here."

## Vanished Sisters

*

MARK AND PETE came in as the six o'clock national news began. Anne sat on the sofa with a glass of wine, her eyes swollen and red from crying. Mark gave Carrie a kiss and went to Anne. He sat beside her and swept her into his arms. "I'm so sorry this had to happen."

Pete knelt beside her and took her hand. "Anne, over the years, I've worked with the FBI, and I can tell you the size of the egos at the top level is enormous. The CIA and the FBI can't work together without someone getting their knickers in a wad. They'll make a big deal of this, and then it will all go away. The only thing you can do to help David is to stand by him and have faith."

"I suspect his superior is pissed because David resigned before he had a chance to fire him. Remember when the terrorists captured Mark? David was asked by his superiors to back off and pretend he knew nothing. He wasn't even supposed to follow them to see where they relocated. How dumb was that? David decided to work with the CIA and continued to help keep tabs on the terrorists. He knew he would be fired when it came to light because he ignored a direct order."

"Pete is right, Anne; we worked with David in Kansas as well as here. He's the only FBI agent I've ever met who didn't have an attitude. I liked him from the first day I met him, and this arrest doesn't change my mind about him in the least. David will come out of this on top; you wait and see."

Everyone turned their attention to the news as the announcer, Ted Booker, said, "We have breaking news out of North Carolina. A huge meth and marijuana bust went down last evening in the sleepy village of Poplar Creek, in the mountains of North Carolina, near Asheville. Facts are sketchy at best, but a local law enforcement officer informed us that the CIA, FBI, and SBI were teamed together to smash this operation. When the battle was over, seven drug dealers were dead and two FBI agents. Another two agents remain in the Asheville hospital in critical condition. Three others were treated and released.

"The strange twist to this story is that the local director of the CIA, Adam Bradford, and the local director of the FBI, David Durham, were both arrested today by federal marshals and taken to Washington, D.C. No one locally has any idea why they were arrested. We have our Washington reporter, Monica Mathews, on the scene at the FBI building in Washington. Monica, what have you been able to uncover?"

The screen switched to an attractive woman reporter standing outside the federal building. "Thank you, Ted. Unfortunately, both the CIA and the FBI are being close-mouthed about this unexpected turn of events. I was witness to the arrival of the two prisoners behind this federal building. The CIA was waiting, papers changed hands, and both men were turned over to the CIA. The director of the FBI did not look happy. Federal marshals surrounded the scene and refused to grant us an interview. However, we were able to film the transfer of prisoners."

Immediately, the film of David and Adam getting out of the FBI vehicle filled the screen. They were both handcuffed as if they were criminals. Anne gasped and wiped away her tears as she stared at the screen. Everyone in front of the TV watched as papers changed hands, were verified, and the men released to the CIA. Jason Greenstreet stomped off into the Federal building. The CIA made sure the press filmed the cuffs being removed from both David and Adam. They were placed in a different vehicle and sped away. The reporter was back. "There you have it, Ted; we will continue to pursue this and hopefully have more information soon. Back to you, Ted."

"Thank you, Monica. We now have an eyewitness to the battle that ensued as the sting went down last evening in Poplar Creek." The second news clip of a farmer, wearing overalls, a dirty plaid shirt, brogans, and a hat dating back to the Civil War, appeared on the screen. The reporter held a microphone in his unshaven face.

"Can you tell us what you witnessed last night?"

The man smiled, obviously pleased with himself, showing his rotten and missing teeth. "Lordy, mercy," said the farmer, "hit was like watching a war agoin on. My son, Rafe here, and I wuz a raccoon hunting when'st we seen the hel-of-a-copters all over tha place and heard the gunfire. We slipped up at ridge thar, dropped to our bellies, and watched. Hit seemed to go on forever. Wes knowed bout tha marjawana. Figered hit would cause trouble sooner or later. We knowed em ferners wuz up to no good. All of a sudden, tha house blew up in a far ball. We wus covered in cinders. Ain't seen nothing like at since Nam."

"Did you report the marijuana fields to the authorities?"

"Well, no. We's believe in a-minding air own business. Don't need no law stickin' ere noses in our business."

"There you have it," said the reporter. "The locals knew, but said nothing. Back to you, Ted."

Anne had to smile along with everyone else. The guy was funny. "They were probably all stoned on free weed.... Why report it and kill the goose who laid the golden egg?"

Mark was happy to see Anne smile. The report made him feel better too. Knowing the CIA was in charge now was a good sign. David was going to work for the CIA. They take care of their own. Hopefully, David would be home soon.

Mark's phone rang. He saw it was David and excused himself. He went out to the back porch to answer the call. If David had bad news, he wanted to receive it alone, not with everyone watching him. David sounded beat. Mark knew he had had only two hours of sleep in the last thirty-six.

David's main worry was Anne. He was afraid of losing her. After seeing the news report, he was sure everyone would think him guilty of slaughtering the, now referred to, drug dealers in cold blood. They would never know how many innocent lives he had saved.

David poured his heart out to Mark. Mark listened and could, at times, hear the tears in his voice. This was a man who had tried to do the right thing all his life. He had put his life on the line many times for his country and his fellow man. He didn't deserve to be humiliated this way on national TV. Yes, he had disobeyed an order, but he had to follow his heart, his brain, and his common sense. Not to mention that protocol put Adam in control of the sting; therefore, placing David under Adam's jurisdiction.

Mark assured him everyone was behind him 100 percent. "Anne is upset, but not with you, only because you have been unjustly treated and she's afraid of losing you. Anne loves you and will be behind you no matter what the fallout. What do you think will happen now? Will this go to trial?"

"If Greenstreet has anything to do with it, it will. The government doesn't want the real story to come out. This is purely a case of smearing my name because I disobeyed an order—a bad order—and resigned before they could fire me. If I hadn't had the terrorists followed, it would have taken months to find them again. The only reason we found them in the first place was because you decided to build a summer home on property where they had stashed their weapons. By now, the airports would have been bombed, and who knows how many lives would have been lost?

"I'm in a hotel now, not in custody. I'll meet with my legal team in the morning and discuss our options. At the very least, I think I'll have to go before some kind of special commission that will investigate the entire incident and make a ruling.

"Adam says he isn't worried and we'll probably be back at work next week. It's a total farce, according to him, and I agree. But because Jason Greenstreet has formally brought charges against Adam and me, we must go through the progression of legal procedures and see it to the end.

"Greenstreet's only objective is to ruin my reputation, and he will definitely succeed in doing that. He doesn't know I've chosen a totally new field of law enforcement. I'm sure when he discovers I'm an employee of the CIA and will, more than likely, cross his path again sometime, he will be thoroughly pissed. That is my only consolation."

Mark looked up at the kitchen window and saw Anne watching him. He motioned for her to come out on the porch. To David, he said. "Anne has surely figured out that I'm talking to you. Are you ready to talk to her?"

"Yes; thanks for letting me know how she feels. My conversation with her will be much easier."

Anne took the phone, and Mark slipped back into the house to give her privacy. She wanted to climb through that phone line and hold him. Instead, she said, "Hey, David; how are you?"

"Oh, Anne...." He had to wait until he could get his emotions under control. Her heart went out to him. She felt so helpless. "I'm fine; really I am, at least physically. Emotionally, I'm a wreck. I'm consumed with so many emotions right now...anger, disappointment, disbelief, and a good portion of self-pity—to name a few. I'm sure a good night's sleep will improve on a few of those, but I couldn't go to bed until I talked to you. I need to know you truly believe I've done nothing wrong."

"David, I can save you a lot of time. I love you, and I know in my heart you are not capable of doing anything wrong. We will get through this together. I don't care what people think; they don't know you.... I do. Will you be able to come home soon?"

"Yes, right after my meeting in the morning with my legal team that the CIA has provided. They'll tell me what's going to happen and what's expected of me. Then I'll be on the next plane to Asheville. You'll never know how much better I feel just hearing your voice and knowing you care."

"Call me with your flight plan; I'll meet you. I don't want you going back to an empty apartment alone. Come here and stay with us for a few days. You need to be around people who love and support you."

"I'll call you as soon as I have a flight. I love you, Anne."

"I love you too, David, and I pray you get some sleep tonight." He said goodbye and hung up. Anne had a little cry and said a prayer to thank God for turning Mr. Greenstreet's vicious plan around. She knew God had a plan for her and David. Today was not a stumbling block but a test of how strong their love was for each other.

## CHAPTER 21

MARK, WITH HIS team of medical examiners, had finished with the autopsies, but he needed to return today to listen to their notes and dictate the final reports. Pete insisted on helping before driving back to Mississippi. They were sure that, between the two of them, they could knock out the reports in a couple of hours. Both had gotten a good night's sleep after being reassured David and Anne were going to be okay. Mark envied Pete being able to get in his car and put all this behind him. He, too, was ready to get back to a normal routine in the classroom.

Carrie would get her casts off tomorrow and have her final checkup with the obstetrician before going back to Mississippi. They yearned to get back to their normal lives where the word "terrorist" wasn't in their everyday vocabulary. Mark needed to hold his son, Tucker. He had talked to him almost every day, but it wasn't the same as being there with him. Tucker was infatuated with Carrie and eagerly accepted her as his mom. He considered Aunt Mattie his grandmother, and he was thriving in his newfound family. He was no longer alone when Daddy had to go away on a dig. He would be so happy about the prospects of a new sister or sisters or sister and brother.

Carrie had fallen in love with Tucker the first day she met him. The fact that Tucker had Down syndrome was never an issue with her. The bond between them was strong. At times, Mark airport.

    David drove to his apartment to pack some clean clothes. They held hands as they entered the elevator and ascended to the third floor. As he opened the door, he warned her he was not the neatest housekeeper in the world. They laughed as he closed the door behind them, and then he took her in his arms again and gently kissed her. As he released her, he noticed his surroundings...as did Anne. "David, I know you said you weren't much of a housekeeper, but I think your apartment has been ransacked."

    David couldn't believe what he was seeing. The apartment was a total wreck. Someone had totally destroyed the place. Every drawer and closet was open and their contents strewn all over the floor. He stood with his hands on his hips as Anne said, "Why would someone do this?"

    David put a finger to his lips, telling Anne to say nothing. He mouthed, "Bugged," as they stepped over things and inspected the rest of the apartment. In the bedroom, he picked up an opened suitcase thrown on the floor. He began throwing things into the bag. Anne could tell he was upset, his jaw was clenched, and his face flushed. He took her arm to leave and locked the door behind them.

    "You drive," he said as he tossed her the keys. "I would probably kill us, I'm so angry. Greenstreet ordered this. He was looking for something to use against me in his investigation, most likely my computer. It's in my hotel room in Marion. We need to stop by there and see if they've found my room and confiscated my computer and iPad. He has requested a special prosecutor to look into my actions and decisions of the night before last. I'm afraid both Mark and Pete will be required to give depositions as to how things went down and their opinion of what happened."

    "You don't deserve this, David. Why does this man want to ruin you? Shouldn't he have a warrant to enter your apartment?"

    "I have no doubt he had a warrant. Greenstreet goes by the book. It's a long story, and I would be divulging top-secret information if I tried to explain it in detail. Let's just say that Mr. Greenstreet and I have very different ideas about the security was a little jealous when he had to share her with Tucker. Now there would be two more to claim Carrie's attention. It would be an adjustment, but an adjustment he was looking forward to.

Halfway through their reports, Anne called to say David was landing in Asheville and she was on the way to meet him. She talked to Pete and asked him to stay one more night. The guest room had twin beds. She felt sure Pete would be the perfect person to put David's mind at ease about the arrest and news reports. "You made me feel better as you shared your experiences with the FBI. I know those stories will make David feel better too," she said, begging him to stay. "You'll be much fresher in the morning to face that long drive, and if you leave, David will think he pushed you out. Besides, you're part of this family and we're going to have a big family dinner tonight. You have to stay."

Pete was convinced. He almost lost it when she said he was part of the family. This was the *only* family he had now, and he *was* leaving to make room for David. He thought he would be in the way. Tears stung his eyes as he agreed to stay another night. He really did need to get back, but family came first.

\*

ANNE ARRIVED TWENTY minutes before David's plane landed. She was nervous and afraid their reunion would be awkward. She knew when she was nervous that she talked incessantly about nothing. She said a little prayer that God would give her the right words to put David at ease and return them to their normal, friendly, and warm relationship.

She was watching planes land, lost in her own thoughts, when someone tapped her on the shoulder. She turned; he was there. For several seconds, they stood, eyes locked, each waiting for the other to make a move. As a tear trailed down Anne's cheek, David reached for her and enveloped her in his arms. They knew not how long they held each other, but neither wanted to let go. Finally, Anne slipped her arm around his waist and said, "Let's go home." David was unable to speak. He laid his arm around her shoulder and together they walked out of the of this country. He sits in his office in Washington and dictates orders that put this country at great risk. He, like our Madam President, is soft on terrorism. They refuse to believe another 9/11 is inevitable. I'm afraid that's all I can say about the situation, and I need to make a call to Adam." David began dialing Adam's private number.

"When is this investigation going to happen?" Anne asked.

"No date has been set yet," David said as he waited for Adam to answer. "Greenstreet is trying to select a prosecutor of his choice, and the CIA is doing the same. It's a pissing contest. He can't win this battle and he knows it, but he plans to make it as uncomfortable and embarrassing as possible for me. He will mess his pants when he finds out I'm going to work for the CIA."

Anne had to snicker. This was a new side of David she had not seen before. She had never seen him angry. For some reason, she was glad he could get mad. He was always so easy-going. She was relieved to see him mad and ready to fight back if need be. She reached for his hand. "I'm with you all the way, love. We will survive. How is your family taking this?"

David held up his index finger to let Anne know Adam had answered. "Adam, have I caught you at a bad time?"

"Not at all; what's up?"

"My apartment was ransacked. Do you think Greenstreet would do that?"

"In a heartbeat; I'll check to see if warrants were obtained, but I can bet you they were. With your permission, I'll send someone over to take pictures and make sure the place isn't bugged. Did he get your computer?"

"No, I'm sure that's what he was looking for—copies of my reports, explaining every decision we made. Without those, we could be in trouble. He could accuse us of anything. Thank God, it's in my hotel room in Marion, and Greenstreet has no idea where I was staying. I'm headed there now. I won't let it out of my sight."

"You back up, don't you?"

"Yes, but my backup files are also in the hotel. I had no

idea Greenstreet would be after my files."

"David, take my advice; when working with government, keep a backup in a very safe place away from your apartment. Don't even put it in a safe deposit box; he could get a warrant for that too."

"Thanks, Adam; I'll do that, and you have my permission to check out my apartment. I'll give my superintendent a heads-up that you're coming. Thanks, Adam."

"No problem. Greenstreet doesn't know what he's up against, but he's going to find out. The fact that he went for your computer tells us he's desperate. Hang in there, buddy."

After David disconnected the call, he turned his attention back to Anne.

"Sorry, Anne; to answer your question, my mom is in a retirement complex back in Kansas. I've filled her in and warned her about the news reports. I called her last night to let her know everything had been resolved. She was relieved to hear I have a new job with less danger involved. I'm second generation FBI, so I'm sure my dad is rolling over in his grave. He was a highly decorated agent. She didn't want me to follow in his footsteps. Excuse me; I need to make one more call."

David dialed his superintendent's number. Kevin answered on the first ring. "Hey, Kevin; this is David Durham in 315."

Before he could say another word, Kevin interrupted. "David, what's going on? I thought you worked with the FBI? They came in here yesterday, flashing badges and pushing us around. They had a warrant so I had to let them in. Sorry. What did you do to make those guys mad?"

"I guess I forgot to fill out the required three forms to go take a leak.... I keep forgetting. Anyway, don't touch anything because the CIA will be by today to take pictures. They have my permission, so let them in. I'll be back in a couple days."

"You aren't going to jail are you? I heard you were arrested."

"It was a bogus arrest to create a show for the press. I've done nothing wrong except hand in my resignation. The FBI director is pissed off because I resigned before he had a chance to fire me. I've been by the apartment to pick up a few things. I'm staying with friends in Marion for a couple days. Call me if anyone other than the CIA shows up. Thanks, Kevin."

\*

ADAM CALLED THE Director of the CIA and brought him up-to-date. Damon Wentworth laughed. He knew if Greenstreet had stooped that low, he was desperate to find something to charge David with. He had David's reports and they would substantiate Adam Bradford's reports. The Attorney General named the CIA as lead investigator of the Boone cell. David complied with this ruling and made no decision without Adam's approval.

Greenstreet was more interested in his career than the safety of the United States. Any time the CIA and the FBI collaborated on a case, Greenstreet tried to give all the credit to the FBI and downplay the CIA's role. He whined and complained to the President. She always took his side because she knew she could control Greenstreet and dictate her policies. The CIA was a different story.

Damon Wentworth, the Director of the CIA, was a seasoned veteran. His climb to the top was earned by his performance, dedication, and brilliant mind. He could smell a terrorist plot in the wind before his subordinates had a clue. He could get in a terrorist's head and figure out what he was up to even before he was sure himself.

The President ordered a stand-down after Greenstreet advised her that the terrorists were on the move. The capture of a local cop as well as an anthropologist working for the FBI was not even considered in her decision. Greenstreet gave David the order to stand down without checking with the CIA. If he had, he would have known the two undercover agents imbedded in that cell were already dead. The President knew, but she chose not to pass on the information to Greenstreet.

Greenstreet ignored the Attorney General's order placing the CIA as lead agency over the Boone cell. Because the FBI had stumbled on the Dovecote cell and that cell had joined the

Boone cell, Greenstreet considered himself in charge of both. He knew he was wrong, but he felt sure the President would back him. His grave error was in using the President's name when ordering the stand down. When all was revealed in the investigation, Greenstreet would not be the only one with egg on his face.

*

WHEN DAVID AND Anne arrived home, Mark, Carrie, and Pete were waiting and received David as if he were family. It was the reassurance he needed, so he began to relax and bask in the warm, protective cocoon that a family provides to one of its own.

The evening was happy with lively conversation, good food, and wine. No one mentioned David's present situation. Mark knew David was not at liberty to discuss a federal investigation. Mark was well aware of the bureaucratic pandering involved in every politically-charged federal investigation, and he was impressed with Adam Wentworth; he knew Adam and his director would stand behind David in this investigation. Mark had observed, during the traumatic decision-making process of confronting the terrorists, that Adam and David were a team. They were equal in experience and knowledge of the terrorist threat. It was obvious they respected and trusted each other since both sought the other's opinion and suggestions.

The combined talents and efforts of these two had saved hundreds of lives. Mark knew he could rest easy at night because men like Adam and David were out there trying to stay one step ahead of the bad guys.

While they ate, Carrie announced that the house plans had finally arrived. After dinner, they were spread across the dining room table for everyone to see and comment on. Carrie couldn't wait to give Mr. Tate his copies. He was eager to begin on the foundation. Materials had been delivered and workers hired as he anxiously awaited the blueprints from the architect.

Pete wanted to check out the apartment over the garage. He had already claimed it as his retirement home. He would be caretaker for most of the year and travel in the summer to give

## Vanished Sisters

the family time alone in their summer home. Finally, he was looking forward to retirement, now that he had a family to look after.

David, too, had secret dreams of being part of this family. He knew he was in love with Anne. The way she came to his rescue, standing by him when most women would have politely backed away, only reassured him that he wanted to spend the rest of his life with her.

Before he could even think of a life with Anne, however, he wanted the stigma of this investigation behind him. He was confident the CIA would support him, but he also knew Greenstreet had the President's ear. There were too many unknowns. If this investigation went badly, he could be looking at prison time. At the very least, the CIA might back away from hiring him because of the media publicity surrounding this investigation. He was afraid the President and Greenstreet were planning to try this case in the media, before the investigation even began.

David would fly back to Washington in two days to meet with CIA lawyers, as well as Damon Wentworth. Lawyers were already busy preparing his case for federal prosecution. The Attorney General's office was the superior authority, to which the CIA, FBI, and Homeland Security reported and would ultimately name a prosecutor. Everything hinged on who had the most influence with the Attorney General. David was afraid that would be the President.

When Anne and David finally said goodnight, David slipped into the single bed across from Pete's without turning on the light. Pete had been in bed for over an hour, thinking of what he wanted to say to David. He turned over to face David when he heard him getting into bed. "I'm not asleep, son; I wanted to talk to you before I went to sleep. I'm leaving early in the morning, so I won't get another chance.

"I just wanted to say, in my years as coroner, forensic anthropologist, and adviser to law enforcement at all levels, I have had to testify in many federal cases. The bureaucratic bull and political games occurring in these federal investigations tend to obscure and confuse the truth until, in the end, it's hard to remember why you're even there. My advice to you is, above all else, ignore these games they play and keep to the facts. Don't be led into rabbit traps. Stick to the facts, even if you have to repeat them over and over again. The truth is, you disobeyed an order, which is not a criminal offense. It may be in the military in time of war, but you're not in the military. The CIA will prove you ignored the order because you had information your superiors either didn't have or chose to ignore. You were in the right; they were wrong.

"After this is all over, no one will remember who you are or even the fact that you, supposedly, busted up a huge drug ring. No one today cares. The public moves on to today's news and yesterday's is forgotten. Sadly, that's the world we live in. Your life will be pure hell for the next couple months because of the animosity and political ambitions of Washington bureaucrats. I want you to look at this as a lesson in how to survive. You will learn much, be wiser, and be more proficient for having gone through this awful ordeal. You will put this behind you and go on with your life. I promise."

David had listened quietly in the dark, knowing this was sage advice. "Thanks, Pete; in my heart, I know you're right. It's just the getting through this quagmire of bureaucratic bull that's difficult. I know the Lord is putting me through this for some reason, and hopefully, someday I will know why."

"That's my boy; always look for the lesson in any obstacle the Lord puts before you. The lesson is always there. Sometimes hard to see, but it's there. Now get some sleep, son, and stop worrying about it. You're going to be fine."

"Thanks, Pete; goodnight."

\*

THE NEXT DAY, the CIA gave Mark and Pete a call. A federal lawyer would be by to take a deposition from each. Pete was on the road back to Mississippi when he got the call. Arrangements were made to meet with him on campus the next day.

Mark and Carrie were on their way to Asheville. Today, the casts were coming off and she would have her final visit

## Vanished Sisters

with her obstetrician before going home. From Asheville, they planned to go to Dovecote to deliver the blueprints to Mr. Tate and walk the property, taking many pictures, one last time. They had hoped to get an early start home the next morning, but now they needed to wait until after the deposition.

David knew it would not look good for him to be there while the deposition was taken. Anne was disappointed; she had hoped to have some time alone with David after Mark and Carrie left. Now, she would be totally alone for the first time in eight weeks. She was not looking forward to the empty, quiet house. It reminded her of when her husband died and the terrible feeling of being totally alone.

David got up early and had breakfast with Anne. She gave him a ride downtown to pick up his car. It remained where it was parked the day he was arrested. Anne had offered to take the day off and help him put his apartment back together. David wasn't sure the photographers had been there; if not, the apartment could still be bugged. He would be fine and promised to call her every day and keep her aware of how things were progressing. He was headed back to Washington the next morning and needed to wash clothes and repack before catching the early flight to D.C.

They sat holding hands in her car as the little town of Marion came alive around them, preparing for another busy day. David hated leaving her as much as she hated to see him go. "Thanks for taking me in, Anne. It would have been so depressing to face that apartment as soon as I got back to Asheville. Just being with you and your family has given me the courage to face whatever comes my way. I know now I can handle this, and as Pete said, I will be the wiser for having gone through it.

"I don't know when I'll be back; it all depends on what needs to be done in D.C. to prepare for this travesty. I'll call you tomorrow when I arrive in D.C. and get settled. This could take months; Washington moves at a snail's pace, especially when they want to drag something out in the press. Don't watch the news; it will only depress you, and I need you to keep me up."

Anne had promised herself she would not cry. She had to be positive for David. He had enough on his mind without worrying about her being depressed. "If you can face terrorists and defeat them, I have no doubt you can handle Greenstreet. You are a brave, wonderful man, and I love you very much. Someday, we will look back on this and laugh at the absurdity of the whole situation."

David took her in his arms and kissed her right there in the middle of downtown, as people walked by on their way to work. They didn't care; this was goodbye for who knew how long. He released her, looked into her eyes, and said, "You're my rock, Anne. I love you. I'll call you tomorrow." He opened the door and walked away. She sat there watching him as he unlocked his car. He turned and waved goodbye one last time before driving away. Now Anne could cry, and she did, all the way to work.

\*

THE DEPOSITION TOOK two hours. It would be noon before Mark and Carrie could get away. Carrie stayed in the bedroom with her ear glued to the door. The lawyer was recording as well as videotaping their conversation. Even with the deposition, Mark would probably be called to testify during the trial. He wasn't worried; he had done this many times in his career as a forensic anthropologist. Trials usually followed finding a body. It was just part of the job.

A lawyer with the CIA arrived early to represent and advise Mark. "I will say, 'Don't answer that,' if the question asked is unnecessary, inappropriate, leading, or self-incriminating. You have the right to say, 'I don't know' if that is the case, and you need not give any explanation after making that statement."

The lawyer for the FBI then arrived. After setting up his audio and video, he asked Mark to lay his hand on the Bible and swear that everything he was about to say was the truth. After asking Mark to speak slowly and distinctly, he began. "Tell me how you became involved with the Dovecote terrorist cell, what you were asked to do by the FBI, and your version of how the confrontation between the terrorists and the joint task force evolved."

## Vanished Sisters

Mark began at the beginning with how Carrie and he had investigated the Hawkins' property in hopes of buying the place and building a summer home there. Their first inkling of anything amiss was when the bullet passed over Mark's head as he tried to look into the well. The story progressed as Billy and the ranch came into the picture and then the proof that the sisters were indeed, or had been, down in the well.

Mark continued the story and explained in detail how the story progressed from Dovecote to the Boone safe house and then to the village of Poplar Creek, including his and Danny's capture and rescue. He described his offer to work with the FBI and the SBI to process the barn at Billy's ranch, the sisters' house, and the Boone farmhouse where the bodies of the CIA undercover agents were found. From there, he began his narrative of how all agencies came together to infiltrate, observe, and take out the three combined cells at Poplar Creek. Mark took the deposition through the entire day, from the time the terrorists left for Charlotte that morning until the decision was made to bomb the Charlotte airport the next day and move again to a Raleigh safe house. "This decision was made," Mark said, "because Shahin was afraid the escaped convert would go to the authorities. It was at this juncture that David informed Adam Bradford of the imminent threat to bomb the Charlotte airport. The joint agencies concurred, the decision was made, and procedures were put into motion to move in and try to capture the terrorist."

Here the lawyer interrupted Mark. "Please explain in detail how the agencies learned the information about the bombings."

Mark explained how the encrypted report left by the two murdered CIA agents had given them the locations, but not the specific targets. "However," he continued, "we didn't know the how or when until the CIA got a break in the case. A terrorist was arrested as he crossed the Mexican/U.S. border. He was sent by Hamas to the Poplar Creek cell with specific instructions on how and when to bomb the two airports. Hamas considered this information too sensitive and detailed to be communicated over a cellphone."

"What did the CIA do with this man?" asked the interviewer.

Mark looked at the CIA lawyer before saying, "I have no idea where this man is now." He continued his story. "A CIA agent, posing as this man, took his place. The documents were altered to give us more time. The imposter informed Shahin they must visit both sites to observe the most populated areas as well as the busiest times of day. While they were away from the house, Pete Gunter and I were able to get in and process the entire house. The FBI agents, who were imbedded in this cell as field workers, then bugged the house with audio and video."

"So you're saying everyone left the house? No one was left to watch the house except two field workers?"

"No, all of this was possible because the one meth lab worker, who was left to continue his work and watch the house, decided to escape. He was a local convert who got himself into this mess and knew he would never get out alive. He ransacked the house and ran. He was arrested by FBI agents and held in protective custody. He was released to his family after the bust went down. His cooperation with the FBI indicated he was just a kid, taken in by Muslim extremists and their promise of glory.

"Upon finding that the meth tech had decided to desert, Shahin made the decision to move up the Charlotte bombing and postpone the Raleigh bombings until later. They made the decision to bomb the Charlotte airport the next day and move to yet another safe location where they could re-group and plan the Raleigh bombing."

"How did you obtain this change of plans information?" asked the FBI lawyer.

"We watched it all, as it was happening, on David Durham's iPad. Remember, the house was bugged with audio as well as video. David and Adam then gave the signal for the imbedded agents to get out as soon as possible. When they were given the all clear, Adam, using a loud speaker, announced they were surrounded and needed to come out with their hands up. That did not happen.

"We watched as the terrorist escaped through a tunnel leading from under the living room rug and exiting a hundred yards behind the barn. Unfortunately, we did not find the tunnel

as we processed the house. We waited as helicopters were called in to illuminate the area. The helicopters sighted the terrorists attempting to escape. They came out fighting, and for a while there, it resembled a war zone. They must have planted a bomb under the house in the tunnel. It was ignited as the terrorists realized they could not escape and refused to be captured.

"When all gunfire had ceased, all terrorists and two FBI agents were dead. Two agents were hospitalized, and three others were treated and released."

"In your opinion, Dr. Goodman, was proper protocol used at all times? Were you aware that an order from FBI Director Greenstreet had been given for the FBI to stand down?"

"No, I did not have that information at the time. When the cell was discovered in Dovecote, the SBI called in the FBI, which took over the decision-making. After the Dovecote cell moved to the safe house near Boone, they became a part of that cell, which was being followed and infiltrated by the CIA. The FBI then, according to protocol, was officially under the CIA's control. If protocol had been properly followed, the Director would have immediately informed the CIA of the existence of the Dovecote cell as soon as it realized it was dealing with foreign terrorists and have asked the CIA for instructions. Greenstreet failed to do this.

"The reason given by Greenstreet for ordering a stand down was because the CIA had two imbedded agents in that cell. Greenstreet was not told the agents had been compromised because first, the President didn't tell him, and second, he did not consult with the CIA before ordering David to stand down. David followed protocol and checked with Adam Bradford. Bradford rescinded Greenstreet's order and informed David that the two agents were dead."

"How do you know the FBI Director didn't know the agents had been compromised?"

"Director Greenstreet told David Durham the order to stand down came directly from the President. The reason given was the two CIA agents imbedded in that cell. The CIA had informed the President the two agents were dead. The President neither informed Greenstreet, nor did she ask him to consult with the CIA before ordering the stand down. David Durham wanted to save his two captured men before the terrorists killed them. He talked with CIA and received orders not only to try to recapture his men, but to follow the terrorists to see where they were relocating."

"What is your relationship with David Durham? Are you more than professionals working on the same case?"

The CIA lawyer immediately stepped in. "Supposition. Do not answer that question."

The FBI lawyer tried a different tact. "Have you ever worked with David Durham before?"

Mark's lawyer gave him a nod. "Yes, we worked together on a case in Kansas a little over a year ago. I was impressed with his leadership qualities and ability to work in multi-agency situations."

"Is your sister now dating David Durham?"

"Do not answer that question," said the CIA lawyer. "It has no bearing on this case."

The FBI lawyer then announced he had all the information he needed and the deposition ended.

# CHAPTER 22

CARRIE CAME OUT of hiding to meet the CIA lawyer. "So, you were thrown down a mountain by the terrorists? You look pretty good after suffering that fate."

"I just got the casts off yesterday. I had a broken arm and leg."

"Plus," Mark added, "we learned after the ordeal that she is pregnant with twins who also managed to survive the trip down the mountain. Carrie is tough and I suspect our babies will be too."

They shook hands, the lawyer left, and Mark began packing the car to leave for Mississippi. They stopped by the garden center to say goodbye to Anne and tell her about the deposition.

"Maybe," Anne said, "you had better warn Pete."

"Pete is a veteran when it comes to depositions; he'll be fine. He can handle lawyers. He knows how to answer a question without answering the questions, just as well as they do. I'm sure we'll both need to go to Washington to testify. The FBI lawyers will attempt to get us to contradict what we said in the depositions. It's all a game, but the fact remains that Greenstreet hasn't a leg to stand on. Unless he wants to say the President didn't tell him about the dead agents, and we know he won't do that; it would be suicide for his career.

# Rachel Poe

\*

THE HOMECOMING WAS a complete surprise for Carrie and Mark. Banners saying, "Welcome Home" covered the front porch. Mark's parents were there, and Pete joined the party to celebrate their homecoming.

Aunt Mattie was first to hug Carrie. "Am I seeing things, or are you pregnant?"

Carrie gave Pete a look. Pete held his hands up as if protecting himself. "I promise I didn't say a word. Did I, Mattie?"

"No, he did not. I haven't seen you in two months. Did you really think I wouldn't notice?"

Tucker hugged his dad and turned to Carrie. "What does pregnant mean, Mom?"

"It means you're going to have a sister to play with, maybe even two." Carrie knew that was as much information as he could process at one time. She and Mark would explain more later. After everyone was hugged, they went inside and enjoyed a wonderful dinner, prepared by Mattie and Rosa. They stayed up late describing all they had been through in the last eight weeks. That is, as much as they were allowed to say.

Mark's parents were thrilled at the prospects of another grandchild and just as thrilled to hear Anne was dating someone Mark and Carrie held in such high esteem. It was great to get back in their own bed, and especially great the casts were off and they could finally be close again.

The next morning, Mark's parents left after a big breakfast and everyone settled down to a normal routine.

\*

PETE AND MARK had lunch the next day to compare notes on the depositions. Pete's lawyers were a little less friendly than Mark's. "I was asked basically the same questions, but when the FBI lawyer asked about my relationship with David, the CIA lawyer objected. Like your lawyer, he said it was speculation and not to answer. The FBI lawyer became indignant and insisted it was not speculation. He argued I knew whether I was a friend of David or not. My lawyer then allowed the question, and I answered I was no friendlier with David than with any other person I had worked with on this case.

"Then the big stink came when he asked about the relationship between David and Anne. My lawyer told me not to answer, and the other lawyer pressed on as before. This time, my lawyer held firm and insisted it had nothing to do with the order to stand down or whether it was obeyed or ignored. The other lawyer, red-faced now, said if David were having an affair with your sister, it could definitely affect how you and I felt about David and influence our opinion of how well David performed his job."

"I held up my hand for quiet and said you and I had worked with David one other time in Kansas. My lawyer tried to stop me, but I continued. We were both impressed by his professionalism and ability to work in a multi-agency situation. Whether he is dating Anne or not wouldn't affect David's decision making, or our opinion about his decision-making capability. Now the FBI lawyer tried to stop me; this was not what he wanted to hear. My lawyer was now smiling. I ignored the FBI lawyer and continued. David Durham acted in this case just as he had in the Kansas case. He was professional and worked closely with the CIA, which was the agency in charge. If David had obeyed the order to stand down, it is my personal opinion the Charlotte airport would have been bombed before we could have discovered the terrorists' new location and stopped them.

"I was wound-up and barreling ahead when the FBI lawyer cut the audio and video off. My lawyer objected and stated: I must warn you, sir, if any part of this videotape is removed or altered, I will personally see that you're indicted for tampering with evidence. A complaint will be filed immediately, stating you cut the tape because you didn't want a favorable reply to your question."

Mark was surprised. "I'm worried the FBI will take the position that our testimony should be thrown out because our opinion of David is prejudiced by the fact that David was seeing my sister. Did you talk to your lawyer after the deposition was over?"

"Yes, we had a long conversation, and he has the same fears. He feels this whole case has been trumped up to hurt David and ruin his career with the FBI or any other law-enforcement agency. He says Greenstreet is a very vain, pompous, career-oriented bastard. The FBI Director thinks, because he and the President are in accord, he will have her backing and succeed in ruining David's reputation.

"Did you see the news last night? They're referring to the terrorist confrontation as a bloodbath. They are accusing David of killing these men in cold blood. Of course, the word 'terrorist' was never mentioned. The entire incident was referred to as a methamphetamine and marijuana operation. It was insinuated that the entire case was mishandled and two FBI agents died unnecessarily."

*

ANNE SAW THE news and was very upset. How could David defend himself against such allegations? She switched to the local news only to see the same news clips she had just watched on the national news.

Her phone rang. It was David. She tried to answer without letting him know how down she felt. "Hello, David; how are things going?" she asked.

"Actually, I think this may all turn out okay. My reputation will be ruined, but the CIA has a plan. I can't really talk about it, but I want you to know I'm in good hands. The CIA is ready to defend Adam and me, and they feel confident they'll win. They assure me they have a plan that should bring this whole case to a head as soon as possible. They suspect the case against Adam and me will be dropped completely. Say a prayer and cross your fingers."

"What good news. If the case is dropped, it will soon be forgotten. All the locals I have spoken with aren't happy that a drug operation of that magnitude was being carried out right under the public's nose. They're grateful the CIA and FBI took the operation out. They feel that if these men had gotten away, they would have relocated in a different place and continued as usual. The news may be sensationalizing this whole story, but the locals are with you."

"I'm glad to hear it. I think you're right about the story going away if the case is dropped. I'll be home tomorrow, but unfortunately, I won't be able to see you for a while. It seems the FBI is trying to use our relationship to get Mark and Pete's testimony thrown out. Of course, all FBI agents are afraid to comment because their jobs and reputations could be at stake, too. Therefore, we'll only have the statements of the CIA and SBI operatives who were there. Greenstreet is pitting the FBI against the CIA. This is very dangerous for this country right now, when we should be working together to stop any threats against our homeland."

"I understand, David; we'll get through this one way or another. Call me when you can and keep me informed. I'll be praying for you."

"Thanks, Anne; we'll stay in touch daily. I need to go. I love you very much. Goodnight."

\*

THE CIA HAD had enough pandering, posturing, and whining from Director Greenstreet. A decision had been made. This had gone on for over a month while the press made Adam and David look like criminals. Monday morning, the Director of the CIA would make a formal request of the Attorney General, in accordance with the United States Department of Justice, to appoint Independent Counsel. Since Greenstreet had stated that the order to stand down had come from the President, she needed to be questioned about her motives and Greenstreet's influence. This was all a ploy, of course, in hopes of getting the President and Greenstreet to back off and dismiss the case against Adam and David.

David and Adam had been trained well. Both always saved copies of reports sent to their superiors daily. In these reports, David had confirmed that Greenstreet's order to stand-down came from the President. It also confirmed that the CIA had rescinded that order because it was not only based on false information, but the CIA was the agent in charge and Greenstreet had no authority to give the order in the first place. If the President had contacted the CIA, which she knew was in charge, she would have been reminded that the operatives were dead. She knew this, which is why she used Greenstreet.

Thankfully, David's computer and iPad were in his hotel room in Marion, not at his apartment when it was ransacked and bugged. He had never mentioned to Greenstreet that he was staying in Marion because of the heightened terror alert. His computer was never out of his sight now, and all reports had been backed up and were safely in the hands of his lawyers.

*

WHEN THE PRESIDENT was informed that Independent Counsel was being appointed, she flew into a rage and sent for Greenstreet immediately. Greenstreet's exaggerated self-importance was only heightened by the President's request. He informed his personal assistant to cancel his morning appointments; the President needed him.

As the FBI Director entered the Oval Office, he smiled with the self-confidence of one who enters the den of a trusted friend and confidant. His smile was erased immediately as a paperweight sailed past his head. "You stupid fool! How dare you use the name of the President of the United States in a mundane order to a subordinate!"

"But, Madam President, you did order me to give that order."

"Yes, you fool, I did, but I did not give you permission to use my name. You have no proof I told you anything. You decided to use my name to make yourself look important. The cell has been eradicated now and my contributors are not happy. I have the next election to worry about. The CIA has requested Independent Council be appointed. They want to question my reasons behind asking for a stand down when terrorists were plotting to bomb the Charlotte airport. I can't very well tell them contributors to my last election ordered me to back off. I want a confession that you used my name without my permission.

I want this lawsuit dropped against Adam Bradford and David Durham and your resignation on my desk within the hour. Now get out, before I have you arrested and thrown in jail."

*

    FBI DIRECTOR JASON Greenstreet made the evening news, but not for the obvious reason. He did admit and apologize for using the President's name without permission. He did call his legal team in and announce the lawsuit against Adam Bradford and David Durham was to be dropped. His resignation was written and a copy sent to the President, the CIA, FBI, and Homeland Security, but that was not the end of his story. After packing up all his personal files and having them sent to his home, he committed suicide in his office. He could not face the world a fallen man.

## CHAPTER 23

RICHARD HOFFMAN CALLED Mark's cell phone. Richard had been the rookie reporter with *The News* in New York, who had finally been awarded the writing of the Kansas story. After many failed attempts to get into Carrie's hospital room and find out what was going on at the Masters' farms, he had finally won Carrie's empathy and she had given him the story. Since then, he had been promoted to lead reporter on the evening news. His tenacious determination and his genuine, warm personality were a winning combination. He had steadily moved to the top of his field.

Mark recognized Richard's name on the Caller I.D. and answered. He remembered Richard with mixed feelings. He was a constant aggravation as Carrie tried to recover. Mark had felt he used his allergy attack to get sympathy from Carrie and worm his way into convincing her to let him do the story. However, it was a good decision, and as promised, Richard had been very sympathetic of Carrie's condition and told the gruesome story with accuracy and just the right amount of tenderness.

To repay her for letting him have the story, Richard had talked his editor into giving her an interview on *The News* just before her book came out. The interview sent her book sales soaring, and overnight, Carrie was an accomplished writer.

"Richard," Mark's voice boomed into the phone. "How

are you and Mazy doing, and when are you coming to see us?"

Mazy had been Carrie's office manager when she was in the interior design business. Mazy had run the Thomasville, North Carolina office from Carrie's hospital room in Kansas while Carrie convalesced. She'd stuck by Carrie and even helped her write the book. When Carrie's book became an overnight success, Carrie had decided that writing was her calling, so she had closed her interior design business, leaving Mazy without a job.

Richard and Mazy had met and fallen in love while Carrie wrote her book and recovered from surgery. Six months before they had come to look at the sisters' house, Mark and Carrie had flown to New York for Richard and Mazy's wedding. Now, Mazy worked for the publisher of Carrie's first book.

"We're great, Mark; hope we can get down to Mississippi next summer. Mark, I ran across your name, as well as Pete's, on the list of possible witnesses in the trial of CIA agent Adam Bradford and FBI agent David Durham. The news of their indictments and upcoming trial has monopolized the evening news for over a month. I was wondering if I could get a comment from you on today's suicide of FBI Director Jason Greenstreet?"

For what seemed an eternity, Mark stood holding the phone and saying nothing as mixed emotions flooded his brain. *Could this whole debacle be over?*

"Mark, are you there?"

"Forgive me, Richard; I hadn't heard about Greenstreet's suicide. What does this mean for the indictment and trial?"

"Mark, it's all over. Before Greenstreet committed suicide, he admitted he had misused the President's name in his order to stand down; then he ordered his lawyers to drop the lawsuit, resigned, and committed suicide. Quite a day's work if you ask me. All this happened after he met with the President in the Oval Office. His career was obviously over. I was hoping to get a comment from you and Pete about what really went on down there in North Carolina."

"We processed the house where the drug dealers lived and worked," said Mark, thinking as fast as he could. He knew he couldn't mention the word *"terrorist"*, and he didn't want his and Carrie's part in the fiasco to be publicized on the evening news. He had to keep his answers bland and get to Pete before Richard got him on the phone. "We expected to be called to testify, but neither of us has received a summons. About all we could say is how impressed we were with Adam and David as they worked together in an interagency sting operation.

"We never understood the stand-down or why it was ordered." Mark was walking as he talked, on his way to Pete's office. He didn't knock, just barged in. Pete looked up, surprised as Mark motioned for him to say nothing. "Richard, I'm afraid we had a very small part in this case, just our routine everyday job."

"How did you get involved with this case? Aren't you a professor in a university now?"

"I just happened to be in the mountains looking at property to build a summer home. We ran across David Durham, whom we worked with in Kansas; next thing we knew, we were dusting for fingerprints. Just that simple." He tried to change the subject. "How's Mazy doing?"

Pete's eyes grew huge as he realized whom Mark was speaking with. He knew Mark was walking a tightrope. Richard could smell a story a mile away. Mark pointed to Pete and to the cell phone, asking if he wanted to talk to Richard. Pete waved his hands as if to say, "No way." He wrote on a piece of paper, "Talk about the house."

Richard was telling Mark about Mazy's recent change in jobs; she had left the publisher of Carrie's book and was now working with a huge publishing house. Mark used the opening to say, "You two need to come down. We're building a house in the little village of Dovecote, not too far from Asheville. We'll be ready to entertain guests next summer. We would love to see you and show off our new home."

"We will, Mark; sounds perfect. Mazy and I love the mountains. That's where we fell in love. We'll definitely make plans. Thanks for taking the time to talk to me. We do need to get together and catch up since the wedding."

"No little ones on the way yet?"

"No, we aren't ready for children. How about you?"

step outside right now—the press is going wild. They're camped on the doorstep of our hotel. I feel sad that Greenstreet committed suicide; it makes me feel a little guilty about being so happy. I'll call you with my arrival time. I love you, Anne."

"I love you, too, David. I'm so happy this is behind us."

\*

RICHARD HOFFMAN WAS no pushover; he knew when he was getting the run-around. There was a story here, and it was much more than a drug bust. His instincts told him to get himself down to those mountains and quietly nose around to see what he could find. After he was sure he had a story, he would confront David Durham. It was for sure he wasn't getting any information out of Mark, and Mark would get to Pete, so that was a dead-end. Although he was glad he had called because he could read between the lines, and Mark was definitely hiding something. He had kept changing the subject, and Richard could sense that Mark wanted to get him off the phone. His gut told him it was something big. He picked up the phone and called his travel agent.

Mark had said he was going to build in a village called Dovecote. That must have been where he ran into David Durham. What was an FBI man doing in a backwoods mountain village? He remembered Mark, saying. "We ran across David Durham.... Next thing we knew, we were dusting for fingerprints." Something must have happened in Dovecote. That was as good a place as any to start.

\*

RICHARD PULLED HIS rented SUV over and checked his map again. He was lost. He saw Dovecote on the map.... He was on the Hudlow Road.... Where the heck was it? As he sat on the side of the road, a huge truck passed him and turned in at a dirt road a short distance from where he sat. He was delivering building lumber. Thinking there must be new construction down that road, Richard pulled in behind the truck and followed

"As a matter of fact, we're expecting twins in a litt[le] four months." Richard was surprised, so they talked abo[ut ba]bies for a few minutes until the conversation ended with a[n] promise to come down next summer.

Mark clicked the phone off and sat down as if exha[usted]. Pete shook his head and said, "Wheeeee, that was a close [one]. Do you think he believed you?"

"Have no idea; I'm not even sure what I did tell hi[m.] I do know it wasn't interesting enough to write an article o[r he] called to get our comment on the Greenstreet suicide this m[orn]ing. I didn't even know about it. It must have happened afte[r I] came to work."

"Oh, Lord, he committed suicide? What does this m[ean] for David Durham?"

"It's all over; turn on the news and let's see what's go[ing] on."

Mark called Anne to see whether she had heard the ne[ws.] When Anne came on the line, Mark couldn't contain his exci[te]ment. "It's over, Anne; have you seen the news? Greenstr[eet] committed suicide this morning, but before doing so, he drop[ped] his lawsuit against David and Adam."

Anne had not heard, and tears came to her eyes as [she] listened to Mark explain about the suicide, and all that had ta[ken] place beforehand. She couldn't talk as sobs wracked her bo[dy.] Could this really be true? She had to hear it for herself on [the] news.

"Anne, are you there?"

"Yes, Mark," she sobbed. "I can't even talk. I'm tur[ning] on the television now. I have another call, Mark; it's David[. I'll] get back to you."

Anne clicked on the new call. She was still sobbi[ng as] she heard the excitement in David's voice. "Anne, my love[, it's] over! The lawsuit has been dropped! Our lives can return to [nor]mal! Are you there, Anne?"

"Yes, David; Mark just called me. I'm afraid I'm a [bit] distraught. I can't stop crying. I'm so happy for you, for us[, and] for Adam. When will you be home?"

"I hope today; there is so much going on here. We [

it for about a mile. He was right, and he bet this was Mark and Carrie's house. In a backwoods place like this, how many new construction sites could be in progress? He got out and walked over to the man who seemed to be in charge.

"Hello. I'm looking for Dovecote. Could you point me in the right direction?"

"Well, hits to tha right of this here driveway. Don't go and blink er you'll miss it. Only thing thar's a post office, general store, and fillin station."

"This wouldn't be Mark and Carrie Goodman's house you're building, would it?"

"You'd be right there, feller. Mity fine folks, they are."

"I'm visiting friends in Asheville and thought I would see if I could find where Mark's building his new summer home. Looks like you're just getting started? From the foundation, I can see it's going to be a pretty big house."

"Hit's a gona be a whopper. Say, you's a friend of Mark's?"

"Yes, sir. My name is Richard Hoffman. Mark said to check out Dovecote and see if I could find his new house. The view is going to be spectacular. How did he find this place?"

"My name's Tate, Alvin Tate. Nice to meet ya." They shook hands as Alvin said, "Mark used to stay with his grandpappy and granny every summer, right down thar in that there valley. He nowed tha two old ladies at once lived here. They wus murdered in er beds by gunrunners. Herd tell Mark found ere bones in tha well."

*Funny, Mark forgot to mention that little bit of information,* Richard thought. He was right; there was a story here. Dovecote and Poplar Creek weren't that far apart. Could there be a connection between the so-called gunrunners and the drug dealers in Poplar Creek? "Sounds interesting; tell me more."

"Don't know no more. Ain't a from round here, mabe the locals can tells ya more. Just a sayin what I heard."

Richard offered his hand, thanked Alvin for the directions to Dovecote, and left the way he had come. He turned right out of the drive, topped the crest of a hill, and headed down the other side. He soon came to a few older homes, and at the bottom of the hill, he found the small village of Dovecote. Alvin was right; you didn't want to blink or you would miss the three small buildings.

The old brick buildings of the post office, general store, and service station were well over a hundred years old. Richard wondered why the village was there at all. What attracted people to this out-of-the-way, long forgotten little village? Richard pulled into the service station. No one was around, but he could hear banging coming from out back, so he walked that way.

As he rounded the station, Richard saw an old railroad depot down behind the stores. The tracks had been removed years ago, but the small depot stood forlorn in a field of weeds. The old sign hanging from the eaves squeaked as the breeze slightly moved it back and forth on rusty hinges. Years ago, before the weather and time eroded the sign, it had said, "Dovecote." Now, unless you knew what it was supposed to say, it was unreadable. *Why would there be a train station in this small village?*

Richard followed the banging and found a mechanic working on a tractor, the same vintage as the depot. He watched the laborer until the man looked up, wiped his hands on a rag, and came over to Richard. This man was neither old nor young, and the name on his uniform said, "Butch." He was hatless, and his graying hair looked as if it hadn't seen a comb since last Sunday morning. His wide smile was friendly, albeit missing a few teeth. He offered Richard his greasy hand and Richard took it. After all, he planned to pick this man's brain, so he couldn't afford to offend him.

A woman appeared from under the tractor and brushed off her bib overalls, wiped her hands on the same dirty rag Butch had used, and came to meet Richard. She was tall and slight, as was Butch. Another grubby hand came out to greet him. At first, she appeared to be a young woman. Her hair was drawn back in a ponytail with a handful of freckles scattered across her nose. On closer examination, the crow's feet, graying hair, and the beginning sag of jowls along her jaw became visible. Richard guessed she was Mrs. Butch and placed their ages at fiftyish.

"I'm Butch Morgan and this here is my better half, Ruby. Sorry we weren't out front; can we fill up your tank?"

# Vanished Sisters

"Sure," Richard smiled and pointed to the tractor. "That's a classic; you restoring it?"

Butch looked puzzled. "Restore it? I'm just trying to get the darn thing running again. I got jobs to do." They all walked out front. Ruby started the pump, while Butch cleaned Richard's windshield, checked the air in his tires, and his oil level. "Mister, you could use a quart; it's a bit low." Richard was impressed; he hadn't had this kind of service since, well, he couldn't remember when. He would have filled it himself if there had been a place to stick his credit card. The pump was an antique like the whole village, but it still worked. He suspected he had better find some cash in his wallet because it didn't look like plastic was an option here.

Richard paid the bill and said, "You know who's building that new house up the hill?"

"Sure do; Mark and Carrie Goodman, good people; they only plan to be there in the summer. He teaches at a university in Mississippi. He sort of grew up here in the valley, spending summers with his grandparents, who were highly respected around these parts. Addie was a railroad man and Lizzie was one of the best cooks in the county. They won't be forgotten any time soon. We're mighty glad to have Mark and Carrie as neighbors. For a while there, we were afraid they'd been scared off the property."

Richard's ears perked up. This was what he had come for—the real story, he hoped. "Scared? Scared of what?"

"Well, we had some excitement around these parts a little while back. Some foreigners moved in on one of the old farms. Had a drug ring a-goin' and even weapons. Killed the two old ladies who lived on the property Mark bought. These foreigners wanted to hide weapons on the Hawkins' property. That's Mark's property now. It's called the Hawkins' property 'cause of the old ladies. The gun runners thought the property wus deserted, ya see; it had no 'lectric power or running water and it looked like it was mite-near a-falling down. They didn't know the two old ladies were still a-living there; they wus in their nineties. Lived there all their life, never married, but neither one of the sisters wus much to look at. When they surprised them one night as they moved a shipment of guns into the house, they had to kill 'em. Threw their bodies in the well. Can you imagine?"

"You don't mean it?" Richard replied. This was getting better by the minute. There had to be a connection between this incident and the drug bust in Poplar Creek. Richard wondered whether these folks had a TV or even took the paper.

"I read in the papers about a drug bust in Poplar Creek; that's not far from here, is it? Did the two have anything to do with each other?"

"Shore did; the FBI, SBI, and local law enforcement tried to catch 'em here in Dovecote, but they slipped away and relocated up near Boone and then moved again to Poplar Creek. That's where it all ended in a heap of fireworks. According to the news, they killed all of 'em and lost a couple of their own men. Tha news kinda made the good guys look bad, but us locals is mighty glad they cleaned house."

"You didn't mention the CIA. The papers said the CIA was in on the bust. They usually handle foreign affairs. Why were they involved?"

"Probably 'cause these men wus A-rabs—from the Middle East, ya know. The sheriff said they probably come across the Mexican border. They come in here to get gas in their four-wheel vehicles. Didn't know much English and not very friendly. They gave us the creeps, didn't they, hon?"

"That's the truth," Ruby agreed. "I didn't want nothing to do with 'um. Sneaky, wouldn't look you in the eye. I knowed they was up to no good. They kidnapped Carrie and threw her down a mountain to get the SBI off their tails. It worked, too, and they got away. Mark found the old ladies' bones and the whole community gave them a real good burying."

Richard knew why Mark had left out the important facts. He didn't want their personal story on the evening news. Richard was trying to put all this together. There had to be someone who would sit down with him and share the entire story from beginning to end...but who? Anyone having anything to do with law enforcement had been told to say nothing except what was covered in the news stories for the past month. Richard knew these were no ordinary drug dealers. He was becoming very suspicious that these men were terrorists. If this were true and the truth had been kept from the American people, he would blow this story wide open.

Richard ventured one more question. "Butch, while all this excitement was going on, did you ever hear anyone use the word 'terrorist'?"

"Lordy, no! This here's America. We don't got no terrorists on American soil. Them heathens that hit New York City was a warning. That can't happen again here in America. I hear tell America is on high alert to keep that from ever happening agin."

Richard stared at Butch. Could anyone be that stupid? He was sure they had terrorists living among them and never suspected it. Maybe they didn't want to know. It was probably beyond their capacity to grasp. He made a lame excuse and asked whether the General Store had cold drinks—anything to change the subject. Butch sent him over to meet Minnie Sue Winkle and get one of the coldest drinks in the county.

Richard pulled open the squeaky screen door and entered the General Store. An unusual smell accosted his olfactory senses. It wasn't an unpleasant aroma—a sweet and spicy odor mingled with the smell of old wood, lemon oil, fresh produce, home-baked bread, and the mustiness of the old building. Richard peered into the depth of the long, dimly lit, narrow store and realized the General Store was also a barbershop. Part of the smell was coming from the barbershop area. Probably still used hair pomade from the '50s.

Richard stood in the warm store, letting his eyes adjust to the dim light, and suddenly, he became aware of how quiet it was. The only sounds were the clip, clip of the barber scissors and the click, clack of the ancient fan in the tin ceiling above him. As his eyes focused, he became aware of two coal black eyes watching him.

She was no more than 4' 6", and the counter was at least that or more. The top of her head was almost even with the counter. She said nothing, just peeked over the counter as she watched him. Her face was a roadmap of wrinkles. Her white hair was pulled back severely and twisted into a bun at the nape of her neck. Her black eyes darted here and there, and he ventured to guess that she missed nothing. Her hands were gnarled and twisted into unnatural angles. They held on the counter as she peeked over at Richard. "Good afternoon. Butch says you have the coldest drinks in the county." A smile eased across her face, unveiling a picket fence of missing teeth and making her eyes squint and twinkle. Guess there was no dentist in Dovecote.

"If'n there's a colder one in this county, I don't know it. We got Coca-Cola, Grape, Pepsi, and Truade Orange. And today, we have homemade fried apple pies; also the best in the county."

"Let me try one of those orange drinks and a fried pie." He sat at a small table, between the end of the counter and the old potbelly stove. Richard would bet money that in winter the old, wood-burning monster could run you out of there. Minnie Sue delivered his drink and pie on a paper plate with a plastic fork. The anachronism of paper plates and plastic forks in the midst of a hundred-year-old country store was comical. But he could see the need, and Minnie Sue didn't look like she could reach a sink to wash dishes.

Minnie Sue sat down across from Richard and stared at him while he tasted his pie. "We don't get many strangers come through here. Where you from?"

With a mouth full of the most heavenly-tasting apple pie, Richard hurriedly chewed, swallowed, and said, "New York. Visiting friends in Asheville. Decided to try and find a friend's new house. Mark and Carrie Goodman. We're old acquaintances."

Minnie Sue immediately became his best, new friend. "We love Mark and Carrie. This old village needs new blood. Can't wait to see those twins running around here. Been a long time since we had a baby in Dovecote; now we gonna have two. Every evening after all the workers leave, the whole village walks up to see how many bricks they laid today. We're keeping an eye on the place for 'um. They ought to be coming up in the next few weeks to check on the place."

"Really? Maybe if I'm still here, I'll get to see them," Richard said as he shoved another bite of apple pie in his mouth. "I think I'll take two more of these pies to go. They're really good. We don't get homemade in New York. Butch next door said you had some foreigners living here a while back?"

"I'll wrap 'um up fer you. Baked 'um myself this morning. Oh, the ferners, yes we did, but they's all dead now. They wus a living on Billy Burgess' farm. We wus suspicious from the start when Billy came home from Texas after his pappy died. All of a sudden, he was rich and a pushing folks around like he owned the whole dern county. Ferners killed the two old sisters and Billy too. They got out of here just ahead of the law and kidnapped Mark and a policeman from Marion. You going to see Anne?"

"Sorry?" Richard was in a daze. Could all this really have happened? "Anne who?"

"You never met Mark's sister, Anne? She lives in Marion, about twenty-five miles from here. Keep on the Hudlow till you git to the highway. Turn right and keep a-gitten it. You can't miss it."

Richard felt like a gift had been dropped in his lap. Mark's sister would know everything. Maybe he could convince her to talk to him. "Do you have an address and phone number for Anne? I definitely want to go see her. She'll know exactly when Mark and Carrie are coming."

"Never been to her house. Only seen her here or at the garden store. She owns Anne's Garden Center in Marion. It's on the right just before you get to town. You can't miss it. She'll be there."

Richard took his pies, said goodbye to his new friend, and headed to Marion.

## CHAPTER 24

DAVID STEPPED OFF the plane in Asheville, breathed a sigh of relief, and walked toward baggage claim. He was home—it was over—his life was again his to plan and live. Anne had wanted to meet him and again bring him back to Marion with her for a few days rest, but he didn't think it was a good idea for him to be alone with her; without Mark and Carrie there, Anne's reputation could be blemished in a small town like Marion, especially after all the publicity. For a while, he wanted to keep their relationship as quiet as possible. Just until things calmed down on the local scene. He didn't want his bad publicity to cause her any unnecessary grief. He was surprised there were no reporters waiting to accost him at baggage claim. Hopefully, Pete was right. The fickle public had moved on to today's big news story, which was the Greenstreet suicide. But as he turned around with his bag, a microphone was instantly in his face.

"What is your reaction to FBI Director Greenstreet's suicide?"

Before he could remember his planned answer, another reporter joined the first and asked, "Why do you think all charges were dropped against you?"

As David took a deep breath, he noticed a crowd gathering to see who he was and what he had to say. He closed his eyes and silently said a prayer. *Please, dear Lord, let this be over.*

*Help me to say the right thing.* "I was very saddened to hear about Director Greenstreet. We had only worked together for the past few months. I was transferred here from Kansas. I'm, of course, delighted to hear he dropped all charges and apologized to the President. I'm just sorry he didn't feel he could handle the fallout from this one misstep made hastily and obviously regretted. My heart goes out to his family. He was a good man and I highly respected him." David tried to pull away, but the two reporters had him hemmed in on either side.

"Is it true that you resigned before the charges were brought against you? Why did you resign from the bureau?"

"My resignation had nothing to do with Director Greenstreet. I'm making a career change; out of respect for Director Greenstreet, I waited until my last case was finished before announcing my intentions. I am moving into the field of Criminal Mind Study and will be working with the CIA when I've finished all my studies."

"Greenstreet accused you of killing those drug traffickers in cold blood. Why would he make an accusation like that, if it were not true?"

"My full report, along with Adam Bradford's report, has been thoroughly scrutinized and found accurate and truthful. The recent actions of Director Greenstreet indicate he was having difficulties of some kind. I can only conclude that he made a hasty mistake, which he regretted to such an extent that he felt he had to take his own life. That is all I have to say, and I wish you both a good day." David forced his way past the reporters, cameras, and the gathered crowd. Without looking back, he exited the airport to look for his SUV.

*

ANNE WAS EXPERIENCING mixed emotions. She was elated that the charges had been dropped, but saddened that David felt he needed to keep distance between them for a while. She remembered how, several months earlier, she had backed away from a closer relationship with Blake, fearing her reputation in the community would suffer. Was David being overly cautious because of the publicity surrounding him right now? Or was he afraid of making the same mistake that Blake had made? Anne pondered this, with a hose in hand, as she did the never-ending chore of watering plants. Deep in thought, Anne wondered whether David was home and hoped he would call her tonight. She looked up as a shadow crossed her face. An extremely nice-looking, young man was staring at her, probably wondering where her mind had wandered off to. "I'm sorry; may I help you?" she asked.

Richard could see the resemblance between Mark and Anne—that same self-assurance, those same deep blue eyes. He had been standing there for two minutes. She seemed in a trance as she automatically performed the mundane task of watering. "Performing boring chores does have its perks," he said. "You can let your mind wander. Are you Anne, Mark Goodman's sister?"

"Yes, I am. How do you know my brother?" A wave of caution came over her. David had warned her about reporters. For some reason, she immediately knew she did not trust this nice-looking young man. He was smooth and self-confident, with a little bit of sneaky thrown in for good measure. She instantly liked him, but she definitely did not trust him.

"I met Mark back in Kansas. My name is Richard Hoffman. I fell in love and married Carrie's office manager. We now live in New York. You may have heard Carrie talk about my wife Mazy?"

"Yes, yes, she has. It's nice to meet you, Richard; I'm Anne Goodman-Frost. I would offer my hand, but I'm afraid it's rather dirty from handling this hose. Carrie is working on a new book, and many times she has become frustrated and wished Mazy were here to help her through her stumbling blocks. Mark and Carrie have gone back to Mississippi. I'm afraid you've missed them."

"I know, but he told me about his new house. I was in the area, so I decided to see if I could find Dovecote. I did and met some very interesting people. Mr. Tate, Butch, and Ruby Morgan, and of course, Miss Minnie Sue Winkle, who asked me if I was coming to see you. I thought, 'Why not? It's on my way

## Vanished Sisters

back to Asheville.' Minnie Sue told me about the garden center, said I couldn't miss it. She was right. I'm staying with friends in Asheville, so I think I'll pick up a posy for my hostess while I'm here."

Anne felt obligated to offer him a bottled water and chat for a few minutes since he was a friend of Mark's. "Can I offer you a cool water in the shade before you select a plant?"

"That would be wonderful; lead the way."

After they were settled in her office with a bottle of ice-cold water, Richard immediately veered into a field of discussion Anne was not comfortable with, saying that Mark had told him about the drug traffickers and Carrie's kidnapping by terrorists.

Anne knew "terrorists" was a word Mark would never use, not with anyone except her, Carrie, Pete, and of course, David...but no one else. Was this guy a reporter? He could have gotten his information from poor, sweet, unsuspecting Minnie Sue or even Butch and Ruby. He was fishing and she was not going to bite.

"Carrie fell down a mountain, but I don't know where you got the idea she was kidnapped by terrorists. How ridiculous. Sounds like something Minnie Sue would conjure up. Her mind is not always in the present and, sometimes, not even in the realm of reality. But she is very sweet and makes delicious fried apple pies."

"Actually, I tried one of her pies and have two more in the car. They are out of this world."

"And so is her mind at times. I wouldn't put much store in her ramblings."

Richard knew he was being stonewalled, and it made him even more suspicious. When he had used the word "terrorist," Anne's eyes had dilated as she stared straight into his, looking to see whether she could read his mind. She wanted to know what he knew about the terrorists. She was a dead giveaway.

Richard tried a different tact. "I've been following the news, and this area is famous because of the huge drug bust and the accusations made by Director Greenstreet. Do you know this David Durham? The one accused of killing the drug traffickers in cold blood?"

Anne hid her trembling hands in her lap. She wanted to reach across her desk and cut his tongue out. What was he after? He was definitely after something. He was trying to elicit a reaction from her. She was afraid the expression on her face had betrayed her, but he would get no confirmation of that. How could she get rid of him? She needed to talk to Mark and David...now!

"Richard, I learned a long time ago that you can't believe everything you read in the papers or hear on the evening news. Politics has made its way into everything today. Now let's go see if we can find you a flower for your deserving hostess." She rose and opened the door for him to leave. She gave him no choice. As soon as she waved goodbye out front, she headed back to her office and called Mark.

Mark was livid and confirmed that Richard was a reporter for *The News*. Richard had not believed Mark and headed straight for Dovecote to see what he could garner from the locals. The fact that he used the word "terrorist" scared Mark. To tell the truth, Mark didn't understand why the public was being kept in the dark about the terrorists. If more people knew, they might be more apt to come forward and report unusual behavior and suspicious people. Mark didn't understand the reasoning behind the deception of the American people, but he had given his word, and he would respect that promise.

He told Anne he didn't think Richard would be back since she gave him no information. He praised her for doing a good job of not revealing anything and told her he would call David right away and warn him to expect Richard on his doorstep.

*

WHEN DAVID ANSWERED Mark's call, he was happy to hear from him. "I've missed you guys. How's our little mother doing?"

Mark gave him a glowing report of how Carrie had taken to motherhood and was being pampered by Aunt Mattie and Rosa. Then he quickly moved on to the problem of Richard Hoffman. David was upset to hear the reporter had tried to deceive Anne, but proud of how she had handled the rogue.

Mark explained how determined Richard could be when he was on the scent of a good story. "He's like a turtle who sinks his teeth into you and won't let go until it thunders. I'm not really clear why the American public needs to be kept in the dark on this, but that has been decided, and I, for one, don't want to be the one who lets that cat out of the bag.

"Richard smells a story, and the fact that he used the T-word tells us he either knows something or is trying to confirm what he has heard from the locals. He definitely thinks there may be a story here to snoop out. Either way, he won't be put off. My advice is to send him to Adam since the order not to use the T-word came from him."

David agreed, even though he knew the *word* came from the President, not Adam. He promised Mark he would call Adam as soon as they hung up. He and Mark talked for several minutes, discussing David's new lease on life and how things were finally turning around for him. "If you can take the time, bring Anne and come down for Christmas. Do you good to get out of there, relax, and have a few laughs. We would love to see you both. Let me know about Christmas and what Adam has to say about our tenacious friend."

\*

ADAM WAS NO stranger to Richard Hoffman. "He's like having two Geraldos rolled into one person. So, you're putting him on me?"

"No, I just want your advice on how to handle him. What do you want me to say and not say?"

"The order not to use the T-word, as you know, came from the top, and frankly, I agree with you and Mark. You can't keep this lid on forever. It's just a matter of time before they succeed in blowing up a major airport or government building. I guess they'll then have to admit the enemy is among us. Tell you what—you send him to me, and I'll send him straight to 1600 Pennsylvania Avenue. She's probably the only one who can keep Richard quiet. I guarantee that if any reporter can get in to see her, it's Richard.

"While I've got you on the horn, I was going to call you and congratulate us on our reprieve. Can you meet me in Washington next week? The boss wants to see us. It has something to do with your new position."

David was instantly nervous. He was afraid the CIA director would change his mind about hiring him because of all the publicity. It was standard procedure for the government to give you time to calm down after the hullaballoo and then hit you with a whammy. David made arrangements to meet Adam next Wednesday; he might as well get this over.

David then called Anne. He needed to hear her voice again. He so wanted to be near her, but right now, especially since reporters seemed to be coming out of the woodwork, he had to keep distance between them. He didn't want any more reporters down in Marion bothering her. Maybe getting away for Christmas would be a good idea. They could relax, away from Marion and the chance of running into reporters. He would run it by Anne.

She was thrilled with the trip to Mississippi. She would have him all to herself on the trip down and back. They made plans to meet at Sarah's apartment and leave Anne's car there. That way, if reporters were watching them, they would not be seen leaving together from Anne's house. Maybe by Christmas, all this would be old news.

\*

DAVID AGAIN TOOK the early flight to D.C. Adam met him at the airport and took him to his favorite hotel. They made plans to meet with the Director of the CIA at nine the next morning. They were going out tonight to have a few drinks and dinner to celebrate getting their lives back.

\*

# Vanished Sisters

DAMON WENTWORTH ALWAYS walked into a room with an air of superiority, confidence, and authority. Today, he left no doubt about any of the three aforementioned qualities. He would make a good President; he knew how to take charge and get things done. He immediately took charge of the meeting and got down to business. "David, good to see you again. I hope Adam is taking good care of you. He shook hands with both David and Adam. Didn't I tell you I had an ace up my sleeve? I knew if I gave them time to get overconfident and then hit them with Independent Counsel, they would panic and fold. I was not surprised at Greenstreet's reaction either. He was never up to the job, just a yes man for the President. Madam President likes pushing men around, and Greenstreet was only too happy to accommodate her.

"I asked you two here today to run something by you. The Study of the Criminal Mind is a needed and innovative way to read and understand a criminal's predicted behavior. It will aid law enforcement in apprehending the criminal before he can do the most damage. I want this program up and running as soon as possible.

"David, I know you need to finish the classes you're taking, and that's fine, but I want you on the payroll now, and I want the two of you meeting at least twice a month to start planning, organizing, and interviewing prospects for this project. When you finish your training, I want this program ready for you to step in and take control. Eventually, you will head a team that travels all over the world to crime scenes to obtain the needed information to hunt down and take into custody criminals who execute appalling crimes against humanity. Does this sound like something you two can handle?"

David was thrilled. This was just the kind of program he wanted to see in action, and he had lots of ideas about how to accomplish the results the director wanted. David looked at Adam and got a positive nod. "Yes, sir, Director; we can get started on our first planning session while we're here in D.C. Adam and I talked along these lines last night over dinner. I think we can put together some preliminary ideas for you to look at in the next couple of weeks."

The director was visibly pleased. "That's exactly what I wanted to hear, and I'll make myself available when you're ready to sit down and talk."

"Adam has informed me," the director continued, "that Richard Hoffman is trying to write a story on terrorists in this country and how they're operating under the radar. I think that's great, but we don't want him to know we think so. We're going to use him to get the story out without having to take heat from the President ourselves. David, this is a great chance for you to use your psychology techniques on this young man's brain. Let him come to you, and tell him, without telling him, where to find the information he needs to get this out to the American public."

David was grinning from ear to ear. He had been given permission to aid a reporter in writing a story that would wake up this country—just what Americans needed before they decided whom to vote for in the next election. "I'll do my best, sir."

\*

AFTER HIS MEETING, David called Mark for two reasons: first, to make arrangements for the Christmas festivities, and second, to enlist Mark's help in steering Richard in the direction they wanted him to go.

\*

RICHARD LEFT THE garden center with his flower for no one. What was he going to do with a flower when he didn't even have a room yet? His conversation with Anne was disappointing, but it made him even more convinced they were all hiding something. Maybe it was time to find David Durham, but he had one more trick he wanted to try on Mark after he checked out Poplar Creek.

Poplar Creek was no bigger on the map than Dovecote. There would be no hope of a room there. Between Marion and Poplar Creek was a place called Lake Lure. Richard followed the signs and found a room across from the beach and several restaurants. He had a nice trout dinner on the lake while watching the sunset behind a magnificent mountain range. He tried to put together the few facts he had garnered from the cautious avoidance of the facts. They didn't lie, just avoided the questions, usually by changing the subject. The accounts he heard in Dovecote couldn't be all imaginings. Butch and Minnie Sue actually concurred on their stories.

After dinner, he strolled down to the boat docks where you could rent rowboats and kayaks. An old man was hosing down the boats and checking to see that they were securely tied to the dock. Richard watched him for a while and walked over to ask about renting a boat. His real purpose was to talk to a local and get the local's opinion of the drug bust.

After the old man rattled off the rental fees, he asked Richard where he was from. "New York," Richard replied.

"We get people from all over, but not many from New York. Your family here with you?"

Richard decided to be truthful and admitted he was a reporter trying to find out the truth behind what had happened in Poplar Creek. The old man stared at him for a few seconds and asked what he meant by "the truth."

"I think the drug dealers were terrorists. What I do know is they were from the Middle East and they had an arsenal of weapons on that farm. I think they were selling drugs to finance the arms and plan attacks on Americans, but I can't prove it. I can't print it unless I have proof to back up my story. I'm going to go to Poplar Creek tomorrow and look around to see what I can find. What do the locals think happened there?"

"Well, I can tell you that you won't find anything on that property to back up your story. The house and barn have been leveled, bulldozed as if they were never there. The foreigners blew themselves, the house, and the barn to pieces when they realized they weren't going to escape. There won't be any clues there to find. Even the fields of marijuana were pulled up by the roots and the earth poisoned in case they missed a root."

"How do you know this?"

"The locals weren't ignorant of what was going on. Every weed smoker from Asheville to Marion was buying from a local farmer who helped himself at night. The fields weren't guarded, and they were everywhere. The farmer knew how to dry and refine it and make it into joints, as well as many other forms. It's much safer to buy from a local grower than take a chance on the stuff coming up from Mexico, which could have anything in it and has been known to make people sick. No one would tell because the weed was cheap and good. You need to go see Rupert McKinsey. He has a farm, if you can call it that, in the next valley, south of the farm in question. He shares your opinion and may be able to help you."

"Why didn't the locals just buy from the foreigners?"

"They sold the whole plant to refiners and wanted no contact with the locals. They wanted as little attention brought on themselves as possible. According to Rupert, they made meth too, but they never sold it locally. They sold to big distributors up north." The old man drew Richard a map to Rupert's place.

\*

RUPERT MCKINSEY SAT on the front porch of a dilapidated farmhouse, which was so far back in the woods that Richard thought, several times, he must be lost. Mr. McKinsey relaxed in a vinyl recliner that had once graced his parlor but had since been recycled to the front porch. As Richard stepped from his car, he could hear Rupert snoring fifty yards away. His beard rested on his obese stomach, which was clad in bib overalls, with no shirt, and opened on the sides to accommodate his rotund physique. His bare feet, with toenails curled over the ends of his toes, were propped up as high as the recliner would allow. A double barrel shotgun rested by his side—the ultimate picture of tranquility.

Richard stood still when he saw the shotgun. Should he clear his throat? Should he call out his name? As he decided the best way to wake Mr. McKinsey, an aging hound dog raised his head from the porch floor and let out a howl that would wake the dead. Rupert, in one fluid motion, stood, grabbed his shotgun, and pointed it at Richard.

Richard raised his hands and announced. "I'm Richard

Hoffman with *The News* in New York City. Mr. Brad Bowers in Lake Lure said I should talk to you. I'm unarmed and only want to talk about the drug bust."

Rupert relaxed. He liked being interviewed. Richard wasn't the first reporter to come-a-calling. "Thought at air wus old news?"

"No," Richard smiled. "We now think those foreigners might have been terrorists."

"Well, hell; I done told 'um at."

"Maybe those reporters didn't want to believe you, but I do, and I want to hear why you think they were terrorists."

An hour later, Richard left with a notebook full of notes, a smile on his face, and a renewed spring in his step. The next morning, he checked out of the hotel and headed south to Mississippi.

\*

MARK DISMISSED HIS class and gathered his notes as he left the classroom to meet Pete for lunch in the cafeteria. He was taken by surprise as he came face to face with Richard Hoffman. He thought to himself, *Oh, shit*, but he remembered his conversation with David. He didn't need to lie to Richard. Well, not unless you call setting up someone a lie. Pete was in on the scam, so Mark asked Richard to join them for lunch.

Pete was waiting outside the cafeteria and looked worried when he saw Richard and Mark coming toward him. He locked eyes with Mark and received the nod, which meant, *Show time*. Richard shook hands with Pete, and they all took a tray and headed down the chow line. They settled in the faculty dining room where they had reasonable privacy.

Mark asked Richard if he was still on the trail of terrorists in North Carolina. "Actually," Richard smiled, "I've found them.... All I need is validation." Richard began his story: "I have a witness who was a local convert to Islam. He was a heavy marijuana and meth user and easily brainwashed by the brothers of Islam. They were preparing him to be a suicide bomber and also took advantage of his ability to make methamphetamines.

"According to his father, he got cold feet and ran. The FBI surveillance team took him into protective custody. After the drug bust, they questioned him extensively and released him. He had no place to go and no money. His only option was to go home. He told his father what the cell of terrorists were up to, so his father sent him to Tennessee to live with his aunt for a while. He was to hide there until they were sure no other terrorists were operating in the area."

Mark was not expecting this. He knew the boy had escaped from the cell. This was the key reason the terrorists stepped up their plans, causing the authorities to move in. "How did you find the boy?" Mark asked.

"So you don't deny he exists and you knew?"

"I don't think we should talk about this here. Why don't you go on out to the house and see Carrie. I'll call her and tell her you're coming and staying for dinner. Pete and I have two classes this afternoon, but we should be there around three. We'll talk then. And to answer your question, yes, we knew about the boy and the terrorists, and we need to get something straight right now. What we say cannot come back to haunt us. Because of our jobs in this liberal institution, we never spoke to you. Is that understood?"

"Completely.... I was never here."

Mark and Pete cancelled their next class and barricaded themselves in Pete's office on a conference call with David.

David was surprised the boy had surfaced. This would take the burden of the story leak from the shoulders of the CIA and FBI. They needed to think of a way to direct him to the President without involving Adam or David. When the story broke, David wanted blame going straight to Pennsylvania Avenue. He wanted to make sure Madam President couldn't shift the blame to the CIA or the FBI.

The only way to do that was for Richard to see a copy of David's report confirming Greenstreet's statement that the order to stand down came from the President. He also needed to see the report where the CIA appointed Independent Counsel to question the President as to why she had told Greenstreet to order a stand-down. David also needed somehow to let Richard know the order to eliminate the word "terrorist" from all reports came from the President. He had nothing on paper to prove that, but he knew who did. Greenstreet for sure had a copy of the order. Maybe, if he packed up all his personal documents and sent them home before he committed suicide, his wife might have the proof Richard needed. Richard knew the rest of the story. Greenstreet was fired...the lawsuit dropped...Director committed suicide...end of story.

David was quiet for a minute, and then he told Mark and Pete to send Richard to him. "I think I know how to accomplish our objective. Tell him I'm distrustful of reporters and would never give him an interview, but if he just showed up at my apartment, he could probably talk his way in because I'm really a pushover. Tell him he needs to get up to Asheville tomorrow because I'm headed to Washington day after tomorrow. That way, it'll look as if I wasn't prepared for him and had not had time to remove all evidence from my desk. Richard, being a snooping reporter with no scruples whatsoever, will see what we want him to see. And he will never have to admit he snooped where he should not have snooped. I have a plan I think will give him time to find everything he needs without being discovered."

\*

EVERYONE WAS ON the porch having iced tea when Mark and Pete arrived. Carrie, Richard, and Aunt Mattie were repeating the Kansas story to Rosa, who was trying not to let on that she had heard it many times. Rosa was a good soul.

Mark and Pete thought they had their story straight, and they wanted to get this behind them. When they joined the group, Rosa jumped up to get them an iced tea. They spent a delightful afternoon sipping tea and catching up on each other's lives. Mark hoped they could get through this and remain good friends for Mazy and Carrie's sake.

\*

AFTER DINNER, THE three men went into Mark's

home office and shut the door. Richard continued his story. He explained how he had found Rupert McKinsey, who had told him about his son and his near fatal escape from the terrorist cell. While Richard was there, Rupert had called his son and confirmed that Richard would come to Tennessee to interview him about his time spent with the terrorists. His name and face would not be revealed, and he would be paid for the interview. The young man confirmed he had knowledge of weapons and plans to bomb the Charlotte and Raleigh airports.

"Why," Pete had to ask, "didn't the father report this information to the authorities?"

"Because he was making a fortune stealing marijuana from the fields at night, refining it into many forms, and selling the stuff to locals from Asheville to Greensboro. He made so much money; he will never need to work another day of his life. He is perfectly happy to sit on the front porch of his dilapidated house, sip moonshine, smoke weed, and nap. He's in hog heaven."

"What do you need from us?" asked Mark, venturing into dark waters.

"I need to be able to verify his story with government documents. If this young man is as backwoods as his pappy, the whole story could be dismissed as a fabrication by an over-zealous reporter—me. My reputation as a creditable, knowledgeable journalist would be ruined. I can't go with this story unless I can prove the government agencies knew they were dealing with terrorists."

"So you need something stating that the President knew and ordered the stand-down?"

Richard's eyes bulged. "What...did you say?"

Mark and Pete stared at each other as if afraid they had said the wrong thing. No one said a word for a whole minute. Mark then said. "I think you need to go talk to David Durham. I think we have said too much. We need to stay out of this. We were just technicians used to process the crime scenes. We have no access to documents, and we don't want to get ourselves involved in this story. We gave depositions for the would-be trial and expected to be called to testify in court, but that was the extent of our involvement.

"David could help you, but he's in a scary position, and so far, he has kept the real story quiet. Greenstreet ordered the FBI to stand down and said the order came straight from the President. He wasn't supposed to say that. The President didn't give him permission to let anyone know she was involved. He thought it would make him sound important and close to the President to add that she had personally ordered the stand-down."

"This is monumental. It could affect the next election. How can I get my hands on those documents?"

"We can't help you there. The President is also the one who ordered that the word "terrorist" be eliminated from any press releases. The public was to be kept in the dark. She felt it would cause panic. I know David Durham didn't agree, but he had no choice but to follow orders. The CIA also disagreed with her, but its hands were tied. David is very leery of reporters. If you call ahead, he will not give you an interview. But, I think, if you just show up on his doorstep, you can talk your way in, and he might have some suggestions on who and where to look for proof. I can't promise, but I think it's worth a try. What do you think, Pete?"

"I think David's a push-over. He avoids reporters like the plague, but I've noticed that when he is cornered by one, he usually cooperates, within reason. Richard can talk his way in, I'm sure of it. Isn't he going back to Washington soon?"

"Yes, day after tomorrow," Mark answered. "Can you get up to Asheville tomorrow?"

Richard had taken the bait—hook, line, and sinker. He was practically on his way. Mark and Pete decided to shut up while they were ahead. As soon as Richard's car pulled away from the curb, Mark called David and warned him that Richard was on the way. David would be ready and waiting.

*

DAVID'S NEIGHBOR HAD been alerted. She had agreed to help. David explained the situation and what was needed of her. She was elderly and always home. David often helped her with getting groceries up to her apartment. In return, she collected his mail and paper when he was away. He trusted Maud; she was a retired court recorder and had given David advice when he had needed to testify in court.

*

THE NEXT DAY when his buzzer rang, David was ready. His desk was cluttered and his computer was on. He called Maud and quickly said he thought this might be the man. David hit the button to release the lock on the downstairs door. He heard someone coming up the stairs. As David answered the knock, Maud came out into the hall and said, "David, I need your help for a minute. It's that troublesome commode; it's stopped up again; please hurry."

David looked at Richard and then at Maud. "Stay here; I'll be right back," he told Richard. David hurried to Maud's, leaving Richard standing in the hall with his apartment door ajar.

Richard pushed the door all the way open and looked inside. He immediately saw the cluttered desk with the computer staring at him. He knew unplugging a commode would take at least a couple of minutes, so he ran to the computer. He made a few clicks and was into David's personal files in seconds. He searched quickly for daily reports and clicked again. As he scanned the reports, he knew the one he wanted would be the last or next to the last report sent to Greenstreet. He kept one ear on the hall, but he heard no one coming. He clicked on the ones he wanted and hit "copy." It only took seconds for the copier to spit out the last two reports. Another click and he was back to the screensaver. He shoved the reports in his briefcase and returned to the hall where he was leaning patiently on the doorframe when David came out of Maud's apartment, drying his hands on a paper towel.

"Sorry about that; were you looking for me?"

"Yes, I'm Richard Hoffman with *The News*. Could I ask you a couple questions?"

David frowned and acted irritated. "Only a couple; I'm

very busy finishing a paper for a class I'm taking."

"I understand completely. I talked with Dr. Mark Goodman yesterday; we know each other from Kansas."

"Really? I'm from Kansas, and that's where I met Mark."

"That must be why he sent me to you. I've had a young man contact me who swears he worked for the drug traffickers in Poplar Creek. I'm going out to interview him tomorrow. He says the drug traffickers were actually a terrorist cell. They were here to blow up the Charlotte and Raleigh airports. He claims this cell had extensive weapons, including a shoulder-held grenade launcher. Can you confirm or deny his story?"

David stared at Richard and pretended to be having an inner "come to Jesus" meeting with himself. After a minute of silence, Richard cleared his throat and added, "I take it you either don't want to answer, or you can't answer; am I right?"

"You're right. I can neither confirm nor deny this young man's story."

"By refusing to confirm or deny, you have confirmed his story. I respect the position this must put you in, so I would only ask one other question: Whom should I go to for validation?"

"If I were you, I'd pay Mrs. Greenstreet a visit. Before Director Greenstreet committed suicide, he had everything in his office packed up and sent to his home. I've heard that Mrs. Greenstreet was ordered to return those files or a court order would be obtained. She's a very smart lawyer and might be willing to help you, but you didn't hear it from me."

"Thank you, Mr. Durham. Be assured; I always protect my sources. I will not bother you further." Richard could not believe his luck. He was on the next plane to Washington, D.C.

*

THE GREENSTREET RESIDENCE was a fortress with a guard. Richard pulled up to the gate. This was not going to be easy. The armed guard stood stalwart at Richard's window and ordered him to reveal his name and state his business within.

"I'm Richard Hoffman, and I have information about the terrorists Director Greenstreet was searching for when he died."

He hoped the word "terrorist" would interest Mrs. Greenstreet enough to let him in.

The guard did not answer, but he went to a phone and called inside. He talked for a short time and then returned to the car. "I will accompany you to the house."

He went around the car and got in the other side. Richard was uncomfortably conscious of the revolver resting at his side. The gate opened, and Richard drove slowly up the drive as the gate ominously closed behind them. There was a rock in the pit of his stomach.

A butler answered the door and escorted them to a huge mahogany-paneled office. The house was as quiet as a tomb. Richard entered. The guard firmly closed the door behind him and Richard could feel his sentinel presence on the other side of the door. *Why do I feel trapped here, never again to see the light of day? I've handled lawyers before; I can do this,* Richard thought.

Mrs. Greenstreet was tall, thin, and unattractive. Her eyes were piercing and black. Her mouth puckered, accentuating her sharp, narrow nose. She glared at Richard, and he stared back to show he was not intimidated. For several heartbeats, they continued with this staring contest until finally she said, "I know who you are. You're with *The News*, and I have nothing to say to you."

Richard thought to himself, *If she had nothing to say to me, she wouldn't have let me in, in the first place.* He took a deep breath and began. "I know the President caused your husband to commit suicide. She used him to keep the truth from the American people. The order to stand down and not use the word 'terrorist' came from her. I have a young man who was a local convert and lived with the Poplar Creek cell. He has agreed to be interviewed, for a price, and he has admitted they were terrorists and planning an attack on the Charlotte and Raleigh airports.

"What I need from you is documentation that he's telling the truth." He sat perfectly still and let this information sink in. He was not going to say another word until she either threw him out or agreed to help him. They stared for more heartbeats, and the rock in Richard's stomach grew heavier. He wished he had taken time to eat lunch. After a full minute, his stomach growled loudly and a smile cracked Mrs. Greenstreet's face.

"Where is this young man?"

"I can't tell you. I fly out to meet with him as soon as I see evidence that he's telling the truth."

"He is, and I have the proof you need. I will help you. I will do anything to show the world the kind of power-hungry woman who defiles our White House. My husband was a smart man, but his narcissism ruled him. He made foolish decisions, hoping to advance his self-importance and career. It was his downfall."

# CHAPTER 25

THE TOUGHEST ANCHOR for *The News* was Phil O'Malley. Phil asked the questions every other anchor didn't have the nerve to ask. When he asked a question, he already knew the answer, or at least the answer he wanted. If he didn't get it, he not only butted in and answered for the guest, but he also insisted the guest agree with him. Even though Phil and Richard were on the same side, Richard was scared senseless. Phil was arrogant. He surrounded himself with an unapproachable attitude to keep everyone at arm's length. No one dare question his authority.

For two months, they worked together to prepare for this news special. A team of lawyers worked round the clock to authenticate the documents and ensure the station had the legal right to break this story to the public. Finally, they were given the okay to proceed.

The news special was advertised for weeks in advance, but the content was only hinted at. The station wanted the content to be a total surprise. They feared if the political world knew what was coming, it would try to stop the show from airing.

The news special began with Phil O'Malley, alone and somber, as the camera panned in to a close-up of his face. Phil looked straight into the camera and began: "*The News* has uncovered a national scandal, the magnitude of which is mind-boggling. Tonight we bring this scandal to the attention of the

## Vanished Sisters

American people. This station has always prided itself on reporting the truth, no matter how ugly or controversial. We give you, our followers, the facts and opinions from both sides of any issue and allow our supporters to make up their own minds.

"Tonight's story has only one viewpoint because you already know one side of the story. Our task tonight is to prove to you, the public, that...it was all a lie. The American people have been deceived. This administration has given the nation a false sense of security, because, it says, the public will panic if it knows the truth. Panic or not, tonight the public will hear the truth.

"Richard Hoffman," the camera panned wider to show Richard sitting beside Phil, "who is a top reporter for *The News*, has been working on this story for months. He first became suspicious when the story broke of a multi-organizational sting, which received national attention.

"Recently, a small war was waged in the quiet, little village of Poplar Creek, North Carolina. The CIA, FBI, SBI, and local police joined forces to eradicate a huge marijuana and methamphetamine operation. At least that is what the public was told, but we have, as Paul Harvey would say, 'the rest of the story.' Was this really just a routine drug bust, or was there much more to this story? Tonight, Richard Hoffman will share with you 'the rest of the story.'" The camera zoomed in on Richard as he began his story of how he, piece by piece, uncovered the huge conspiracy.

Richard began by first re-running clips from the news coverage of the Poplar Creek drug sting. He presented the news clips in order to give the public a summary of how the sting played out and the consequential arrests of David Durham and Adam Bradford. "I first became suspicious when I saw this clip," said Richard as he rolled the film of the farmer being interviewed. "The farmer stated that he 'knew those foreigners were up to no good.' Nowhere else, in the entire coverage of this drug bust, were the perpetrators referred to as foreigners. I decided to find this farmer, as well as other locals, and ask them to describe these foreigners to me. Here are several clips of interviews with local people."

The farmer turned out to be Rupert McKinsey, Sr. His face was blurred out and his statement was short and to the point. "They was A-rabs, and I knowed they was up to no good."

The next face seen was that of Butch Morgan, saying, "They looked like people from the Middle East. They just appeared one day, and no one knew where they lived or why they were here."

Next were two FBI agents who agreed to be interviewed, but insisted their identities be protected. Each admitted it was common knowledge to the CIA, FBI, SBI, and Homeland Security that these were indeed Muslim Extremists.

And then the blurred face of Rupert McKinsey, Jr., saying, "They were terrorists and planned to blow up the airports in Raleigh and Charlotte. I was a converted Muslim, a member of their terrorist cell. They were grooming me to be a human bomb."

The interview with Rupert McKinsey, Jr. (better known as Ruppie) was professional from start to finish. With face blurred and voice altered, he told his story. Richard had worked for hours to help him come across as intelligent and truthful. He was glad the public couldn't see his pimply, weasel face or hear his mountain twang. His story, while sad, was intended to awaken and shock the public. It unmistakably demonstrated how easily an unloved loner, who was unaccepted by his peers, could be turned into a human bomb.

Ruppie held his head down as his story evolved. About a year ago, he had converted to the Muslim religion. The local mosque taught him to pray and read the Koran. It also instilled in him how highly worshipped and revered were the martyrs of the Muslim religion. He had finally found a group of caring friends who loved and accepted him into their inner circle. For the first time in his life, he belonged. It didn't take long before Ruppie wanted to impress his new friends with his decision to be a human bomb. They would never forget him, and he would, for eternity, be among the most honored in not only his mosque but the entire Muslim religion.

When the terrorists arrived in Poplar Creek, they prayed with Ruppie at his mosque. He finally achieved his ultimate goal.

He was asked to join a terrorist cell and become a respected member. His talents as a methamphetamine technician (the title he was awarded) gave him even more importance in the cell. He worked hard and never left the farmhouse. The terrorists constantly praised him and spoke of the time when he could truly prove his value to Allah. His martyrdom would place him on the highest level of religious importance. His reward in heaven would far exceed anything his human brain could imagine. Ruppie was being brainwashed.

He told of the weapons the cell purchased with the money they received from the sale of drugs. He was allowed to touch the weapons. He was privy to their plans, which made him feel important. Ruppie shared with Richard their plans to blow up airports, taking as many casualties as possible. At that point in time, he truly believed the infidels needed to die.

He had volunteered to stay behind and guard the house. He was honored when selected to remain behind, while the rest of the cell traveled to see the target sites. It also made him aware of how close they were to actually accomplishing their goal. Then it suddenly dawned on him that he was going to die. He had always been afraid of dying. He knew there was no turning back. This was his only chance to change his mind. There was no doubt in his mind he would not be allowed to live if he backed out now. He had witnessed the killing of a fellow convert who had questioned the terrorists' motives. If he wanted to live, now was his only chance to get away. Ruppie decided to run.

FBI agents working in the fields and pretending to be members of the terrorists' cell immediately arrested him. They told him he would be protected from the terrorists if he told them all he knew. He cooperated, and they released him after the devastating confrontation with the extremists.

The FBI was convinced Ruppie had been brainwashed and now saw the error of his ways. He went straight to his father and explained what he had done. His father had no idea his son was living with the very people he was stealing marijuana from. Realizing the danger Ruppie was in, he hid him and slipped him out that night, across the mountains on trails known only by mountain men. He made his way to Tennessee, where he would hide until his father was sure there were no other terrorists in the area. His father had told him how close he had come to being killed. He had described to him the confrontation between the terrorists and government agencies the night following Ruppie's arrest.

Ruppie explained how his Pa had stolen marijuana from the fields at night and sold the refined product to locals. His father was a simple man, he told Richard, and didn't want to give up the chance to make big money, so he didn't report the marijuana fields to the police. He had no idea the marijuana growers were terrorists planning to bomb local airports. He only knew they were foreigners.

Phil O'Malley took over again. He explained the terrorists' decision to escalate their plans to bomb the Charlotte airport and move to a new safe house, causing the CIA to take immediate action. He described the battle, which ensued. Documents, provided by Mrs. Greenstreet, were then read, giving a moment-by-moment commentary from the time the terrorists were found in Dovecote, through the decision to take out the cell.

Richard then explained these reports in further detail. He took the audience through the order given to Director Greenstreet to stand down by the President of the United States. He explained the CIA's rescinding of that order, because it was based on false information, and the subsequent arrest of two agents as a result of disobeying Greenstreet's order.

Richard told how he, with a little help from Mrs. Greenstreet, approached several agents involved in the sting. Two were convinced to come forward and be interviewed. Again, faces were blurred and voices altered as the agents confirmed both David Durham and Adam Bradford's reports as being accurate records of how the bust went down. Both agents had been observing the terrorists for weeks as the Dovecote cell joined the Boone cell and then moved again to join another smaller cell in Poplar Creek. They also confirmed that Ruppie had ransacked the house, tried to run with a sack over his back, and was arrested for his own protection.

Mrs. Greenstreet was also interviewed. She stated she believed her husband sent pertinent documentation home to her, before he committed suicide, because he wanted the truth to come out. She testified that the new acting director for the FBI had ordered her to turn those papers over, or a warrant would be obtained.

The documents confirmed the President had informed Director Greenstreet that he was the senior authority in charge of the combined agencies. The President ordered Greenstreet (against normal protocol) to advise the FBI and CIA to stand down because the CIA had agents imbedded in the Boone Cell. A second report from the CIA proved the President had been informed, days before, that the agents were already dead. She ordered a stand-down anyway, for no reason, which could have resulted in the bombing of two airports, if the order had been followed.

Mrs. Greenstreet also stated the FBI, CIA, and Homeland Security, in a private meeting with the President, were told to avoid using the word "terrorist" in any report to be shared with the media. She had documented proof.

As the report ended, many news clips from various stations were shown as they reported the killing of drug traffickers in Poplar Creek, North Carolina. The word "terrorist" was never mentioned in any of the clips from previous broadcasts. Phil O'Malley concluded the report by thanking Richard for his efforts to bring this to the attention of the American people.

*

THE SPECIAL REPORT aired during the holidays. Carrie and Mark were hosting a family weekend. They all watched the special report and were pleased with Richard's commentary. David, Mark, and Pete were relieved that the truth was finally revealed, so they no longer needed to feel secretive about their part in the confrontation with Muslim extremists. No one knew what the fall-out from the report would encompass. Time would tell. The ball was now in the public's court. They hoped the public outcry would call for the President's resignation and impeachment. At the very least, David felt sure her re-election was unattainable.

Mark's parents were visiting, as well as Anne and David. They were impressed with the entire news special. When they switched channels, they were not surprised how quickly the other news agencies were picking up the report and showing major clips that repeated the story. David was sure the Independent Counsel would be renamed immediately. The President would be forced to answer questions about her decisions and whether campaign contributions from Middle Eastern countries had influenced those decisions.

\*

FOR ANNE, THE trip to Mark and Carrie's house had been wonderful. It was the most time alone she had ever had with David. They talked about their dreams for the future. Anne's first marriage came up and she was as honest as possible. Ken had been her first love and she would never forget him. David seemed to accept this without feeling jealous of her memories.

Anne's parents were meeting David for the first time, and they seemed to get along great. Anne noticed, at one point, her father and David on the front porch, having a serious conversation. It made her a little nervous, but she took it as a good sign.

Carrie was so happy to have everyone together for the first time. She had not slowed down since the casts were removed. She was editing her new novel, which she had been working on, non-stop, while recovering from broken bones. She became proficient at typing with her index fingers. She had five more weeks to go. She wanted this novel ready for the publisher. Once the babies arrived, there would be no time for writing.

After dinner, everyone gathered around the tree to open presents. It was the week after Christmas, but this was the weekend everyone could get together. The real Christmas had been a week earlier with just Carrie, Mark, Tucker, and Aunt Mattie. Rosa always visited her sons for Christmas. As Carrie handed out presents, she had her first labor pain. She reached for Mark's hand and doubled over. He helped her to a chair. Christmas was forgotten as everyone focused on Carrie and, with much confusion, decided to get her to the hospital to be checked out.

## Vanished Sisters

The waiting room was crowded, but no one was leaving until they knew Carrie and the babies were okay. She was five weeks early, which worried everyone, especially Mark. Then her pains stopped after having only two in one hour. The doctor announced they were false labor pains, due to the excitement of having the whole family together. He decided to keep her overnight for observation just to be on the safe side. Mark stayed with her and sent everyone home, promising to call if there were any change.

Around three in the morning, one of the babies developed a rapid heartbeat, so the decision was made to perform a cesarean section. Things began to happen rapidly, and before Mark knew it, they were wheeling Carrie into surgery. When they closed the surgery doors and left him to wait alone, he was faced again with possibly losing Carrie and one or both of the babies.

He called Anne, told her what was going on, and suggested she and their mother come on down, adding, "I'm not sure we can get everyone in this small waiting room. Why don't we call and wake everyone when the babies are here?" Anne agreed. She tiptoed into her mom and dad's room and quietly woke her mom. They managed to slip out of the house without waking anyone. When they arrived, the doctor was with Mark. They waited outside the glassed waiting area, trying to read the expression on Mark's face. He looked serious, but not sad. Anne and her mother bit their nails and waited for the doctor to leave.

Mark motioned for them to come in. "Would you explain this one more time for my mom and sister. I'm afraid I need to hear it again, too."

"Sure," the doctor began at the beginning. "We have identical twin girls. Both survived the cesarean section, both Mom and girls are doing fine. The babies are very small and one has a heart murmur, which could be temporary. We have moved all three to ICU as a precautionary measure. Carrie will be moved to a regular room probably in a few hours. The girls will remain in ICU for a couple days. One is three pounds and the other is three-and-a-half, very small, but not critical. They should both be fine.

"We just want to be cautious, especially for the first twenty-four hours. I'm going to let Mark in to see them, but no one else just yet. He can take their first pictures and send them to everyone. As soon as the girls have recovered from the trauma of a cesarean birth, a barrage of tests will follow to make sure each baby is perfectly normal. They're both receiving nourishment through IVs and breathing on their own. There is no reason to be pessimistic. You have two fine but very small daughters."

As the doctor left, Anne noticed her dad and David peering through the glass looking very anxious. She gestured to them and they quickly joined the others. The situation was explained again, and then Mark said, "Now I have to go see Catherine and Elaine."

"Elaine?" said his mom, stunned to hear her own name.

"Yes, Mom," he said, kissing her on the cheek. "The girls are named after you and Carrie's mother."

Then Mark left to go see his new family.

\*

THE GLASS-ENCASED little room beeped, buzzed, hummed, and blinked. How could Carrie be sleeping with this cacophony of instruments, each playing its own tune? Mark washed his hands and was given a sterile gown to place over his street clothes. He eased quietly into Carrie's room, leaned over, and kissed her forehead. Her bright blue eyes popped open. "Have you seen the girls?"

Mark smiled to himself. For the rest of their lives, they would be known as "the girls." *Where are the girls? Call the girls to dinner. Are the girls home yet?* He felt so happy, so blessed. "No, I had to see how Mommy was doing first."

"I'll call the nurse; maybe they'll let me go with you to see them."

The nurse helped Carrie sit up and draped her with a sterile gown. The babies would be brought to her, one at a time. The Neonatal Intensive Care Unit nurse would help her try to feed the girls for the first time.

When the first baby arrived, Mark was allowed to hold her for a minute. "Which one is this," asked Mark, "Catty or Laney?"

Carrie looked confused. "I don't know; how will we tell them apart?"

The nurse handed Mark two bracelets, one for Catherine and one for Elaine. "Problem solved," the nurse smiled at them. "These will go around their ankles for now, and by the time they need a bigger one, you'll have learned to tell them apart."

Mark held out the tiny little foot while the nurse clipped the bracelet on. "This is Catty," he said as he placed her at Carrie's side. He moved to the other side and the nurse helped Carrie try to get Catty to latch on to the breast for the first time.

Catty, no bigger than your hand, rooted around, grunted like a puppy, and finally found the nipple. Carrie's eyes grew big. She laughed and cried at the same time. Mark had tears in his own eyes as Catty held on to his little finger and wouldn't let go while she tried to get nourishment from her mommy. Mark couldn't help but remember the vision he'd had of how the baby would look. His memory also went back to Tucker's birth, remembering how his first wife refused to have anything to do with Tucker because he was born with Down syndrome. The love Mark felt at this moment as he watched Carrie nurse their little daughter was overwhelming.

"The sucking will help stimulate milk production," the nurse explained. "By tomorrow, you will feel the milk coming in, and the nursing will ease the uncomfortable fullness."

The same procedure was repeated with Laney, which left Carrie exhausted. She immediately went to sleep, knowing the girls were back in the NICU being cared for. Mark slipped out of the room to give the family the good news. Both girls were very small, hungry, and doing fine.

The waiting area had gotten more crowded as Aunt Mattie, Pete, and Tucker joined the rest of the family. Mark showed pictures of Catty and Laney on his cell phone. Everyone drooled over them and couldn't believe how small they were. Tucker was totally confused about why they were so small, but he was sure the two new sisters were his presents from Santa Claus.

Santa must have forgotten to leave them on Christmas Eve.

Carrie was moved to a private room that afternoon, and everyone took turns slipping in to say hello. Even Pete slipped in as a relative with an arm full of roses. Carrie would come home in a couple of days, but the girls would stay a week or until they each gained up to five pounds with no complications. Laney's heart murmur had disappeared as predicted, and both girls passed their tests and were pronounced healthy, but very small.

*

DAVID AND ANNE left for home the next day. They were in no hurry and had mapped out a scenic route far from the busy interstates. They stopped in several small towns to wander the gift shops, looking for the perfect gift for Carrie and the girls. They talked of funny things and serious things. They acknowledged that even though they had been friends for several months, they really didn't know each other. Each was sure of his or her love for the other, but wanted time to be sure. Neither was in any hurry to rush into anything. David would be busy going back and forth to Washington, setting up the new division for the CIA, while finishing his classes at UNC-Asheville.

Anne would concentrate on her business, while David finished his studies. Each knew deep down that things were going to work out for them. Right now, she had to be patient; their whole future depended on this new venture David was pursuing. They planned to email and talk daily. Anne agreed to come to Asheville for dinner when he had a free evening, and he promised to come to Marion when he had a free weekend. Their time together would be sporadic but cherished.

*

WHEN THE GIRLS were two months old, Mark and Carrie called Anne to say they were coming up to check on the house. Tucker wanted to see the house and hoped Aunt Anne would have snow so he could make a snowman. Anne, who hadn't held a baby since Tucker was born, went into panic mode, trying to get everything ready for the twins and Tucker. Anne need not have worried because Carrie had everything under control. The girls slept together in one portable bed in Mark and Carrie's room. Carrie was still feeding the girls once in the middle of the night. Tucker had become very protective of the girls and considered them his personal responsibility.

David was able to spend time with Anne and the family while Mark and Carrie were there. They were both mesmerized by the babies. Anne carried one all the time, and David had the other. Carrie had been substituting a bottle of formula occasionally to give herself a chance to get a sitter and begin a writing course she had planned to take.

David and Anne each had a baby, a bottle, and a rocking chair. They were babysitting while Mark and Carrie took Tucker to see the new summerhouse. "Do you think we'll make good parents?" David asked out of the blue.

Anne had to smile at his remark. "Of course we will. I just hope we aren't too old to experience this for ourselves."

David smiled at her. "We will experience this, I promise."

\*

THE NEW HOUSE was under roof, so Mark and Carrie could walk through and see the different rooms. It looked so big. Now the carpenters would be able to work on the house all winter. Hopefully, in the spring, they could start moving things in. Between the furniture Mattie had shipped from her house in Kansas and Carrie's own furniture, they had enough to furnish the entire house. It sat in storage, where it had been since Mark and Carrie's marriage. Aunt Mattie had planned to go into a retirement community, but somehow, she had never made the move. Mark, Carrie, and Tucker liked having her with them.

Carrie walked through the new house, placing furniture in her mind. If the weather held, they would spend this coming summer in their new home. She was so happy with the quality of workmanship she saw all through the house. Anne was their landscape artist; she had already designed flowerbeds and natural areas around the house.

Pete made the decision to retire at the end of the school semester. He was as excited about moving to the mountains as they were. He spent as much time with the girls and Tucker as he could. God had been good to him and given him a second chance to have a family. That day in Kansas when he had walked up to Aunt Mattie's porch and shaken Carrie's hand for the first time, it had felt like coming home. Somewhere, long ago, in his mind's eye, he had seen this house, the twin girls, and Aunt Mattie, all there in this summerhouse in the mountains. Had it been a premonition, or just a hopeful dream come true?

*

THE INDEPENDENT COUNSEL was in full swing. The President had fought the situation with every ounce of pull she had, only to be stonewalled. Her own party did not want her to win re-election. Everyone wondered whether impeachment would be an option, but no one wanted to predict the outcome.

The Secret Service was having a rough time with her. She was not in the greatest mood of late, and she took it out on the agents. Her temper tantrums were more frequent, and she defied those, who were supposed to protect her—in every way she could. Her team of lawyers frequented the White House daily, and daily, one could hear things breaking in the Oval Office. Copies replaced many of the valuable artifacts (especially those small enough to throw) in her office and private rooms to protect them for posterity. Her poor husband, showing signs of senility, took to his own rooms and avoided her whenever possible. He was too embarrassed to go out in public. The special report had aired months ago. Since then, the news agencies had reported her every move. The public was angry and wanted her out of the White House.

The President had filed lawsuits against *The News* after the Special Report had aired and was picked up by every other news agency. The station's lawyers had expected this reaction and were prepared. After the Special Report aired, the country was in outrage. How dare the government hide the fact that terrorists were plotting destruction in every state in this country? The latest polls indicated a whopping 70 percent of voters wanted her impeached. Her own party begged her to resign quietly and avoid the public display of all the illegal donations she had accepted. Like many before her, she thought the President of the United States could do as he or she pleased. No one would dare question the President.

Just before her appointed appearance before the Independent Counsel, the President faced the nation in a hurriedly announced news conference. She looked frazzled, her face swollen from crying. Stone-faced, her husband stood beside her and looked off into the distance. The Vice President and several of the President's Cabinet (those who remained faithful) surrounded them as cameras loudly clicked and flashed.

The President tried to speak but her voice faltered. She cleared her throat and tried to begin again. "Today, the saddest day of my life, I must announce my resignation as President of the United States. At twelve o'clock today, the Vice President, Mason Woodward, will be sworn in as your new President, followed by a state luncheon." Cameras continued their rapid clicking as she spoke. Reporters hovered, hoping she would allow questions. The Vice President tried to look humble, but he didn't quite pull it off. She took a deep breath and continued. "I regret some of the decisions I have made, but I applaud many others. I have not failed as a President. I have failed to communicate my wonderful plans for the future of this country. Future historians will look back on my plans and history will be kinder to me than my own constituency. I feel confident my Vice President, as President, will implement many of my plans and dreams for this country."

The Vice President's eyes looked perplexed while his mouth forced a smile. He wanted this over. For three years, she had totally ignored or degraded him in cabinet meetings. Now, she thought he would continue her failed plans? She was here today because she would not listen to him or her cabinet. *Let her posture*, he thought to himself. *Tomorrow, I will begin my own campaign for re-election. My plans will be implemented, not hers.*

The First Husband's expression had not changed. His stone face continued to stare off into the distance, showing no support or condemnation. One had to wonder what was going through his mind. The President droned on: "My election was a landslide. The country was ready for change, and I succeeded in turning many failed programs around and have implemented many others. Despite what the news media has said, I have kept this country safe. Never, in the history of this nation, have our relations with the Arab countries been better. I sadly regret all I was not allowed to accomplish in this term, and all I had hoped to accomplish in my second term. To all my many supporters, I thank you for your loyalty and your vote of confidence. There will be no questions at this time."

She turned and walked away from the podium and back into the White House. Her husband and entourage followed. The news reporters of all the different agencies took over and repeated her statements, adding their own comments. Those who had supported her were favorable, and those who did not were cruel. One even stated she had ruined any chance of a woman ever being elected to the office again.

## CHAPTER 26

IT HAD BEEN over a month since Anne had seen David. He had finished his classes at UNC-Asheville and received a degree in Psychology of the Criminal Mind. Since then, he had been in Washington, working to establish the new division of the CIA, which he would head. He and Adam were collaborating to get this team up and running as soon as possible. Mark sent him one of his best students who had both a degree in Psychology of the Criminal Mind as well as a Ph.D. in Anthropology. He was young, single, and enthusiastic about working for the CIA. He was immediately hired after his background check proved squeaky-clean.

The program was up and ready to go. A few bugs needed to be worked out, but the basic plan was ready to put into practice. The director came into David's office one morning to see how things were going. David was surprised to see him; he usually had to make an appointment with Damon Wentworth to discuss a problem or questions. David stood and said, "Come in, Director, and have a seat. What brings you down in the trenches today?"

The director took a seat and said, "David, I wanted you to know how pleased I am with the speed and quality of your work in setting up this division. To tell you the truth, I expected it to take at least six months. You have been diligent, and I am afraid you have had very little life of your own since we started this project. Adam tells me you are thinking of getting married. I want to encourage you to go ahead with those plans. You deserve some time off, before we get this thing up and running. I want you to take a vacation for four to six weeks. Rest, do something fun, and get married. I want you rested and ready to put this division in action when you get back." As he voiced the last sentence, he was already out of his chair and headed for the door. "See you in four to six weeks." He was out the door and David sat there wondering whether he had imagined his visit.

David called Anne. She had just walked into her office when the phone rang. David answered her "Hello" with: "Number one, will you marry me? Number two, we have six weeks from planning to honeymoon—can it be done?"

Anne pinched herself to make sure she wasn't dreaming. Her wildest dreams had just come true. "Yes, to the first question, and I think so to the second. Why so sudden? What's the rush?"

The director has just given me four to six weeks off before we implement this program. Now is the time, love; what do you say? I'll be on the noon flight to Asheville. Meet me and we will discuss plans and have dinner."

\*

WHEN DAVID'S PLANE landed, Anne was there waiting. She saw him running up the exit ramp and ran to meet him. A guard saw her coming and was poised to stop her, but David got there before she reached the rent-a-cop and ruined his whole day. She flew into his arms, and they kissed like two teenagers experiencing first love. They were off like two kids on an adventure.

\*

WHEN THE PHONE rang, Mark saw Anne's name and answered. It was early and Carrie and the girls were still asleep. "Hey, Sis; what's up?"

"Are you sitting down?"

"Yes, but don't tell me we have a problem with the house. Carrie has everything planned and ordered. When she plans something, she expects it to move along as smooth as silk, and it usually does."

"No problems at the house that I know of, but she will need to work a wedding into her plans and soon."

"What? That's great!"

"What's great?" Carrie came in with one of the girls on her shoulder and the other on a hip.

Mark reached for one of the girls and said, "Anne and David are getting married soon. Here, give me the girls, and you can talk to her—weddings don't come under my job description."

Carrie exchanged babies for the phone, and said, "Anne, what great news. When is this going to happen?"

"As soon as Mom can get it together. I need you to stay on her and help me keep it simple and small. David has a small window of time when he can be away from Washington. We need to stay in that time frame. You know Mom, Miss OCD. I need you and Mark to help me here. I'm coming down next week to sit down with her and make plans. I want you two to be there to support me and not let her talk me into something I don't want."

"Anne, we will be there; you know Elaine and I get along great. I know we can get this thing put together in no time. I am so happy for you both. I've felt you two belonged together from day one. I even noticed the way he looked at you in my hospital room the day you met him. He was smitten at first sight."

\*

ANNE'S MOM SAID it couldn't be done. Elaine had three weeks to get it all together, and she just didn't know how she was going do it. *Anne is just like her father; laid back and doesn't worry about a thing, because they know old mom will handle everything. His only job is to give the bride away,* she muttered to herself as she worked on the guest list.

# Rachel Poe

Mark's job was to go over and have a talk with their mom after Anne went back to Marion. He had promised to reiterate the need for simplicity. Elaine was in a tizzy. She tended to look at the whole picture, instead of one part at a time. "Mom, sit down and talk to me." Mark could see this wasn't going to be easy. "Mom, if you think this is too much for you, we'll have it at our house. Anne just wants family. Look at it as a family dinner, not a wedding. You know you can handle a family dinner. You could do that with your hands tied behind your back. Throw in a minister, a few flowers, and you have it."

If looks could kill, Mark would be dead. He was not handling this very well. His dad felt sorry for him and came in to back him up. "Mark is right, Elaine. If you don't calm down and stop trying to make this into what you want, instead of what Anne wants, you're going to cause your daughter to elope and leave us out of the wedding altogether. Is that what you want?"

Elaine sat down, tears in her eyes. "I just want this to be a nice wedding. One she will remember for the rest of her life. What will our neighbors and friends think if we don't invite them? If we invite one, we need to invite them all."

"Mom, if you don't tell them until after the fact, they will just think the Goodmans are having a family dinner. You don't seem to understand what Anne wants, and who cares what the neighbors think? If this is such a big deal for you, we'll have it at our place and all you will need to do is show up."

"Mark, you know Carrie can't handle a wedding with those two babies. Men...you just don't understand. Oh...all right, we will just have a glorified family dinner. Preacher Spencer has agreed to perform the service, but I really need to ask his wife. It's expected. Other than that, I guess Pete is the only other outsider I can invite. How about the Taylors? They've been our best friends forever."

"Mom!" Mark said in unison with his father's, "Elaine!"

"Okay, okay—just family. I have the picture. Now get out of here and let me start making lists."

Carrie would do a follow-up visit in a couple of days to see what she could help with and make sure Elaine had not deviated from the original plan.

David's mother, Hilda, was insisting on coming. According to the nurses, she was more than well enough to make the trip. Hilda was already telling everyone her son was getting married and she was going to fly to North Carolina for the wedding. David's cousin, Ruth, and her daughter, Alice, were coming with Hilda and would arrive the day before the wedding and leave the day after. Carrie insisted they stay with her and Mark to keep Elaine from blowing a gasket. Aunt Mattie would bunk in with Rosa. Between Mattie's room and the guest room, there would be plenty of space and everyone would be out of Elaine's hair. Carrie and Rosa were going over, early the morning of the wedding, to arrange flowers and help in the kitchen. Carrie had finally convinced Elaine to let Rosa do some of the cooking.

*

HILDA, RUTH, AND Alice arrived without a problem. Rosa had insisted on preparing a dinner for everyone the night before the wedding. It gave Hilda a chance to spend some time with her new daughter-in-law to be and her parents. Anne and Hilda were fast friends within minutes. Hilda was so happy she had lived to see her son finally married.

Elaine had calmed down now that everything was arranged and prepared. She could relax and enjoy getting to know David, his mother, and their relatives. The dinner was a huge success. It put everyone at ease, which would make tomorrow more relaxed and fun.

Anne and David slipped away to the front porch to have a few minutes alone. "No regrets?" David whispered in her ear as he stood behind her and held her in his arms.

"No regrets; I must be the happiest woman in the world right now. How about you?"

"No regrets here. I just wish we had done this sooner. I knew the first time I saw you that somehow we were going to be together. I dismissed the thought at the time, but it kept coming back. When you accepted my last minute invitation to have dinner the night of our first date, I knew it was fate. We were meant to be together. It just took me a while to trust my heart."

# Rachel Poe

"I think you're right, darling. Every objection I ever had about dating, after Ken died, just melted away when I met you. It was as if the Lord were telling me, 'Yes...this is the one.'"

David laughed. "That's exactly how I feel." He turned her around and kissed her softly. Anne snuggled her face under his chin and they held fast to each other.

\*

THE WEDDING DAY was upon them. Anne and David had separate rooms at her mom and dad's house. David slipped out early to avoid seeing the bride and to have breakfast with his mom. Rosa and Aunt Mattie were preparing a big breakfast. The plan was for him to dress at Mark and Carrie's and return with them for the wedding.

The hours had slipped away and it was time to dress for the big moment. Everyone scattered to dress and then meet back downstairs. They all managed to squeeze into three cars, including Pete, who came for breakfast and dressed there as well. Rosa had volunteered to stay home with the twins. Before they even left, Tucker, who had received a camera for Christmas, was snapping pictures of everyone and everything. No one was sure whether he even had film in the camera, but it didn't matter. It made him feel important and part of the wedding.

They had called ahead to make sure Anne was upstairs getting ready before David entered the house. Once they arrived, Carrie rushed upstairs to see Anne and help if needed. Anne looked beautiful in a tea-length, pale blue dress. The dress was simple but elegant, and it looked stunning on her. Elaine was putting finishing touches to Anne's hair. Anne had decided to wear her hair up to please her mother, who thought it showed off her beautiful neck. Carrie agreed it gave her just the right sophistication. She hugged Anne and told her she looked beautiful.

Anne did look glowing and she felt glowing, without the least bit of nervous anxiety. Her father tapped on the door and announced it was time to go. Elaine placed a lace veil over Anne's head and secured it with a crown of simple baby's breath. Her father smiled and said his daughter looked radiant. When he offered his arm, Anne took the bouquet from Carrie and walked with her father to the top of the stairs. Elaine and Carrie gave her a kiss, hurried down to take their places, and gave Aunt Mattie the signal to begin the wedding march.

Everyone was watching the stairs as the music began. Aunt Mattie had been the church music director for years and still played beautifully, even with her arthritic hands. David drew in a breath as he saw Anne. There were no words to describe his feelings at that moment. His happiness and love shone on his face as he watched Anne walk down the stairs and come toward him. He took her hand as the candlelight reflected in their moist eyes and together they turned to the minister.

Carrie and Mark held hands and wiped their tears as they remembered their own wedding. As the minster pronounced David and Anne husband and wife, they kissed and turned to face their families. A huge round of applause went up for the newlyweds.

The dinner was served and soon everyone felt stuffed with Elaine and Rosa's delicious food. It might have been a small wedding, but Elaine had insisted on a three-tier wedding cake, which was a work of art. The photographer filmed the entire ceremony and the cutting of the cake. After the cake cutting, Hilda stood to say a sweet toast for her son and his new wife. *Maybe*, she thought, *I will live to see a grandchild.*

Aunt Mattie was back at the piano with a flute of champagne by her side. David took his new wife in his arms and asked her to dance. They glided around the living room, hall, and dining room and invited others to join in. The dance floor became crowded, but no one noticed. Pete asked Hilda to dance, and she accepted. They flew around the room, like two spring chickens, to the waltz that Aunt Mattie skillfully played. It would be a day remembered by everyone.

The entire party was getting a little tipsy from champagne as David and Anne slipped away to change before saying goodbye. Pete had disappeared a little earlier to decorate the car with whipped cream, old cans, and shoes. Before leaving, David hugged and kissed his mother, promising to visit as soon as his new job allowed. She had tears in her eyes as she wished them well. The entire inebriated party gathered out front to throw birdseed and wave goodbye to the happy couple.

The interstate beckoned to the newlyweds, but first they had to find a carwash. After a quick cutting of strings and a drive-thru wash, the couple was on its way to Asheville and the Grove Park Inn. They had decided on the inn because neither had ever stayed there and it would make it easy for them to pack up David's apartment and move his things into Anne's house. They then had four glorious days of getting to know every detail of each other while relaxing in the beautiful mountains they both loved.

## CHAPTER 27

PETE WAS ENJOYING his second winter in the mountains of North Carolina. He loved the solitude of his cozy apartment over the garage. The community, like welcoming arms, had surrounded him with brotherly love and accepted him as one of their own. He attended the community meetings and was included in all their dinners and celebrations. He had even joined the ancient church, where the sisters were buried. Occasionally, he was sure he saw the sisters in the fields, or the graveyard, as he helped maintain the church and grounds in his spare time. He helped Butch work on his tractor, regularly had coffee and a fried apple pie with Minnie Sue, and an occasional game of chess with Lester. When the snows came, he settled himself in his favorite comfy chair in front of his stone fireplace and read all the books he had never before had time to read.

At least once a month, he had dinner with Anne and David. Anne was now pregnant with their first child. After two years of trying to get pregnant, they had given up on having their own baby and had applied for adoption. Before the adoption was completed, Anne happily became pregnant. She was healthy and no problems were expected, even though she was pushing forty. David was a different story. He couldn't believe he was actually going to be a father. He treated Anne as if she were sick and needed to quit work and rest for nine months. Anne, along with her doctor, tried to convince David that pregnancy was not an illness and he needed to relax.

Anne and David regularly made time to visit Hilda in Kansas. David took Anne to see the farmhouse where Carrie's mother and two half-brothers had lived, as well as Aunt Mattie's old farmhouse. After reading Carrie's book, *Secrets from the Attic*, there were many places Anne wanted to see. The bizarre story of Carrie's mother's life and the events that took place as Carrie and Mark tried to find the graves of her two half-brothers had put Farmington, Kansas on the map. Mark had also written a book, which gave a forensic anthropologist's view of the case. It had become a textbook for future students to read and learn from.

They had tried to get Hilda to move to Marion and live with them, but she would not leave Kansas. She had been born and raised in Kansas and she felt it too difficult to make such a change at her age. David hoped, now that Anne was pregnant, Hilda would change her mind. She was thrilled at becoming a grandmother, so she agreed to come visit for a month after the baby was born, but she made no promises beyond that.

Anne had taken Sarah as a partner. They shared the work, responsibility, and profits of the business. It gave Anne time to travel with David on some of his assignments, if no danger was involved. David and Pete went hunting in the winter and fishing in the summer. They enjoyed each other's company; Pete had become David's surrogate father and future grandfather to his children.

Pete looked forward to the kids coming. He worked the whole first winter, when the weather permitted, building a playhouse for the girls and a treehouse for Tucker. The kids pleasantly interrupted his solitude, as they wandered in and out of his apartment. His company was constantly needed as the kids investigated the woods surrounding the summerhouse. They were not allowed in the woods without either their dad or Grandpa Pete.

Mark and Pete were designing a barn and chicken coop to be constructed about a hundred yards back behind the garage. Mark wanted to have a pony for the girls and a couple of horses for him and Pete to ride the mountain trails around Dovecote. Carrie wanted to have a few chickens and a couple of goats. Pete had grown up on a farm as a boy and was experienced in taking care of animals. They had enough pastureland for grazing, and the goats and horses would keep the weeds from taking over. Pete had found a man through Mr. Tate to build the barn. He looked forward to having animals to care for. He had even adopted a stray puppy, which he named Sparky, to keep him company. Sparky followed Pete's every step, even to church, where he patiently waited outside the door for his master. They hoped the new buildings would be completed that summer so they could add the horses next fall.

Billy's ranch was finally sold to a horse breeder from Tennessee. He was famous for the breeding and training of award-winning horses. Buyers came from all over the world to purchase his horses. He had placed Dovecote on the map. Pete was introduced to the new owner and had been to the ranch several times to look at his horses. Preston Sterling, the new owner, assured Pete that he also bred working horses, which was what Pete and Mark needed to investigate the trails around Dovecote.

Carrie and the kids were to arrive the first of May. She wanted to plant her vegetable garden as soon as she was sure the fear of frost would be behind her. Pete had hired Butch to plow the garden and have it ready to plant when Carrie and the kids arrived. He had been to Marion to pick up the tomato plants and seeds Carrie had ordered from Anne's Garden Center. He also took the initiative to build a picket fence around the garden to keep the critters and kids from getting in the vegetables.

A deal was struck between Carrie and Pete. He would help her plant the garden if she would give him lessons in fly-fishing. Carrie's father, he had learned, had been an avid fisherman and had taught Carrie to fly-fish when she was a little girl. She had agreed wholeheartedly and looked forward to fishing the river that ran through their valley. Pete had stopped in a fish and tackle shop in Marion to pick up all the supplies they would need. He had dinner with just Anne since David was in Arizona, collecting evidence in an assassination attempt on an American diplomat by a foreigner.

Anne was happy to see him. They were excited about Carrie and the kids coming the first of May. When Pete explained his fly-fishing deal with Carrie, Anne agreed to come out and play with the kids while he and Carrie went fishing. She needed the practice; her baby was due the first week of August. Pete asked whether Hilda was coming out for the birth. Anne smiled. She knew they had become friends when Hilda came to Mississippi for the wedding. Pete always asked how Hilda was doing, so Anne begged him to write to Hilda and convince her to come out for the entire summer instead of waiting until the baby was born. She and David had asked many times, but Hilda was afraid she would just be in the way. Pete agreed and promised Anne he could convince her to come out as soon as possible. Anne asked him to assure her there was plenty of room for her and the new baby.

Pete liked Hilda; they were about the same age. Hilda had gone into a retirement community because she was alone. David was an only child and her husband had been gone for several years. She had her own cottage and was still able to cook when she wanted and drive where she needed to go. She felt David and Anne were just being kind to include her. This was their first baby, so she was sure they didn't need an old lady around at this special time in their lives.

When Pete arrived home, he immediately sat down to write Hilda. He hoped he could convince her to come. He had no plans to travel this summer. He just couldn't get enthused about traveling alone.

Within a week, Hilda wrote to Pete and Anne, saying she was packing her bags and would call with her travel plans. Pete's letter to Hilda had worked. She was coming for the summer, and Pete was sure he could convince her to move permanently to the North Carolina mountains. He would persuade her that she needed to be here to see her grandchildren grow.

\*

THE DAY CARRIE, with entourage, arrived in Dovecote, the sun was shining and the mountains were coming alive with traces of that special yellow-green of spring. Across the mountains, the dogwood and redbud trees were bursting into bloom. The pansies Carrie had planted, with Anne's help, around the front porch and entrance gate were blooming to greet them. The van was filled with kids along with Aunt Mattie and Rosa. Everyone was excited to be back in the mountains. Anne, Pete, and Sparky were waiting on the front porch as the family pulled in front of the house to unload. Tucker ran to hug Pete and immediately fell in love with Sparky, as did everyone else. Catty and Laney wanted to hug him too tight, causing Sparky to let out a yelp, but he seemed to understand they were little humans and didn't know any better. He was going to be a wonderful addition to the family.

Anne received lots of hugs and congratulations on the soon-to-be blessed event. She had lunch ready with sandwiches, iced tea, and strawberry shortcake made from the results of Pete's berry-picking at a local berry farm. The girls were running through the house screaming and laughing as Tucker tried to herd them into the kitchen for lunch and, hopefully, a nap. He loved his sisters, but they exhausted him sometimes. He felt very protective of them and was never far from where they were playing. He hoped they would go down for a nap so he and Grandpa Pete could go check out the treehouse. He liked to play in their playhouse too, but they were too young to go up in his treehouse. That was all his until they were older.

*

THE SUMMER WAS an endless sequence of get-togethers, parties, and picnics. Carrie was planning a huge Fourth of July party, to which the whole town of Dovecote was invited. Last year's Fourth party was such a success that she had decided to make it a tradition.

Carrie and Pete found time to get away and do a little fly-fishing. They convinced Mark to come along on the second excursion. Pete had taken to fly-fishing like a pro. Every time Carrie tried to instruct Mark, Pete felt the need to add his own advice as well, as if he had been fly-fishing all his life. She couldn't be annoyed because, after all, Pete had caught more fish on his first outing than she had. In no time, they had Mark's line flying above his head and landing just where he wanted it. To their surprise, Pete had discovered that Hilda and her husband used to fly-fish together. After that, Carrie was no longer needed. Pete and Hilda had been on several fishing/picnic outings together. Mark and Carrie felt a little left out, but they were thrilled Pete had found a friend.

The children were wild and free, having a great old time. Pete had added a swing set and slide beside the playhouse. The kids now referred to this area as the playground. At home, the kids were restricted to the yard and constantly warned not to go in the road. Here they had acres of space to play and investigate. The girls were growing and thriving in the mountain air. They were two and a half and followed Tucker everywhere. The time would come when they would intellectually pass him by. Mark and Carrie worried how they would explain this to the girls. The doctors had put Tucker's intellectual level at about six years old. Tucker would always be a six year old, but that had its good side too. He would never leave them and would always be their wonder-eyed, loving, precious boy. The doctors assured them Tucker would not even realize he was not as smart as the girls. The girls loved him so that they would never do anything to hurt Tucker's feelings.

*

JULY WAS ALMOST upon them. Plans for the Fourth were underway. David, Mark, and Pete would have three cookers going with hamburgers and hotdogs. They were expecting around fifty people. Everyone insisted on bringing a covered dish, and Aunt Mattie had volunteered to coordinate the food. Picnic tables on the lawn were being used, weather permitting; if it rained, they would move the dinner to the community center.

Butch and Elvis were handling the fireworks while Minnie Sue and Lester would coordinate three ice cream freezers. They were going to use the kids to crank the freezers; each child would crank a ten-minute turn. Carrie's electric ice cream freezer was rejected because everyone said the ice cream was better when the kids worked for it. Minnie Sue was planning on peach, strawberry, and chocolate chip.

The community was excited about the plans for the Fourth. No one could talk of anything else.

\*

FINALLY, THE DAY arrived and the weatherman promised a perfect day. Mark, Pete, and Carrie were up early mowing grass, setting up tables, and decorating the house, porches, and trees with red, white, and blue streamers. They wanted most of the decorations up before the kids woke and wanted to help. Carrie had saved streamers for the kids to decorate the treehouse and play yard.

David and Anne arrived early to help. The guests would arrive around five for cider and finger food. Dinner was planned for around seven, with homemade ice cream and cake to follow. As the sun began to set, Elvis and Butch would take over with a display of fireworks.

As the guests began to arrive, Anne, Aunt Mattie, and Rosa took their covered dishes and arranged them on two long, covered tables. Hot dishes went to the kitchen to be kept warm in the oven. Cold items were placed in coolers under the tables until the meat was about ready.

Carrie was putting the finishing touches to the flower arrangements for each table with red and white-checkered tablecloths and napkins.

The children's laughter was contagious as they ran helter-skelter through the guests chasing each other. The whole evening had the feel of a huge church social. The neighbors saw each other almost every day, but they talked and laughed as if they had not seen each other in months.

Mark, Pete, and David were setting up their cookers and getting them ready to light. Minnie Sue and Lester were organizing the kids and getting the ice cream churns started. Elvis and Butch were out in the field, setting up the fireworks. Butch was a volunteer fireman and had parked the fire truck in the field just in case. If it was needed, it was there; if he got a call, he was ready to respond since all his volunteers were here at the party. The children were all over the fire truck, so Butch had to shoo them away.

As Anne made her umpteenth trip into the kitchen, she stopped to hold her back. What was that nagging pain in her lower back? She dismissed it and continued on into the house. As she handed a cake to Aunt Mattie, she felt water running down her leg. The weight of the baby had caused her to lose control a couple of times, and she felt embarrassed as she admitted to Aunt Mattie that she had peed on the floor. "Oh, dear; I can't seem to stop peeing."

"You aren't peeing, dear; your water has broken. Sit down and I'll get some towels. Are you having any pains?"

"I had a low back pain suddenly hit me as I was entering the house. It's gone now. Are you sure my water has broken?"

Aunt Mattie looked down at the water dripping from the chair. "Oh, yes. We had better get you...."

"Ohhhh, I'm having a real pain now.... Oh, dear, what do we do now?"

Minnie Sue came into the kitchen as Anne said this and ran to her side. "Are you in labor, Anne?"

Aunt Mattie answered for her as Anne held her abdomen and groaned. "Yes, she is, and her water has broken; we need to do something fast."

Minnie Sue took off out the door and hollered back for Aunt Mattie to time her pains. She found Carrie and Mark and yelled at Butch to come into the house. Not knowing what was wrong, all three followed her back to the house.

As they entered the kitchen, Anne was having another pain.

Mark took control and carried her to the nearest bed. Aunt Mattie followed and informed him that Anne had had two pains only minutes apart and her water had broken. Mark told someone to get David as he examined Anne. The baby was coming and there was no time to take her to the hospital. They were twenty-five miles from the hospital, and he didn't want to take a chance on her having the baby in the back of a car.

David arrived. "What's wrong?"

"You," Mark replied, "are about to become a father, and it won't be long."

Minnie Sue, who was standing at the bedroom door, ordered Butch to go get Bessie. Butch didn't wait for permission; he was out the door, running.

David, who was in shock, asked, "Who's Bessie?"

"Bessie McKurry," Minnie Sue informed him. "She's delivered most of the folks in Dovecote. Best midwife in the county. She lives back in the woods a ways. Butch knows where she lives; he'll be back before you can say scat. I can tell you what she is going to say right off. You need to get her lots of sheets, not towels—they're too rough—and keep one real warm to wrap the baby in unless you got a clean baby blanket handy. She's gonna need lots of boiling water and strong, black coffee."

"What's she going to do with the coffee?" David asked.

"Drink it.... What did you think she was going to do with it?"

Another pain wracked Anne's body. It had only been twenty minutes since the last one. David took her hand and talked softly to her, reminding her how to breath as the pains began. She focused on David's face and did as he said. They had taken lessons, and David was planning to be her coach, but he hadn't planned on it happening at home. He wanted a doctor, but there wasn't time. He prayed the midwife would know what she was doing and would hurry. Anne wasn't due for about four more weeks. At their age, this might be their only chance to have a baby. *"Please, God,"* he kept praying silently. *"Please let Anne and the baby be okay."*

Mark was a doctor, but not the right kind of doctor. Still, he had studied everything he could find on the Internet about birthing babies when Carrie was pregnant. He was sure he could deliver the baby if he had to. He knew enough to know that this baby was coming soon.

Pete had been informed and had enlisted Lester and Elvis to help with the cooking. No one knew what was going on inside the house, and they wanted to keep it that way as long as possible. Lester appointed one of Elvis' older kids to take over the ice cream job and keep the crank going. The fireworks were set up and ready to go. Aunt Mattie and Rosa were manning the kitchen with Ruby's help and would see to it that everything was served on time.

\*

BUTCH FOLLOWED THE rutted dirt road up the mountain. He started blowing the horn when he was within hearing distance. As he pulled into the yard, Louis McKurry stepped off the porch. Louis was tall and lean. His overalls stood out from his body so far that there was enough room inside them for another person. His white hair looked like a halo on his bald, dark brown dome. A corncob pipe hung from his large lips. Butch thought to himself, *He could win an Uncle Remus look-a-like contest.*

"Bessie is a gittin her bag; is we having a baby? Didn't knows of anyone specting?"

"You met Mark and Carrie, our new folks in Dovecote? It's Mark's sister. She isn't due for four weeks, but the baby is coming too fast to move her."

The screen door creaked open and slammed shut as Bessie waddled across the porch. She weighed at least two-fifty and was almost six feet tall. She wore her hair pulled severely back in a knot at the nape of her neck. A tie-dye scarf wrapped around her head with gold loop earrings dangling from her ears. She wore a white, starched uniform that looked more like a tent, and on her huge feet she wore flip-flops. She always wore a smile that stretched from ear to ear. Butch had never seen her without that smile. She gave Louis a peck on the cheek, told him not to wait up for her, and hefted herself into the seat beside Butch. Butch felt his side of the car rise five inches. "Evenin', Mr. Butch. Who be having a baby?"

Butch explained the need for a midwife as he turned the car around and headed down the mountain as if he were running moonshine.

\*

# Vanished Sisters

AS THEY PULLED into the drive, Bessie's eyes became big and her mouth dropped open. "What's goin' on here?"

"It's the Fourth of July, Bessie. We were having a cookout for the neighborhood."

"I must a lost my invitation."

"Until today, Carrie didn't know you existed, but I bet you get invited next year. They're good people."

Bessie entered the house, barking orders as she was led to the bedroom. Minnie Sue was right and they had everything ready for her. David was on one side of Anne and Carrie on the other. Mark stood at the end of the bed as if he were ready to catch the baby if it popped out. Bessie assessed the situation and asked Mark whether he was a doctor.

"Yes, Miss Bessie, but the wrong kind of doctor. I can do autopsies, but I've never delivered a baby."

"You can stay; at least you'll know what to give me when I axk for it. Who are you?" she asked David and Carrie.

"I'm the father; can I stay and coach my wife?"

"Coach! This ain't no football game, honey. We havin' a baby here. You pose to be pacing the rug outside. This ain't no place for a Daddy right now."

Anne tugged at David's arm. "Go on, honey; I'll be okay. Do as she says."

Anne was scared and this huge woman was not helping. She wanted her doctor. This was not how things were supposed to happen, but she was not all that sad to see David leave the room. She had never been comfortable with the natural birth classes. David made her nervous. She wanted to be able to scream if she felt like screaming, and with David there, she was afraid of looking like a wimp. But he was so thrilled to be part of the birth that she hadn't had the heart to tell him how she really felt. On the other hand, she wasn't sure about Miss Bessie, either. Part of her wanted David there to protect her from this drill sergeant.

To tell the truth, David was thrilled to get out of that room. He had been trying to convince himself that he was not going to faint. His head throbbed and he had a ringing in his ears. He had been sure he could do this until the time came, and now it was a different story. It just wasn't what he had expected. He saw himself in a white sterile gown in a sterile, clean delivery room with doctors and nurses all around them. This just wasn't the way he thought it would be. He hated to let Anne down; they had faithfully gone to all the natural birth classes.

Carrie was thrown out, too, but ordered to bring Bessie a cup of black coffee. She came out of the room, took one look at David and his mom, and all three broke into hysterical laughter. Carrie put an arm around David and Hilda. "Let's go get a cup of coffee before you start pacing."

Bessie examined Anne and came around, pulled a chair over, and took her hand. "Now, honey, how you feelin'?"

She spoke in an entirely different voice as she stroked Anne's hand. Anne immediately relaxed and was mesmerized by her soothing voice. Bessie smelled like lemon and vanilla. "You doin' jus fine and we gon have you a fine baby boy here real soon."

"Can you tell the sex already?" Anne was shocked.

"No, but I knowed the minute I seen your belly, it was a boy. I ain't never been wrong. Now, if you listens to what I tells you," she continued to stroke Anne's hand and speak softly, "this will be over afore you know it."

"Okay, Miss Bessie, but I think I'm beginning a.... Ooooh."

"Dat's good, honey, but don't push just yet. I tells you when to push. Take little short breaths and it help to ease da pain." Anne did as she was told. "That's my girl. Yous doin' jus' fine." Bessie felt her stomach and listened to the baby's heartbeat. "He sounds fine." She took oils out of her case and gently began to rub them on Anne's stomach—she was feeling the baby and massaging him through Anne's stomach. She then sat down to drink her coffee. Mark, not sure he trusted this midwife, took a look and reported that he could see something. "I know, honey, but it ain't quite time; dat little boy is still movin' around to get in just the right position. He be there soon." She continued to drink her coffee.

Mark couldn't tell you why, but he decided he trusted this woman. He couldn't guess her age, but if she had deliv-

## Vanished Sisters

ered most of the people in Dovecote, she had to be in her seventies. He watched her with interest as she soothed Anne into relaxing as she calmly went about assessing the situation. She wiped Anne's face with a cool cloth and told her she was going to check on how things were coming along.

After reexamining Anne, Bessie calmly began to give orders. "Now, Anne, when you have the next pain, I wants you to bear down as hard as you can. Mr. Mark, I want you to hold her hand and let her squeeze it as she works through the pain." She sat back down and finished her coffee.

"Here we go," Anne yelled as she grabbed Mark's hand.

"At's my girl. Push...push...push. Good one. Now rest a bit 'til da next one. His head be almost out. One more push and wes get to meet dis little fella."

The next one came fast. Anne dug her nails into Mark's hand as she screamed and pushed with all the strength she had left. She heard a cry as another pain seized her body. With this last push, the strength she thought was gone was there again, and she felt a swoosh as the baby was born. "We has a fine baby boy, just like I tol' you," Bessie announced as she laid the screaming baby on Anne's chest wrapped in a warm baby blanket.

Bessie continued to speak calmly to Anne as she helped guide the baby to Anne's breast. Her work was not over. She gave Mark orders, and he handed her the needed instruments for her to cut the cord and collect the afterbirth. Stitches were required, and she skillfully sutured the torn places. Mark was surprised; this woman was a skilled professional, not only in technical knowledge, but also in her ability to calm the mother and ease her fears. Mark wanted to hug her and planned to do just that before the evening was over.

\*

OUTSIDE THE DOOR, David, Hilda, and Carrie were going mad. They heard the baby cry and wanted to be in there. Carrie could stand it no longer. She peeped in and asked whether Bessie was ready for the warm water. "Yes, ma'am; I needs two pans of warm water. One for da baby, one for Miss Anne, and tell Mr. Daddy he can come in and meet his son."

David timidly entered. When his eyes met Anne's, they both began to cry as David eased over, kissed Anne, and peeked in the blanket at his son. While examining all his toes and fingers, they laughed and cried together. David asked whether he could hold his son. Bessie was there by his side, showing him how to pick the baby up and how to hold him so his head was supported at all times. "Since you already have da baby, you can give him his first bath."

Mark motioned to Carrie and they quietly slipped out of the room to let the new parents get acquainted with their new son.

David paled and shook his head no. "I'm afraid I'll drop him."

"Dat's why you need to do dis; I shows you how. Come on now; you be real good at dis; I kin tell."

Bessie stood on one side of the shallow pan of warm water and David on the other. Bessie held her hands under David's and guided him through his son's first bath. "He's so slippery," David said with a shaky voice.

"You doin' fine; jus' be sure you support de head and you can lets de rest of him sit in the water. See, he likes his first bath. Ifin he be afraid, he be squalling right now."

Anne watched as Bessie eased David through the baby's first bath, tears streaming down her face. David was going to be a great father. Bessie gently showed him how to dry and dress the baby. By the time David successfully attached the first diaper...after three tries...and dressed him in a gown from one of the twins, he felt like a pro. He was so proud of himself.

Bessie suggested that David walk the baby around and sing to him while she gave Anne a bath and helped her into one of Carrie's nightgowns. Bessie smiled and winked at Anne as David tried to sing a lullaby that his mother had sung to him. The tune was right, but he had forgotten some of the words. He did the best he could as he walked his son and held him close.

*

## Vanished Sisters

CARRIE AND MARK joined their guests out front and announced that Anne had just given birth to a precious baby boy. When someone asked what they had named him, Carrie looked at Mark. "I don't know; do you?"

"I don't," Mark confessed. "All we know is he weighed seven-and-a-half pounds, he is healthy and beautiful...and I was allowed to assist in my first delivery."

The crowd cheered and Lester proclaimed, "Let the fireworks begin in celebration of this new life."

\*

BESSIE FINISHED HER duties and slipped out of the room to let the new parents enjoy their new son. With case in hand, she went outside to find Butch. She was ready to go home. As she came out on the porch, everyone stood and cheered the woman-of-the-hour as the first fireworks exploded above the Goodmans' summer home. Bessie blushed, but she enjoyed the attention.

Mark took her arm and escorted her to a table where a plate of wonderful food was placed in front of her while Carrie ran to get her a fresh cup of coffee. Bessie enjoyed herself. She knew everyone there—had delivered many of them. Mark and Carrie sat with her, savoring their ice cream and cake while watching the fireworks. When the fireworks ended and folks began to leave, Butch came over and asked Bessie whether she was ready to go home. "I shore is, honey. This old lady is ready for bed. I shore do preciate de food." Carrie jumped up to fixed a plate for Louis, as Mark made sure she had been compensated for her night's work. "Yes, sir, Mr. David done took good care of me; I thank ye for axin."

Carrie returned with the food for Louis. "Next year, Bessie, you and Louis must plan to join us for our next Fourth of July celebration." Bessie took the food and held Carrie's hand. "We will, and I see you be needing me pretty soon. You give old Bessie a call. Dese boys gonna be about seven months apart, and I predict dey gona be close friends for their entire life."

Her prognostication floored Carrie. "Bessie, how did

you know I'm pregnant? I haven't told anyone. I haven't even had it confirmed by a doctor."

"Bessie nose des things. De Lord talks to me.... He say you gona have a fine son in 'bout seven months. You mark my word, honey."

Butch left with Bessie, and then Mark and Carrie said goodbye to the rest of their guests and began the clean up. Lester and Elvis, along with Pete, chipped in and helped. They did all that was necessary and left the rest for tomorrow. When everyone had gone home, Pete joined Mark and Carrie to check on the new family. Rosa put the twins and Tucker to bed after seeing the new baby. The baby was crying as Granny Hilda helped Anne learn the secrets and pleasures of breastfeeding her first baby. David watched with pride. He couldn't take his eyes off his new family.

Everyone sat around the huge kitchen table and had a last cup of coffee while reliving the eventful evening. This was a day no one would ever forget. The stories would be repeated for years.

David came out and sat down after pouring himself a cup of coffee. Everyone bragged about what a good job he had done bathing and dressing the baby. Everyone wanted to know what Anne and he had decided to name the baby. "We've decided to name him after my father and add my mother's maiden name as a middle name. Joseph Forester Durham." It was obvious that Hilda did not know until that moment. Her eyes filled with tears as she kissed her son and said his father would be so proud.

# EPILOGUE

CARRIE WOKE BEFORE the sun was up. She quietly slipped out of bed, tiptoed down the stairs, fixed a cup of coffee, and proceeded to the back porch. On the way, she listened at Anne and David's door to see whether she could hear any sound. All was quiet. She hoped David and Anne were getting a little rest. She had heard little Joey crying a couple of times during the night.

Watching the sun come up was her favorite summer thing to do. The valley was still, the corn was high and taseling, willow trees along the river dipped their tendrils in the cool water, and cows grazed quietly in the meadow as the birds began to awaken and sing their morning song. Over the mountaintops across the valley, the sun was just beginning to soften the darkness of night. She sipped her coffee and waited for that first golden haze to seep over the entire dale. Then would come the first peek of the sun, as it scintillated over the horizon, sending beams of wonderful sunlight to fill the sky and streaks of multicolored light across the hazy valley.

This was what she was waiting for as she rocked in her favorite chair and sipped her coffee. As she quietly waited, Carrie felt more than heard someone behind her. Mark kissed the top of her head and sat down beside her. She reached out her hand for his without saying a word. The miracle was about to happen, and neither wanted to miss the spectacular display of light. Even the birds quieted as if waiting for this morning miracle. As the sun peeked over the mountains, Mark kissed her hand.

They waited until the sun was fully up before they spoke. Carrie smiled at him and shook her head. "I never tire of seeing the sun come up. Did you watch the sun come up as a boy?"

"Yes. I usually found Granny sitting on the porch waiting for the day to begin, just as I found you. She would already have biscuits in the oven and country ham fried, but she had to take a moment of quiet to watch the sunrise."

They were silent for a while, just enjoying the beautiful valley and thanking God for their many blessings. Carrie turned to Mark and said. "Do you think the sisters took the time to watch the sunrise every morning?"

"I'm sure they did. They were in the barn before the sun was up, ready to milk the cows. How could they miss such a spectacular occurrence? Do you ever feel their presence here in the house?"

"Yes! I thought I was the only one who could feel their aura; do you feel it too?"

"Oh, yes. I know they're here. Pete is convinced he has seen them walking in the fields and in the cemetery. Once, when I was in the root cellar, I felt someone touch my shoulder and thought it was you; when I turned around—no one was there."

Carrie was not surprised. "Once, as I was working in the garden, I saw them too. They were watching me. I smiled at them and then they were gone. I kept telling myself, *It's just my imagination,* but I know they were there."

"We are truly blessed, Carrie. We have two angels watching over us.

They were quiet again for a few moments. Carrie squeezed Mark's hand and said, "I guess they just couldn't leave this place."

He kissed her and asked, "When were you going to tell me you're pregnant?"

"I haven't been to a doctor to confirm it yet. I suspected, but Bessie's pronouncement was a shock to me too. I didn't want to say anything that might diminish the anticipation and joy of the birth of Anne's first baby."

Mark stood and pulled her up from her chair. They held each other as they enjoyed the sunlit valley below. "I couldn't be happier. I love you, Carrie; you're my soul mate and a thoughtful, considerate sister-in-law."

The screen door slammed as the twins came running to them. A new day was beginning and the peaceful moment had passed.

THE END

# AUTHOR'S NOTES

THE SISTERS ARE based on real people, who actually lived on a mountain, in a tiny village that overlooked the valley where my grandparents lived. In reality, I was Mark, walking down that dirt road with my older sister. The old sisters actually lived on that farm, just as I described it. As far as I know, they both died peacefully in their own beds, after living well into their nineties. The little village of Dovecote still exists today, under a different name. The post office is the only business still in existence.

The memories of time spent with my grandparents in that valley will sustain me until the day I die. It was not just the beautiful mountains, but also the real, God-fearing, good people who lived there. They were not proficient in speaking the King's English, even though some had college degrees, but they spoke from the heart. They tried to live by the "Good Book," and if you needed anything, they were there to help.

My father was in the Second World War when I was born. My mother, sister, and I lived with my grandparents until I was three. My father—a stranger to me—came home from the war, and we moved away. My grandparents came to get us the day school was out, and we stayed in that valley every summer until I was seventeen and had my first job.

As I get older, I find my mind drifting back to that peaceful place where life was simple, neighbors were friendly, and doors were never locked. Time gone by—never to be recaptured, except in our memories.

# ABOUT THE AUTHOR

RACHEL POE WAS born in the mountains of North Carolina. She has a degree in Interior Design and owned her own business for many years. She is a self-taught artist and works with oils, acrylics, and watercolors.

*Vanished Sisters* is her second novel and a sequel to her first novel, *Secrets from the Attic*.

Rachel is now retired and enjoys writing, painting, and spending time with her eight grandchildren.

# SECRETS FROM THE ATTIC

IF YOU ENJOYED *Vanished Sisters*, you're bound to love *Secrets from the Attic,* the story of how Mark and Carrie met and fell in love....

When medical examiner Mark Goodman and Carrie Whittaker meet in a graveyard, over a pile of bones, they're thrown into a mystery that sends them on a roller coaster ride neither wanted to take. The bones found in North Carolina lead them to Kansas and a forgotten farmhouse of fear, horror, and sadness.

Their chance meeting was predestined for more than one reason. Mark joins Carrie in uncovering family secrets and supports her as she grieves for the lost souls of those she never had the chance to know.

Evil awaits them in Kansas. Their original discovery leads them into an even more complex and emotional mystery as Carrie experiences the same tragedy that occurred there thirty years earlier.

While they struggle to understand what happened, and fight to reclaim their sanity, their souls are joined as each tries to resist the magnetic pull of two hearts fated to be together.

CPSIA information can be obtained
at www.ICGtesting.com
Printed in the USA
FFOW02n2359060616
24728FF